DEAD WORKS

BROOKLYNN DEAN

ISBN 978-0-578-29550-3

Edited by Kereah Keller

Cover design by Steve Rice

"That which hath been is named already, and it is known that it is man: neither may he contend with him that is mightier than he."
Ecclesiastes 6:10

DEAD WORKS

The Anti-Gospels Book III

BROOKLYNN DEAN

Prologue

The rip in the sky grew. It seemed to tear further with every flicker of violet lightening, with every angel or demon or god that fell through it.

As angels stormed this earthly battleground, they manifested their divine spirits into flesh and blood. These bodies, physical and made of matter, tore through the once-whole blanket of the sky. New rips formed. The sky tore each time an angel, fiery and furious, manifested into matter and burst through its atmosphere.

The angels sought out purer souls. They came together, adjusting to the gravity of the earth and the feel of it upon their new bodies, to save those remaining who could be saved.

The antichrist freed demons, though, and for every soul saved by an angel, two more fell to the temptations or the terrors of the divinely mutated.

She was risen.

Death seized any soul who would not bow before her. Hurricanes and volcanic eruptions claimed countless lives. The ripping of the skies continued as the antichrist gained more and more momentum, ruling over Hell and sending her Brethren out into the world as she plotted and planned for her revival to the earthly plane.

Survivors of the broken skies, of the antichrist and her demons, those that saw the face of God in Torrence's gleaming eyes and heard the gospels in plump lips fell to their knees before her.

These souls who had bore witness became enraptured. Her countenance regal and entrancing, her voice authoritative and melodic, and the power that emitted from her in palpable ripples through the air surrounding all within her proximity, billowing its tingling, fiery pressure against those caught in storming winds of the broken skies.

If their knees did not buckle under the enormity of this great turbulence, they fell to all fours in witness and worship of Torrence.

She praised those strong enough to withstand the tempests, offering them her hand and asking only for devotion in return.

After branding them, she committed to them a tutor, one of her Brethren, for a week or two of intense study, often titling Skeet or Freddy or Michael her most knowledgeable disciples.

Monuments had been resurrected in her image. Across the lands of darkness, great statues bearing the likeness of the Unholy Savior replaced those of angels. They struck down the marble crosses and erected in their stead the elegant features of Torrence.

A church formed in southern Pennsylvania, and the newly-appointed leader of the congregation instructed the disposal of all angelic countenances in the attached cemetery.

A sculptor crafted a great effigy Torrence, her long hair flowing as if gravity did not press down upon it, her lips parted to command or to consume, her arm outstretched, palm upward, offering to clasp the hand of a newly-fallen follower or reaching for the throat of a God-fearing angel who refused to bow before her.

They scattered about her feet the broken hunks of marble angels, and across the path, which led to the church's door, on an elevated but shorter stand, was the likeness of Conrad, Great Awakener to their Unholy Savior's destiny.

Three hours away, another sect formed in glorification of Torrence. From the broken bits of angels, they crafted the Unholy Savior in a seated position, her legs hanging from the pillar on which she sat, feet pressed into its fluted column. Draped around her head was a veil-like hood. The stone had been shaped with such masterful artistry that the face appeared about to move, the eyes about to blink, the hood seemed fabric thrown about the statue, protecting her from unworthy eyes. She was beautiful, she was serene, though she smirked. Her elbow rested upon a bent knee, and hanging between her legs, she held onto a Bible, a Bible bursting into flame.

Nearer to the ocean, somewhere in Florida, the sects placed their graven images near the ocean. Gargantuan creations, the great statues of Torrence stood within the waves of tumultuous seas. Beacons they were. Warnings. Ominous eyes glared into the distance as her hands held within bloodied fists the wing of an angel.

Overseas, poets glimpsed her. They watched her ravage their towns. Her Brethren desecrated thousand-year-old churches, dismantling the pews with the swinging of axes, spray-painting the horned serpent—Torrence's emblem—over the faces of the Virgin and of the Saints. They smashed golden angels and wore their wings like costumes.

These poets either drank themselves to death in the pain of history destroyed, or they came forth to honor her.

Without working technology, these artists used pens to write their worship of her into hymn. Long-since drained of modern oil ink, these pens had to be dipped into ancient concoctions of mineral and plant inks from the small jars in which they had been blended.

Onto old papers these were penned. Onto the backs of how-to manuals and even onto coffee filters. Often-times these poets would seal their work with a thumbprint of their blood, sending the finished papers off into the gusting air as offerings to their Unholy Savior.

Less artistic souls merely wept before her glory. They cried. They stood paralyzed and slack-jawed, in awe of what they witnessed.

They gathered in old cemeteries and worshipped the dirt, sharing her stories to those who had not seen her or one of her Brethren, explaining the unholy communions, their power, the evocation of the violet lightning.

They told of Torrence taking this phenomenon into herself. They told of Torrence lapping at the blood of the virtuous upon their respective deaths. The slowed time of the sacrifice. The capturing of this blood as it coagulated within the atmosphere, caught within the time warp as her Brethren were caught within it. The vials, seven in total, full of blood, human blood, yes, but representing all that was pure and holy.

They recreated these communions by slicing open their own chests. High priestesses would lick the wounds.

In some denominations, those that saw Wesley as divine son or unholy ghost or simply human extension in some way to their great antichrist, the priestesses would select a successor, male and always shy of nature, with whom to consummate the ritual. The man lying in freshly-disturbed cemetery dirt as the high priestess would mount him, chanting out praise to Torrence from lips stained with wet, glistening blood. Around the pair knelt the rest of the church, watching this replicated act of their new God and her right-hand man, and when the high priestess achieved her climax, all would dig up from before their knees a vial of some other follower's blood and consume it.

Throughout the lands of what once had been modern and technological societies, old hymns became the method of communication and of storytelling. Instead of live streams and video clips, they told of Torrence and her brethren around a fire and in their travels. Electronic images were replaced with portraits. They crafted from the broken beams of collapsed homes tiny crosses, and stuck them onto scraps of paper where they wrote the lyrics of their hymns.

In other parts of these same countries, the sun could still be seen. Only an angel or two had broken through the clouds and their vast expanse over these towns. They came for the demons who were traveling now to conquer the souls within those city limits. Battles would arise in all areas of the earth; this was merely the beginning of them.

CHAPTER ONE

"There's never any music on." He stared at his wife's fingers as they pressed button after button. "Julie." He scoffed, turning off the radio and silencing the static. "Why do you insist on listening to that buzzing?"

"Sometimes you get a voice." Julie shrugged from the passenger's seat.

It was true, but not true enough.

The human need for connection, to be heard, to be known simply so far as to say, "I exist," to be acknowledged in that way outweighed all else, including the end of days.

A person locked away in their basement with the outdated technologies their parents kept in the damp, dark areas riddled with spiderwebs and rat droppings, too attached to the glory days of their youthful experiences with the modern miracles to simply get rid of them, might have found a way to rework the wires and make an obsolete machine new.

Someone, who had been rushed into an old police station or veterinary clinic by an angry mob of looters and murderers, might have seen the old phone systems with their intercoms and multiple lines and, out of sheer boredom, picked up the dusty handset to see if dial-tones still existed under broken skies.

And sometimes, well, sometimes the old radio hosts and disc jockeys, the reporters of ink and paper, and the creators of so-called news online would come together in a mutual respect for the way of the old world—that is, for the communication of facts and information, or even slanted truths of scandal—and form a sort of gang themselves; one of ego, yes, to be heard still, to be important, to have the acknowledgment of those they'd knew know existed, but also one of communication. They wanted to share the news. They wanted to share with anyone, even someone stuck in their basement with only an old tape-player as their company, what it was that they saw and experienced and felt here in the end of days.

Sometimes they would take old tape recorders to the street—outdated handheld systems advertised to children of the 1990's through their favorite film about a young boy forgotten at home while his family traveled abroad; the microphones of these ancient artifacts of modern culture and civilization were thrust into the faces of those people remaining alive on earth and brave enough to walk the streets and seek supplies from stores as if the skies had never separated.

"Kate Marks, formerly of KDA Action News, reporting. Please tell us what you've seen here since the skies have split and life as we knew it failed."

Many of the tapes made by Marks & Co., the little coalition's self-given name, had never been heard. The decades-old tapes were brittle. Merely removing them from the device would break them. Others would warp on playback, as if some great force had not wanted this or that particular sighting or message to be spoken of or heard.

They recorded rumors of this very phenomenon, supposedly occurring even before the skies broke open. The story went that there was a boy—no, a man, some argued—who had been taken by demons, and the exorcism of these entities failed, for it had not been a demon—an external force of altered divinity—but a personal daimon, the very essence of human soul too broad and too heavily-weighted for most physical bodies to withstand.

All storytellers agreed, however, on one thing: that an old VHS tape existed of this supposed exorcism, and that anyone who tried to replicate it failed.

Tapes would burn and warp. Phones would explode in the hands of those recording their televisions. Discs cracked as they attempted to copy the video. Entire computers would burst into flame.

Kate and company considered seeking out this boy, this man, whoever he was or had been, but none of them were blessed. None were evil. None had some bigger part in the apocalypse, perhaps, than the attempt to document it.

"Not everyone has a role in this story," she told her company. "But we can still record it."

Julie had never heard Kate's new reports. She found lost souls in their garages and their basements. And while her husband found the entire thing absurd, writing the untrained voices off as con artists, for the skies above him were blue, darker blue and the sun shone within them for only a few hours a day, but they were blue.

"This apocalypse business is ridiculous," he said. "Evacuating for what?" He looked at the long line of cars ahead of them. Horns blared in the frequent jams. They were nearing the tunnel that would mark the city limits of their hometown, and head where? Somewhere safe? He thought the world had gone up in flames. Where was safe? He huffed. "Sky looks fine to me. Fucking ridiculous."

"The apocalypse doesn't take the world in an instant, Tim," Julie replied as she, too, looked out the window to the winding road out of the city. "It spreads as infectious disease from person to person, slithering through the lands as a great serpent."

"Where'd you hear that?"

"The voices," she said, staring into the sky. "Looks like rain."

"It's gonna rain angels, right?"

"You shouldn't mock them," she warned, leaning forward to turn back on the radio.

After some tuning, words could be heard. It was Kate's voice breaking through the nothingness.

"Change in temperature…Shelter right away…Storm…"

The voice was lost to static. Julie worked to recapture it, but it faded as swiftly as it had come.

"See?" She looked to Tim. "They come through, and they give us warnings."

"Yeah, of imaginary storms. This is bullshit, honey. I'm sorry. But all of this is fear mongering. It's—."

Over the static came a low, growling sound. It filled the sky and reverberated inside the tunnel, shaking the stone. A streak of lightning, violet and white-hot, broke through the darkening sky, tearing open the atmosphere in its quake.

Another roar of thunder encompassed the city. Windows came down. Gasps came from inside the cars. To the left of their car, Julie and Tim saw a great crack form in the concrete wall of the tunnel.

Darkness spread across the sky in waves, streaking the blues and whites with its dulling gray before encompassing the expanse entirely. Blazes of silvers and deep crimsons streaked the skies. Large, human-like creatures broke through the atmosphere, seeming to ride these bursts of energy down to the very earth itself.

They crashed into the road before the tunnel, sending large hunks of pavement hurling through the air in all directions. Stoplights short-circuited. The static in car speakers became high-pitched, war-piercing screams.

Standing before and behind the entrance, these creatures stood in enormity, too large it seemed to even enter the tunnel without having to contort their already-jagged spines.

Their titanic hands were adorned with shining rings, emeralds and rubies the size of gold balls glistened upon their bulbous knuckles. Their irises were lovely hues of purple and pink, and even those with more than two eyes appeared angelic for it. Long lashes curled over their eyes. Their noses were straight. Beneath their noses were plump, pink lips. They were dressed in sleek, black clothing, wielding weapons of gold, which shimmered in the headlights of the cars.

Terrifying yet beautiful, these creatures seemed as vicious as they did regal, and the humans in their cars, bearing witness to their monstrous allure were stunned, seemingly transfixed by shock or awe.

From between the two creatures standing guard at the tunnel's exit came two figures. Both human. One female, commanding, and attractive. She walked through them and onto the hood of the car centered in the front of the tunnel. The other was male and holding a handgun. He stood next to the vehicle upon which his companion strode, his eyes scanning the cars as she raised her hands.

The engines of the cars all died out. Gasps came for this, but eyes rose to the figure who seemed to cause it.

"Children of the broken skies," she spoke, her eyes connecting with the fearful faces in the now-inoperable cars. "You inhabit a world in which your welcome has run out." Thunder roared in the skies above her. Lightning cast its glow upon her lovely features. Then silence spread throughout the tunnel. "Your god has raptured those worthy of paradise or summoned them to the holy lands of angels. Your presence here only proves your insignificance." She paused, her eyes and the eyes of her handgun-wielding companion connecting with the eyes of the fearful, the trapped. "My children stand before you in their enormity. They exist because I willed them to, and you shall live if I will you to, if you bow to me now, if you surrender."

Somewhere in the far left of the tunnel a shaken hand

emerged from a car window. Between the open palms came a terrified face, the features tight and hesitant. "I…surrender…" he stammered as he gazed upward to her.

A sinister gleam in her red eyes seemed to spread through her delicate features; its evilness, pushing at her stern brow until it slanted somewhat eagerly and uplifting a corner of her mouth into an eerie grin.

She lifted a hand toward this man, her palm upward, fingers unfurling. The first two of her fingers moved, signaling for him to come to her.

A shaken hand went to the handle, and when the door came open, the hand rose submissively again. The man trembled as he approached her, pausing only when he saw shadows move across the concrete, human shadows, shadows that seemed to slip out from behind the large shadows cast by the giant creatures in the bursts of lightning.

The man looked up to her, her hand still outstretched for him. Her eyes were serene, calm, and indomitably inviting.

"Yes," she said, her voice reassuring and tender. "Place your hand in mine."

The man swallowed harshly. He inhaled deeply the hope of bravery, trying with all his might to at least project the air of confidence to her as he lifted his hand to her offered palm.

"Good," she said, staring to him, encouraging him. The gleam in her pretty blue eyes sparked, burst into flame, and became entirely red.

He winced, recoiling as he looked away, but she gripped his hand tightly. As the fire rose in her eyes, she pressed her free hand to his wrist.

He gasped at the connection. Her hand emitted heat, fiery heat, heat that did more than burn his flesh, heat that sank inside it. Forehead wrinkling as his face twisted in the pain of it, the man cried out. He looked up to her, her eyes were fixed to his.

"What's your name?" In both soft and energetic pulses, the

question came against his ears. It was as if multiple voices left her lips at once, some wanting to calm him, others to terrify him.

"Isaac." His features loosened; as the heat seemed to dissipate, confusion replaced agony within them. "Isaac Masters."

"Well, Isaac Masters," she said, releasing his hand. He stumbled backward slightly, eyes finding the spot she touched. The scent of singed flesh lingered on his arm, rising off of a brand-like wound there in the shape of a serpent and horns. He looked up to her and a brow arched over a scarlet eye. "Welcome to the afterlife."

She looked back into the faces of those in the cars. "No one else?" Aside from the storm, only labored breaths and heavy heart rates came to her ears. "Understand this," she yelled, but her face was calm, untouched by disappointment or anger. "There is no salvation but mine. No savior but me."

From behind her, moving in between the giants and lining the threshold of the tunnel, came more human beings. Mostly male, but not all.

"These are your new saints."

They stood around the car their leader used as a pulpit, all angled toward her, but not entirely facing her. Their eyes scanned the crowd of cars as the man with the gun had done. They raised from holsters on their thighs great, shining blades and slapped led pipes into their palms. One wrapped barbed wire around his fist. One shoved a piece of fabric into an old wine bottle. They had not come with their weaponry ready because they seemed to like the looks of fear in the faces of the people who watched them preparing.

"Brother Michael, Brother Freddy, Brother Skeet," she said as she gestured to her left then she extended her hand to the right. "Brother Jason, Sister Jocelyn, Brother Jack. Wesley, your Eldest Brother, the right hand of the devil, stands next to me, your new god."

"Most High," all spoke, save for Wesley. He had parted his

lips to join in the devotions, but a faint throbbing in his head clipped the words. He blinked purposefully, allowing the darkness of his closed eyes to absorb the pain, then he joined the others, gazing up to her. "Most Powerful. Devoutly we praise you. Your will is our law."

"Somewhere in the shadows, your patriarch, Conrad Sawyer, lurks. Do not tempt him with your demise. He seduces even the most devout. He binds angels in chains, sterilizing their human forms of all divinity. When you see his face, you will cower in fear or you will genuflect in awe. Please him, feeble mortals, for his contentment please me."

"Before the Awakener we fall," came the choir of sacrilegious saints, "for us, to the Unholy Savior he prays."

"Most of you will not survive this night." She paused, listening with preternatural ears for the gasps of worry, the spiked heart rates of terror. Tears came.

She could feel the suffering and the sadness and fear. Grief for the physical world that would fall away, and despair for the spiritual realm that awaited them.

Closing her eyes lightly, she breathed it in—absorbing the litany of last-minute prayers, invigorated by the fitful melodies of melancholy and misery. After a moment of this spiritual, sacrificial sustenance, she opened her eyes of erratic flame onto the earth again.

"I tell you this in the chance you live," she said, "for you will know my name and the names of my brothers. The name of my consort. Regard me with fear and wonder. Venerate the saints before you. And tell all who have not bore witness what you've seen."

She looked down to Wesley, who smiled lovingly at her, his hazel eyes ablaze with adoration. Palpable and vicious, she basked momentarily in the intensity of his desire. She grinned.

Her eyes moved to her brothers now, to the saints of her unholy creed. "Break what you must, be it bone or flesh or spirit, but remember, little brothers…" the words lingered as she spoke them; her voice slow, seductive. She swiped her tongue across her lips as if to taste the horrid flavor of the command as it hung upon them. "Destruction is the only fate for those young enough to have been born beneath the broken skies."

"Yes, my Lord," said Jocelyn, her gum snapping inside her smiling lips.

"Gotcha, Boss," Jason practically growled.

"Go on, then," she said, lightning emblazoning the sky behind her.

When the accompanying thunder roared, so too did the creature on her right roar. Its plump, bow-shaped lips opening wide, its jaw unhinging to accommodate this. Saliva clung to its sharp teeth and sparkled against their white enamel, then it looked about the road to its kin. All bellowed in return, the same fearsome manner expressed by myriad monstrosities shook the vehicles as they sat in disrepair. Mirrors cracked. The stoplights before the tunnel burst.

Cackling came then. Screams wrung out. Human figures moved through the tunnel, aiming knives and brass knuckles to the people fleeing this city, as the creatures rushed to rip the roofs of cars away.

Watching his brothers, Wesley remained by the center car, near the Unholy Savior, his gun firing only when a human sprinting for escape came too close to her.

This was his duty. The most precious of the merry men, his place was one of witness and rule. He looked up to Torrence, felt the heat circulating around her, watched it blow through her dark hair as the lightning bounced off of her cheekbones and her lips and reflected in her eyes. She appeared almost angelic in this golden glow, but Wesley could not consider angels. Not now. Not at the precipice of his full conversion.

Do not move. The sentence resounded in Wesley's mind. He'd heard it in Hell with Torrence, in the angel chambers full of wrought iron cages and Latin commandments.

Since that night in Hell, he could hear them—the angels. He could do nothing to shut them out. He figured he'd somehow opened the floodgate within his mind that separated his internalized world from their respective ones, but he didn't know how, so he could not undo it. He was helpless to it, to them and their intentions, their feelings. They could think things, words or images, memories, it didn't matter, and they could inject these thoughts into his brain.

It must've had something to do with this innate goodness everyone accused him of harboring, the purity consisted of what? Bloody dealings in broken-into homes and sexual excursions on hallowed grounds? He scoffed as he stood here in the presence of Nephilim and the demonically possessed.

Mythology had come alive around him, creating a fantasy world of logical reality. And now angels spoke to him in silence and with severity.

Their thoughts were not as human thoughts. Their internal monologue more representative of their immense spirits than of physical vocal chords and audible sound.

They came to Wesley in violent currents. Pressing upon his skin in waves and seeping into his ears, the energetic torrent flowed rapidly down his auditory canal, broke through his tympanic membrane, and collided with his cochlea.

Wesley not only heard the voices, he felt them. They tore through the matter of his body, breaking open the physical bonds that tied the mind inside its flesh, and pierced his brain. Severe, acute, overwhelming.

The first time it had happened, he thought he'd been stabbed by a white-hot blade that had just been sharpened for the kill. Punctured by static and electrocuted by thought.

He'd grown more accustomed to it now, but this familiarity did not lessen its physical repercussions, for it inflicted agony upon him with each syllable, and even in the all-encompassing noise comprised of car alarms and rumbling thunder and screaming, dying people, the whispered words were deafening.

The prophecy, came a thought.

"Ah, fuck!" Wesley's upper lip raised as he cried out, his lips parting, eyes closing firmly.

"Are you all right, Precious One?" Apart from a faint crease in her forehead, Torrence's face remained still. Adoration lilted her voice ever-so-slightly.

"Yeah," Wesley said, straightening his knees. He squared his shoulders to crack his back, then his neck. "Good."

It must come to pass, shot into his brain, but this time he'd been prepared enough by the first message to anticipate impending blows. He suffered, therefore, in a silence of tension and gnashing teeth. He tried to keep his eyes open, tried to fix them onto a specific point in the tunnel, but the channel of these messages flowed outward as well as inward.

When Wesley would look upon the face of a bleeding woman, the angels would weep. Their cries were shrill and echoed inside his skull, threatening, it seemed, to shatter the very bones surrounding his brain.

He'd blink away and open his eyes to some other point, but all around him was chaos. Eyes were torn from flesh and false lashes. Teeth were smashed against headlights.

Michael, having found a baseball bat in the trunk of an Honors Student Mother's SUV, transformed the instrument of athletics into a weapon of religious war. He shouted out prayers to Torrence as he smashed car windows with it, reigning down upon those inside a hailstorm of glass shards and splintering wood.

The angels hated this, they screamed at Wesley now, begging him to use his weapon against these people, for they were no longer people but servants of sacrilege.

He brought his hands to his ears, the cold metal of the handgun causing a sudden chill to roll over his spine. This attempt to silence all did little good, however.

The gang members laughed and taunted. From car to car they jumped, as if this assault were one fantastical game.

The creatures, with their muscular arms wrapped in opalescent armor, moved in the same pursuit, but more slowly, more controlled, as if fueled by mission more than fun. They groaned and made incomprehensible sounds as they did so.

Some of the saints responded to them. The one identified as Jason stood with a giant to the immediate left of Tim and Julie, and instructed it to find someone else. The pretty blonde in the white jaguar, he said, was his.

Witnessing this in awe-stricken terror, Tim and Julie could not tell if these creatures were communicating in an understood language or if they were merely speaking some animalistic tongue, interacting with the humans as a barking dog might interact.

"What is all this?" Tim gasped.

"The end of days," Julie murdered. "Should've left weeks ago. Before they forced us."

"Didn't think it was serious," Tim answered, still awestruck by the creatures and by their chaos.

As they moved throughout the tunnel, Tim noticed their varying eyes and digits, or lack thereof, their graying skin, accented by deep, stone-like purples and blues that speckled their cheekbones as if they possessed freckles made of gemstones.

Aside from their skin and their size, one final quality seemed shared by all. Upon their muscular backs were two large, oblong scars that ran half the length of their spines on either side of the protruding bones.

"Quattuor!" Jocelyn shouted from atop a red truck.

One of the giants turned to her, tilting its head as it awaited further instruction.

"The roof, honey," she said, kicking at the windshield. "Please."

As the being identified now as Quattuor made for the truck,

it responded in its unusual language, but ended the sentence with a human word, her name.

With little effort, Quattuor tore from the truck its roof and threw it behind his great shoulder.

It slammed against a wall of the tunnel, the tin cry of its bending metal echoing through the enclosed space with the car alarms and crying.

Jocelyn chuckled at this. "Go help Freddy, would yah, sweets?"

Quattuor nodded, moving back and to the third lane of cars, standing before a handsome man with dark hair and watching as he attempted to light a match in the windstorm.

Freddy looked up to the monster. He grinned when their eyes met.

Quattuor took from Freddy the cloth in his left hand and stared to it. After a moment of concentration, it burst into flame.

"Toss it out front," Freddy told him. "Tunnel's lined with gas. Torrence wants anyone fleeing to run straight into the fire."

Responding then nodding, the creature hurled the fiery cloth down the tunnel. It soared over the figure still standing on top of the center car at the tunnel's entrance. Behind her, the fire spread across the road in a controlled line, then an explosion shook the foundation of the structure and almost knocked Wesley to his feet.

Torrence stood there, draped in the darkness of the tunnel, face illuminated by flickers of orange and yellow as the fire contorted in the raging winds around her. She began to move.

Thankful for her departure, Wesley gasped out all the breath he'd been holding in. He was able now, in Torrence's distraction from him, to try to fight the shrieking inside his mind.

In electrical currents that cut through his mind in migraine-like waves, Wesley continued to absorb the melodic voices. His knees began to buckle. He fell into the car where Torrence had been standing, his body sliding down the side of it until he was no more than a crumpled ball on the road, violently shaking as the stabbing pressures of angelic voices thudded against him.

Do not move in this manner, the voice instructed him, as it so often did, but the sharp, shrill nature of it never grew more bearable. Instead, the inhuman wavelengths through which it moved worsened the experience of it with each blow to Wesley's already-pained head. Then came the commands of his leader, then the raging storm outside, then the innumerable sounds of people dying. All this combined with the unbearable heat blowing over him and into the tunnel as great gusts of wind pushed through the flames behind him.

Someone screamed. The sounds of people gasping for air became common within the concrete. A man stuck his head out of the rear window of a car, vomiting and crying.

Move for God, the piercing voice instructed, Save them.

Wesley's hands clasped onto his ears. He gritted his teeth and groaned, his eyes shutting tightly. "Can't do shit with you filleting my fuckin' brain!" he bellowed as glass burst around him and bones snapped and echoed through the enclosed road.

He yelled out again, but all those within the tunnel yelled. Whether it was battle cry or blood-curdling scream, all human vocal chords expressed the inner-workings of the souls inside their flesh.

People still tried to flee, but they were jumped on by the saints—stabbed, throats slit, punched by fists wrapped in barbed wire, or kicked with steel-toed boots. Giants smashed their hands through windows and pulled people from their cars, tossing them aside or crushing them in their grasps.

"Jesus!" someone shouted. "Dear God!"

"God?" Skeet responded. "Not here."

He kicked the woman, then thrust his blade into her stomach. Blood spilled from the torn flesh onto the pavement around her. A man running from Jack slipped in it.

Skeet rose from his crouching position before the gutted

woman and stuck his blade into this man's neck. A sharp wail came from him. Gurgling.

Wesley tried not to focus on the physical sounds. They caused the spiritual ones to rage. He wanted, instead, to focus on the warmth, perhaps. Yes, it was warm. It was suffocating heat.

No good, though. Too many of his senses were being targeted to ignore reality. The scent of burning flesh overpowered every inhale. The taste of his own sweat as it ran in streams down his face was too salty not to acknowledge. His skin felt sticky. He saw violence all around him. Then came something else—an unusual sight for this type of environment.

Through the flames came a figure. Wesley could see its shoes as it stepped inside the tunnel. It paused before him, gazing to him as he shook there on the road. He felt the pressure of its eyes, and found within himself the strength to look up at it.

"Fuck," he whispered sharply, his head falling forward as the pain of this small expression seized his tormented body. He gasped for air and looked up to it again. "Angel."

Armideus sent me, he responded in the silent, brain-piercing manner that only Wesley could hear. Each word another knife into his mind, a purposeful torment by an angel who had a manifested mouth and functional vocal chords. I am Formaadoria. I have been freed from Hell.

"Who? What the—?"

You may know him as 'War'.

"War?" He groaned. "He freed you?" His words, though barely audible in the chaotic echoes of the tunnel, were gruff and deepened by his aching body. "What are you gonna—?"

End this. The angel looked forward now, stepping away from Wesley. He attempted to heal injuries, to save those close to death from dying, but it had been bound inside Hell in Latin-riddled cages for months, and was weakened by it. The energy necessary for the angel to have located the antichrist and then show up at the threshold of her destruction was almost all the divine being could muster.

Bodies scattered the tunnel, no souls within them to be saved. The dying were spared a second or two of suffering, perhaps, by the focused energy of the angel, but they died still. And if Torrence had touched them, they would be sent to her Hell.

The angel stepped cautiously through the tunnel, slowly but with great authority. He moved with purposeful intent—save souls that were not lost to the antichrist and find a way to end her. Destroy her saints, undo this end of days.

Though he was but one angel, he considered as he grabbed the wrist of Jocelyn, he could injure the antichrist even by destroying just one member of her flock.

"What?" Jocelyn turned to find the source of her stifled arm. She cried out when the angel tightened his grip, the great pain that seized her combined with his glowing eyes and shiny, iridescent skin. He gleamed in the flashing headlights and blazing flame, radiating glory, yes, but contempt for all he witnessed here as well.

"You will torment no longer," he said to Jocelyn.

"Who the fuck are you?" Her voice was softened by her suffering.

"I am the bringer of your retribution." He squeezed more tightly, a mere flinch to him, but an indomitable pressure to the delicate, human wrist.

Jocelyn shrieked as her bone crushed. "Get off of me!"

"It is time to close your eyes to this world," he said. "You shall return to Hell. Do not fret. But no longer shall you torment. Your eternal fate is to become now one of the tormented."

He lifted his opposite hand. From its palm came sparks—small, incomprehensible flickers at first, which flowed forth from his flesh in gentle bursts, chiming as they broke the atmosphere. These small sounds grew in enormity as the specks of energy became beams of it. Wind blew around him now. He stood, it seemed, inside the focus of a human-shaped tornado, one that had broken loose from a great steeple, its large church bell, which rang out within the storm its ominous tolls.

"To Hell!" he yawped, his voice mighty yet lost to the chaotic clangor of the tunnel.

"With you," came a smooth, dulcet voice.

The angel turned to face its source and found reddened irises adorned with black lashes set inside irresistible, tanned skin.

"Festering spirit," the angel hissed out.

"Most people call me 'handsome'." Conrad's perfect, bow-shaped lips curled into a smirk.

"I am no person." Raising his now-free hand to strike at Conrad, the angel released Jocelyn. She staggered backward but Freddy, who jumped across the hood of a car to aid her, grabbed her waist before she could fall.

"You will be," Conrad said, his hand rising as quickly as the angel's and capturing within an iron, Latin-clad cuff his wrist.

"No!" The angel yanked free of Conrad, busting the Awakener's perfectly-sloped nose with the whipping chain. His hand and its great light grabbed at the iron locked around his wrist. "I will not be taken captive! Not again!"

Conrad's head had been thrown back by the blow, but he stood stern, facing forward again quickly. He lifted a hand to his gushing nose, studied the blood upon his fingers as if he hadn't known he could bleed, then he looked at the angel.

"You were a part of a plan. You should've played that part compliantly." Conrad's voice was easy, patient; honey for the ears as always, delicious and smooth, but oppressive—easily drawing anyone who might hear it in and ensnaring them inside its viscous nectar. "You would've gone back in mere shackles."

His head tilted, neck cracking. He stalked toward the angel, feet crashing into the pavement and leaving potholes in their wake. As his eyes flared, red glowing all around him. A fiery oblong formed a bastardized halo above the crown of his head. His plump lips opened, forming, as their corners slithered upward into his cheeks, a maniacal smile. "Now you go back bloody."

When he lunged at the angel, exhilaration gripped Jocelyn, distracting her from her broken bones. "Fuck him up, my Lord! Break his face!"

The angel cried out as Conrad exerted in brutal elation his monstrous fury, sending pulses of shrill thoughts into Wesley's mind as the giants and the unholy saints continued their assaults.

Thunder raged still. The lightning had not ceased.

While the chaos struck fear into most within the tunnel, it emboldened others. Skeet was quick to claim the fighters. He stood in silence before an anger-fueled almost-victim, wanting to feel the sensations of his own lip busting open when a human exerted all his physical strength upon him. It tickled. He liked that. After a chuckle or two, Skeet lifted his axe and buried it into his chest cavity or neck.

Tim and Julie, and those few still alive inside the tunnel, witnessed all in paralyzing dread.

A boot came down onto Tim's hood then. A body was before him and before Julie in the passenger's seat. These boots, black and shining where the blood of those evacuating this city had stained them, were mere inches from his face, from his family.

Trembling, he leaned into the steering wheel, his knuckles white as his sweaty palms gripped it tightly, and he lowered his head into his shoulders.

He peered up to her, this beautiful woman with savagery in her elegant features, as she shouted out orders to human and monster alike.

As people fled from their cars, running by Tim's window, being shot down by arrows and bullets and thrown-knives alike, torn limbs flew through the tunnel. These giants ripped at people's bodies, tearing them in two, and the humans who accompanied them seemed to dance in the blood that rained down around them.

"Torrence," yelled Freddy. "I got one!"

He held up by the ankle an infant, throwing it into the air and smirking as the great hand, sparkling and radiating its own twisted, divine magic, of a giant caught the child in its spell. In an instant, the child, lost inside the chiming bells and slowed time that seemed only to exist near a Nephilim exerting its will into the atmosphere, disappeared; crushed inside the large, glittering, gray fist.

Another gasp came from Tim, prompting Torrence's eyes to dart downward to him.

His eyes widened at this attention. How could she have heard this small noise with such screaming and crying and chaos all around them, echoing from the concrete walls of this tunnel and vibrating through it as one collective noise of agony?

It did not matter how she heard it, for she had heard it, and a brow arched over her left eye as she found Tim's gaze upon her.

"Oh, ye of little faith," she said, smirking. "A doubter." She knelt down, her forearms resting upon her knees, which were spread wide in a rather masculine taking-up of space. "You know, doubting the great godly father is the first step on the path to me." Her head tilted as she stared intently at him, the angle rendering all loveliness about her face eerie now and somehow inhuman. As her eyes narrowed further, she practically purred. "You know who I am?"

"No," he stammered almost inaudibly, his head backing into the headrest, desperate to create a greater distance between him and this woman.

With the blink of her eyes, the whites and blues vanished, replaced immediately by a glowing red streaked with quick, violent shocks of yellow. She smirked. "I'll allow you a guess."

"I…No…It can't be—."

A scream from the backseat interrupted his disbelief. He trembled in the presence of this undeniable evil. Sweating and gripping at the steering wheel, he seemed spellbound. He heard the cries of his children, but he could not break the connection of this woman's gaze. Her pupils like the skits of those of a serpent or even a predatory cat; her demeanor encompassing both attitudes perfectly and all at once.

"Sweetheart," gasped Julie. "It's okay." Turning toward her children, she continued to speak, but before she could finish her attempt to comfort them, a gag came from her lips. Blood followed. Gurgling.

Tim pulled his attention from Torrence and looked over to his wife, witnessing her clasping at an arrow lodged within the flesh of her throat. It bled as she attempted to breathe. Her children screamed and sobbed.

"Not to worry," Torrence said after a small cough of death encompassed Julie. Tim looked to her, her eyes still fixated upon him as a gargantuan figure appeared beside the passenger's side of the car. "The tribulations of this world are no more for her. We should be thankful for this."

Her words, punctuated by shattering glass as the giant, man-like shape thrust a fist with seven fingers through the widow next to Julie's corpse, were soft, like that of a minister consoling a family after their loss.

He jumped at this, at all of it, his eyes witnessing the unusually-large hand reaching into the vehicle. It grasped Julie, ripping her through the opening as if she were a mere doll, the jagged remnants of the glass tearing at both her clothing and her flesh as she was drawn through it.

The creature looked at the filleted body with its multitude of eyes, drew it closer as if it could not perceive it from the distance of his arm's reach, then sniffed it.

Looking to Torrence, who nodded very slightly toward the burning world behind it, the creature tossed the body over its shoulder. It moved, then, toward the back of the car as the corpse thudded against the hood of someone else's vehicle. Repeating the action on the back window, this giant reached now for the children in the car.

All three humans screamed. Tim moved now for his daughters, but from Torrence's boot came her knife. She pressed a release button on its black handle and a silver blade seemed to burst from within it.

With great force, she shoved the blade into Tim's shoulder, pinning him to the seat of his car. He cried out in pain as he attempted to break free of it, but she kicked the weapon violently, shoving it deeper into his shoulder. Half of the handle was inside him now, further opening his wound, pinning him down more securely.

"You could've died with them," she said, her tongue swiping over the fresh blood spattered upon her lips. "But now for your disobedience you will watch them die before you do."

She looked up to the creature, which held a child in each hand, and eyed first the older one. She shook her head, and the giant tossed the girl upward, then opened his palm. Her body caught in the wave of the time-loop its divinity thrust into the air. The glistening sparks of angels came forth next, pinging against the child, covering her in glitter and adorning her cries with the ringing of small, elegant bells. Then, with a flick of his wrist, she was gone, tossed aside. Her body thudded against the concrete wall of the darkened tunnel and splattered beneath the pressure of it.

Torrence delighted when Tim screamed. For all Tim knew in this moment was that his daughter had just been killed.

Pain had always been enjoyable, yes, for the power of it; Torrence had been able to cause such an intense emotion in another person, and that person had no control over the experience of it.

But, this was prophecy. It had been written that he, born beneath the broken sky, was the sole spirit able to end the apocalypse, and Torrence, who ruled here on this broken planet, now ensured that they, whoever they were, could never reach the potential of that prophecy, which stated the antichrist's reign would end after a mere forty years, by not allowing anyone young enough to fit the aforementioned time-frame to live that long.

Torrence's eyes moved to the younger one now. The infant. Her eyes seemed to glow, for the space around her became illuminated in a deeply-red hue.

The giant seemed to understand what this meant, and it thrust inside the loop and glittering air the screaming baby, then crushed it in its palm.

Torrence moved toward the giant, climbing on the roof of the car. Extending her hands to the creature's face, Torrence smiled and kissed its forehead. "Good boy," she said, petting its cheeks. "That's my good, little abomination."

She moved away from the monster now, looking about the tunnel. Car alarms blared. People were sobbing and screaming. Some were gurgling as they died.

Through the ribcages of running humans, these giants, these Nephilim created by her force-breeding of angel and human, shot from their golden bows glistening, silver, diamond-encrusted arrows.

As the thunder rumbled, the wailing died out. Screams became sighs. The last breaths of final moments faded. Life had been extinguished here.

It was enough relief to allow Wesley control over his body again, and as he released his tightened muscles and unclenched his jaw, he heard Torrence's voice, even above the continued cries of intrusive, external thoughts.

"Any more, Little Brothers?" Torrence shouted.

"None here," Jocelyn yelled from one side.

"Got 'em, Boss," came Jason's voice.

"None!" Michael shouted.

"Just a trophy," Conrad said, shoving forward the angel he'd bound at the wrists with spell-laden chains. "Tried to sneak in with the Nephilim."

"Pesky little insect," Torrence said.

"Disgusting abomination." He gasped when Conrad struck him, then sucked the human sound into his teeth. He looked back up to Torrence. Human-like blood oozed from his nostrils, his ears. His left eye was bruised and already-swelling. His busted lips curled, revealing his teeth in a defiant snarl. "Forty years."

"No prophecy against the Savior shall ever come to pass," said Conrad. "He that is born beneath the broken skies will not live long enough to see his first birthday, much less end the supposed-forty years of the antichrist."

"'Forty,' says God," Jocelyn said with a smirk. "'Eternity,' says Torrence."

She smiled, sinister and sincere, then she noticed Jocelyn's wrist in her hand. "What happened there?"

"It's broken."

"Give it to me," Torrence said, taking Jocelyn's arm into her hand and using her deviant divinity to piece the bone back together.

"The angel," Conrad said to Torrence. "He's suffered for it."

"He'll suffer further in Hell," she said to Conrad, her eyes boring into the angel. After a moment, she looked about the tunnel, locating her brothers one by one as they came toward her. "And where is Wesley?" she asked, ready to complete the routine she'd been enacting for what seemed like ages now.

"Ready for you," he said breathily, moving through the burning cars and broken bodies slowly. No, do not move. "As always."

"Good," she said.

"Torrence?" came a voice unrecognized and weary.

She turned to it immediately. In a car stuck in the traffic jam beyond the tunnel sat a man.

He blinked his narrowing eyes as he climbed out of the window of his collapsed and smoking car.

"Todd?"

"Hey!" He smiled widely, approaching her with his arms

outstretched.

Two of her Brethren caught him before he could near the car upon which she still stood. Michael secured his arm while Jason drew back a chain-wrapped fist.

"Easy, gentlemen," Todd said, his palms open and upward to signal submission. "I was a follower before you were."

"Unlikely," Jason said, scoffing.

"Let him go," Torrence said as she jumped down from the car. "His word is good. I knew him long before I knew any of you."

"Who the hell is he?"

"Jason," Torrence said simply, and he apologized.

"Can I try again?" Todd asked, extending his arms as he moved to her.

She allowed him the friendly embrace, even returning it with a bit of enthusiasm.

"What happened to you?" he asked. "I mean, not now. All those years ago. What happened?"

"I had to get away."

"Yeah, I get that."

"Destined for grander things, you might say."

He chuckled. "Well, you knew that back then. We all knew it. But you just left us. Didn't even tell us where you were going."

"I didn't really know where I was going. Not if I'm being honest."

"You could've taken us with you, though. We would've followed you anywhere."

"You can still," she said, allowing her blue eyes to gleam red.

"It's true," he said in astonishment. "You really are the antichrist."

"You've heard that I was?"

"No," he said. "I've seen the desecration of cathedrals. I'm a photographer. Worked for a few newspapers. Kind of followed in the footsteps of your—." He broke off, looking away. His hand rubbed at the back of his neck. "Nevermind. I just…I've been traveling anywhere they reported an incident, and I've been compiling a book of the new monuments. As soon as I saw the new images painted over the ceiling of a cathedral in New Orleans, I knew it was you. It looked too realistic, too much like a photo, to be someone else. So I…I started going to wherever weather incidents were being predicted. Kind of hoped I could meet up with you."

"What about Aaron?"

"He didn't survive the skies," Todd said.

"So, you remained close?"

"Of course we did. Think of all we've been through."

"How'd it happen?"

"Hurricane. Can you believe that? Who'd think we'd have ever seen a hurricane back home?" He chuckled nervously. "Of course you can. You probably sent it."

"No," she said quickly. "Some of the storms are mine. Others are just side effects."

"Side effects?"

"The demons, the angels. The energy they emit when they break through the atmosphere, it can cause all kinds of things."

"So, only the killings are yours, then?"

"At least they serve a purpose now."

"To fill your kingdom? Hell? I don't want to die, Torrence, but I will gladly follow you. I always have."

"You were a mere boy then. Why do you think, as a fully capable man, you'd submit again? And so willingly?"

"I knew you before all this," he said. "If I followed you then, why wouldn't I follow you now? You're even more powerful than we ever could've imagined, but you always said what we were doing was your career." He smiled, then his face became more solemn. "Genuinely, you were my best friend. After Perry…I mean, you were really there for me. You understood what I was going through. No one's ever understood me the way you did."

She stared at him for a long moment, eyes and energy all scanning him for signs of deceit. When she found none, she nodded, then a small smile came to her lips. "Okay, then." She extended her palm to him. "Give me your wrist. Wear my brand."

"Brand?" he asked nervously as he worked the sleeve of his jacket upward and offered her his arm.

She gripped his wrist tightly, jerking it toward her. Placing her fingers over the veins there, Torrence focused her heated energy onto the spot.

Todd gasped as his skin tingled, warmed, then singed beneath her touch. He stared down to the burning flesh, but he did not budge.

Torrence's eyes were fixated on his skin, too, but slipped away from the forming horns of her serpent to find his shaken hand. She stared into his palm as he trembled, her brow arching when she saw the scar there. His old commitment to her rendered a mortal memory now by this new, everlasting one.

"Fuck." He exhaled painfully when she released him. He looked up to her. "That's it?"

"That's it?" Jason asked from behind Torrence, his brows furrowing as he stared to the still-burning skin. "You thought it'd be worse than that?"

Inhaling the smell of his burning flesh, Todd swallowed thickly, then he chuckled. "Yeah," he said. "We used to have to bleed."

"We still bleed," Wesley said as Torrence took him by the hand. "Only our wounds are not so material."

"For real, Boss?" Jason asked. "One of us, just like that? He doesn't have some dedication test? Some show of loyalty?"

"He's proven himself time and time again," Torrence said. She stepped out of the tunnel, eyeing the distant trees and mountains that set over the evacuating city. "But what about a little bonding? Brotherly bonding."

CHAPTER TWO

The sole of Torrence's combat boot stamped into the muddy dirt as she exited the car.

"Fuck, I'm ready for this, Boss," Jason snarled out. He clapped his hands, his body bouncing its weight onto one foot then the other. "I like this damnation shit as much as the next guy, but I'm ready for some good, old-fashioned fun."

"Me, too," Michael said. He wrapped an arm around Freddy. "You're going to actually go crazy with us this time, right?"

"Yeah," Freddy said, his confidence returning with his enhanced strength and power, with his returned beauty, all thanks to Torrence. "Yeah, I'm ready to get back to the fun."

"Say the word, Boss," Jason said to Torrence, his grin eager and maniacal and in the worst, most beautiful way thanks to the final communion and his loyalty rewards.

"You have six minutes," Torrence said, smirking, leaning back against the hood of the SUV, her arms crossing as she watched her brothers run toward the home. She looked to Todd. "Have fun, my returned brother."

"Fun?"

She withdrew from the holster on her thigh a great silver

blade. Offering it to him, Torrence grinned. "Like the old days."

As he stared at the blade, Todd slipped off his suit jacket. He removed his tie and opened the first few buttons of his shirt. A sinister smile spread across his lips and infected the rest of his face with its eerie glow. "Like the old days," he confirmed, taking the knife and following his new Brothers toward one of few homes in the city that seemed to still contain life.

Leaning against the car again, Torrence watched Michael kick at the door, busting it open after only one attempt now that he was gifted some semblance of Torrence's demonic energy, when in the whole-sky days, it would've taken him three. He and Jason and Todd ran in, unbridled and eager, while Freddy crossed the threshold with more control. She wondered if he'd burn the house to the ground when they'd finished their work.

"Any reason you're not rushing in?" Torrence asked without looking over to Wesley.

He stared at her, his head lowered, always ready to bow to her, always looking for some semblance of affection or security before he said something unsavory. It didn't come. "I guess it just isn't as fun as it used to be."

"Why's that?"

"I don't know, Tor. We're different now. Everything has some grand scheme to it, some prophecy or fate. Feels wrong to do things for no reason once you've been given a purpose."

"Not everything is about work, Precious One."

Wesley snorted. "Right. You've got no plan here but to have fun."

"Sometimes you have to let loose a little." She winked.

"Yeah, but I don't know if letting loose for me is killing someone or assaulting them or breaking their expensive china."

"Then why did you come?"

"Because you invited me."

"You're required to accept every invitation now? Since when?"

"Since always."

"Then it's a requirement you put upon yourself. You could've gone home with Conrad and the Nephilim." Turning her head to look at him now, Torrence glowered. "I thought you might enjoy this—a return to the old ways."

"Oh, you do things for other people now?" He chuckled.

"You step out of line now?" She looked to him, her face free of emotion, merely studious.

He shook his head, smiling as he lowered his head. After a moment, his features became grave. He looked forward, stern-faced. His brows came together. "I hear the angels," he said, eyes concerned but unafraid. "The ones in the cages. They whisper to me."

"They do? What do they say?"

"They say I shouldn't let you touch me. They say you mark people that way—you mark their souls that way—and when we sin together, I'm in the perfect position spiritually to be marked by you."

"I can't mark good souls unless I catch them in an act of sin, you know that."

"I do," he said. "My question is just…why haven't you marked me already?"

"Why would you want me to? You realize marking a soul means marking it for Hell."

"Yeah, obviously. Hell is where you are. Hell is your kingdom. You don't want me with you eternally?"

"You misunderstand my motivations. Just as War does."

Wesley's nostrils flared. War. "So, what happens to me, then? When I die? I just go to Heaven regardless of all sins and violence and lust? Or I go to Hell anyway, just without your approval?"

"I don't know, Wesley," she said, looking over to him now. "I'm not God, no matter how much I profess to be."

"What does that mean?" He recoiled, lips curling in their confusion.

"It means that whatever I am, it's part of a prophecy I didn't create. I rule in Hell, but I don't choose who goes there, not unless I lure them in."

"And you haven't lured me in? You don't think taking me away from a normal, legal life and—."

"I didn't take you away. You let me."

"Of course because you promised me—."

"I've delivered on all of my promises, but don't confuse your decision for my manipulation. You would've followed me regardless of what I offered. You would've followed me had I offered nothing. Love in general is your downfall, Wesley. Not love for me specifically."

"That's not…No, that isn't it."

"You're sensitive, and your heart is open and always searching," she said. "You would've gone with any woman who promised to love you."

"Okay, wow," he said, uncrossing his arms as he moved away from the car. He took only a step or two toward the house before he stopped and turned back to her. "No, you know what? No," he said. "I might have gone with another woman. I might have explored any opportunity I had to fall in love and feel loved back, but I wouldn't have gone to this extreme, not for just anyone. You…you know the hold you have over the people around you. I bet you've done it your entire life. I mean, who's Todd? He's proven himself time and time again, right? Well, when? Because I've known you for years, and I've never seen him. So, why?"

"Why?"

"Why pretend like you care about me? Why pretend I'm more than the others?"

"Because you are more than they are. I don't pretend. Not with you. I've never been anything but honest with you."

"Then be honest now. Why do you want that angel?"

"I want him for the same reasons I wanted you."

"Wanted me. Not want."

"Wesley."

"Whatever, Tor." He withdrew from his thigh holster the same gun he'd been carrying since the communions. "Is this okay? Do I use one of the few remaining guns on the planet on someone we kill just for fun? Is there some ritual to make sure one of us completes?"

She stared to him, her face stoic, her body straight and stern, her shoulders squared inside her cropped, faux-leather jacket.

"You know the prophecy. If one of those inside qualifies, kill them. Kill the ones that won't join you. Kill them even if they will. Just loosen up, will you? Your mental constipation is giving me a headache."

He shook his head, throwing up his hands. "Fine." Stalking toward the house, he muttered as he withdrew his gun. "Kill 'em all. Fine, Torrence. Whatever."

Though she heard this, she did not engage with it. She had to encourage Wesley in this manner. He'd always been emotion-driven, even when he was rough or angry or violent.

Her brothers, well, all they needed was the promise of it. Go in there, break in, bust the windows, hurt the people, make them bleed, feel alive because they're dead and you made them that way.

Oh, they were all so easy for their trauma, and Wesley, for his lack of it, for his broken heart—the worst suffering he could experience, and how trivial such a trauma was to his brethren for what they'd endured—well, Wesley was difficult.

For Wesley, love was always the end-goal. Love had always been the ultimate accomplishment.

Wesley grew up on pop culture, on the movies and the songs that described oneness in another. He'd never imagined, even after he'd obtained his degree and secured an impressive career, that he'd be successful—not fully. Complete success required love. It meant marriage to someone like Wesley. Success was only internal so far as shared emotion was concerned. Success was a woman and her love for him.

It was easy for Torrence to offer love to Wesley. He was

beautiful and smart and undeniably devoted. She remembered the beauty of her first love when she looked at Wesley, and she thought of the glorious physicality of War.

Torrence had always been a sucker for a beautiful man, for a solemn man, for downcast eyes within handsome features, the silent type, sure, but not the strong. These men were few and far between, however, so genuine lust, even when mistaken for love, didn't occur much at all for her.

There were attractive men, sure, and there were attractive women. She'd have taken Jason or Freddy in this manner if she had had to, if that had completed some goal of hers, but it took more than proximity and physical appeal to create an actual sexual want within Torrence, and she wanted Wesley when she provided intimacy to him. She wanted War.

Where Wesley differed from War was in his willingness. She learned originally at eighteen-years-old, and now again at thirty-three, that her sexual proclivity for goodness was merely an extension of her desires to destroy it. The love of her life all those years ago had been an alter-boy, the son of a preacher, a jock at a Christian high school who was shy and pensive and artistic, instead of fitting the outgoing and rather obnoxious stereotype of an athlete.

He had been beautiful, of course, blond and blue-eyed and slight of frame. Oh, Torrence had wanted him. Tempted him. Possessed him. But when her tendencies became others' actions, he was too fearful to fall in line. What a waste.

She supposed she saw reflections of him within War, back when she thought War was a human. He'd been so faithful and devout, she'd imagined him a strict Catholic, and though she hadn't realized it then, it was the same desire to possess through corruption the appeal of that righteous spirit.

She didn't want to be righteous, but she wanted anything that was alluring, even if it was innately good.

Besides this, the object of her first lustful desire, like Wesley, then like War, had never been intended to follow as the others had. They were to be devoted and subservient, of course, but their position was planned for her side—a position Wesley claimed to want now, though he'd never stepped into it.

She felt inclined to blame Wesley for this, for taking away from her the one shot she had to make a good soul her sinful consort, for it had been his choice to join the ranks and inflict pain through violence. He could have said no. He could have denied Torrence.

Her lips pursed in intrigue—was the thing she desired most in those around her the very thing that turned her off? The term was a romantic partner, after all. Sexual partner. Not romantic inferior or sexual submissive.

Was this why she dismissed War now? Why Wesley no longer held the same appeal he had when she'd first seen him? No. Plans for them, plans for both of them. She considered her brothers in the house. Plans for all of them.

But regardless of Wesley, or anyone else, or the need to dominate and control, Torrence understood with undeniable clarity that War was not appealing in the way Wesley had been. War was something entirely different, and whatever she felt for him ran far deeper than any emotion a human had caused in her, even if it was something as fickle as lust or desire.

But these were contemplations for a later time, maybe some day when War came to her with wings extended and freckle-like stars exposed.

Tonight was not that night. Tonight was a night for chaos.

Torrence waltzed toward the home. Much like the olden days of full skies, or even those days of snagged ones, Torrence was but a leader tonight—not of demons or nearly-fallen angels, but of human monsters; monstrous men.

"What's it going to be?" she whispered to herself as she strolled up to the door, which had been splintered so that the dull brown of its original state became visible in its red paint through jagged lines. It became a lovely representation to Torrence of nature overpowering mankind, of a natural state breaking through the synthetic mask.

She felt she was donning the mask again—the human one, the one that painted full lips and gleaming blue eyes onto the soul of the devil—but she didn't mind. Not only did her brethren, her demonically-gifted human men, deserve a release of pent-up, apocalyptic planning, but the residents of this home—a lovely, devout couple—potentially had something Torrence needed for her hellish take-over of the planet.

A child.

A child had been born. This was prophecy. New life in the end of times. The life's beginning shared a date with the world's end.

"And within that new life breathes the life of us all, for the dealer of death cannot prevent; he can only destroy." This was what the demonically-possessed teenager cried out in a church basement. He'd been bound to a chair. His father stood by, weeping, as a Father of the church prayed over him. It was no matter though. The daimon that existed around Conrad, his higher-self, his soul's full form, well, it had already begun seeping into the cells of his human body at this point, even though viewers of the old VHS tape might not have known it. The Father and his father surely hadn't known it then.

But the dealer of death he'd prophesied was his great, Unholy Savior, the one he'd grown to awaken to full glory in his thirty-fifth year of life.

He knew she'd be powerful. He knew she'd be beautiful. He knew she'd be some years his junior, for Christ was thirty-three at crucifixion, and Biblical prophecy always seemed aligned with literary symmetry. Oh, the antichrist would be thirty-three during the final of her seven communions, so he spent many years awaiting her, planning for her, studying for her, ensuring he'd be not only her Awakener, but her adviser, her confidant, her most knowledgeable and well-versed prophet. He was all of those things, and even more.

But now was not the time to think of Conrad, to remember his youthful face in that old tape, still beautiful beneath the blood and bruise. Now was the time of prophecy he'd spouted through demonically-infested vocal chords, creating a voice that shook the very foundations of the church in which he had been captive.

That prophecy was of life anew, and Torrence would not have such a thing as that. So she sent her brothers in to destroy those who would not evacuate their home—another couple, and another child.

She ascended the staircase, hearing the voices of her brothers.

"Prepare yourselves," Freddy said.

"She's coming," Wesley added.

Amongst the crying and the pleading came a sharper sound, a smaller one.

"What was that?" Wesley asked.

"Kid, maybe," said Jason.

"A kid?" He turned toward the door and saw Torrence standing there. "Just for fun, huh?"

"Michael, go take care of that baby."

"Torrence—."

"Wesley," she interrupted him sharply.

His chin raised, eyes glistening as they fixed on those of Torrence. His lower lip moved into his teeth as his jaw clenched, and he took in more air than necessary to inhale. He shook his head lightly as he stared at his ruler here, his friend, his lover. When he exhaled, his shoulders lowered, his deflating as his defiance fled his lips with the expelled air.

Behind him, the man who resides here began to shift, to rise. Wesley stared Torrence, his nostrils flaring briefly, lips pursing in disapproval, then he turned quickly and shot the man between the eyes.

He fell onto his wife who screamed. Wesley raised his gun to her, his brow stern over his hazel eyes, eyes that bore into the woman's eyes. They were blue, swollen by tears and spattered with blood.

Her child screamed in the other room as heavy footsteps drew nearer to it.

"Damn it," Wesley said, gritting his teeth. In one swift motion, he holstered his gun and made for the door.

Pausing when he got to Torrence, gazing into her raging eyes with a soft, worried disobedience, he lowered his head as he moved by her.

"Freddy," Torrence said, "break her legs. Then set the place ablaze."

Wesley stopped in his tracks, shuddering when he heard the snapping of bones and its subsequent wails.

He followed the sound of the crying child around a corner and then down a long hallway.

He heard his brothers' feet moving about the house. He heard the softer steps of Torrence, her smaller feet, shorter legs, smaller stride.

Glass broke somewhere behind him. Screaming came again. Torrence laughed, and the roar of flame, so recognizable to those who lived within the borders of Hell, tore through the room, which was far behind Wesley now.

He didn't know what he was doing. He didn't know why. To any regular human being, he was simply doing what was right. He was rescuing a child from two terrifying men, even if he left their mother alone in a room with the antichrist and her pyromaniac companion. Baby steps, perhaps, but toward a very uncertain and entirely unknown destination.

A laugh came from the room at the end of the hall, inspiring Wesley's steps to press on more quickly.

Sweat beaded on his smooth forehead. The air around him grew hot as the fire ravaged through the home.

His hands gripped onto the door-frame when he reached his destination. He stared inside the room, watching Jason and Michael as they hovered over a crib.

"Guys, don't—."

"Don't what?" Jason asked, turning toward Wesley, revealing the contents of the crib.

Wesley stared to the display, only noticing now amongst the sounds of the crackling fire and busting glass, that the small crying had died out.

"Let me guess," Torrence said from behind him.

"What?" It was more an exhale than a spoken word. His hands, still pressing against the door-frame, became fists.

"You rushed back here because you wanted to do it." Leaning in over his shoulder, her voice was low with cruelty and seemed to float from her lips in a purr. "You wanted to be the one who destroyed some holy prophecy for the sake of your savior."

His lips curled, but he tried to smile through it. "Yeah," he said, sucking in his breath as his nostrils flared, his arms falling away from the door-frame. He looked over his shoulder to her. "You know me so well."

"Maybe I do," she said, her hands slithering around his waist. She rested her chin on his shoulder as she pulled him roughly against her.

His eyes closed in response to this jerk, rolling as they opened only to watch Jason ignite the blankets of the crib now.

"Maybe that's the problem," she said, kissing his neck as her nails grasped at his shirt, ripping through the fabric and scraping at his skin.

"Torrence." Freddy gulped at the air as he approached them from the opposite end of the hallway. "The entire downstairs is burning. It's coming from both sides."

Wesley's brows raised as he looked down into the hallway on his left then on his right.

Michael and Jason came to the door, witnessing the flames that were coming toward them.

Torrence moved away from Wesley, standing before Freddy now, glaring at him for a long moment until she felt the fear pulsating within his frame.

"I'm sorry," he said finally.

She looked about the hallways, felt the heat of the flames and saw the golden illumination on the walls of the staircase. "Well," she said, an eager twinkle in her eyes. "This should be interesting."

"If we die in here," Jason said to Freddy, "I'm gonna spend our entire afterlife beating your ass."

"Easy," Wesley said. "Look." He nodded upward toward an attic door. He pulled the cord and lowered its small, wooden stairs. "There's a window up there, I'm sure."

Torrence climbed them first, then Wesley, then the band in no particular order. Oh, it had been the way of things since the skies were solid, but it was an unspoken order then. Now, it was the hierarchy of Hell.

Instead of a window, the attic had sliding doors. As the glowing heat blazed light into the dark room from its small, squared entrance, the merry men rushed to the glass, breaking it with an old Christmas decoration instead of opening it.

All moved onto the balcony, gripping at the banister and staring downward at the grass and the pavement.

"Well, would you look at that?" Excitement flickered in Torrence's eyes. She looked up to Wesley. "A leap of faith." Her brow arched.

"You want us to jump, Boss?" Jason asked from Wesley's opposite side.

"I want you to trust in me."

"I do," he said, beginning to move.

Wesley's hands came to him, a palm flattened on his stomach and a fist gripped the back of his shirt. "Whoa," he said, glancing back to Torrence. "That'll kill you, man. We're stronger, but not immortal, not invincible."

"You don't trust me?" Torrence's head, eyes narrowing.

"I trust you, Boss!" Jason said. He climbed onto the railing, and Michael and Freddy followed suit.

Panting, Todd entered the attic, a few stolen treasures swaddled in his coat jacket. Just like the old times.

Wesley watched Todd move toward the men, these strangers, which had, moments ago, become his brothers. He looked to Torrence, brows creasing over pained eyes.

"You don't trust me in the slightest," she said to him. "You really think I'm the monster."

Tension ravished the muscles of his handsome face, shaking his plump lips, which tightened in an effort not to cry. He really had thought she was a monster, the monster, the end-all evil. Perhaps she wasn't.

As he approached, Todd looked to Torrence now, his face, though slightly-aged since she'd last seen him, looked all-at-once boy-like again. He moved onto the railing with his brand new brothers as if he'd known them his entire life, as if he'd been following Torrence steadily from the age of sixteen straight-through his years until this very moment.

Torrence looked up to him; love seemed to radiate from her, tangible and felt by all around her.

It troubled Wesley at first in his perception of it, but he realized rather quickly that this affection was as self-adulating as it was focused on Todd. Yes, climb the rail for me, Wesley imagined her thinking, Jump for me, die for me.

She blinked to Wesley, a brow lifting in arrogance, in acknowledgment of his conjecture. It was cute, his perception of her. She liked how evil he thought she was. Unadulterated evil, and with no redeeming qualities, perhaps, than her affection, which only existed within her soft spot for his handsome face.

Oh, there was no use trying to argue or alter this idea. Torrence knew he'd only see her attempts as manipulation.

Besides this, she liked being seen as bad, liked the thrill of it, the way it stopped people in their tracks and silenced them; the way it made people, in either fear or admiration, do whatever she wished of them.

Torrence looked up to her band of merry men, her eyes finding Jason's then Michael's then Freddy's. When they came to Todd's eyes, he nodded, his face free of worry or concern. He smiled to her—his restored leader now his new god—and he opened his arms and allowed his body to fall back.

Next was Jason, who tossed himself from the ledge. Not wanting to be outdone by this new recruit and his loyalty or his guts, Jason jumped into the air with his hands together over his head as if he were diving into a swimming pool, not concrete and grass.

Freddy looked to Torrence. "I love you, T," he said.

"I love you," she replied, watching him jump.

After a smile, Michael, in his strong silence, dove into the air.

Wesley had climbed swiftly onto the railing, reaching for the men as they fell, but he caught no one.

Torrence joined him, her brows raised as she watched them.

"You want us dead, Torrence?" Wesley asked, his face aghast.

"The minute you're born you're dead. It's inevitable."

"Unless you're you."

"What?"

"You can't die," he said, exhaling a fearful breath. "Can you?"

"No, and because I can't, neither will you." She grabbed the collar of his jacket with both hands and jumped.

Caught in the air it seemed, Wesley looked about the sky. He was trapped there, almost as if the sky had thickened, though it wasn't hard or uncomfortable. A blink, slow and easy, seemed to take more time to complete than typical, and he realized in that, as he looked over toward Torrence, that he was experiencing that same type of time-loop he'd been stuck inside after the communions, the sacrifices.

He saw his brothers tumbling slowly, carried downward, not thrown or plummeting. He looked over to Torrence, who moved freely inside these loops of time. Arrogance angled her chin upward as she drew him into her, wrapping her arms around his shoulders and nestling her cheek against his hair.

"Holy shit," Wesley said as they landed, their brothers falling gently around them in the same protective fields of Torrence and her abilities. "I thought you manipulated blood. What the hell?"

"Matter," she said. "All things are matter. I've been practicing. Getting stronger. This is why I told you planning was better than diving right in."

"You're right as always," he said, reaching for her hand and bringing it to his lips. He kissed it, then brought it to his chest and kept it there. "My Lord." He smiled.

"Boys," Torrence called, hearing them grunt around behind her and at her side. She sat up, moving atop Wesley as she looked around from Jason to Michael to Freddy. "Run along home. Mommy and Daddy need a few moments alone."

"Aren't they our brothers?" Wesley asked, hearing their footsteps, the sounds of doors and a car engine.

"Sometimes," she said. "Sometimes they're only children."

"And that makes me…?"

"Whatever I want you to be."

"What do you want me to be right now, Torrence?"

"Inside me," she whispered, leaning into him.

Wesley grinned at this response, eager to commit whatever lustful trespass Torrence offered, especially in these moments after a violent one.

When she climbed atop him, draping her legs around his hips, pressing her center into his center, he tried to ignore the smell of smoke around them. He blinked; looked up to the moon. He tried to picture the only illumination in the great field as that of the silvery, pre-tear moon. Don't focus on the fire, the flame, the heated rolling off of the burning home, its yellow, deviant light.

The light of Hell itself.

"Your eyes," Torrence said, rolling her hips over his.

"I know." He groaned, half in response to her body against his, and half in response to the chastising words.

"No." She chuckled, gripping his jaw and forcing him to look at her. She saw within their human colors the innocence of angels; the purity of War. Within Wesley, his distaste for demonic red irises and the destruction blazing behind them, that trait of true appeal—purity.

Disgusting as it was within the populations of human and angel alike, when found within the eyes of a handsome man, Torrence could deny its enticing beauty.

Perhaps it was the chase of it, of conquering that which should remain pure, she wasn't certain. But unadulterated innocence was an aphrodisiac, and the only thing more pleasurable than conquering it was chasing it.

Follow me, children, she thought, but Fear me, was an even better consideration. Run from me, for I am the unholy, I am the strength to coerce and corrupt, and you will either bend to my will or flee in fear of it.

After all, what could God do to an unholy soul? Did He have the power it might take to convert it? To make righteous what has so-long been sullied by the freedoms and fun of sin? Torrence was stronger than God for this. Torrence could convert. Even angels fell willingly into her bed, and even the one who'd denied her longest eventually gave in.

And Wesley, who laid beneath her now in a field of moistened grass, allowed her murder, arson, infidelity, even as he wept over these very acts.

Willing love. Yes.

When he looked up to her, Torrence's brows raised slightly.

Though the blood affected him, ignited within him his spiritual strength, bestowed upon him the demonic gifts of the antichrist's most beloved followers, it did not seem to take hold of him as it had the others of her flock.

His eyes, which stopped her briefly in her assault, were the same lovely hazel they'd always been. They weren't red. They weren't fire and brimstone. They were human and deep and ever pensive.

She reached for him, touching him, running her fingers through his hair, and resting her hand at the base of his neck.

Letting her fingers delicately massage him there, Torrence smiled. He really was a beautiful man, a timid one for all his violent ways now, ways that he'd mimicked from Torrence's actions and the actions of the two close-followers she'd had when he'd first met her.

Maybe the angel in the dungeon had been right; it wouldn't have been a surprise to her if it had been. After all, Torrence hadn't been stalking Wesley when she found him, not at first. No, Wesley wasn't a Michael or a Jason. Wesley wasn't someone with a streak of violence in his actions or intentions, and he wasn't someone bullied or beaten down. At first, when Torrence saw him, she wasn't sure there'd be an easy way for her to slip inside him.

His roommate, Dan, had been the object of her stalking. Dan worked out, always playing basketball or soccer in the public courts and on campus, always receiving some flag or foul for unnecessary roughness.

This was what piqued Torrence's interest all those years ago. This is what led Torrence to that college campus, what brought her, as if by fate, to occupy the same space as the stranger who would one day become her most precious brother.

Studying Dan very closely, never taking her strategic eyes away from him, Torrence was caught off-guard when her target became the aggressor in a shoving match on the court, but not because there was a scuffle and not because he was the center of it; instead it had been the man who inserted himself between the bruisers.

Her eyes narrowed in on this man, his oddly-attractive hands pressing against the flesh of Dan's chest; these hands were impressive in size and strength as their force pushed one belligerent man away from the other, but when the brawl subsided, these strong hands moved by different means.

They floated through the air as they returned to their body, rubbing a self-soothing comfort across a strong jawline, then over plump lips.

"Wow," Torrence whispered to no one, maybe to God or to Lucifer, maybe to some unnamed savior she didn't know existed, maybe simply to herself.

Torrence had never been one for romantic notion—not in any traditional or common manner. She used those sensibilities when the situation called for it, but she'd never really experienced some desire that didn't also achieve a goal outside connection, even if that goal were simply to obtain something gorgeous. If she had, it might have only been once, back when she was new to this violence and this leadership, but that had been many, many years ago.

Wesley, however, might have been as close to love-at-first-sight as Torrence imagined possible. He was beautiful. He was athletic. He was not one for violence. He was not what Torrence was here for, but he was what kept her attention.

She found herself losing focus of Dan, of her target, her eyes wandering away from him and his aggression and finding and fixating upon Wesley and this gentleness, this delicacy that wasn't expressed in his movements or his actions, not when he thought eyes were upon him, but that shone through those eyes when his brows lifted and pulled together, when his lips curled into a worried slant. He was a spirit there in motion as much as he was a body in action, and Torrence, something deep within her, wanted that spirit.

After some time turning her attention onto him, while still keeping an eye on her original potential-recruit, Torrence saw very little that encouraged her belief that Wesley was one for the pack.

He was studious, he went to class, worked a job, and frequented thrift shops for old technologies and collector's items from the eighties.

She had considered going into the shop at which he worked part-time and making small talk. She'd considered this only because she'd seen in the small time spent stalking him that he had a significant other already and that her usual sensual approach might not work on someone like him, with this especially considered.

But no. That would not do. Torrence was not the type to make friends; to gather henchmen of sorts, yes, or devotees or even groupies, sure, but never friends. What good was there in friends? Friends denoted some level of equality; with friends, perhaps there could be a leader and a follower, a dominant and a submissive personality, but with friends, no one ever really admitted to their position there.

Torrence didn't like that. She liked to assert her authority and she liked the company only of those who praised her for it.

Not one to give up, however, Torrence considered killing the woman. She didn't really need a reason beyond the fact that she wanted Wesley for herself, but how could making a martyr or a saint out of the woman benefit Torrence?

She knew the time to move had not come to pass, not yet. She knew she'd have to watch, not only Wesley but his girlfriend, too.

"Hey," Wesley said, drawing her attention back to the present. "You okay?" he asked, his gruff voice always low and always submissive.

"I'm okay," she said. "Your eyes are like they used to be."

"I like them better this way," he said, looking down, turning on the bay to face her. "Yours haven't been blue in a long time."

"That's a problem?"

"No."

"You're sure?"

"Yeah," he said, gripping onto her hips and urging them on. "I'm yours, right?"

"Mine," she cooed.

"Then mark me, Torrence." He gasped, lifting one of his hands away from her hips. "Mark me."

"Wesley." She growled the word, blending further the lines of anger and violence with those of love and passion.

"Please," he said, groaning in the pleasures they shared, in the movement of her body upon his, her hands feeling about his neck and chest, nails digging into the flesh draped over them; these jagged lines, a claim in their own right, but not the one he desired. "Tor, please."

"Stop asking," she commanded through gritting teeth, trying to focus on her surroundings, on the flame and fire, the blood spattered across Wesley's plump lips, the radiant, very-human color of his irises. But this purity was more enjoyable to take, to conquer. Sure, submission was attractive, but allowing was far less sinful than taking, and therefore not as fun.

"Why won't you?" Wesley grunted, his hand gripping tightly to Torrence's hipbones as she moved more quickly atop him.

He tried to focus on her beauty—her delicate facial features, the way her shining, black hair fell around them so elegantly, the parting of her full lips, the arch of her brow—but behind this lovely image was evidence of the evil inside it. The flames and falling beams of the home, the knowledge that inside it were a corpse and a broken, but still very alive, body that surely was dying—suffocating—in excruciating pain while he, the cause of this great suffering, experienced the height of physical pleasure.

It was too heavy a burden to bear, especially for what ultimately felt like nothing. He hadn't been claimed by Torrence, not as his brethren had, and wasn't he supposed to be her most precious one?

"Tor?" he asked, his lips rolling into his mouth to clip off whatever audible expression of his inner-turmoil vibrated around inside his throat. He closed his eyes. Breathed very consciously for a moment.

She ignored him still, her eyes either closing in ecstasy.

"Tor, please," he said finally, removing a hand from her hip and reaching for her shoulder.

In an instant, her demeanor changed. Her chin lowered so that he might better see her eyes, which opened suddenly, casting down upon him the same heat of the fiery destruction behind her. She took hold of his hand, squeezed it tightly.

Wesley gasped, the bones of his fingers snapping under the strength of her hold. "Tor," he tried to cry out, but his voice was a pleading whisper instead.

"Do not move," she said, digging into the skin of his breaking hand her sharp fingernails. "Do not speak unless I tell you to." She flung his hand aside, ignoring the distress that came from him as a result of this.

Fearfully, he nodded. His brows raised above his worried eyes, and he brought his broken hand tightly to his chest. His other hand came to it, but the slightest touch caused further injury.

Torrence rolled her eyes, exhaling exasperatedly. She reached, without any semblance of tenderness, for the injured hand and used her abilities to piece together the bones again.

"I'm sorry," she said, eyes flickering away from him as she muttered the words. "I didn't mean to."

He nodded, rubbing at his healed hand. "I know," he said, swallowing thickly, hoping she couldn't perceive how little he believed that, how exacerbated his fear of her had grown in the last few months. At least their activity provided an excuse for a fast-beating heart and loud, heavy breathing.

She looked back to him, eyed him for a moment, then she

moved away from him to lie next to him.

Remaining entirely still, Wesley only watched her. He said nothing, did nothing. He didn't know what he should say, what he wanted to say, if anything. He only knew that he had been commanded not to say it.

She stared into the flames before them, watched glass windows break and give out. She closed her eyes, centralizing her concentration on the souls within the house. Both were dead now. Both were in Hell, awaiting her.

"Come here," she said, opening her eyes finally.

"What?" he asked lowly.

"I don't want to force you," she said.

"You don't," he said. "Force me, I mean."

"Then show me that you want me," she said, raising her knees, parting them, an invitation for him to move atop her now, for the very first time.

Hesitantly, he sat up. "Okay," he said softly. He bent toward her, his fingertips brushing over her knee, then down her thigh.

Her teeth gritted, nostrils flaring slightly, but she allowed this; she knew she had to. She knew Wesley was being seduced by the silent songs of the angels, and that her abuse of his body would only aid their cause.

He looked up to her when his hand found her hip. He grabbed onto her tightly there, licking his lower lip nervously into his mouth. He knew what she expected, what she offered, but he questioned it. "Torrence?"

"Yes, Precious One," she answered curtly, but tried to seem sincere.

"What do you want me to do?"

"I want you to have me as you'd like to."

"Okay," he said, looking down to his grip on her body. He looked back up to her, biting his lip, then he used his hold of her hip to pull her toward him. He moved onto his back again, and brought her into his lap as she had been.

Torrence chuckled, triumphant still, but surprised. "This is what you want?"

"It's what I've always wanted," he said. "Own me."

CHAPTER THREE

War stood nervously in the center area of Torrence's private salons. He didn't expect her to receive him here with open arms, but he could not leave this place as she'd instructed.

As he sat down in a velvety chair, his hands tracing the ornately-carved, golden lions adorning each of its arms, War craned his neck enough that he might see inside her bedroom.

Oh, that room with its painted angels and its baldachin bed. That damned bed. Its lovely sheets and soft pillows, the thin satin that hung from its tall canopy. He'd felt so secure within that bed, closed off from the world, from the heavens, from the Hell that laid just beyond the room's door. Safe inside the luxury and comfort. Safe with Torrence.

He'd let himself slip. After what felt like an eternity of denial, he let desire consume him. He succumbed to it. And in less than one human year. But time was different on earth, was it not? It passed differently to him here. A day felt like an eternity. Months felt like eons. He'd denied and denied and denied for could've been a billion years in Heaven, but in that earthly time, he surrendered. He sinned.

And after all her pursuing, Torrence had abandoned him

before he could experience even the entirety of a singular moment inside her.

He'd chased her when she exited the room. It replayed on his mind on an endless loop. Tore me tint him. Guilt-ridden, ashamed. Abandoned and afraid, and lost to all those gods glorious enough to command him.

Even his voice reverberated in his mind.

"Torrence—." The sound of this one, small word, so telling. It was hollow and weakened. Desperate, he'd been, and so very alone. She hadn't cared, though. Or so it seemed.

"War, let go of me," she said, her voice low, controlled, and passing through clenched teeth.

"I'm your servant," he said, removing his grasp of her arm. "But I want to hold onto you."

"No, you don't. Leave."

"Leave?"

Even as she turned and moved about the spiraling ramp of despair, he followed her.

"You want me to leave, Torrence? To go out into the apocalyptic wasteland you created, and as a human? As a godless human? Just end my life now. Why prolong it by mere hours or by days?"

Torrence stopped at this. "As a human," she exhaled lowly. Her eyes clenched shut. She turned. "A godless one?"

"I've committed a sin," he said, approaching her slowly. "Willingly. Defiled my eternal grace with the flesh of mortality. I am no longer God's son, Torrence, and if you banish me from Hell, I've nowhere to go but the desolation outside this manor. When I die, I shall return to you…as a demon." He flinched. "What will become of an angel rejected by God if he becomes a demon rejected by the devil?"

"Your God does not abandon you," she said. "See your stars. They glisten still. If you won't leave on your own, I'll summon you an escort."

She turned again, and he reached for her, but in remembering her command, his fingers only brushed against her wrist before he let his hand fall away.

Behind War came the growls of his fallen brothers, the heat of their exhales, the glowing cast of orange from their eyes in his peripheral vision. He turned only briefly toward the new sensations, and in that small space of time, Torrence had departed.

"Come now, little brother," a hissing voice spoke over War's shoulder. "Keep your wits about you."

"Do whatever you wish," War said. "I'm not leaving, and you cannot overtake me."

"Even if we could, you're safe under boss's orders. Can't do anything." He moved slowly, standing before War now. "But you can."

"What do you mean?"

"I mean, dear brother, that the choice is yours."

"Choice?" His breathing shook, eyes still glistening with sorrow and concern. "What choice?"

"Leave righteous," the demon said, waltzing gaily toward one of the archways adorned by Cupids and cherubs and blazing open with a fiery swirl, "or stay and sin."

War's chest was hollow and as full of pain as it was of air. If Torrence did not want him, it was because of his purity, his angelic grace. He knew this, and he hated himself for it. "Oh, God in Heaven," War whispered, exhaling his uncertainty as his head fell forward. "What do I do?"

The demon tsked him. "Now, now, Armideus. These types of prayers will not do here, and I am not so certain they can even be heard from such a plane as this. But then again," he said, ushering the hesitating War closer to the doorway, "maybe you're hoping for that."

"I can't—I don't want to go in there," War said, his heels pressing into the sloping marble of this rounded stairwell.

"Come, delicate, little brother," the demon snarled, pulling him into the doorway. "Come."

Another demon stood before a bound woman on a slab of rusted, blood-stained iron. He lifted a great blade into the heated air, stepping upon heaps of rotted flesh which shook as if alive by the myriad maggots feasting upon it.

The demon brought this blade to the woman's cheek, nicking it quickly, a torture of the mind, this, in terrified preparation for the physical torment and when it might begin and when it might end.

"This was a lustful soul," the demon holding War's shoulders still whispered to him. "You know about lust, brother, do you not?"

"Vaguely," War whispered, tears welling in his eyes as he watched this torturous demon continue his acts.

Reaching for the woman's shoulder, the demon's claws pressed into the flesh there, and then he moved the hand which held the blade down her chest and across her navel.

"Wait," said the demon with War. "Go no further."

"Wait?" the demon growled in response.

A clawed hand squeezed tighter on War's shoulder and the other extended out to the torturous demon. "Give it to me," he said. "Oh, better yet…" he withdrew his hand now and pushed War forward. "Give it to him."

"Him?" The demon's head drew back as he laughed. "What is the meaning of this, Avalux?"

"He lusts after our Master," Avalux said, chuckling and scoffing, his growling voice teeming with cruelty. "But he still serves God."

"Oh, you can do both?" The demon sneered. "Funny that I was cast down, stripped of my pristine armor and divine sight when I chose to bed a beloved human." He glared at War. "And this one is graceful and clean after loving the antichrist."

"Calm now, Anahhuv," Avalux said. "Let the little saint make his choice as we've made ours."

"Yes, little saint," Anahhuv said, grabbing War's shoulder now and shoving him toward the sobbing, fearful woman. "Do you want the Master or do you want goodness?"

"You cannot have both." Avalux sneered, dangling before War the key to the chains which held the soul against the slab. "Set free this soul, little angel. Take her away from here. I'm sure she's repentant now. Set her free. Choose goodness."

"Or sink the blade into her womb," said Anahhuv, taking War's lovely hand into his distorted palm and settling the knife's handle inside it. "Choose Torrence." He moved behind War now, peering over his shoulder.

"Choose her bed," Avalux taunted, moving to War's other shoulder, whispering into his ear as he stared at the terrified woman. "Choose her."

"Who taught you in the ways of temptation?" War's brows lifted as he stared down to the blade. "It wasn't Torrence." He looked up to the soul now. "If it had been, you'd be better at it."

He jerked his shoulders away from the demon's grasp, stepping toward the soul on the slab.

"It's all right, child," War whispered, his breath shaken and his eyes full of tears as he gripped more tightly the handle of this torturous blade. He wondered if that eased the poor soul before him, if this vision of an angel and his creamy skin and iridescent eyes, surrounded by the gentle music of church bells put her at some sort of ease.

"Please." She sobbed, squirming against the slab, confined to it by iron cuffs and great chains.

War looked up to the pleading woman, his head tilting, eyes narrowing. His brows came together in contemplation.

This soul seemed fragile here, as fragile as her physical body had been, and she was suffering, fearful. It was all so distasteful. In his earthly manifestation, the distaste became something more, something emotional. It had become painful for him.

But Hell and punishment for sin, all this that was surrounding him now, had been created in some form, for some reason, by God. And it was He who had commanded sinful souls to exist in eternal suffering here. Did this mean that this agony, this torment was somehow God's will?

War looked down to his hands, eyes flickering from the key in his palm to the knife in his other. Back and forth, right and wrong, good and evil, God or the devil—God or Torrence.

"Psalms 20:30," War whispered. In his trepidation, his voice seemed very human. Slowly, his eyes rose up to the woman's face. His fingers gripped the blade more tightly. Resolve replenished vigor into his downtrodden features. His brows creased. Lips thinned. He began to raise the knife, his shoulders squaring. He focused his divine intent upon his fist, warming the handle of the weapon and flowing down into the blade.

As he shifted, the minuscule motions of hesitation preventing him from moving as swiftly as necessary in this moment with these demons, a voice came into the room.

"Gentlemen." The word floated in a gentle wave, smooth and calm and superior.

War's nostrils flared for the interruption. He quickly lowered the weapon, and turned toward the doorway.

His fallen brothers gazed toward it, their eyes finding its source in the lovely visage of Conrad and his plump, bow-shaped lips.

In acknowledgement of him, they fell, bowing their heads as they bent their left knees, kneeling as knights might have knelt before their king.

Slowly, with an air of assertion that was neither obnoxious nor unnecessarily cocky, Conrad entered the room.

He looked down to the demons, running his fingers through the shiny black locks of Avalux's hair as he walked through them.

"Up," he said, and they rose instantly behind him.

He appeared serene as he stared at War, but then that was the way of Conrad. Always calm, moving in fluidity and with elegance, even when his eyes tapered in concentrated focus onto one pestering   point of inconveniencing interest. His head tilted slightly, lips always open, always so close to being closed, but too eager to smile or speak or perform some equally alluring act to whomever was lucky—or unlucky—enough to find his fancy.

From this slightly-downcast angle, Conrad's lovely, dark eyes gazed upward through his lashes. His brows remained even, creating a more extreme display of this heavenward stare. He was handsome, yes, but within him the spirit reigned, always arranging his body in the most appealing positions and aligning his already-alluring features into the most seductive expressions.

His eyes glanced briefly to the weapon in War's hand, then they blinked up in a flicker of golden-red phosphorescence that melted slowly into the human, but radiant, brown of his irises. "What have we here?"

"We were attempting—."

Conrad lifted his hand, and the demon went quiet. "I wasn't speaking to you," he said, his head turning slightly. When he looked back to War, he spoke again. "I was addressing the angel."

"I owe you no explanation," War said, his face free of anger or contempt. Stoic in expression and his stance austere, only the depth of his uneasy blue eyes gave any hint of his concern.

The corners of Conrad's lips slithered upward. For a moment, he appeared to War so very human. So very fragile. The skin wrapped around him, the bones inside of him, these hadn't been manifestations of a demon, no. These had been born from flesh, created by woman and by man.

As he regarded Conrad, War imagined that young boy, that troubled young man who had been chained up inside the basement of church by priest and by father, all so very human and so very afraid.

Was that boy still housed within the prison of his ever-dying body? Or had the daimon that was Conrad's full spiritual essence taken over whatever mortality remained?

The silence was chilling. He wondered if Conrad could sense his musings, for he could not gauge those of Conrad. It did not mean Conrad was entirely inhuman; it simply meant that he was not a good human, that his heart had blackened at some point in his small existence, in some thirty-five or thirty-six years that were but a second's passing to a being such as War, and suddenly sensation crept into War's thoughts, overtaking any logical conjecture with the encompassing shroud of intense emotion, which always seemed to cradle its victim gently before submerging him into the dreaded experience of it.

Air came into his lungs through a slight parting of his lips, and he blinked away from Conrad, who stood in patient study, waiting for this moment of emotional fluctuation.

"You blinked," he said, the words slow and smooth, wrapped in some melody that made them seem a purr.

He stepped closer to War now. The two divine beings, stuck inside skin, mere inches from one another. Their eyes, gleaming respectively the opalescent hues of Heaven and the incandescent tones of Hell, saw beyond the creamy allure of high cheekbones and defined jawlines.

Conrad's lips twitched, a smile gracing them for a fleeting second. "You smell good," he said. "I don't know how Torrence can stand it."

"You smell good, too," War said. "Masks the decaying spirit within you."

Conrad laughed, an elegant sound that almost made War want to join him. It was contagious, yes, but it was cruel.

"Nothing rots here," Conrad said gently. He lifted his hand toward War, who stood in strength to absorb whatever travesty rolled off Conrad's connection and sunk into his skin. Nothing came, though. Only the very-physical sensation of a simple touch. "You see?"

"Do not touch me." War's teeth grated.

"Tread cautiously with your commands," Conrad said, his voice lightened by patience. "Look at where you stand."

"I stand in Torrence's Hell. Who are you but another of her servants?"

"I am more than that, and you know it."

"Regardless, I answer to no one but her."

"As do I." He chuckled now, something darker and deeper than the expression of humor, but it was tempered ebullient still. "Humor me, though, little angel." He stroked his chin with his finger and his thumb, the digits slipping over his features fluidly but with a careful exactitude. "Why are you holding a demonically-charged blade? Why stand before a soul with it in your glittering palm? What is the plan here?"

War shrugged. "I don't have a plan. I thought I came here with one. I realize now that I've been acting on impulse and reverie, not logic or conviction."

Conrad's fingers moved over War's hand now, slipping inside its grip to free him of the blade. "This is an impulse?"

"An unwanted offering," War said. "None of my impulses urge me to torment."

"Ah, then let me save you the trouble," Conrad said, taking the weapon into his fist. It was warm still, from War's grip, yes, but nothing so human as body temperature. Angels did not operate at a perfect ninety-eight-point-six.

His focus went to the knife for this warmth. His forehead creased in the rising of his brows. Again, the sinister nature of his soul uplifted the corners of his mouth. When his eyes moved up to War, he kept his head down, angled still toward the knife in his hand.

"And what's this?" he asked, his tongue moving about his lips like that of a snake.

"I need to explain your own weapon to you?" He was insolent. He hoped the melodic nature of his angelic voice did not conceal it.

Conrad looked back down to the knife, every motion from his blinking eyelids to his lowering chin was calm and unhurried. He snickered as his eyes moved upward to War's eyes, a low sound reverberating in his throat. As he lifted his head, it grew, deepening and thickening until his lips parted, releasing from behind his smile full-bodied laughter.

As abruptly as the sound stopped, Conrad's body moved, breaking the silence of the room with the distinctive squall of a blade slicing through air. Then came a sharp breath, the sound of something thick and sticky peeling open, parting, separated from itself by a great force.

War jumped, his eyes finding the soul behind him, and Conrad's hand still holding the handle of the knife, which had been thrust inside her bare stomach.

Sneering, Conrad jammed the blade into the woman more deeply. Twisting it as he stared into her screaming face, Conrad grunted, exerting in great fun all his force upon the blade,

When he released the weapon, Conrad took a step back. He stood in-line with War as both men regarded this soul, the agony in her face as jagged lines of silver, glistening and reflective, splintered in all directions from the wound.

The woman squirmed. Her bound feet attempted to kick, her hands in their chains reached violently for the source of the injury, but failed to even near it.

She cried out, tears streaming from her eyes, as the graceful divinity forced into the knife by War's hand, intended for the demons behind him, discharged into her. It crept slowly at first, but the quickening of her terrified heart forced the energy to flow faster.

This energy, the manifested glory of War's divine strength, was too powerful for her flesh to contain. Her skin began to heat and bubble. The silver lines of graceful power were obstructed by paths of boiling flesh. These boils burst. Sores were left in their stead, gaping open, full of pus, but emitting the most beautiful, gleaming light.

War stood before the bellowing woman, his eyes widening in the repercussions of his decision. Oh, he should have stabbed her himself when he'd had the chance. Why try to fill the blade with his magic and strike a demon with it? What was he going to do after he'd knocked them dead, anyway? Release this soul? To where? Where could she have gone but here?

His brows furrowed as he watched his glory consume the woman's flesh, illuminating it from within until she was less a person or a soul than she was a human-shaped beam of light.

Silently, he prayed for the salvation of this damned soul, trying consciously to ignore the automatic thoughts that acknowledged the impossibility of this.

"Please," he whispered in solemnity, "forgive me."

"I don't think so," Conrad said, placing a hand on War's shoulder as the soul before them burst into hunks of shimmering flesh. It fell around them; some tiny fragments fluttering through the air like snow while larger pieces slapped onto the ground in great clumps of glitter-dipped, bloody meat. "Forgiveness isn't really a thing here."

War's chest rose and fell harshly. He tried to back away from this turmoil, but Avalux was on him, his claws digging into the fabric of War's t-shirt and scratching at his shoulders.

From beside him came Anahhuv, a box in his distorted hands. War had seen this type of box before, black and covered in Latin spells, when he'd first entered Hell, when he walked the darkened hallways with Torrence, when he made his way to her bed.

He watched the demon capture in its claws the halo-like presence of the spirit and shove it into the box.

When the lid slammed, War jumped, causing the claws of Avalux to sink into his skin. He hissed and jerked away from the demon, his skin rolling off his bones in curling ribbons that stuck to his fallen brother's nails. War watched these tendrils of his own flesh fall into the mess of matter on the floor.

War's chin lowered. He wanted to look at the tears in his shirt, at the wounds in his flesh, but his eyes were fixated on the piles of humanity, destroyed in Hell by his own graceful power. He watched Conrad take the blade from it, a small clump of flesh falling from its point as he moved.

War swallowed thickly. The harshness of this act brought his awareness to his physical form—he swallowed. His throat was dry. His skin had been peeled off of his bones and little red pinpoints of blood seeped upward into the pink lines of tissue.

A second of sin with Torrence and already he was falling from divinity; becoming human.

"Don't worry," Conrad said, his fingers slipping down the scratches in War's shoulders. "It's a spiritual reaction to the room. The torture chambers make the immaterial material. You can't stab a soul, after all." As his fingertips brushed against the frayed shirt, Conrad wrapped his fist in the fabric, then he tore it away from War completely. "Perhaps we should take this knife, now that it's free of your purity, and thrust it into your stomach. See what happens to you here."

War's lips snarled in his disgust as he glanced to the blade.

"Oh," Conrad said, his brows raising with his tone. "We can clean it off before we gut you with it. Don't worry." His eyes stared into War's as he brought the knife to his own lips and licked away the blood from it. "Is that better?"

"Sir, wait," Avalux said quickly. "I apologize, but this is the angel from the Master's bed chamber. This is the one she freed."

Conrad's head fell back slightly as he took in a great breath of exasperation. He knew War. They'd spent time together here in Hell, when Torrence dressed the angel up in a little tuxedo and paraded him about the pre-ritual ballroom like a doll—one that she'd pretended to heal so that the human souls might consider her the Second Coming before she killed and therefore claimed them.

Conrad turned swiftly and stuck the blade into the demon's shoulder, ripping it free so that its glistening blood, black but pristine, like liquefied onyx, spattered the floor in its absence.

"If our Lord freed him, what is he doing in here?"

The demon hissed as he grabbed at his injury, an unusual feeling for his kind, but spirits had bodies in these rooms. "My apologies," Avalux said through gritted, snarling teeth. "I thought we were helping her. She wanted him, did she not? If he enacted sin by choice, he'd fall for her. He'd be her human and, upon his death, her demon."

Conrad's brow arched. He turned to look at them, his eyes falling onto Avalux first, then the other two demons.

"You know this?" His voice grew now, plumped by the magnitude of his rage. "You know what causes the fall of angels and you said nothing?" Conrad grabbed the demon by his bleeding arm and hurled him onto the ground. Low came his voice as he knelt down over Avalux. "I should let him smite you where you sit."

"Sir, forgive me. I know because he knows. He worried. He considered it. His thoughts were not entirely comprehensible to me, but when they were dark and very intense, I received flashes. Choice. He'd thought it in the hallways with the Master. Choice is the downfall. I was hoping to test the theory, Sir, before I came to you with it."

Considering this, Conrad's chin lowered into a deviant slant as he pressed the point of the blade into the tip of his first finger and rotated the knife as if it were a toy to ease the boredom of absentminded contemplation.

His eyes came up to War's now. "Enacting torture would cause the fall of an angel?"

"In specific, yes," War answered.

"And in general?"

"In general, the choice to sin."

Conrad stood. "Witnessing sin weakens angelic spirits, does it not?"

"It does," War said.

"Consuming blood weakens angelic spirits?"

"Weakens, yes."

"But these things will not contribute to their falling from glory?"

"Contribute, perhaps in some indirect way. Weakening the spirit weakens its resolve to some extent, but if the angel still rebukes sin even in the face of it——."

"Even if forced to participate in it?"

"In the way of your force-breeders?"

"Yes."

"If they rebuke the sin even while forcibly engaged, no, it will not cause their separation from glory."

"So, only choice does that?"

"Only choice does it, yes. Willingness."

"You've known this."

"Always. All angels have this knowledge. We've had it since our brothers fell and were transformed. The great fall of the rebel angels is our most renowned cautionary tale."

Conrad's eyes moved to the demons. "You were not aware of this, then?"

"We fell as repercussion of our sin," Anahhuv said cautiously. "We did not know it was the cause or the only way."

"We only knew we displeased God," said the demon who'd entered the room with War and Avalux.

"They don't know," War said, sympathizing with his brothers. "Why would they? They were departed of grace for their actions and they are aware of that fact, but they have not the access to God or to those remaining in Heaven to know of choice in relation to sin. All they know now is choice and sin. Their metamorphosis affects their spirits, their mentality; it is not simply a twisting of features or a blackening of wings."

"Of course it isn't," Conrad said, approaching War now. He

placed a hand on War's shoulder, his fingertips pressing into the almost-bleeding wounds there. The connection of purity and obscenity created a pulse of energy between the two, shared at the site of their touch, which gave them both pause. Conrad considered it, the subtle tingle. He wondered if this what was pulsed through Torrence's body when she conquered Wesley's innately-good spirit through the lustful organ of his flesh. Ah, he decided, Perhaps it was time to try it with a pure soul. But not now, of course. Not this angelic one. It belonged to Torrence.

"What?" War looked at him with obvious contempt. "Speak your thoughts if they bring you the humor your face suggests they do. I do not fear you, even in a room where I am made physical."

Conrad chuckled. "I see why Torrence likes you," he said. "I'm just curious. What were you doing with the key and the blade in your hands?"

"They instructed me to make a choice," War said, his face defiant and willful. "Of all things there are to dislike about Torrence, one can certainly admire her appreciation of free will."

"So, you were defying her."

"By remaining in Hell, yes."

"And by infusing your power into the blade?"

"I did not know we were flesh here. I thought it necessary to escape the demons without summoning all that remains of my power."

"All that remains?"

War looked away now. His skin paled. "I have laid with her." His eyes moved to Conrad's eyes, his words hurrying now. "Only for a second. But perhaps she requires something more drastic to make my status here more permanent."

"Something like stabbing this woman? Were you going to thrust this blade in the physical embodiment of her soul? Was that your form of falling from grace, your way of choosing to sin? If so, why use the blade against your fallen brothers—your brothers, whose kinship would be restored to you should you fall, too?"

War's jaw clenched, his lips tightened for a moment, nostrils flaring to inhale deeply. "No."

"That's what I thought." He looked down to Avalux, who had moved from his fallen position into a kneel.

"Sir, please. I was certain he'd do it. He gave in to lust, had he not? Why not murder? Why not any other sin? Why—."

"Enough."

"He quoted the Bible as he approached her! He referenced Psalms!"

"Which?"

"20:30."

A darkened delight occupied Conrad's face. When he turned to face War again, his chin raised so that could look down on the angel. A grin formed on his perfect lips, rendering the Cupid's bow of their shape more a demonic instrument than a cherubic one. "You meant to scour her of sin? You meant to cleanse her with striking blows?"

"I meant to understand this cruelty through God, who commands it," War said, looking up to him. "I did not mean to justify it. I didn't mean to—. I don't know." He reached for his hair, soothing himself in the feel of it. "I want Torrence," he said after consideration, "but it is difficult to want to submit to her."

"It isn't for most people." Conrad shrugged. "But I guess you're not 'people', are you?"

"Not quite," War said. Not yet anyway, he thought. His eyes flashed to Conrad. He hoped he hadn't perceived that concern.

"Well, you want me to let you in on a little secret? You want me to tell you what I've noticed about Torrence? As a third party, I can see things even your holy bullshit can't."

War stared at him. He was intrigued but stubborn, so he said nothing. Merely gazed at the demonically-charged man in still opposition.

Conrad's lips pursed. One shoulder shifted, half of a shrug.

"All right." He smiled, offering a key to War. "Here. Release an angel or two. We're heading to an evacuation tonight. Some city along the coast in Massachusetts, where I'm from. Tell whoever you set free to find us there. Stop us. All that jazz."

"Stop you?"

"This is just what you tell the angel when you let him go. We both know you don't mean it."

"What?"

"Look," Conrad said, "what you want, what Torrence wants, what we all want is for you to just be a good, little angel, righteous and pure and on the holy side of this war, right? But you also want Torrence and she wants you, but only so long as you remain good. So, you play the part. Release an angel. You know one won't do anything to stop us, but all your brothers in the cages get to see you trying to set them free, get to tell everyone still in Heaven or here on earth in Heaven's name that you're on their side. I catch you before you release too many. Wrap you up in chains. Keep you here. Let you face Torrence when we get back."

"You mean to turn me over to her once I've defied her," War said. "Why bother? She knows what I am. She doesn't want me dead or hurt. She'd have done it already."

"You see things too plainly," Conrad said. "Perhaps it's some aspect of your purity, of the black-and-white nature through which you view humanity and the world inundated by it. Everything is gray, though. Bleaker perhaps than shining white and deepest black, but very gray. Not everything is what it seems. You are God when He said, 'I am what I am,' and she is the antithesis of Him, replying, 'I am what I am not.'"

"You're suggesting she wants the angels freed? She wants goodness?"

"I'm suggesting she wants it, sure, but only when it's wrapped up inside creamy flesh and pretty bone structure."

"She has that with you."

"Yes, but I don't deny her."

"Then you make even less sense."

He laughed again. His tone articulate of humor as well as interest. "I'll say this on the subject: Torrence likes submission, sure. Thrives on it. What's a leader without an army to order around, right? But that only applies to followers and recruits. It applies to me and Michael and Jocelyn. It applies to the demons here. But what about you?"

War's brows came together.

"She seems to like you best when you tell her no."

War's angelic face revealed his contemplation. Mixing with his consideration of this was great confusion. Conrad had a point, did he not? Torrence had tempted War time and time again, even before she'd known what he was, but now as he lay in Hell inside the heavy velvet baldachin canopy of her bed, offering to give up eternal glory for a few fleeing human-moments of passionate affection—this, the greatest submission of anyone's—she refused to take him.

War considered taking this key from Conrad and running straight into the angel chambers to release them—any of them, it didn't matter—so long as Conrad came to catch him and complete this plan.

On the other hand, War did not want to use his brothers in such a way, did not want to pretend to be good. He wanted to be good. He hoped he was still somehow good. And Conrad was demonically charged. He was the Awakener of the end of days. Lies and trickery were as much fun for him as they were natural, quite like breathing to a being such as him. He was a great deceiver of humans and especially of angels, if any were foolish enough to engage with him.

It came down to a simple question. "Why?"

"Whatever pleases my Lord pleases me," he answered plainly.

Sitting here in the chair, awaiting for Torrence's return, for the return of Conrad before her with War's nephews and surely his escaped brother, War considered the choice he'd been offered. He could've chosen Torrence. He could've chosen Hell. He could've chosen Heaven. Had he made the right choice?

CHAPTER FOUR

Celebratory, Torrence came back into her kingdom with a new recruit, an escaped angel, and a returned brother.

Jocelyn greeted the returning gang at the door, excitedly hugging Torrence as she entered the mansion.

"Little sister." Torrence smiled, returning the embrace. "Where's that escaped angel?"

"Back in shackles," Jocelyn said. "I kicked him when Conrad brought him home."

Torrence chuckled. "I'm sure that was terrible for him." She moved by Jocelyn, her brothers following, save for Freddy. He paused before her, placing a hand on her shoulder. "How's your wrist?"

"Fine." Jocelyn raised her arm and bent her wrist up and down, even wriggling her fingers as she did so. "Boss isn't as bad as she seems, right?"

"What do you mean?"

Jocelyn brought her hand to Freddy's face, her knuckles brushing against the smooth, flawless skin there. "Could've left you a fried-up nightmare. Could've left my wrist broken. But she didn't."

"Stop playing," Jason said, wrapping his arms around them both. "Time to feast."

They moved together with their band, following Torrence as she entered into a large dining area.

"So, this is Hell," Wesley said to Todd.

"It's…oddly nice," Todd answered, looking about Hell at its gothic architecture, the murals within peaked frames of gold, the velvet carpeting and marble floors.

"Yeah. Never made much sense to me."

"Makes perfect sense to me."

Wesley's brows furrowed. "It does?"

Todd chuckled. "I guess you didn't know Torrence back in the day." He looked up to the grand ceilings and ornate decorations, the candelabra mounted on the walls, the angels above the doorways. "All this is a little darker than what her parents liked, but their house was so nice it was almost obnoxious. I went to a private school, and their place was more gouache than any of my classmates'."

Wesley's eyes narrowed as he looked up to Torrence ahead of them. She would never give in to him when asked for even her last name, and this man standing next to him knew her parents.

Wesley tried talking himself away from envy. He didn't want to be jealous. He was tired of being bothered, of being upset, of constantly feeling like someone else kept coming along to knock him down another tier on the showcase. He used to be Torrence's right hand. He was her most beloved, her Precious One. It hadn't been a pet name; it had been a title, one he felt he'd earned. He killed for Torrence. Killed for her. Had Todd?

"So, uh, that whole thing about you proving yourself over and over…"

"Yeah?"

"How exactly did you do that?"

Todd shrugged. "Lots of ways, I guess. Helped her build from the bottom. Helped her recruit people. Helped her scare the ones that didn't join. Eventually helped her kill them, but that came way after we first met."

"How did you meet?"

"We met at—." Todd's words were interrupted by a deep intake of air. His eyes moved to the ground, focusing now on his moving feet. "We met at a cemetery." He looked up to Wesley, his eyes opening a bit. "I went to an all-boys school, so I was still pretty awkward around girls. I was awkward around everyone honestly. I mean, except Perry."

"Perry?"

"He was my best friend," Todd clarified.

"Was?"

A painful smile came to Todd's lip. He tried to laugh through an obvious sadness the memory recalled in him. "He died," Todd said, lowering his head. "When we were sixteen."

"Oh, I'm sorry."

"Yeah," Todd said, the word sharpened by a jolt of pain. He shrugged, but the sorrow was still evident in his face. Perry was more than Todd's best friend, Perry was an inspiration to him. He was sensitive, poetic. He used his talents to create beautiful prose work and was never hesitant to share his creations with their English classes.

Perry wasn't overly-confident, however. He was surrounded by structure and order and trapped inside a uniform, ready to walk whatever path was assigned to him.

He'd been sent to the private school solely because it was a school for boys. His parents did not want him distracted by girls; they wanted him to focus on his studies so he could maintain his 4.0 and go on to school and become something great, like a businessman.

Perry intended to do just that. He intended to follow the path his parents set for him, writing off his passion for poetics as his parents wrote it off—as a hobby and nothing more.

But suddenly a new life was breathed into Perry's passions.

Todd wasn't sure from where it'd come—none of their friends were—but Perry began talking to them about their paths in life, about whose dream it had been for them to become bankers or businessmen. Was it their dreams? Was it their parents'?

"Perry was sneaking off and doing poetry readings, going to open mic nights, stuff like that. He was doing that when he should've been doing extracurriculars. Dropped out of a lot of stuff his dad wanted him to do, you know? Said he knew what his destiny was now, what freedom was." Todd shrugged half-heartedly.

"When his dad found out, he told Perry he was pulling him from Calvary and sending him to a military school where he couldn't hide his books of poetry or sneak away somewhere to write his own. Perry…" Todd exhaled something akin to a laugh that had been stifled by raw pain, his hand rushing to his mouth and trembling there briefly. "Perry went into the woods outside his house, and he…he hung himself."

"Damn." Wesley's hand went to Todd's shoulder.

"It's okay. Torrence was there. She was putting flowers on her cousin's grave. Her cousin died when she was really young so her parents didn't let her go to the funeral or anything, so she always brought him flowers when she got older, you know, but had to hide it from her parents. That's why she was there so late."

Wesley's brows furrowed now. His head remained low, angled respectfully toward Todd and the seriousness of Todd's story, but his eyes blinked up to Torrence, still walking ahead of them. Cousin? Torrence didn't have cousins, did she? Well, she had parents, so maybe she did. But Wesley couldn't help but notice the similarity of the stories—the stories of Perry, who had been Todd's best friend, and of Torrence, who had become his new one.

He wondered if Todd had considered that—surely in the fifteen or so years since they'd met, he had. Wesley now wondered if he thought it was merely coincidence or something more, something akin to fate. He was sure that was how Torrence would've sold it, whether it had been happenstance or Torrence's very purposeful, planned-out doing. Wesley couldn't really tell anymore what was true about Torrence and what was carefully crafted lies; who she truly was and who she pretended to be. Maybe she didn't pretend. Maybe she didn't lie. Maybe the divinity within her, awakened or not, had always carved out perfect paths for her eventual takeover. He couldn't be sure.

He wondered how long she'd been in the business of building a brotherhood, how long she'd been lying or manipulating her way into the hearts of those most desperate to be loved. Had Todd been the very first? If not, how many came before him? And, either way, how many were there after him—between him and Wesley?

"She came up to me, and asked if I was okay. We spoke a bit. She just really understood what I was going through, what Perry was going through. She got me, you know?"

"Yeah." Wesley frowned a bit, his face full of emotion for Todd, yes, his new brother. Todd, who had known Torrence when she was teenager. Todd, who'd lost someone precious to him and was taken in by the warm embrace of the devil herself. Funny how she knew to provide trust and loyalty to Wesley, to offer love to him, how she gave Jason women and Jocelyn drugs, to Freddy she restored a long-lost confidence, and to Michael she provided revenge. Todd and his friend, these private school boys with controlling parents, perhaps she'd offered some sort of freedom. "She really sees you, doesn't she?"

"Yeah," Todd said, smiling now, interpreting Wesley's observation with a less sinister implication than he'd meant it.

When the band rounded the corner to enter the great room, Torrence stopped suddenly, struck by something in the air, something that did not belong in her Hell, something pure. Her brothers all stopped when she did. Wesley moved through them to reach her position. He placed a hand on her shoulder. "Tor, you okay?"

Heightened by the slayings, the storms, the violence, all her abilities seemed to focus upon was the shot of purity bursting through the heats of Hell. Her eyes moved about the room as she tried to place this energy, tried to sense it more clearly. After a moment, it registered.

"Where is he?" she asked through gritted teeth.

"Here, my Lord," Conrad called out to her as he entered the room with the presence of two angels. He held onto War by the shoulder of his t-shirt but yanked Formaadoria into the room by the chains on his wrists.

"Avalux caught him releasing angels." Conrad shoved War closer to Torrence. As the angel's feet staggered in their chained proximity, his footsteps echoed through the grand room, shaking the chandeliers above the antichrist and her bad-boy band of unholy saints. "The one in the tunnel," Conrad continued, jerking the chains in his hands so that Formaadoria fell onto his knees. "He'd come by his doing."

Torrence's boots smacked against the marble as she made her way to War, the swiftness of her steps throwing mud in all directions from where she stomped.

Elegant as she was, her angry pace created an intoxicating air about her; one that raged onward with authority, yes, but one that highlighted the swaying of her hips, the way they curved out and inward and back out as they became her waist, her side, her torso.

War wasn't sure if he should fear her or if he should fall onto his knees in worship of her.

After all, he'd resigned himself to disobedience now, disobedience in all forms. He'd walked into Hell willingly and laid down with its ruler. He wanted God's forgiveness and he wanted to remain righteous, but Torrence was god too, was she not? Were demons not his angelic brethren? Were they as ideologically attached to her as they'd once been to God? Why couldn't War remain a figure of both stations? Couldn't he keep his love for

God and his lust for the devil?

War would not inflict torment or torture or pain in any form. He would not make bleed the suffering humans nor would he convince those alive above-ground to turn their backs on God. He wouldn't, and he knew he didn't have to.

The god of this place did not offer rules or regulations; no absolutely-wrong or absolutely-right existed in a place where sin was decadent and delicious and where saintly behavior was either eradicated or deemed erotic.

He could be the conquest of the fallen. He could be the sacrosanct on his knees in prayer, who chastised all the devil did while he kissed her lips in praise of them.

He'd worship this new god as he'd never been allowed to worship his previous one. God Almighty in Heaven could take of War his spirit and his worship, but this god, the devil's son in creamy flesh and divinely-structured bone, Torrence herself—this god could have the body; "and the angels which kept not their first estate, and how they sought after this strange flesh." War was fine with this. It was Biblical.

He wasn't sure if it was the tone of Hell itself or if it was merely Torrence and her appeal, but he felt liberated. He was free here to explore whatever desires his flesh beckoned him toward; he could choose, make his own decisions, plot his own course, but still he had a god here, a ruler, a divine governance to whom he could be loyal and subservient and submissive.

War realized now that angelic traits weren't as much righteous as they were devotion to the righteous, and in God's overpowering will, War wondered exactly how righteous He was.

This was blasphemous. War shuddered. His hand rose into his hair, this grasping of the physical locks somehow his expression in the flesh for his spiritual uncertainty. He cursed himself. He wondered if this guilt and this shame and this disgust with his sinful decisions would lessen as he adjusted to his new role.

"What are you doing here?" Torrence demanded, more War's adversary now than she'd ever been. She reached for the chains upon his wrist and ripped them away from his arms. Tossing them aside, they changed upon the marble floor, causing a shudder to run the length of each spine in the room.

"You," he said, staring at her, impressed by this visage now; the old trappings returned, a hunter-green crop top and high-waisted, black jeans. She was more human Torrence now, or at least appeared that way, and without the opulence of some ungodly ruler, she became even more beautiful to him. Humanity within her, as it had been from the moment of its creation, was beautiful. Fragile, vulnerable, mortal. Wasn't this the very basis of affection—this ability to be broken, be it a breaking of emotions or of bones or of metaphorical hearts, but trusting someone else to keep intact what pieces of the other had been given them?

War supposed he'd never really felt that way about her, not even when she was human, for her indomitable strength was always evident as such, and his entire being was built only to worship.

But now came a new worship, a loving one, one of desires and sinful thoughts, a new worship to a new god; not the deified Torrence, but her flesh.

"I want to touch you," he said finally. It was simple and ineloquent. It was not spiritual or poetic. He did not know how else to say it though, not in some way that left no room for interpretation. Easing his hands toward her, War wanted only to feel the heat of her skin, its soft texture, the divinity radiating from its pores, but something else was present there, too. "Oh," he said, his voice breaking audibly, even in the short word he spoke. His eyes fell away from her.

Torrence's eyes narrowed on him, a grin forming on her lips. "What?" An eyebrow raised above a gleaming crimson eye. "Feel something?"

"Lots of things," War said. He bit his lip. Nerves seemed to dance beneath his flesh in stabbing, sharp motions. "Violence," he said, looking up to her carefully, "and love." He glanced over to Wesley. "This is exactly how you used to feel when you'd leave me in your bed in the middle of the night and then come back." His brows furrowed tightly above his downcast eyes. How strange it was to attach a name and a face and a spirit to this sensation.

His lips curled, trembling, and his hand moved into his hair again. After a contemplative moment, he inhaled the anguish building within him, this knowledge that he'd given himself in such an irredeemably sinful manner to a person who took such pleasures in other people. He supposed he'd always known this, even if he hadn't related it to himself in such a way, but it also seemed plausible that night when he was lying atop Torrence, sinful organ almost breaching a boundary to which it never should have come so close, that after he'd offered this intimacy she wouldn't have needed it from others.

Perceptibly, War felt anguish that was not his own. It burst forth from one side of the room and spread into its great space like bolts of jagged lightning, heating only for an instant the chilling air through which it traveled. He looked in the direction of this troubled spirit and its turmoil to find Wesley, who stood in silence and solemnity, staring at Torrence with widened eyes beneath the uneasy slant of his pulled brows.

"Does it hurt you to hear this?" War asked him. He felt Torrence's eyes light on him in anger now, but he didn't meet her gaze. Fixated on Wesley's eyes, studying their exact dilation, their full expression, War's eyes fluttered in his acknowledgment. The full understanding of Wesley's reaction filtered through War's human perceptions—these senses, the sight of Wesley's parted lips and the sound of his breath as it shook through them—and translated within the cells of matter to the language of the spiritual being within it.

"Oh," War said softly, his eyes falling to his feet again and burning in the mental exploration of this emotional impression.

He soothed himself with another grip of his shimmering hair and felt his own chest shake upon air intake; only this time, he seemed to be breathing in Wesley and his concerns and thoughts and worries, the conjectures in his mind about Torrence and her relationship to War, the images he'd created like photographs of the two of them in the throes of a passion for which War never provided her engagement, much less release, and every renewed wave of agony each of these considerations thrust upon the man; everything about Wesley which could not have been seen with the eyes or touched with the hands. War seemed to be filled with this experience of him.

"I did not consider your reaction to the idea of us," War whispered, more to himself in astonished realization than to Wesley in conversation. "Only my reaction to the idea of you two."

"Wesley is fine," Conrad said with confidence. "Worry for those on your side who reside here, not for those who chose it."

"I'm afraid that isn't an option," War said, his eyes moving from man to man, for within the group he felt something perceptible that did not come from Wesley, which meant another among them had been pure or good or at the very least touched by it. He hoped it hadn't been in some violent act or its destruction.

His eyes came eventually to a face he had not seen before—a new face here, but one that pulsated with knowledge of Torrence, with familiarity of her.

"A new recruit," War said quietly to Torrence, but his eyes remained on Todd, who stared back at him somewhat in awe.

"A returned brother," she replied, narrowed eyes never leaving the angel.

"He's as dark as the others," War said, a distasteful confusion furrowing his brow. He looked over to Wesley. Except for you, he thought. His eyes went back to the returned brother. There was a sensation emanating from him and flowing back to him; a current circulating between him and—when War focused upon its path, he realized—Torrence.

He was taken aback. His brows immediately rose over blinking eyes. A shock springing forth from him, his energy filled the room to those with the ability to perceive it.

Something pure radiated between Torrence and her old friend, this Todd. Something pure, something good, something indomitably innocent. But what?

Lowering his head as he considered this strange current, he peered upward to Todd, from whom he could feel nothing—no thoughts or desires or sensations—then he blinked back to Torrence, whose inner-workings were only perceptible in the way those of other angels were, in the way those of demons were; it was nothing human, for what was human within Torrence was not good.

But something good existed here between Torrence and Todd, something that was separate from them both, but nearby to them, close to them, touching them and leaving upon their bloodstained bond its own spiritual residue—all glittery and golden and dripping over what should've been a dark, deeply-red connection.

War's eyes went to Torrence, to her face; not the features of bone and flesh, but the spiritual one—the recognizable, individual view of her eternal soul.

What had been so good and so near to her? So near to her follower? A follower lying dormant, left in her past only to be uncovered here in the future, in her present.

Perhaps this goodness was there lying dormant, too. War wondered how he could see the soul from whence it'd been wiped; how he could come into contact with this soul. He wanted very much, to satisfy his own curiosity, to bear witness to its physical form. Had Torrence destroyed it? Or had she loved it?

He looked over to Wesley, the good so loved by Torrence and yet so sullied by her. She was, after all, the destroyer of virtue, the bringer of death, controller of chaos. But this merely explained Wesley's tarnished soul. It did not explain Torrence's affinity for what goodness remained within it.

War looked to Torrence again, a sincere yearning in his gaze. "Why tenderness after such violence?"

"Who says it's tender?" she asked.

"Is not all intimacy innately tender?" His brows raised in genuine curiosity. "Why else participate in something so attentive and so affectionate?"

Torrence's grin fell away, her lips softening, as did all her features, and slipping into a gentle smile. Genuine warmth came from her now, though War wasn't certain with her new abilities if she could feign something so well that it felt sincere, and she felt, all at once, as if she could breathe for the first time since the night of their almost-sin.

Oh, the innocence of War. The way it shimmered inside the charred flesh of a weak human body attempting to house the might of universal infinity.

"What?" War asked shyly, raising a shoulder toward his lowering chin. He looked up to her innocently, his teeth nipping at the inside of his cheek.

"Nothing," she said after a long moment of silent appreciation. "Nothing. You just don't belong here."

"I belong with you," he said, his eyes worried even when he tried to appear controlled and convicted. "You have everything you require from everyone in this room. Everyone save for me. Yet you deny me when I offer it to you."

"I don't want it."

"You've always wanted it. You've pleaded for it, demanded it, feigned love and offered safety for it."

"Feigned love?"

"Torrence, you've put your hands on me in violence, and you've given others permission to lay their hands upon me in the same manner, and in passion you've touched me. In lustful intent, your fingertips have coursed the length of this body to which I am bound, and in pursuit of some unimaginable sin, you pushed toward it even as I asked you not to. Do not tell me now that you suddenly don't want it, not after all we've experienced in need of it."

"You don't want it, War, so your desire now is just as baffling, perhaps, as my lack of it."

"It was never a matter of want, Torrence, and you know that. You knew I wanted to. Don't tell me that you didn't feel me writhe beneath you, that you didn't see the pleasure in my face or feel it in my kiss."

"I did, and blended with it always was an undeniable pain."

"A pain, Torrence, because I could not give it to you."

"For your love of God," she said.

"I love God in fear of punishment; I love you despite the threat of it."

"Torrence," Conrad said lowly, "he has provided the key to your experiments."

"Oh, he has?"

"Yes. It's choice."

"What is?"

"Fallen angels. Humanizing them. They must choose it. Regardless of the tortures we enact upon them, we force them to enact, if they do not do these things willingly through desire of the act they will remain angelic."

Torrence's eyes moved to War. "And you're choosing to——?"

"Love you. Stay here with you. Touch you," he said. "Please, let me. Before I lose my nerve." His hands came to her shoulders. He held them there for a long moment of contemplation, of reflection. He tried to focus on the smoothness of her skin, its softness. He tried not to think that she was the antichrist, that she was the devil, and he especially tried not to think that he was an angel.

He looked up to her, swallowing thickly, his hands moving up her neck so that his thumbs could brush across her jawline and her lips. "This isn't dirt." He frowned, staring intently at the blood staining her shirt and her chest and collarbone. His eyes moved up to hers. "Let me wash you. We can go into that heavenly bath together, the lion and the lamb."

Her narrowed eyes bore into War an intensity that seemed to ravish his spirit. It was as if he could feel internally her consumption of his flesh.

Her heated gaze slid down his nose, traced the shape of his lips, the lines of his jaw. Her own lips parted as she took him in, breathing in through them as if she didn't want to scent the air now that his goodness invaded it.

"Why so pushy, little angel?"

"I am an angel no more."

"Lying is a sin, but not one damnable enough to send you here."

"I am here anyway, and by my choice—choice, the very concept I should not be able to experience. You've given me that. There is no other explanation. Through your own divinity, whatever it may be or whoever it may have come from, you've affected my own. It bends to you, even when it fights itself in the endeavor."

"It didn't bend to me in the past."

"You weren't you in the past. It was easier to deny human flesh when the spirit only fought a soul. Now the spirit fights a god. The battle is exhausting, Torrence. I surrender to it. And when I surrender all logic and consciousness, I am left only with impulse. Impulse keeps me here. It wants me to submit to you, your divinity. You may not be God, but you are a god. Let me praise you as such."

His fingers, clean and cool and delivering small shifts of atmosphere around their movements, fluttered along her jaw, her chin. Across her lower lip brushed his thumb.

Unconsciously, she leaned into him, her eyes closing in the relief of his temperature as it cooled the flesh of her cheeks, which had been heated by rage and by temptation. She raised her chin, her being reacting instinctively against his chilly touches, his soft fingertips, his heavenly scent. A small hum sounded in her throat, her hands swiftly finding his waist so she could take into her fingers the flesh of his hipbones.

Though he felt her reach beneath his t-shirt, heated fingertips exploring his body, sullying the purity of his flesh with dirt and blood and violence, he remained focused on her and the expressions of her face as he spread his spirit across her skin and let it slip into her pores.

"Torrence," he whispered, his eyes intent on her parting lips and gently-closed eyes. "Let me cleanse you of all this. Please."

"You wish to cleanse me so that I might defile you?"

He blushed.

"Perhaps fully this time," she said.

Expecting to see mischief on her face, or at least some sort of entertained grin, War was shocked to see Torrence wearing such a serene expression. Her brows creased ever-so-slightly, her head tilted as if she were studying his features—as if she'd never seen him before.

"We don't…" He paused in a hesitant confusion. "We don't have to…"

"I have an angel awaiting me," she said abruptly, her brow arching over newly-emblazoned eyes as she looked to Formaadoria.

He swallowed thickly, knowing she surely meant awaiting to be tortured. He couldn't think on this or its implications though, not if he wanted Torrence, and he never could deny his desires for her. "I've been waiting for you," he said. "And you've waited for me even longer. Sacrifice one sin for another. Instead of asking me to bend to your will, could we try giving in to mine? Just once?"

"The angel will get you bloody again," Conrad said, his dulcet voice undeniably smooth, heavenly even to War's angelic ears.

"No reason why you can't have his brother wash away that of some unremarkable humans."

"All humans are remarkable," War said. His jaw clenched. He couldn't help himself. He looked to Conrad. "As you were."

Conrad chuckled. "As you will be."

War looked back to Torrence, her stoic energy alarming, as it had never been her usual.

"I'll be whatever you want me to be," War said. "Your human, your angel. I would be your demon."

Torrence looked to Conrad, who grinned at her. "He releases angels. He gets demons to willingly relinquish to him their weapons, even as they torture souls. He seems simple, doesn't he? Yet he is cunning."

"There is no deceit between us," War said. "We know what the other is. We know who the other is."

"Who?"

"Yes."

"You concede, do you?"

"What else can an angel do?"

"Fine," she said. "Conrad can tend to the angel. You…" Torrence said, raising her hand to recall to her the chains. She clamped them onto War's wrists, locking them tightly against his flesh to make him gasp. "You can tend to me."

She took the chain into her hand, turning to her brothers. "Show Todd a warm welcome, boys. Celebrate a night well done."

They thanked her in a riotous release of their tension, embracing each other or moving to the table to feast.

Torrence led War away from this by the chains. He moved a step behind her, sharing a look with Conrad as he passed, ready, once again, to descend further into Hell with her.

CHAPTER FIVE

"No more games," Torrence said, her arms crossing before her. "What's your angle?"

"Angle?"

"Don't play dumb. You want to stay in Hell? You want to give in to me? To worship me? Why?"

"Because I love you." His brows creased. "Is it so shocking? Doesn't everyone worship you? Hasn't everyone your entire life given in?"

"People," she said calmly. "A person, an observant person, an articulate person, a person with a very keen understanding of their fellow man can coerce and overcome almost anyone. It's simply two people at the end of it, two human beings with limited senses and familiar wants." Her fingers came to his flesh now, the delicate skin that draped over a high cheekbone. She pressed her thumb into the freckles of black expanse trapped within this flesh, which had burned holes into the fragile, physical matter. From these charred openings came the light of the spirit within, glittering even in the slight movement of his slowly-blinking eyes and illuminating the skin around them. "You are not a person, though."

He exhaled through a half-hearted smile. Embarrassed of himself, he could not meet her gaze when it billowed onto him so intensely. "Neither are you."

Her hands moved down his arms and over the metal shackles binding his wrists. Her fingers traced the chiseled Latin upon the cuffs, which bound his essence and therefore his magic, into his physical form. "Conrad is stronger than you?"

"A moment of weakness," he said, watching her hands as they caressed his own, "is all it takes."

"A moment of weakness?" Her brow arched. "If you were fallen, it'd be an eternity of weakness, would it not?"

She lifted her hands from his, raising her pointer finger between them, then tapping it upon the cuffs. They shattered beneath the touch.

"Yes." War trembled at this immense strength, at the growth of her abilities or even simply the harnessing of what was already there, the mastery of it.

"Conrad would be stronger than you at all times, then. I would be." He watched in worry as those same, powerful fingers moved up his wrists, his arms, until her hands ran up his shoulders across his t-shirt.

"You are," he said.

"I wonder why you're so convinced you've sullied your spirit."

"I know I haven't completed the transformation, but it is happening."

"You can feel it?"

"I don't know what I feel." Trembling and hesitant, his hands moved to her. He had no body part in mind, no article of clothing, he only knew he was near enough to Torrence, after so much time apart, to touch her. She was filthy, her skin spatter with blood, drying mud caked upon her boots and jeans. His fingers went unconsciously to her jeans, to her belt loops. They slipped inside these tiny pieces of fabric, his knuckles brushing against the worn pleather belt around her waist, his fingers hooking around the loops, holding onto her this way.

He wanted to move her closer to him, kept trying to find the right angle or the right grip to coax this from her, but after some exploration of his fingers, he touched something warm and sticky upon her hip. He recoiled quickly, hands rushing to his pants where he unconsciously wiped them. A shaken breath passed through frowning lips. "Let me cleanse you of all this." His brows furrowed tightly. "I can't focus on our discussion with it."

"Yes, our discussion." A brow arched as a smirk of serene, but arrogant, playfulness came to her lips.

"I'll cleanse you of it. I'll—." He couldn't finish his sentence. The air had been taken from him and rather abruptly. A fraction of a second passed in blurring vision and pricking skin. Then something warm encompassed him. It yielded as quickly as it had consumed him, releasing him from its suction while remaining all around him.

As he adjusted, the sound of water falling entered the disorienting silence. As this auditory recognition leveled, other sensibilities came back, blooming around War in sharpened images and faint, but heavenly, aromas.

He recognized this place immediately. Torrence's grand bath. As he blinked, the murals came into focus. Angels, his brothers, depicted in open fields beneath blue skies. Rendered so masterfully were these works, War thought for a moment he could feel the sun of the unbroken sky offering its warmth upon his skin. Oh, it was, indeed, a lovely experience.

Water sprinkled gently against his back. Then soft, easy waves, the waves of water accommodating matter, caressed his chest and came over shoulders.

Fingers fluttered across his sides as arms came around his waist. A body behind his body, pulling him into its embrace. Hair brushed across his shoulder as lips caressed his neck, his ear.

He smiled, turning his head toward her, his hands moving to her hands and keeping them tightly against his midriff.

Had he done it? Charmed the devil? What would this mean for him, and for the world at large?

She chuckled against him, her lips offering their devotion to his shoulder now. A hand released his hand, slipping up his wrist and arm to grip him where her lips had just been.

He turned now, looking into her eyes. She hadn't cast them in her once-natural blues, though everything else about her seemed so very human. Her eyes were red, dark, and deviant, even inside the lovely skin about them.

He lifted his hands to her cheeks now, brushing the moisture from his thumbs across the spattering just below her left eye. Staring to the spot intently, brows knitted, lips tight and pursing, War worked hurriedly to rid her beautiful features of any signs of destruction or death. He only wished she'd aid him in this. Replace the deeply red irises with their human blues. That was all he needed now to slip inside the fantasy of it all, of Torrence somehow in Heaven and able to love him there.

She blinked slowly as she watched him, allowing the water to wash away all evidence of her sins. Her hands went to his waist again and she coaxed him into her, wanting to create as much intimacy here as possible, especially when he was so focused on the bloody remnants of his beloved humanity upon her face.

He let his body, slipping weightlessly through the warm water, press against hers. A hope within him, too, that some desire of his own might stem from this connection, but where he'd expected to feel skin against skin, inviting space along invading organ, he felt only fabric.

Looking down at the water as it expelled in a rolling gush from the closing gap between their chests, War realized more consciously now that Torrence hadn't stripped him of his pants. Only his shirt had been removed. Her small, cropped tank top remained over her chest, though it had tightened against her breasts to reveal by shape alone their curvature, humble peaks, budded nipples.

Though his features donned the attitude of great confusion, Torrence could sense the consumption in his eyes. She shifted so that the water rolled gently away from her, revealing her more visibly, playing into the attraction as best she could. She didn't want to relieve the angel of his divinity, this was true—not yet, anyway—but she couldn't deny the thrill of lust, of any of those tried-and-true old seven deadly's, when they emitted so intensely from a soul so close to her.

She decided that she could play with this angel, for whom she had such deep affection, if only she practiced a great deal of self control—something that had never been her strong suit. Still, she expected that she could do anything, so she pressed on.

She raised a leg then, allowing the flesh of his flank to feel the bare flesh of her thigh. No, she hadn't stripped them both. She hadn't needed to. The angel was here to cleanse her body, wasn't he? He hadn't come to partake in intimacy with it. But he was appealing; his thin waist and small chest always offered, like a Valentine from her eyes to her brain, a burst of chemically-charged emotion, and there had been no reason to deny herself some enjoyment while she contemplated his motives here.

"Torrence," he whispered gently, his hand instinctively finding her thigh and gripping it tightly. He leaned against her, their foreheads connecting, his eyes closing. "May I kiss you?" Though the question had been ardent and breathy, the melody of its soft yet somehow gravelly expression undeniably heady, there was a patience to his voice. As he awaited an answer—any answer—he exhaled through his parted lips, then licked them closed.

"Yes," she finally responded, simple and serene.

He closed his eyes gently, leaning further into their embrace, and brushed his lips against hers.

Motionless in this small connection, neither rushed to heighten or hurry their passion. They merely took pause, each of them for their own reasons, to absorb every sensation their togetherness created.

"Oh, to be manipulated by an angel," she whispered against his lips. "What trickery is this?"

"No manipulation or deceit, Torrence," War said gently, easing the human side of her mind that still wandered into fearful territory where the metaphorical heart was concerned. As if with an unseen chalice, he used his angelic abilities to lift the water from the bath around them, and slowly commanded it to cascade against her dark locks. "Only truth. Only honesty. You should know me well enough by now to see that all I do is done for you."

"I know you well enough to know that isn't true," she countered, fighting the comfort in her body to release her from such a docile state. Her eyes came open slowly; ease in her features, though the hellish irises raged in flame. "You could overpower me if you chose," she said.

"We both know that isn't true."

"It isn't true in general," she said, lifting a hand to his glistening cheeks, touching the radiant stars and smiling at the sounds of the dripping water on her fingertips as it evaporated in the constellations' great heat. "It's true as we are now."

"Here in this bath? Water is not a weakness of the antichrist, only the antithesis of her Hell." He brought his fingers to the flowing water, allowing them to trace the path it took into her hair, then he brushed his fingers through the tendrils. "So many souls cry out for merely a drop, and we lie together in a pool of it. Hedonism seems rarely as sinful as it's made out to be, but in this case perhaps we should feel badly." He licked his lower lip into his teeth as his brows furrowed. Glancing to her now, he exhaled. "Regardless of the element surrounding us, I could only overpower you if you allowed me to."

"Maybe I should," she said. "I'm tired, War."

"Tired of the violence?" He looked up to her, his eyes as exquisitely hopeful as they were bright.

A vicious glance of her eyes revealed the answer.

"Right," he said lowly through a thin smile. His brows came together, lifting as he brushed her hair behind her shoulder. The nail of his thumb trailed the punctuated path of a scabbing wound there. "Why don't you heal this?"

"Why should I?"

He licked his lower lip into his mouth, his eyes still staring at the injury. Slowly, a very dim light issued from this thumb. He brought it down against her flesh. "It's just—."

She struck his hand, pushing it away from her forcefully. His eyes followed his hand instinctively, then he looked up to her.

"I have always hated that."

He nodded. "I know. I'm sorry."

He lowered his chin purposefully as he looked up to her, readying his hand to emerge from the water and take into his palm the flesh of her shoulder again. This time, he would not press. He lifted his brows to suggest this to her. She allowed it.

"Of what do you tire, then?" He commanded the water over her shoulder now, slowly taking away the sweat of the night's activity, the grime of it.

"Look at what I've done. Look at all I've created and all I've conquered. To use this immense power and such great force upon children seems a waste. To use force upon children at all is grotesque. It feels like weakness. I hate it. I am not weak nor is my congregation."

"I know that."

"I have such plans," she said, releasing a bit of her stress in an easy sigh. "But it seems something, be it angelic spirit or prophecy, keeps getting the way."

"You don't have to murder the children," War said. "You could take them captive. Keep them here. Let the mothers in your hybrid chambers tend to them, raise them as their own and for you."

Her eyes opened, a brow jumping upward. So, War wanted

to impress upon her his own will. Laughable. He knew nothing of Hell, she realized, no matter how ancient or angelic he was, and this meant that he knew nothing of here. But this ignorance, like all things irritating when found in others, was somewhat endearing within War. It draped him in the naivety so commonly-associated with innocence that she found him rather charming in the moment. She loved him for it, for his lack of understanding the enormity of her plans, even in his innate knowledge of them; how similar they proved to be in this moment—despite their obvious and intense differences—for they were utterly in sync without trying, without even knowing it. God's son, refusing sin as he begged for it from its master, and the devil's son, refusing compassion as she delighted in the embodiment of it.

Undeniably, however, his idea of her as ultimately-cruel was appealing, too, so she did not correct or castigate him. Instead, she used the opportunity to dig a little deeper into his motives.

She hummed in response. "Raise the thing that would destroy me?" She huffed.

"Think on it. You've raised the offspring of angels to do your bidding. Surely you could raise human children with the same indoctrination."

"Devious angel," she said, turning in his arms so that her back was against his chest now. She brought the hand at her shoulder more closely to her chest, her neck. "I think, after all, you wish for my demise."

"Never." He winced, but she didn't see it.

Instead, she felt him as he held onto her more tightly, drawing her more closely into him. His arms around her chest now completely, he nestled his face into hers, kissing her hair, her ear, what bit of her cheek he could reach from this vantage point. "You'd have an army, though."

"You keep pressing."

"Hear me out?" He placed a tender, but open-mouthed, kiss

on her ear, warm and lingering and wetted by the teasing of his tongue.

She said nothing, but he decided to continue. After all, hadn't Torrence always accepted his silence as his consent?

"Gone would be the days of recruiting and converting. Your army is raised from birth to praise you. You control what they learn and what they see and read and hear. You'd control what they thought. You'd tell them what to think."

"And I suppose this pesky little angel running about Hell without my permission wouldn't try and poison their minds with purity or the promises of redemption?" She smiled now, something genuine and unconcerned for the first time in a long time. "Have I figured you out?"

She'd been plotting, yes. She'd been murdering and violating and sinning and damning. She'd been away more than she'd been home, and she was tired of it, even if the desire for simpler times went as abruptly as it had come.

Oh, these tender moments with the fragile War, what comfort she'd always found in them.

After a communion, he'd enclose her with his arms and his humble chest, the creamy flesh wrapped 'round these body parts always smooth and soft and inviting when her muscles ached and her mind tired. Their positioning now brought her back to those times, times when she thought him a human. Oh, how she wished he had been merely that, or that he had succumbed to her lustful pursuits before she'd found out that he wasn't.

"You've figured me out a long time ago, Torrence. You figure everyone out."

"Not you," she said.

"If that's true, don't feel bad about it. I don't have myself figured out. Not beyond the basics."

"Which are…?"

He inhaled deeply, bringing her more tightly into him once again, nestling his cheek against her. "God is good. You are not good. I am good but fallible. And I enjoy this flesh more than any spirit is supposed to."

"So, why not give in to it when we first met? Why tempt me now?"

"Tempt you?" He chuckled. "Yes, an angel tempts the devil. I like that."

"An angel? I thought you were resigned to human now."

"I thought I was." He raised a hand to his own cheek now, feeling about the charred holes and the heat they emitted. His brows furrowed. He had spent a fraction of a second within Torrence, true, but he had been within her. Wasn't that point? Or was there some minimum time requirement upon sin? He exhaled, exasperated and uncertain. "I am your angel, Torrence," he said, "I would be your demon. Your human. Just tell me what you want."

"I want you," she said, turning to face him. Torrence reached up to him, the wetness of her fingertips fizzling as they traced the jagged edges of his spiritual freckles. "I can't imagine looking at you and not seeing these." She stared into his eyes in careful observation. "Oh, your irises. Your hair. Everything pure and inhumanly perfect. It seems unfair that I shouldn't be able to own it—to own you."

"You can," he said.

"But not as you are. I want you as you are."

"As I am." He blushed at this, then a worry overtook him. "Torrence, I've entered you in lust already. What happens if the fall still commences?" A shiver gripped his body. His eyes rose hesitantly to hers, and he bit his lip. "God has no use for a fallen angel, and you don't want me as a demon."

She brushed his glistening hair from his equally-iridescent eyes. "Look at your reflection in the water. You're you."

"But, Torrence—."

"War, you were filled with worry that night. I felt it. I'm sure God felt it if such vibrations can rise as far. Or perhaps He can't perceive at all what happens here—."

"He perceives all. He knows all."

"Then you'd have always been a demon. Then falling into such a state wouldn't be possible."

"What?"

"If He knows all, then He knows who would fall and who wouldn't. If He already knew of the fall, why create the beings capable of such a thing? Maybe you give Him too much credit. Maybe He doesn't know even half of what you think He does."

War's lips curled in disgust at this blasphemy, but why argue? Torrence was God's antithesis, and it was entirely possible she said what she did now, not as her belief, but as a tool of manipulation.

"Why do you want me so assured?"

"Assuring you is bad?" She laughed. "What do you want from me, then?"

"Merely this," he said, lifting a hand to her cheek and wiping away the remnant dried blood there. "Serving the lord is all angels know, and I don't think God would want dominion over me any longer. It's you, Torrence. It's only you. It will only ever be you. Even if I wish it weren't."

She brought her hand to his, stopping his motions. Nestling into the coolness of his divinity, Torrence manifested a small, annoyed growl in her throat.

"You feel so good," she said, using her other hand at his shoulder to move him nearer to her. "It feels so bad."

"Natural aversion," he said in accordance and understanding, even as he submitted to the suggested proximity. "But even instinct cannot control desire."

The words fell from his lips in a shaken exhale as he closed the small space between their skin. Connecting in mutual desperation, in the shared longing intensified only by a forbidden, distasteful, idiotic craving, the lips of the devil's child pressed wantonly against the lips of a Son of God.

Without hesitation, War returned the affection, pulling Torrence into him more tightly. His fingers gripped the flesh on her body, holding her with his hands, his arms, his lips, his tongue.

Hell wasn't Heaven, and this new God would not be praised as the previous one. Now love was romantic and sexual, no longer agape and pure. Devotion was quick words whispered between kisses, not dutiful prayers. Lust was pious, and virginity merely a body wasted.

War tried to ignore the pit forming in his stomach; tried not to listen to the voice in his mind, his human-esque mind with something akin to a conscience, urging him to stop the physicality he could avoid.

But he didn't want to. How sinful. He'd had a mere taste of pleasure after a year of experiencing such desire, such lust, and he knew that small grazing of flesh within flesh was enough to damn him.

Oh, strip him of his wings. Pluck each of the six from his back, feather by wretched feather. Break the bones, rip them from his spine. He did not care.

He wanted Torrence now. He wanted her as he always had wanted her—close, connected, intimate—but now this needed expressed, and War could see no easier or more human way to show her his affections than through the sins of the flesh.

As he gripped at her neck to deepen the embrace of their panting lips, War pressed his body against hers, moving his hips awkwardly, but suggesting successfully nonetheless, toward his intention.

All around them came the lovely chiming of gentle bells. Cool air floated around them. The atmosphere seemed to shine.

Noticing this, Torrence opened her eyes. She looked about at these small miracles, the spiritual manifestations of War's physical pleasure, and chuckled against his lips.

He pulled away at this, his brows creasing. "Have I done something wrong?"

A serenity came into her features. A patient hand brushed his hair very slowly from his eyes. "Look around you. Listen."

He looked up at the shimmering air around them, the rainbows created by the flowing water where his essence had expanded into the stream. "I'm sorry."

"It's okay. I'm not angry. But I don't need to assure you now. You see that your divinity is intact."

"Break it, Torrence." He moved into her again, reclaiming her lips in his tender, unskilled way. He took hold of her body, drawing them against each other to attempt a reigniting of that just-lost passion. He'd come too far, too close, to fail now. "Fragment it. Trying to remain whole has grown too tiresome."

"Accepting this is far too tempting," she said.

A ringing came to his ears then. Familiar. His body felt cold suddenly. His feet were no longer suspended in weightlessness. The bath had gone from around him. He blinked until his vision came back. His hand went to the throbbing in his head. Dizzying, this trick of hers, but here he was, standing on the marble stones of Hell, fully clothed once more. From the silence this quick movement caused came sound once more—the sound of clicking heels on the marble.

"Get out of here, War," Torrence said, walking by him.

"If I leave then I leave in your name."

She turned back, crossed her arms, an amused expression on her face.

"Leave for whatever reason you'd like," she said. "Don't act so Biblical about it, though. You're an angel, but one that was just begging me to help you fall."

"I meant that I'll leave as your follower."

"You will not."

"Torrence—."

"You'll spread my message?"

"Your messages?"

"You'll go out into crowds of the faithful and preach my

sermons?"

"Well, I—."

"You'll tell them that I am God, that I have Risen, that I am He who is resurrected to guide them into paradise?"

War's lips tightened, trembled. He stared into Torrence's eyes defiantly, regardless of the tears welling inside his own eyes or the sorrowful slant his brows provided them.

"You don't want to be here, War."

"No, I don't," he said through gritted teeth. "But I want to be with you."

"Why?"

She was indomitable, strong and god-like. All-powerful. Demonic, yes, but he fashioned that a form of divinity for it had once been angelic grace. Twisted and deformed, but angelic grace regardless. But she was no angel, and she was no demon, and perhaps these facts alone were the reason War felt so inclined to follow, even when his faith did not align with her system, even when his beliefs opposed hers.

It was not as if Torrence was a deity of ancient religion. It was not as if she were agnostic or atheist. Torrence was, within his very belief system, the antithesis of all he valued, all he believed, all he knew as righteous and true.

But she was a leader, a divine one. She was preternatural now, and she sat upon a throne in the realm beyond the living.

It was nature to follow such a god. He was created with perfect submission, designed to desire only the wishes of his God. He wondered now, not if Torrence had become his God, but why.

It might have been proximity alone; his essence as a spiritual servant perceiving so near her essence as a spiritual leader, a divine savior. He, a being comprised of galaxies and energy, feeling only her divinity, regardless of which side of the timeless battle between good and evil she ruled, and submitting before her aggression, her dominance, her authority.

"The first night I met you, I wanted to be near you," he said.

"You were their leader. No one questioned you. They attacked when you commanded, they ceased when you said, they exited when you told them to. And your radiance—in the museum, yes. You shined unlike any other soul. I know now it was the virtuous sacrifice awakening your daimons, bringing more of your spiritual self into your body, where it had not enough room to remain inside without expanding through your pores as a great, shining light.

"It frightened me because I did not recognize it. I only knew that I considered you beautiful, that I wanted to hear your voice and know your name. I am not permitted such knowledge, and I should not be able to experience such desire. I ran to keep intact my duties to God, to goodness, to righteousness, but I wanted to be where you were immediately. But you were there. You were right in front of me radiating your divinity and displaying your authority. I…" He exhaled a fearful laugh. His chin lowered as this worrisome scoff passed through his lips. He was ashamed, embarrassed. He was sinful, but, in reality, admitting his trespasses was the first step on the traditional path to forgiveness, though he wasn't sure he even wanted it. He wasn't sure what he wanted.

His hand came to his hair, still iridescent and shimmering amongst the grays and blacks of Hell's stone walls. "Torrence," he said, looking up to her, "If I hadn't already been on the ground that night, I would've fallen at your feet. I wanted to bow down to you—your grace and your authority. I wanted your favor. I thought I'd won it. I don't know what I did to lose it now, but I am sorry."

"You lost nothing," she replied curtly. "Except perhaps your welcome here."

"But I don't—."

"I've had enough of your complaints and your challenges." Torrence raised a hand to silence him. "You are standing in Hell, surrounded by demons, by my brothers. It will not benefit you to piss me off when I adore you enough to let you leave."

"I don't mean to upset you." War frowned; his eyes fell. Ever the solemn angel, saddened over the loss of humanity, he appeared beautiful in his sorrow. His hair still gleamed its iridescence, his brow loosely furrowed in a regal arch above his downcast eyes, small, reflective specks of light in all colors dancing upon the creamy skin his straight nose from those open-wounds of galactic essence, which lined his cheekbones, and his delicate lips always slightly parted when they saddened.

"Oh, stop it," she said.

He looked up to her, his brows raising in confusion. War hadn't realized he was doing anything, and by mere proximity to Torrence, he was continuing to upset her. He licked his lips as he considered it.

He looked around to the stone walls and the demons lining them. Their armor, though darker, was almost identical to that of the angels. They stood in the same solemnity as War, their faces stoic and their posture pristine. Their eyes looked forward, looked to their angelic brother, then to their devilish leader, but emotion was not present within their eyes as it was in the eyes of Torrence's human companions.

They were, indeed, angelic still, even though that grace had been altered by the choice to make choices; the desire of earthly women, the pursuit of their bodies by angelically-manifested bodies, the combination of the earthen flesh and the spiritual essence—this, the great fall of War's brothers, which ended in their twisted divinity and their stations here.

"So, this is what it's like, then," he said, looking back to Torrence now. "Being your enemy."

"It's what you've always insisted we be," she said. "As I've stated more times than I should have, you're free to go." She glanced at her demons, and they made for War. Each took him by an arm and urged him as gently as they could—which was not very gentle at all—toward the great arch that marked the exit of the antichrist's office-like chamber.

"Release me, wretched creatures." War persisted, struggling against his mutated brothers. "Torrence, please do not cast me out. I—I am afraid to go."

"Afraid?"

"If I fall, then I have no Holy Lord. This leaves me in your authority alone, and if you do not want me either…Without you, I am godless. An angel with no divine ruler before whom to bow, I am not sure how to exist. Even as a human man. I might have remained an angel had I known this was your desire."

"You are angelic," she said. "We all can perceive it."

"The fall is not instantaneous," he said.

"I pulled a wing from an angel," Torrence said. "I'm sure you saw it on your way in. If not, surely you noticed the feathers from its mate spread throughout the murals in my bedchamber and in the bath."

"You used the wing of an angel to create that?" War felt a lump forming in his throat, its consistency thick with nerves and sticky in guilt.

"That angel was human in minutes."

"It can be quick if the spirit is weakened or battered, but I hadn't endured what my brethren endured here."

"Precisely. We completed no sinful ritual."

"But we participated in passion…physically."

"We have plenty of times."

"Torrence, not like that. Not to that extent. You know that. You can deny me, but don't deny the magnitude of what we've done."

"I've done nothing," she said, her brow arching cockily.

"What I did, then," he said, eyes falling. "When I become human, my fate is Hell regardless."

"You are not becoming human," she insisted. "I could perceive it."

"But we—."

"No, we didn't."

"Torrence, I entered you. Even for a split second, it occurred."

She approached him now, taking from her boot her switchblade. When it opened, it silenced all thought within the room.

She stormed toward War with this blade, still covered in the dried blood of the night's victims, clenched tightly in her fist. When she approached him, the demons at War's sides released him. They stepped back in fear of her.

War, gripped by a greater confusion than fear, merely recoiled slightly where he stood.

She reached out for him, grabbing him by his wrist aggressively. Yanking his arm toward her, unbending it, leaving it bare and open and exposed, she swiftly, blindly, shoved the blade into his arm.

He gasped in the acknowledgment of the act—had Torrence really tried to injure him? To inflict such harm upon him? But no pain registered physically. He attempted to pull back his arm, but her grip was too strong.

"No," she said, jerking it back toward her. She tightened her hold of the blade, sinking in further into the meat of his arm, and then she dragged it from its placement beneath the crook of his elbow down the length of his forearm toward his wrist.

"Torrence, what are you—?"

"You're not bleeding," she said, withdrawing the blade.

Light emitted from the gaping wound, but only light.

War looked down to his arm. His eyes widened as he watched the human-esque flesh already beginning to come back together across the tear and heal.

"You aren't fallen. I am sick of proving it to you."

"Then let me fall now." Confusion ravaged him. No thought entered his mind but this: Why doesn't she want me? "Let me be human. Please."

"Why?"

"Why? What do you mean?"

"What makes you want to be human so suddenly?"

"It's not a sudden decision, Torrence. I've endured a great deal since manifesting here the first time and even more since the second. I'm bound to this body. Why not make it eternal?"

"Oh," she said, smiling something sinister as she leaned back, crossing her arms before her chest. "There's a ticking clock over your head. You don't know if you'll ever be given full power again, do you? So you beg me for mortality." Amusement evident in her face, though the sensations he perceived in the atmosphere around her were not so light or so contented. "You ask me for your devolution? Lie to gain it. Say you desire me. You desire the limited years of men."

"I do desire you."

"No. You desire God, and you fear yours has abandoned you here, but I can see inside your eyes and beneath them that He hasn't." She grinned, moving against him now, her eyes gleaming seas of wonder and excitement. "Come now, darling," she said softly but commandingly. Her brows lifted in the eagerness of the potential outcome of her demand. "Show me your wings."

Surprise pulled at War's brows and widened his eyes. His lips parted slightly. After a few fleeting seconds allowed the shock of the request to become understanding, he blushed and looked to his feet. He drew his lip into his mouth, his tongue brushing over it as if the two parts of his body which seemed designed more for poetry and passionate embrace than for the mere but necessary consumption of sustenance worked against his orders when he asked them to respond to her.

"Violence is so different from desire," he said hesitantly. "Both are physical expressions, but one is loving where the other is forceful." His eyes moved wearily toward hers now. "Perhaps you ask to see my wings because you want to rip them away from me."

She smiled. She seemed so amused by him, but his simplicity. "If I want to remove your wings," she said, her tone eerily even, "I'd take you into my bed and let you fall to me as you sink into me. Why do you care anyway? A means to an end. Isn't that what you want?"

"Torment, no."

"Then leave."

"But I—."

The dizziness came again. The auditory loss. The headache. He felt the weight of the demon's claws upon his arms, but as he looked about he recognized this room as the receiving foyer of Hell and the door was getting closer. The demons were dragging him toward it, and he was too spellbound still to fight them properly.

The doors came open, then, and War, uncertain of his stance between Heaven and Hell, between angel and human, was tossed onto the ground.

He groaned, his hand coming to his head while his other palmed the marble beneath him. As he sat there, his knee bent, back aching, he looked up to the doors, watching them as they closed.

CHAPTER SIX

Wesley hadn't been able to enjoy the hedonism that always took place after a battle or a siege or a ritual. Not tonight.

The past was in his mind, a troubling past, a past of which he knew nothing, though he desperately wanted to.

The idea of the past, the possibilities of what occurred within it, distracted him from hunger, from the desire for aged wine, which had become even rarer since the open skies, for the sensual pleasures in which the Brethren engaged. The consideration of Todd and what he knew of Torrence was too great to dismiss long enough to even have a bite of the lavish meal provided.

He stared at Todd, watching the seemingly-hesitant man slouch in his chair. His shoulders were raised slightly, not as an expression of some thought or emotion, but naturally heightened as if he were expecting always some great blow.

He reached tentatively for a glazed bun. He kept his arm tightly against his side even when he extended it toward his wine glass and brought it to his lips.

Wesley scoffed as he shook his head, as he lowered it. Torrence had that type, hadn't she? Michael was that type. Freddy was. The scared-of-their-skin type.

It wasn't that these men were afraid of others or of breaking the law or of punishment. They hadn't feared jail time or eternal damnation. Their worry was far different than these—it was a fear of the self. A fear of their inadequacy, a fear of someone else seeing it. They kept their heads down and their actions as small as their closed-off bodies so they were less likely to draw attention to their many perceived flaws. They did not want others to see how awkward they were, how weird, how every motion from their breathing to their walk was uncomfortable and incorrect.

What easy targets the insecure of self were for Torrence. Easier still, the ones like Jason, who craved the false power of violence. The easiest, perhaps, he realized now, looking down at the untouched beer between his hands, had been those desperate merely for love. Those like himself. Those who wanted a soulmate. Those who found their own validity in someone else, in someone's desire for them.

He sighed quietly, not wanting his brothers to hear or see his contemplations and the upset they caused him, even though he knew they were too busy consuming and imbibing and congratulating themselves to notice; maybe when to care. They were always so excited for the next task, always hoping they had only time for a quick nap before they'd head out again. Destruction and madness and hedonism. What else was there for souls like those of his brethren?

Outside the grand hall, Wesley heard a large gust of wind. He sat up and turned his head toward the doors behind him. Had a section of the manor been ripped away? Why was there wind beyond the dinner hall?

He stood from his seat and made for the door, the party raging on behind him somehow silent in his focus. When he reached the exit of the hall, he opened the door only slightly. The room beyond was still there, still intact. Not a single crack in the walls, nor a broken candelabra or chandelier.

He examined further the entrance room of Hell, heard a bit

of scuffling, of shoes against the marble. The growling of demons, which was merely the sounds of their breathing, became audible, joined by something sparkling, something which seemed to cast upon the darkened walls between burning candles speckles of shifting light.

He stepped into the room, looking toward the sound at his left, witnessing the demons as they dragged the dizzied War through the room and tossed him outside.

When they closed the door, Wesley entered the room further.

The demons looked toward the sounds of his motions, his boots against the floor, the beating of his heart.

"What's going on, boys?"

"Taking out the trash," Anahhuv answered, scoffing as he made his way back toward the spiraling descent into Hell.

Wesley watched the demon move by him, then looked to Avalux. "Why was he so out of it?"

"The Master."

"She didn't want to keep him?"

"Guess not."

"Why not chain him up, then?" Wesley asked as Avalux made his way toward the spiral now. "Hey." He pursued. "Wait, why did you just throw him out? How could you overpower him? He's an angel. Isn't he still an angel?"

"You'll have to ask the Master," the demon said simply, remembering Conrad's wrath in the torture chamber and not wanting to repeat it or have it worsen. He returned to his post, standing guard at Torrence's door—the door that opened into a lounge of sorts, the start of her private salons, which she'd expanded, just beyond her personal chamber.

Wesley shook his head, reaching hurriedly at the command of his intense emotions for the door's handle and jerking it open.

When he entered, Torrence was reading from a large old book. She stood near a bay window with one leg thrown over its cushions. At the base of the window, black streaked the glass.

Fire raged beyond it. She attempted no pleasantry, for she saw the expression on Wesley's lovely face and understood the quickness of his motions as feeling-driven.

"Did you fuck that angel?"

"Excuse me?" Torrence looked up from the book.

"I…" He exhaled, his hands scrubbing over his face. "You brought him to your room when he first came here. He released an angel to stop us in the tunnel, and you brought him to your room. I worship you. I do everything you've ever asked. I never come here."

"No one does."

"Yeah, but I'm not supposed to be like everyone else."

"There's a natural hierarchy, Wesley. Angels and the Awakener, they were created differently from humans."

"I don't mean some bullshit hierarchy of Hell and you know it. I mean your hierarchy. Your favorites."

"Favorites?" She chuckled, her face open and amused. She looked back to her book. "How long do you think the Nephilim in the tunnel will last?"

"What?" His eyes glanced down to the book now, watching Torrence's fingers trace ancient drawings of giants, muscle-bound and beautiful, towering over human-looking women and men with wings.

"They don't seem to last long, do they? My giants."

"Tor—."

She raised a hand to him, her eyes peering upward. "I heard you."

Beneath a weary brow, his eyes became glassy. A weakened exhale fled parting lips. Confusion riddled the handsome face. "Then answer me," he said, the shaken words a desperate plea more than a command or a suggestion.

"No," she said. "That angel is up to something." She looked back to her book, the faded pages crackling as she flipped through them. "Figure out what."

"Excuse me?" Wesley's brows lifted. Genuine surprise gripped him.

"I don't think he wants to worship me for the sake of it."

"Okay, so chain him up. Torture him. Let Conrad or the demons get it out of him—."

"No."

"Why?" His heightened voice leveled. His head shifted when he exhaled, and a hand came to his brow. He looked up to Torrence. "Why is he so different?"

Torrence closed the book. Stepping toward him now, she was the picture of serenity, of calm. She reached for Wesley, offering to his shoulder a tender touch before she rested her palm against his neck.

Glassy, his hazel eyes gazed up into hers. His forehead creased slightly. His face so innocent here, so vulnerable, and she knew it was the uncontrollable outward expression of all he felt internally.

"Because he is," she said plainly, unable to explain, though she preferred it if her favorite human companion thought her simply unwilling. No one needed to know of her struggle, the inner-turmoil, the overwhelming desire within her to own something pure and innocent, but the disgust she held for anything too weak to resist. Oh, wondrous purity could not succumb to her charms—by very nature, it rebuked her every advance—therefore making anything pure enough to desire dominion over indomitable.

His brows creased now. The pain as evident in his eyes as the newly-forming upset. He hated her. He hated War. Mostly he hated himself. "What?"

Torrence leaned into him, her arms slipping around his waist. "You're different, too." A gentle kiss came to his neck. "Don't ever think you aren't." She pulled back now to look into his eyes, and saw that his entire face had loosened. Keeping an arm about his waist, she lifted a hand to his face and brushed her fingers across his cheekbone, his brow line. "You were chosen because of it. He was chosen because of it. You two are not the same because you're flesh and blood and he is only spirit, but you're not much different beyond that. So please, Wesley, my Precious One…"

Tension dissipated from her features, and as it slipped away from them so too did the red slip away from her irises. Blue and human, reminiscent of the time before War, before angels, when Wesley was the only one Torrence trusted, when he was the only one with whom she shared intimacy, her eyes seemed more a window to nostalgia than to her soul. Wesley wasn't even sure if she had one—if she and Conrad ever had them. But she stared into his eyes now as a fragile human, not a powerful god, and she asked something of him. "Please, help me figure out what he's doing. Help me figure out his plans for me, for Hell. Whatever it is, don't worry. We will overcome it. But I hate not knowing what my enemy is planning."

"He's…" Wesley's voice seemed gravel more than air. "He's your enemy now?"

"He's an angel. He's always been my enemy."

"But when you had him in here the first time—."

"The first time was different."

"How?"

Torrence's hands fell away from him now. Her eyes became severe. "Have we entered a universe where I owe you explanations now?"

"Not as a follower, of course not, but I'm not trying to talk to the Prince of Hell here. I'm trying to talk to you, my best friend, my partner, my…" He shrugged, the action small and defeated. "My girlfriend, at one point I thought."

"Wesley, there's a change in War. He says he wants to be human. I can't imagine why."

"Yeah, me neither."

"Leads me to believe there's more to it than he says. I want to know what that is."

"And you don't think the usual methods—?"

"No. So take him out with you guys. See if he really does what he says he wants to do."

"What, fall? Sin? Commit violence?"

"Just see if he's committed to me," she said. "See if he's traded gods or whatever."

"And how do you want me to do that?"

"Make friends, of course."

"Make friends?" Shock pushed his brows upward. "Make friends with the angel you want more than me? My replacement?"

"Wesley, really, this melodrama." She giggled, moving against him. Her fingers danced along his brow, his cheekbone. "The angel is up to something. Just figure out what."

"Yeah," he said, gravelly voice half-broken. Scrubbing his hand over his face, he blinked the sorrow from his eyes. Then he looked back to Torrence, who was already going back to her book. "Okay," he said.

War sat on the steps of Hell—marble and cold—beneath the mural of contorting angels and bloodied souls.

His arms were wrapped around his knees, his fingers loosely hanging from open hands. He watched the trees as souls trapped in an unending loop of their deaths flung themselves from the branches of trees. The sounds of their necks snapping over and over again rang out in the darkness. When lightning burst, the shadows of their shoes projected against the thick fog that hung lowly near the ground. Everything was purple for a moment, glistening in the dewy atmosphere like amethyst, then blackness, punctuated by blurring grays and the occasional shimmer of white, overtook all again.

The door opened behind him but he made no effort to move. It didn't matter who emerged. It didn't matter what they intended to do.

If Torrence would not allow him inside Hell, he'd sit at its very gate until he figured out where he could go or what he could accomplish in this ever-dying, always-decaying new world.

He did not have to worship Torrence to love her, thus was true, and perhaps it was some amalgamation of his angelic subservience with her godly authority that had made him think the two concepts—worship and love—could only exist together.

Fine, he did not have to resign himself to downfall, but he still needed to be close to Torrence, didn't he? Not to love her, no. That could be done from anywhere; it had been done anywhere. When he was in Heaven suffering the punishments of this affection, he loved her still. From a realm away from her earthly plane, he loved her. Within a body or a spirit without form, he would love her. How could a force so inexplicable and yet so understood completely, so intangible and yet so very felt require both body and soul?

The truth, he understood now, was that this emotion, this love that so many who had never felt its encompassing strangle claimed to experience, could be expressed through words, yes, through touches, yes, actions and ideas, of course. But it did not require soul and body. It did not require brain or heart or mind. It simply was. And when two beings were trapped within its often tangled, sometimes spiked, and oftentimes sensually soft web, there was nothing that either of them could do to break free of it. There was no release from this embrace; this sometimes-ecstasy, sometimes-torment. War no longer feared this.

But he could not leave Hell without a monitor, without an angelic presence who had not been strung up and bound by ancient curses taught to evil spirits by the fallen angels. He realized now that his love for Torrence was part of God's plan; that it always had been. That through this love, that was very much the sticky web of two souls connected eternally, was not his love for her, not only that. It also consisted of her love for him. It was mutual. It belonged to them both as much as it bound them both. War loved Torrence and so he sought her out, and Torrence loved War and so she merely banished him when she might have destroyed him otherwise.

This was why God sent him back, he was sure of it now. Wasn't he?

From Hell came the brethren. Freddy and Michael walked by War as if he were not there.

"What have we here?" Jason smirked.

"That's Torrence's angel," Jocelyn said. She leaned against the door-frame, her arms crossed before her chest.

Torrence's angel. Oh, War liked that.

"Huh. Safe," Jason said, moving down the stairs. "For now, anyway."

Skeet came next, walking by War as he shoved at Jason playfully, then came Todd with his head down, staring only to his feet, his hands hovering over his ears as he moved swiftly through the other brethren, attempting to get out of the yard, it seemed, more quickly. Finally Jack, who merely stared at War as if he were something unimaginable, even in this new world of nightmare and myth, came through the door and joined his brothers.

War watched them as they headed down the path, hooting at one another and play-fighting. His forehead corrugated. Where was the final one? The first one, really. The one with whom Torrence enacted all the sins she refused to let War experience.

Slow steps came from the door then.

"See yah, Wes," Jocelyn said before closing it.

Another slow step came behind War, then another, until the perception of a presence towering over him on his left became too obvious to ignore.

"Hey," Wesley said.

War looked over the boots next to him on the porch. His hands on his knees curled into nervous fists. As his eyes moved up the figure's legs, he noted the handgun strapped to his thigh.

He recognized it. It'd been pointed at him once before, back when Torrence didn't know him, back when he was merely another human to them.

Inside this soul, he could sense so much hatred, but not in the typical manner; not in the manner of those who had exited the before him, those whose hearts seemed made of hatred, some shaped by painful events of which they'd been victims, some fueled by the desire to never again feel so weak, and some who had simply been born to hate.

This hatred was nothing of the others'. This hatred did not issue from its source to spread outward. This hatred was reflective; blooming inside the very object of its disgust. Wesley didn't hate War. War wasn't certain if he knew that himself, but War knew it, but it was easier for Wesley to project that hatred onto War, especially if he perceived War as having something he desperately wanted.

As he looked up from the gun, eyes raking over Wesley's black t-shirt and green jacket as they moved upward, War expected to see that hatred in Wesley's eyes. He anticipated the attitude of hatred, the expression of it, but when their eyes met, War was stunned.

Wesley's face was even, stoic. His brows were resting above his hazel eyes. His lips, full and attractive, were merely closed.

"Hey," War replied gently.

Wesley sat down next to War.

War, with his knees together and his chin lowered again, looked over to the man from the corner of his eye.

Wesley's legs, donned in jeans very similar to those of War, were spaced apart, much like Torrence's always were, and there was a natural authority to the shape of his body, the lines of his shoulders, the curvature of his biceps.

Everything about this human was larger than the same parts of War. Everything moved more fluidly. Everything was instinct. He understood how to sit without considering all the minuscule movements the action required, he did not have to make his muscles stretch or tell his bones to bend. He simply thought of sitting and it happened. What control over the machine of human form. What comfort. War envied it.

He looked down to his hands, unfurled his fingers. He let his palms slip away from his knees and attempted, very shyly, to part his legs. He looked over to Wesley, who was watching him very intently, and quickly closed his knees again and placed his palms back on them.

"What are you doing?"

"Admiring the way you sit." Slight crease to his brow as he stared at Wesley and tried to mimic the squareness of his shoulders.

"No," Wesley said patiently, a slight smile loosening his stoic features and illustrating now their immense beauty. "I mean, what are you doing out here?"

War's eyes moved up to Wesley's now, that same concentration still in his features. "I'm banished."

"Yeah, thanks." Wesley shook his head slightly. His tone light, almost humorous, then he cleared it from his throat. "What are you doing, considering your banishment, out here on the steps?"

"Thinking."

Wesley's brows raised, his head rearing back slightly. "About…?"

"The nature of existence."

"Oh, well, if that's all." Wesley grinned when War looked over to him. "Come on," he said, slapping War on the shoulder.

"Come on?"

"Yeah, let's go." Wesley started down the stairs.

"Go? Where?"

"We got a job to do." He turned to look back to War.

Behind him, the shadows of corpses danced from treetops down to their demise.

The image of this man, beautiful in shape and skin, the impermanent house of a brightly shining, though very tarnished, good soul, standing beneath a darkened sky, which only illuminated by fire or storm instead of sun, as spirits died repeatedly around him—it was very wrong. War felt a churning in his stomach, and he committed it as a line upon a mental note he'd been keeping, a note split in two sides: Human and Angel.

"Job?"

"Mission. Is that better?"

"It's not about semantics," War said, though the thought came about to, perhaps, ask Wesley if he'd like to discuss language. He frowned. Shook his head at the idea. He knew better. This man was not a friend here. He was a rival both in spirit and in seduction—the good performing evil for War's adversary, and the man providing intimacy to War's beloved. No, he'd meant only that he needed clarification on this job, this mission. He hadn't meant to engage in friendly conversation with this man, and he certainly didn't mean to learn from him. An exhale deflated War's full chest. He looked back to Wesley. "What mission? What is your assignment?"

"Our assignment," Wesley corrected. "Same as it always is." He smiled. "Raise some Hell."

CHAPTER SEVEN

War found himself in the passenger's seat of a black SUV.

He wasn't sure going along had been the correct choice, but he hadn't had much choice at all. It was either go and attempt to prove some allegiance to Torrence, and perhaps do some good in the process, or remain upon the staircase outside Hell's door, doing nothing.

When he'd risen from the steps, War turned to face the doors, their large, stone lions with manes aflame. He reached for the lion upon the door, brushing his fingers across its nose and at the door knocker in its teeth. He looked up the length of the manor, of this little roofed area before the door, eyes gazing into the faces of disfigured angels and dying humans in the murals upon the ceiling. Then he lowered his head. Fingers brushed the lion once more, and fell away from it.

As he sat in this vehicle now, War considered where they might be headed, what he might witness. He didn't know how he could prevent the impending travesty while pleasing Torrence, he didn't even know if either thing were possible.

Wesley noticed his discomfort; saw the very human signs of unease. The tightening of his fists over his knees before he wiped his palms on his jeans.

"Hey," Wesley said, his voice low and gentle as his eyes moved up from War's hands to his face. His brows lifted, coming together in the center; his features coherent of curiosity and slight concern. "You okay?"

War looked over to him, shocked, it seemed, by the slow words. He exhaled, trying to smile slightly, but unable to fully give way to the expression of any humor or joy. "I've..." He looked out of the window, then his head fell. "I've never been inside a vehicle with such awareness."

"What?"

"My first time in a vehicle, I had just manifested. I wasn't fully awake to the world. Now I am. It is a marvel. Human creativity and ingenuity, it's very similar to the creative force of God. You, with your freedom of choice and your exertion of your will, can dream, and from a dream you can create reality." He looked out the window again, this time just as brief as the first. "I just wish there were a better reality to view from the window of this marvel. That's all."

"That's all?" Wesley chuckled, looking out of the windshield again. There were parts of the world untouched by devils, yes, and parts of the country, too, but everywhere near Hell succumbed to its very presence. Ever-burning buildings, which would catch fire in the gusts of heated winds. Cars that had veered off the road during rapture crushed into trees and store fronts, all missing tires or windshield wipers, entire doors, radios that couldn't work outside the Sun States. Decaying bodies and fresh ones alike laid in the streets, run over by wheels of fleeing cars and pursuing trucks, left to rot and become part of the rubble. Modern roadkill. As he considered it, Wesley pushed his breath from his lips for audible flare. "That's kind of a lot, man."

War nodded, smiling sadly as he looked out of the windshield now.

Wesley's eyes glanced to that wondrous and wandering gaze;

contemplating the world as it had been before the broken skies, its order, its law, its safety. He imagined the angelic being next to him would've liked that—the completeness of it all, the man-made marvels intact, the systems still functioning.

Some were not entirely destroyed, he supposed. The road was still paved. Yellow lines cut through its center to separate Wesley's side from any passing car's side. So many rules unconsciously followed. So very human, he supposed, to simply follow, to be ruled. Even in the end of days, he used his turn signal.

He wished suddenly that he could take War to a movie theatre and see his reaction to film, but awareness of this thought made him wince. His lips pursed, curling in the discomfort of it all, of being so near to his replacement, of being so near to liking him.

"What a mess," Wesley said aloud, scolding himself and his unnerving almost-daydream, but War could only focus upon the mess outside the windows, not the one spattering Wesley's mind with a deluge of conflicting emotions.

"Yes," War said, agreeing as he stared out of the window. Such a distasteful view anywhere he looked—well, anywhere except to his left.

Looking over to Wesley, the angel attempted an unbiased evaluation of the man next to him. Admittedly, Wesley was exceptionally handsome. The skin which draped over wondrously-structured bone was naturally tanned and smooth. His lips seemed ever-pouting above his striking jawline. As noted previously, he possessed impressive muscle-tone and an ideal height. The frame of the body was as pristine as that of the face. The curvature of his arms, the bend at his elbow, the size of his forearm, all attractive in some way. Even the fingers seemed elegant, attached to hands too large to be delicate but too small to be brutish, always strumming at something as if a song were on eternal loop inside his mind and he must play the drums with his fingertips, or maybe it was nerves, for the skin around the nails was torn and bloodied.

Yes, War understood Wesley's appeals—the physical ones as well as the spiritual ones—but he had to wonder why Wesley gave them both away to Torrence so eagerly, so willingly.

War wanted Torrence, too, but not as the antichrist, as the human woman he once knew. Oh, to have a human life with her. To share a detachment from divinity with her; for him to fall to humanity, for her to rise again to it, each forfeiting eternity to share fifty short years together. It was the fantasy of all fantasies, for it not only satisfied his own ungodly desires, but also saved the world from hers. This was his ultimate goal—saving the world, its inhabitants, not only the ones made in God's image, those favorites of His, which War found somewhat barbaric, but all its creatures. If he had to fall from glory to do so, well, he had to repent, had to be redeemed.

But what had Wesley imagined from all this? What had he to gain in it?

As War absorbed the qualities of Wesley, this good soul secluded, as War himself had been, inside the darkness of Torrence's twisted heart, he paid better attention now to positioning of these body parts, the ease of their placements and of their motions, the wrist of his left arm resting on the steering wheel, his right hand settled upon the gear stick.

War did not know the words for these parts, much less their function, but he picked up tiny clues from Wesley, whose mind became conscious of his position and of the various parts when he realized where and at what War was looking.

Looking down to Wesley's hand as it tightened over the gear stick, War's brows knotted. "Gear…"

"Gears. Different gears mean different speeds. You shift into the different gears with the stick here." He tapped the gear stick then, with his opposite hand, he tapped the steering wheel. "Steering wheel is just for direction." He yanked the wheel to the left, jerking the car playfully.

War's hands gripped onto the edge of his seat and onto the handle of the door. When Wesley chuckled, he looked over to him.

"Sorry," Wesley said, his face full of joy and in that expression absolutely beautiful. "Just messing with you."

A small smile came to War's lips then. He looked down to his white knuckles, the cushion upon which he sat, and slowly released his grip on the seat. His hand moved about the leather, fingertips tracing the lines of its stitching until they came to a small hunk of what seemed to be plastic. Curiously he looked to it, let his fingers roam across its surface and push at a little button that gave way at his slightest touch. "Oh," he said.

"Oh, yeah." Wesley looked to War's hand. "Get your seat-belt." He nodded toward the door, and War's eyes followed this direction.

"Oh, this?" He reached up to the polyester chord and felt about it, too.

"Yeah, pull that around you and click it into this." Wesley watched War hesitantly pull at the chord. "Use the little clicker thing," Wesley said. "Here." He reached an arm across War, his eyes flashing back to the road only briefly as he took the latch plate into his hand. "Like this." When he pulled the latch plate toward him, the strap came too, crossing over War's body. The angel tensed for a moment, feeling somewhat bound by this strap, then came the sound of the plate clicking into the buckle. "Now you won't die if we wreck." His brow creased. "Can you die?"

"I don't know," he said, pulling at the strap and unclicking the buckle. He jumped slightly when the polyester shot back into its retractor, then he performed the act as he'd watched Wesley perform it—pulling at the latch plate, strapping the polyester across his chest, and securing it into the buckle.

Wesley found himself laughing again. His face and voice articulate of as much patience as humor. "Come on. You're this big cosmic being, an angel, and you're telling me you don't know what a seat-belt is? How to work one?"

"We see things in Heaven, but not with eyes," War said, his hands running along the strap across his chest, his waist. "We perceive things, but not with skin, not with touch."

"Must be confusing," Wesley said, and when War looked up to him curiously, he added, "being here, I mean."

War's features loosened. He nodded as he looked back down to the seat-belt. "Yes."

As they neared their destination, the calm night skies seemed to burst open around them. Smoky, sheer streaks broke through the darkness of eternal night, as if stroked faintly upon a canvas.

War supposed that's all the sky was once—a canvas, a screen, a ceiling—a solid space which separated the realms of the purely divine from that of the flesh-bound spirit. Now it was broken. Shards of atmosphere rained down upon the plane. Holes torn within its expansive blanket revealed glimpses of Heaven to those trapped on earth—those good who remained for battle but eventually would enter the ethereal and those wicked who never see it any nearer than this.

Though it remained dark, still so unlike it had been in the times before the rituals, it was somewhat calm. Less volatile.

Without accompanying thunder, even the lightning, which pulsated through the blackened sky in slow, jagged shocks of violet, seemed eerily serene, for it illuminated the road and surrounding buildings sporadically without the adornment of ground-shaking sound.

War looked over to Wesley, his features bright and visible in the glow of raging fires and bursting flame, occasionally painted violet in the hues of the storm when the lightning broke through the skies in greater beams.

"What's happening?"

"The apocalypse. You know the stories better than I do, I'm

sure." He exhaled when he looked over to the angel, saw his body leaning forward toward the glass windshield, toward the collapsing world on its opposite side. War's hands gripped onto the polyester around his body. His features were troubled, pained, but loose. "Tornadoes, floods, hurricanes," Wesley said. "Usually when they hit cities in the Sun States, hell breaks loose on its own. Looting, violence, it all starts. We go in and we recruit. We offer salvation from it. If Torrence comes, it's easy for them to believe she's the Second Coming. If she doesn't, we bring a Nephilim or two."

From behind the vehicle on each side came two SUVs just like it. They sped passed Wesley and War, both honking their horns. A man hung out of the passenger's side window on their left and waved, threw up his hands in the display of horns, his tongue hanging from his open mouth, and then, while laughing, offered only his middle fingers.

"Jason," Wesley said, smiling and shaking his head. "The guys will go out and instigate where shit's already tense. Then I come in and convert."

"Amongst the chaos, he is calm and attractive," War said.

Wesley looked over to him, but War's eyes were fixated on the destruction around him. Tremors visibly ran down his spine. His palms against the door, fingers against the window, War's entire body seemed drawn to the displays of destruction beyond.

He never considered himself calm, not since meeting Torrence, but he couldn't deny his longing for some end to all of this. In honesty, he was tired. Always driving, always recruiting, always plotting and studying, then killing, hurting, fighting.

Oh, and the cries of the angels in his skull on top of it all. When Torrence did not have some mission, like this one with War, for him, the angels would not let him sleep. They sang their sorrows through the night, purposefully, Wesley thought, in all those sleepless hours when he'd curl into a ball on his side and try to block out the sounds by wrapping around his head his pillow.

Oh, well, he thought as he parked his SUV in the middle of a street, looking ahead to the other two vehicles. He wanted Torrence, and even if he didn't, it was better in this day and age to be on her side.

He exhaled loudly, his elbow resting upon the door very briefly while he wiped his hand across his brow, cheek, mouth. Tired eyes blinked excessively. When he pushed the dreadful thoughts aside and reminded himself of his task and of the tasks of his brothers, he shifted his expression with purpose, donning again the stoic confidence of Right Hand Man as he opened the door. "Let's go," he said.

Nodding, watching the way the man moved as he stepped out of the vehicle, War opened his door. Attempting to exit the vehicle, he was struck unexpectedly by the locking seat-belt. In knocking the breath from human-like lungs, it jolted him into awareness where he'd been previously trapped inside a paralyzed state of awe and upset.

Buildings had collapsed. Piles of rubble were aflame. Houses and apartments, riddled with broken windows, their doors blowing freely in the windstorms, clanging against broken frames, had been abandoned.

Exiting the vehicle seemed to awaken him to the sounds of the chaos, as if this previous state paired with the borders of the vehicle had isolated him from the full experience of it. He entered the destruction now. He melted into it—a small body amongst bloodied forms and fresh corpses.

In a suction-like wave, the silence seemed to roll by him. All at once came screaming, gusting wind, car alarms, small explosions, the breaking of the glass bottles which had contained their flammable contents.

Fights had broken out in the streets, only one of which featured one of Torrence's boys. The others were composed of various individuals, all of whom were cloaked physically in both the darkness of the night and the scuffling of their bodies, but their souls were so bright to War here.

Pulsating, the energies emitted from the tussling bodies in time with their accelerated heart rates, expanding out from their physical forms as luminous outlines before the next pump of a heart recalls them back into it.

Some of these energies appeared rather blue, though it was hard to tell exact shades for all the violet bursts of lightning, and others seemed outright red, but so were the glowing yellows and oranges of the great flames all around them. War stared at these people, eyes narrowing in on each of them, trying to decipher what energy matched which body.

Someone screamed behind the brawl. Three people pursued two more through the streets, one knocking into War as she ran by and disappeared between buildings.

War lifted his hand to his shoulder, closed his eyes, tried absorbing some of the energy she'd left there, if any.

His brows creased. The touch was so minute it left only trace energies, energies that passed through her clothing and were absorbed by the knitting of his shirt before he could grab it. Still, he closed his palm around his shoulder, focusing on withdrawing the energies, perhaps, from the fabric and into his palm.

His grip grew fiercer, stronger, desperate. From behind the lids of his eyes, he could perceive the light which emitted from his palm when he attempted to use his angelic abilities, the same light that had burned holes into his cheeks and across his shoulders and his upper-back. His energy thrown out of his physical body—the make-up of the cosmos breaching the matter of the earthly plane, had always been too pure for the sensitive flesh. Still, he had to try to pull something from the passing woman, even if it meant melting off a hand-shaped hunk of his own skin.

He trembled, his fingers pressing painfully into his shoulder. Sweat formed across his forehead. A pain came into his skull.

He felt small sparks—two, maybe three. Faintly blue, yes. Another orange. Oh, but all souls have good within them, bad as well. Which had she been mostly? What was she doing here in this open-skied world? Had she even known prior to this night that the sky was no longer a solid boundary between this world and the next?

He opened his eyes. Released the grip on his shoulder. Felt the human body react to the points where his fingers had been. Oh, if he had blood they would've formed bruises. He looked down to his shoulder quickly, seeing glimpses of his flesh through the clawed fabric of his shirt. It seemed, at least for now, he did not have blood within him. Instead, from within his t-shirt glowed in five small, almost-circular spots his angelic spirit.

A sigh of relief, then his focus went back to the world. His eyes readjusted to the city before him, to the fighting men, their energies. Slowly he moved toward them. Glass broke somewhere to his right. More screaming on his left. It echoed from the alleyway ahead.

War stepped sideways, moving around the fight, allowing his hand to brush over one man then a second. Blue. So very blue. As he continued his steady pace toward the alley, the mass of men shifted. His hand touched a third, who turned toward him quickly and shoved his hand away.

"What the fuck?"

"Sorry," War said, his head still down.

A groan came from the man, who seemed in War's peripheral vision to topple, replaced then by another man who flew atop him and pummeled him. Red. That one had been red. War's fingers merely brushed over this one's shoulder. Also very red.

His brows furrowed as he moved beyond the fight, careful not to look back at it, not to see the turmoil, the struggle, the pain. He had witnessed enough of violence in Hell, though it seemed worse when people enacted it upon themselves. At least in Hell War could determine very clearly who was good and who was not. Here, with so many shades of experience, it was difficult to tell.

"What's he doing?" someone said behind him, but it was distorted, faded from his direct focus.

His intention was on the alleyway, on the woman who brushed against him as she ran with a man away from three other people.

He heard footsteps behind him. Shoes sliding across the pavement as the voices of people raged inside the rolling echoes of burning buildings and   the bursts of exploding cars.

When he turned left toward the alley, he saw a shoe on the ground, navy and on its side. It gave him pause, but he continued. Stepping into the alley way now, he saw the shoe's mate—clinging to the woman's foot.

War's emotions passed through his parting lips in a faint breath, above which the following footsteps sounded still, until they stopped behind him.

"What's he doing?" came a whispered voice, different from the first.

"What are you doing?" A third voice.

War didn't look back at them. Couldn't. This woman, lying in the road as her attackers continued down the alley, chasing the man with whom she'd been running, was almost unconscious. The glow around her was dimming. Small were the pulses of blue around her. The energy, so very close to her body, expanded outward with the beating of her heart but barely.

Her languid eyes floated upward to his. When they connected, they widened. It took much of her energy, for her spirit was already slipping away from her body, snapping the two separate entities together briefly and creating a larger pulse in the blue around her.

"Fear not, child," War said, bending down over the woman, careful not to kneel in the spilled blood still pooling about her back and her waist. He took her hand into his hands, gazed into her eyes.

"You…" she whispered, interrupted by a cough.

"No," he said, bringing a hand to her temple. "It's time to rest." A glow came from his fingertips, illuminating her face as the twists of pain slipped away from it.

"You are so bright," she said finally.

"Yes," he said. "Forgive me." Tears swelled within his eyes, but did not fall from them. "I fear this is all my fault."

"Forgive me," she said, "for what parts of it are mine."

"None of this is anyone's sin but my own." He brushed his hand down her face, her neck, placed it finally over her dully-beating heart. "You are absolved of yours. Your energy is virtuous. Heaven will welcome you. I'm sure of it."

A strained smile came to her lips, then from them came her final breath.

The firing of a gun rang out somewhere in the dying city. Then a similar sound—that of a gun, but not the same type of gun.

"Felt weird when he touched me," one of the voices said.

Footsteps again. Car alarms. Screaming.

War brought the woman's hands to her waist and placed them gently over her stomach. He closed her eyes. Shifting in his kneeling position, he posed her splayed legs so they were straight and together, then he made for her missing shoe.

"Hey," the first voice said hesitantly.

War blinked up to this man, one of the blues, very briefly—time to recognize only golden hair and a trim, tall frame—as he moved by him to take the shoe into his hands.

"Hey, who are you?" The man turned when War did, watching him as he bent back down over the woman's feet.

"I wish I knew," War said, replacing the lost shoe.

"What are you doing?"

War exhaled a pained laugh. "I wish I knew."

"What's with your hand? Your shoulder? Your face, That light? Did you do that to me when you touched me? I felt something. I don't know what—."

"You have a good soul," War said, rising from the body. He turned to the man, his eyes drinking in the features now then he glanced to each man on either side of this one. "So does he." War nodded to the man's right.

The man looked over that shoulder, then he looked over the other. "Not him?"

"I can't tell. I didn't touch him. My energy…It's depleting."

"What, like you need sleep?" The man exhaled dramatically, his hand running through his hair. "Look around. I don't think that's happening any time soon. Not here anyway."

"What happened here?"

"Earthquake, then rain that almost flooded the place. Everyone went crazy after that. Bad people came out of the woodworks. Good ones tried to fight them. It's been a wreck for days. New people keep rolling in, thinking they can take everything from the newly-destroyed, the weak. People keep coming talking about the apocalypse, calling us spoiled. They call us Sun Staters, then laugh and say we'll never see the sun again. I thought they were insane, but, uh…" He looked up into the sky, his face raising toward its expanse. Only his eyes came back down to War. "I haven't seen it since."

Another gunshot rang out, nearer to the alley than any have been. War flinched, as did the man and the one at his left. The one on his right spun in place, then he toppled.

"Mark!" the man cried, running toward his friend. He withdrew from the back of his jeans his own gun, raised it, and fired without extreme focus or intended target.

People screamed, gasped for air, wailed. The flames roared and snapped. Glass busted.

War bent down with Mark, placing his hand on the other's shoulder as he knelt.

"Wait," Mark said, "Ryan, don't—don't tell him—."

"I won't," this man, now identified as Ryan, said. His lips rolled into his mouth, brow furrowing intently as tears filled his eyes. He jammed the gun back into his jeans, hissing as the heated barrel grazed his skin.

War sat in a brief awe at this—the very human experience. Emotional injury to human beings seemed always more intense than its physical counterpart. It filled him with hope, a flicker of joy inside so much despair, that the spirit, even when trapped inside tender, sensitive flesh, still reigned.

He looked down to Mark now, running his fingers and their luminescence over his chest. "Rest, child. Your suffering ends here. Your soul is good. I have no doubts that Heaven awaits you."

Mark reached a trembling hand to War, gripping into his wrist. "Is that…Are you—?"

"Yes," War said. "Or at least I was."

Mark's eyes became glassy, then they flashed back to Ryan. "I…I'm sorry…"

"I know," Ryan said. "Me, too."

When Mark died, War closed his eyes as he had done with the woman's, but he let Ryan position him. As Ryan did this, War stood. His shirt shifted as he did so, revealing to Ryan's staring eyes the brand-like scar upon the angel's human-esque flesh. His brows creased at this symbol, but he watched War in silence, in curiosity.

War moved into the street and found a crumpled body, one struck by Ryan's discharging. Light came from his hand and over this woman, too.

Across the way from War, Jason had beaten a man to death. As he stood, he looked to his left and saw the angel.

"Hey, Wes!" he shouted. "What's he doing?"

Wesley, standing stoically in the middle of the street between the SUVs, monitoring, awaiting new recruits, looked to Jason. Jason nodded toward War, and Wesley's focus moved intently for the little angel.

He nodded back to Jason, signaling to his brother to go back to his work. He watched as War moved from body to body, some dead, some dying. His face seemed genuinely pained by the humans at his feet, only relaxing somewhat when the essence of his own spirit washed away their pain.

Unconsciously, Wesley stepped nearer to War. He turned his ear toward him, listening—what was he saying?—until he came close enough to hear War's voice as he issued, it seemed, some sort of final rites.

"Rest, child," War said. He bowed his head for a moment, then he rose.

"Hey," Wesley said from behind him.

War's chin lifted. The tears in his eyes remained, even inside his stern expression. "You can tell Torrence," he said, bringing his hands together before him.

"Yeah," Wesley said. He turned, looking about the chaos, whistled loudly.

Freddy, nearest to his position, called out. "Wes?"

"Yeah," he yelled out toward the direction of the voice, "Fred?"

"Here!"

"Hey," Wesley called when he saw him. "I'm taking the angel on a little field trip."

"Tor's angel?" Freddy asked. "She gonna be okay with that?"

"Well…" Wesley's head tilted, his brows raised. He opened his mouth, but the sentence wouldn't form. He wasn't sure he knew exactly where it'd end, but he didn't think Torrence would mind. After all, she'd instructed Wesley to gauge War's commitment, hadn't she? But should he say that to the others? He looked over to War. He certainly couldn't say it in front of him. But how else to get away with the angel now that the potential of Torrence's displeasure at such a thing had arisen. "Well, I just…I think—."

"He's out here using his magic on souls," Jason interrupted, coming behind Freddy and placing a hand on his shoulder. "I don't think she sent him for that."

Wesley's lips closed. He nodded.

"Don't rough him up too badly." Jason sneered. "Boss probably doesn't want damaged goods, huh?" He patted Freddy's shoulder a few times, then hollered loudly. A war cry, it seemed, for after it left his lips, he ran down the street and into another alleyway.

Wesley and Freddy shared a long look, then both men nodded. Freddy went back to his task—loading the final ingredient into his Molotov cocktail before igniting it and tossing it into a crowd.

"Come on," Wesley said, turning from War and starting his walk toward the SUV.

War turned as well and started to follow.

"Hey, wait!" Ryan's still-shaken voice called from the alley. He held Mark's body, refusing to leave it to the chaos. "Wait, you're going with him? He's leading these assholes who are killing us! They're all following the guys he brought here! Wait!"

War looked over his shoulder to Ryan, issuing from his mind, not his lips, a comforting word. Some numbers.

Ryan's brows creased. He brought a hand to his forehead. "What?" The word was exhaled more than it was spoken. He looked up to War, who nodded gently to him.

He nodded back. He understood.

CHAPTER EIGHT

War opened the door of the SUV. He paused when he looked to Wesley, sitting stoically in the driver's seat, his elbow on the door handle, fingers against his temple.

Wesley didn't look over to War. Didn't move at all, really, save for the expansion of his chest as he inhaled deeply the destruction fluttering into the car through War's open door.

War looked back to the burning city, the bodies in the street. Cries in the distance fluttering into his ears only when gusts of wind allowed him to hear anything but the violent breeze. Ash fell around him; it was taken by the wind, pushed around and circulated, seeping into the air of the city in all places, which made it difficult to breathe. The air was thick with it now and full of stench.

The city, like all cities, had been a marvel of humanity, of their creativity, ingenuity, construction, engineering. It displayed their ability to plan, to structure. It was self-civilization. No god created their barter system. No alien crafted their skyscrapers. The traffic lights did not create a barrier from atop their poles, no; human beings and their brains understood which colors signified a stop and which did not, and though they were able to drive without honoring these devices, the symbolism and its knowledge combined within human awareness allowed an exchange of passage, a safe one.

Now it was all rubble.

"Surely," War said as he lowered his head, "this isn't what Torrence wants."

Wesley leaned his head back, looking over to War from the corner of his eye. "Of course it is."

"What is there to rule, then?"

"The spirit," Wesley said.

War's eyes shot up to him, his face was open, vulnerable, and understanding. A sad smile thinned his lips, and he lowered his head, nodding. "Right." He looked up to Wesley, and got into the SUV.

"She wants them to have nothing to fight for," Wesley added. "Wouldn't her offering, regardless of what it was, look better than this to anyone who survived it?"

Again War nodded. He watched Wesley intently. Watched the way he lifted his hand, how only the finger he used to press the ignition button by the wheel extended from his hand, how it curled with the others when his hand moved for the wheel now. And this button, one small object, the vital, starting piece of this great mechanism. Was this like the mind? The spirit? What, if not his soul, commanded Wesley's fingers, his hand, as he shifted this gear stick? As he drove?

War wanted desperately to touch Wesley. Wanted to feel the essence of his spirit, which seemed so good even when it ruled over such madness.

Usually War could perceive the emotions of the good-souled, but it was different here. He wasn't sure if it was the general state of the parting skies, the storms, the darkening of this Sun State interrupting his abilities, or if it was the darkening of this specific soul, which by nature cut him off from reading it so well.

He didn't think it was humanization of his own essence, for

he was able to still push away pain from the dying and perceive their energies when they exerted effort or felt something intensely.

He only hoped that Wesley, like the good spirits he sensed in the city behind them, had not been permanently altered by all that had come to pass.

War swallowed. His nerves made the typically-unnoticed action seem loud and overdone. He glanced over to Wesley conspicuously, taking his lower lip into his teeth. Slowly his left leg shifted, his hesitant mind only halfway commanding it to separate from his right one. He exhaled, lifting his hand now, placing his elbow on the handle of the door, its arm rest. He wondered if he looked as human in this mimicked position as Wesley looked when he sat so naturally in it. He stole another look at Wesley, who shook his head and exhaled audibly through his nostrils.

"Okay," Wesley said, looking over to him. "I give up. What are you doing?"

"You ask me that when it's obvious," War said, readjusting his legs more overtly now. He looked over to Wesley's and back at his own. Yes, they were spaced apart more humanly now, but it did not feel as comfortable as it had looked. He inhaled deeply, held it for a few fleeting seconds, then released the air. His legs came back together. Muttering, he looked up to Wesley, this supposedly-good soul who seemed as his captor now. "You never ask me when it's not."

"All right," Wesley said, cheery and conceding. "What were you doing with the people in the streets back there?"

"Taking away their pain. You knew that, too, or else we wouldn't be going on this field trip of yours."

"Which leads me to the real question." He looked to War and waited for the angel's eyes to meet his own. They were iridescent and gleaming. Otherworldly, yes, just as Torrence's were, but not frightening. Their immense power only radiated comfort, ease, care. "Why'd you come with me so easily?"

"You're in charge, aren't you? When Torrence isn't around. Or her Awakener."

"Yeah." He tilted his head away from War. The Awakener. Conrad. And War, too. Sure, Wesley was in charge. He was the favorite. But only so long as other favorites weren't around. He supposed being the least favorite of the favorites was better than not being a favorite at all. He grimaced. His head hurt suddenly. "That, uh…" He swallowed his emotions. "That doesn't answer the question, though."

War was silent. He looked out the window, seeing less and less bodies on the streets, watching burned buildings become intact ones. Spaced further apart, the homes became more and more sporadic, then such structures vanished into nothingness.

The trunks of trees, dying without sunlight, broke the bleakness of the darkened sky and decaying world. Though they were not lush or lively, they were, in fact, alive. Surviving. Just as the humans were.

War lowered his head, an act so often performed by angels in reverence now seemed the only effort he had to conceal himself from the distressing world around him. He couldn't look at it, couldn't participate in it, but he also couldn't stop it. Not yet, anyway. Depending on Wesley—whether his silence was the solemnity or the executioner or the sorrow of the saint—he might have a chance sooner than expected. But soon did not make the present feel any better.

"Sorry," Wesley said, his voice gravelly and uncertain. He cleared his throat. His posture, which had lost briefly its strength, realigned to find it once again. "Sorry there's not a better view out there."

"It's not your fault," he said, looking tentatively up to Wesley. "Is it?"

"Some of it, yeah." His lips pouted in his acceptance of this. "Probably all of it if you think about what other people did that I didn't even try to stop."

"People? Not everyone you socialize with is a person."

"Yeah, like you."

"This is socializing? I thought I was facing punishment."

"You're facing a lot right now," he said as the car came to a stop. Wesley's hand moved the gear stick, then his fingers turned off the engine. "No harm in taking a break from it." He opened the door and exited. Mischief graced his plump lips as he looked back into the vehicle at War. "Is there?"

The door closed. Wesley moved around the SUV and began to walk down a muddy path. Too slim was the trail for the vehicle to pass through, War could tell as he watched the man through the windshield. Wesley turned back toward the car, lifting his palms up as he took a few steps backward.

War took the handle into his grip, contemplating this choice briefly. What else was there to do but follow? What worse could be seen than the cruelty of this world, and what worse could be experienced than the punishments of Heaven? He opened the door.

When he closed it, he did so gently, even pressing his palm against the seam of metal when it sealed. Stepping back as he stared to the vehicle, War put his hands into the pockets of his jeans. The human creation, yes. Then he looked up from the vehicle at the trees across the road from it, at the trees behind him. Dead, yes. The natural creation destroyed by lack of sun and the over-saturation of unending storms.

He looked into the sky. Dark, yes, but not blackened, not deeply purple or red. No lightning broke through the blanket of color. Why, it almost appeared as it had in the paintings hung in museums of those times before the slightest tear had torn in it; the times before angels could slip through its atmosphere and visit the earthly plane.

"Don't take too much time eyeing all the half-dead shit," Wesley called.

His voice broke War out of his gazing, out of the thoughts

impending, the tragedy of War's own superficiality—the inability to stop the soul who started this—and here he was now facing some sort of task at the hands of that soul's most trusted human.

He looked down to his feet as he walked the path, careful not to step on any insects that may scurry through the mud there. How amazing, he thought, smiling, That insects still exist here.

His eyes moved up the path before him now. He noticed small specs of green within the mud. Pieces of grass, perhaps. A slight crease of his brow came when he saw it, for all was so dead here, but as he walked the speckled green remained. A leaf blew across the path. A leaf.

He lifted his head. Looked to Wesley, who stood at the end of the trail. His hand rested upon a tree trunk, and from it stemmed large branches, branches that had more leaves. Most were dying, falling away. Some were orange and yellow, but some were green.

A quick, short breath left his lips. His eyes blinked rapidly as he looked to the leaves, the green ones in particular. Still, he moved toward Wesley, toward whatever laid ahead of them at the end of this small trail, for all he could see beyond it were the trunks of fallen trees.

"Come on," Wesley said, grabbing War's shoulder. "Almost there."

War watched him duck under the trunks, bending his knees to follow, but when he did he was struck by the sight of the ground—green. More than just speckles and the occasional leaf.

He moved beneath the trunks, keeping his head down, his eyes staring at the increasing number of tiny blades of grass, tiny blades that seemed to grow taller and taller as he ventured further from the world beyond the fallen trunks. Taller and more visible. Brighter, it seemed. It was confusing but in some exciting way, regardless of what Wesley kept on the other side of this strange little bridge of fallen trees.

Finally, he reached the end of it. The grass at his feet, the mud, it was all so visible now. His brows furrowed as he moved out from beneath the trunks. Was there light here?

Then he stood. Indeed, there was light. Only a bit shining into the trees. It seemed to pour in from behind them, obstructed only by their leaves. Their leaves.

A chuckle somewhere to his left.

He looked up to Wesley now—Wesley, who stood amongst trees.

"Almost there," he said again.

War looked down to his feet. Instead of a few blades of grass here and there within the muddy path, there were patches of grass all around him.

A rather open space here surrounded by trees—trees that perhaps had seen brighter days, yes, but were still living and lush. It was lovely. A perfect space for prayer or for meditation. Oh, how War wanted to sit, even in the mud, so he could be amongst the grass. But there were pebbles here. Stones. Small pieces of gravel, perhaps.

"Another small path," Wesley said. When War looked up to him, he raised his hands playfully. "Super small. Promise."

War nodded, looked down at the gravel, which had been overtaken by nature, and followed Wesley.

When they stopped, Wesley raised his chin. The sun felt good on his face, but he wondered how it felt to an angel. He looked over to War, who had stopped when he had, but was distracted by the gravel at his feet and the grass growing within it.

The sound pulled War from his focus, and when he moved to look up to Wesley, he was caught off-guard by the sight before him.

"Wow," War whispered, an astonishment in his eyes as they drank in the sight before him. His pupils shrank as the light of the sun, still shining and glorious in the blue, unbroken sky, reflected the image of a green, lush field from the reality of the world into his mind's awareness. "It's beautiful." His voice was low and shaken. The small sentence left his lips in punctuated delicacy; his throat, in the constriction of emotion, unable to float the words smoothly into the air.

Wesley's hand fell to the angel's shoulder, causing the human form to jump slightly. "Yeah, beautiful," he agreed. "This is the earth of your Father's book, huh? The one you probably had in your mind when you came here."

"Yes," War said. The word was simple, quick, easy, low. He looked over to Wesley; his eyes scanning the man's face as he stared into the untouched-by-Torrence field.

Under the pressure of this angelic gaze, Wesley looked over to War. He smiled, something genuine and warm. Something each being here in this open space of clean air and bright skies had always wanted, but never seemed able to obtain.

"Well, go on," Wesley said, chuckling as he nodded to the field. "Go touch the grass or something."

War laughed; the simplicity in Wesley, in his words, was refreshing and welcome. He'd grown, over the past few years on earth, to despise poetics and overdone speeches. All beauty in linguistics lost to him. Too many rules. Too many Holy Words. Too many cruelties masked as mercy, and too much pain twisted into poetry.

Everything beautiful and deep and elegant in some human, relatable way was tainted by the very essence of it; the fact of the matter was that here on earth everything powerful comes from pain. What writer had experienced sincerity without observing within its facade the undeniable turmoil which fuels it? What musician had heard an elegant tune without his fingers bleeding to record it? And what painter had seen beauty and been able to keep it?

Isn't this why humans created what they did? Didn't they long to hold forever a single moment of happiness? Of comfort? Wasn't a novel a time capsule of emotion? Wasn't a song an eternal love letter? Was a painting anything more than the artist's desire to capture forever and contain its subject?

Lyricism, so often disregarded by humans as common and ever-present, had grown into something worse for War. It was Biblical and it was the Law of God and it was the commands of Torrence. It was human pain or pain inflicted upon humans by the only spark of divinity they will ever know—their minds.

Oh, what a dreaded feeling this consciousness had become.

War stepped slowly down the gravel road, observing in detail the grass growing over what had once been the trails made by tires. Long out of use, grass had begun to spread through the gravel, cascading around the small rocks like an immovable stream; one that only glistened when the wind brushed through its blades and let them dance.

War looked to his feet as they walked slowly down the path. Up his legs, his eyes traveled. Then he lifted a hand slightly and looked down to it.

He felt the wind blow against his skin. Cool, refreshing, gentle. Touch. What a miracle. Consciousness had been a miracle, not a curse. Maybe it was both.

He remembered that first manifested night and how he marveled at everything to which he'd now grown so accustomed.

War never paused these days to appreciate his hands. He didn't stroll through empty streets at night, absorbing the stripes of white street-lights reflecting rainwater in the darkened streets. He didn't consider the various movements required to walk; the natural and instinctive meat-machine of God's most defined and glorious plan.

He'd lost sight. Lost his way. And when he begged Torrence to take him in, she rejected him. Set aside by God for some unknown task, perhaps one as ridiculous as redemption, and thrown away by the devil for no other reason than her boredom with him, and now he was bored. Bored of a body. Bored of a soul. Bored of this broken world and all the turmoil experienced within it. But then...

He turned, looked over his shoulder shyly.
Then there was Wesley.

CHAPTER NINE

War's brows furrowed above intent eyes. He looked to the ground, deep in his considerations, in the thoughts of Torrence, of her Hell, the new recruit brought back from the past, then he looked up to Wesley.

A nervous smile tugged at the man's plump lips, his eyes falling away from the intensity of War's gaze and the iridescent beauty of his eyes. "What?" Wesley asked shyly.

War stood in silence, awaiting Wesley's eyes. When they found him again, his face was calm in its confusion. "Why did you bring me here?"

"What?" He blinked away, shrugging a shoulder slightly. "It was——."

"It wasn't a mission. Or retribution." War looked around at the open field, its lush grass and full trees, its crystalline sky free of any clouds or smog, the sun shining freely from it. "Torrence wouldn't want us here. In the time of broken skies and rising dead, a meadow like this would be considered a wasteland." He looked back to Wesley now, brows still pulled slightly together. "Why did we come here?"

"I don't know, man," Wesley said, chuckling. His hand scrubbed at the back of his neck as he lowered his head. "I don't know. I just thought…you'd like it." He shrugged, eyeing the weapon strapped to his leg, the nail of his thumb picking at the dried blood upon its blade. "I thought, you know, all the death and decay and even the decadent parts of Hell just don't suit you."

From his lowered head, his eyes looked up to War, but only going as far as his t-shirt. He gestured with his free hand toward the angel with some erratic, noncommittal wave. "You and all your angel stuff. You know what I mean." His eyes fell again, brows knitting together tightly over them. His lips pursed. Inside his mind, he cursed at himself.

A soft sound came from War. More than an exhale, but not quite a laugh, Wesley could only imagine it was the sound of the angels' voices when they sang from the throats of whatever their true forms were. It was melodic and small; a strength inside it, even in its timid, gentle almost-sound.

"What?" Wesley asked him, finally finding his eyes.

"Nothing," War answered, smiling to him now.

"Dude, don't, like, purr at me, okay? I'm just trying to—I don't know—redeem myself, maybe. If…you think that's even possible."

War's head tilted slightly, a seriousness entering the serenity of his face. "You seek redemption?"

"No," Wesley said, turning away from him, shaking his head. "Look, I love Torrence, all right?"

"Of course."

"No, don't patronize me."

"I'm not."

"Just listen to me. I worship her. I'd do anything for her. I have done a lot for her—a lot that I…I don't want you thinking I'm switching teams here. If it's Heaven versus Hell, then I'm sticking with Hell because that's where my loyalties lie. But I'm not—I don't think I'd even be here if she hadn't—." He exhaled loudly. "I had this girlfriend, and she cheated on me, and I couldn't forgive her, and Torrence knew that. I don't know how she knew it. I don't know how she knew half the shit she knew before any of this apocalypse stuff was even a thing, but she knew it, and she knew how to make me feel like she'd be something no one else could be. It wasn't a manipulation like it seems because she really is everything she promised to be. I've never had to worry about anything since we got together. But if none of that had happened, I don't know where I'd be now. I doubt it'd be with her. On this side of things."

"Wesley, God knows what's in your—."

"Never mind." He scoffed. "I'm not here for the 'Jesus loves you' shit. I don't want you to think that I'm falling out of line here. I just wanted you to know that I understand you."

"You understand me?"

"Yeah. You're good. You're righteous. All that she isn't. But it doesn't change what she became to you. It doesn't change what she is to you, regardless of what she is to everyone else. I'm just saying I get that. It's the same for me."

"The same," War said. "Don't take this the wrong way but that doesn't bode well for me."

"Yeah, you don't want to be human. I get that, trust me."

"I sometimes wish I were."

"What? You can't be serious."

"It would just be simpler." He smiled sadly. This wasn't the entire truth of his desire for humanity, but it wasn't a lie." "That's all."

"Yeah." Wesley nodded. "I get that." He looked out into the field before him, up at the sun. "Although, being human isn't always simple."

"I don't imagine it's ever simple," War said. "Since I've manifested, I've experienced a flood of unknown experience and awareness. Consciousness so sharply defined there aren't words to describe it. Emotions. Hearing, seeing." His fingers brushed over the white petals of a small, wild flower. "Touching." He looked up to Wesley, his head tilting a bit as he stared at him intently and with great purpose, as if he were a student of art sitting before a wondrous painting—beautiful, yes; perfectly crafted, but containing behind its pristine aesthetic the answer to many questions. There was depth inside the shallow appeal. Secrets. "I only meant that being with Torrence—." His words were stopped by his own thoughts. He looked to Wesley. No, being human wouldn't have made the choice between good and evil easier. But the choice would've been a choice.

War opened his mouth to speak again, but the image of Wesley here in the sun became unbearable. He was gorgeous here, his handsome features so illuminated by the sun and, therefore, so perceivable; the clean air around him allowed full view of his energy, which was true to its hues, untarnished and unobstructed by the decay clinging to the atmosphere around him.

He didn't want to imagine this man in Hell. He hated knowing that was where he'd go, where he'd want to go. But what if he changed his mind?

"What?" Wesley asked.

"No," War said shyly, focusing again on the flower when his head fell against his rising shoulder. "Nothing. I just…suppose it isn't so easy to be with her, even for a human, is it?"

"Honestly?"

War nodded.

"Between us, right?"

"Of course."

A bitterness overtook his features. Lips trembling, he exhaled more than air. The weight of this worry, this secret, the fear of what admitting fear might bring had all but incapacitated him, especially during so much bloodshed, so much violence.

He thought he'd been doing it for Torrence, for love. He thought she'd rise to power—some Awakener, they'd thought in the early days, sure, but powerful regardless—and next to her, lying in bed with her, would be Wesley, her consort.

Now he seemed more a war hero, a militant of some sort,

taking his vicious warrior-troops into places the sun still shone and instructing them to destroy all that laid in its rays.

It had never been a job he'd wanted—in honesty, he'd never considered having a job back then. He certainly didn't think he'd have one now, yet somehow he'd accepted his position, and he performed its duties wholeheartedly and with exactitude. But only for his love of Torrence, he realized now. For anyone else, he would've refused whatever rank he'd been given. The only title that ever mattered to him was Precious One. And now he wasn't even that.

"No, it's not easy," Wesley finally said, leaning over his knees to rest his elbows upon them. He didn't look at the world or his position in it as his brothers did. He didn't love Torrence because of the power she'd given him or the place in the new world's hierarchy. He loved her because of who she was internally, not who she presented. He wanted human Torrence back. Wanted to hold her without fearing her. Wanted to make love to her without so much destruction around them. He couldn't admit this, though. It was the new blasphemy. To strip Torrence's power from her, the ultimate betrayal to all she'd ever stood for. Still, he wanted it. He felt so guilty for it.

Witnessing such struggle in Wesley, a solemnity came to War, his body exuding now the attitude of an angelic being more than that of a man. Even in his feigned humanity, the divine spirit conquered, eradicating any resemblance of awkwardness or uncertainty. All was fluid now, sparkling and pure and radiant, but very powerful, too. He knew this man needed authority, that he'd trust nothing so unsure as War during his own internal debates. The angel was required now, maybe that was true in general of the world, not just for Wesley in specific here.

"I'm sorry," War said.

"She wasn't always this way, you know? It was easy back then."

"I know." War looked over to Wesley. "I came here only

after the first tear came into the sky, but Torrence was certainly more of her old self then than her current one."

"Her old self? You knew what she was like?"

"I'm given glimpses. The man she brought home with you, there is a perceptible bond between them. It was energetic, spiritual. I could sense something…I wish I could see it all."

"I wish I could see it all, too," Wesley said. He looked over to War, concealing a bit of himself behind his risen shoulder. "I knew when she sent us home that night in your apartment, she wasn't going to kill you. I could just tell."

War's brows creased lightly. "And this upsets you?"

"Yeah." The word was fast but lowly-spoken. He shook his head slightly. "Not like you think." His jaw clenched, nostrils widened. A hissing intake of air lowered his head. "You were beautiful." He looked to the angel. "Isn't that what she told you?" His lips pursed bitterly.

War's eyes blinked away. A slight shrug accompanied his tilting head.

"I wondered how often she saw you. Kept waiting to see you at ritual or have her call some random break-and-enter to initiate you. I couldn't figure out why you never came with us."

"I was never invited."

"Would you have come if you had been, though?"

"No."

"Why's that? You were with Torrence, weren't you?"

War looked to the side, his hand brushing across the overgrown grass.

"Come on, man. I was honest with you. Level with me now."

"I was with her, yes." Suddenly a physical experience came into his chest. He imagined the sensation of a usually-beating heart as it stopped inside the chest of a living human, but he was not human. He hadn't been when he was with Torrence, in those months now that Wesley asked him to recall, but she had been.

Guilt-ridden from this dual betrayal—his disobedience to

God, who asked of His angels to remain pure of human vice, and his exploitation of Torrence's humanity when he'd known he was a divine being and did not reveal this fact to her—War shrunk away. His body became small, tightly closing into himself, but not escaping Wesley's view entirely. It didn't matter. It wasn't as if Wesley's view or lack thereof could lessen or alleviate any of his shame.

War could not escape himself or the thoughts which lingered in his mind long after he'd asked them to depart from his awareness. This, perhaps, was the cruelest aspect of being human—a person had never a second's peace away from his own mind.

"I could sense you," War said, finally glancing up to Wesley. His brow set the tone of his face, orchestrating his features into the visage of a graceful, but imploring, young man.

Oh, so young he seemed for his naivety, for his innocence, but inside him, just beneath the lovely, delicate flesh, cauterizing any matter which compounded into something human, was the rampant and ever-expanding cosmos of eternity.

Wesley could not drink War in enough. He sat patiently, observing every careful motion of this human impersonation, in awe of even the tiniest movement, the softest breath, the stillness of his simply doing nothing.

War tried to smile at the focus, but the silence between them had given him time to find his words, to think, however briefly, on how to deliver these stories, these messages so that they did not cause Wesley any further pain.

"When Torrence would come home, I could always tell when she'd been with you. I don't know if it was because of the intensity of your time spent together or if it was because your spirit is good, but the energy you pressed upon her, left like traces of blood or saliva, was perceptible where you'd touched her, where your fingers pressed into her skin, but, unlike bodily fluids, no length of shower or amount of soap could wash it away before she'd return to the bed with me."

Wesley's eyes moved between War's eyes, the glittering irises of inhuman colors almost lost to how sympathetically his brows curved over them. He huffed lowly, looking away from the angel. His voice only a whisper, though he'd tried to speak properly. "The bed?"

"Yes." War watched the confirmation seep into Wesley's consciousness. Watched him accept it. He could tell by the way the man's lips curled when it sunk in. "We did not share the same relationship you did."

"Did she want to, though?"

When War said nothing, Wesley looked over to him. A sharp motion fueled by his need to know, but his features full of the recognizable prayer of a pained human asking the divine, 'Please no'.

It struck War. He recoiled slightly, feeling the sense of his own tears forming at the sight of these ones.

"Come on," Wesley said. "Did she want to?"

War bent his head. He could not look at Wesley and say it. "Yes."

Wesley nodded, his curling lips donning the indignant smile of his raging emotions. "Of course," he said lowly. "Yeah, of course."

"I'm sorry," War said.

"Doesn't matter."

"It does. Your feelings—."

"Why did you say no?"

"What?"

"Why not do it? Why be with her and not do it? Why do what you're doing now?"

"Honesty still, yes?"

Wesley nodded.

"I'm ashamed of it. I should've told her what I was, but I didn't. I let her think I was human. I never said that I was, but I revealed nothing of my divinity to her, save for an attempt or two at healing the wounds with which she'd return. She hated it." He exhaled through his quivering smile. "I really liked the experience of her, of being with her. I imagined being human and living in that home—truly living there, not slumbering in a human body while on a mission here on earth—and I wondered what it might have been like if she were my mate and had merely come home from work to me." He looked at Wesley, a knowing expression on his saddened features. "Have you ever considered such things?"

Wesley looked away. He felt so vulnerable, so seen. "Yeah. Maybe."

"I knew I'd have a chance to experience it, not only to imagine it, if I gave in to her requests."

"So, you lose your wings if you have sex?"

"Willingly, yes. There are other ways, of course. Any expression of sin. But what others had been presented to me? What others were even tempting?"

"Ah, they're more tempting than you realize."

"Only when she can use your past against you. I don't have a past. I shouldn't have a future to consider. But I consider yours. I consider the world's future, humanity's future. The future God would've wanted."

"It's more than that, isn't it?" Wesley's voice was more audible now. It seemed to carry his words to War on a somewhat roguish melody.

"More than that?"

"You like Torrence. It's obvious." He chuckled lightly. "You don't have to have magical angel powers to sense that."

"I care for her, yes." His brow knitted. "Emotions can be confusing in their absolution, for they are absolute." Careful eyes raised toward Wesley, to his features. How lovely they were, even when his bravery, attempting to mask his pain behind stoic features, made them tremble. "I don't pretend to understand any of it. Emotions are not something angels experience."

Wesley felt the focus upon him, but it hadn't felt like eyes or a gaze. It was deeper than that sensation, more palpable. He looked over to War. Sensed the emotion within him, immediately comparing it to any emotion he'd felt or thought he'd felt from Torrence since her ascension into power, into divinity.

His head fell between his shoulders. He tried to cover the outburst of sorrow by picking at his thumb nail and bringing it close as if he were examining it.

"Lucky bastards," Wesley said, a bitter laugh expelling the words. "You're right, though. About its absolution, I mean. Can't change how you feel. You don't have any control over it, either." He looked over to War, this divinity made flesh. "Or maybe you can? Maybe you, whatever you are here, have a better hold on stuff like that?"

War shook his head, his motions so slight they were barely visible. "I suppose I should've said emotions are not something angels should experience."

"You can't control how you feel either?"

"I'm as powerless to feeling as you are."

Wesley smiled. The delicacy of this angel, a powerful and divine being, was so endearing. The opposition of his natural state of being from itself, a living oxymoron, the blending of all things he'd been told a man should be and all the things he should not, it was an intoxicant more potent than Wesley thought possible.

He blinked away, but couldn't keep his eyes off of War for too long. The way he moved was so gentle, so careful. He approached the world with such wonder, even gazing studiously to a small flower-like weed as if it were in itself a miracle, but he touched it as if the very connection of his fingertip to a petal might cause its disintegration.

Wesley wondered what Torrence might have looked like if her essence had been angelic and not anti-everything. He wondered, very briefly before pushing the thought from his mind, what she might have acted like, how she might have treated him, but he couldn't imagine Torrence admitting weakness, even to something as involuntary as the experience of an emotion.

War looked up to him suddenly, his mind receiving a flicker of Wesley's mind, of Torrence being gentle, being angelic.

"Is that—?" War blinked away.

"What?"

"May I just…?" War lifted a hand to Wesley.

"What are you doing?"

"I just want to see…" He laid his hand on Wesley's cheek, closing his eyes.

Warmth came to Wesley's skin. Somehow cooling, a fresh breeze perhaps, but still very warm.

"What—?" Wesley exhaled. His eyes closed, too. The light emitting from War's hand forced them shut.

He gasped, and suddenly War was filled with the images of his mind. Memories of Torrence hugging Wesley, of her kissing him, of the pair laughing, then all darkened. Torrence's face became reddened, spattered with blood. Her smiles went from serene to maniacal. More memories, yes, dreadful ones. They overpowered the pleasant ones, the ones Wesley seemed to enjoy, but his mind—oh, the human mind—created beauty from darkness.

Visions came next. Daydreams. Torrence without abilities, without violence. A world of blue skies and modern technology, where Torrence curled into Wesley on a soft, gray couch, eating popcorn as a television lit up their faces.

Wesley hadn't wanted this darkness. War figured this from the start. But now it was evident. His fantasies were not of the apocalypse or of power. They were simpler—a comfortable home shared by lovers.

But Torrence was not ever going to be content with such a life. War was sure no part of her had ever even considered it. He knew, however, that the uncertainty of it within Wesley—the hope that somehow he might have this life with her, that she might not be pure evil inside the lovely form of a woman, that she could simply be a woman, and one that would love him—was what kept him where his soul would not prosper.

War's hand fell away from Wesley's cheek and both were brought out of the vision back into reality.

"What the fuck was that?"

"I'm sorry."

"You're sorry?" He lifted his own hand to his cheek. "What did you do?"

"Torrence isn't…She's never going to be the way you want her to be."

"Look, I want Torrence as she is. That's that."

"You want her human."

"No—."

"Good, then."

"Listen—."

"She'll never be good." He shook his head, his hand running through his glistening hair. "No matter how badly we want her to be." He looked over to Wesley. "You're good, though, no matter how badly you wish you weren't."

"Yeah, well," Wesley said lowly, his voice catching in his throat as he looked out into the field. "So are you." He stood, moving down the hill upon which they sat.

"Wesley—." War started.

"I don't know what you think you saw in my mind or whatever, but I'm not weak, okay?"

"Weak?" He turned toward Wesley.

"Stop," Wesley said, putting up a hand. "I can do my job. It's not like…I'm not just in this for her."

"Are you certain?"

"Fuck you."

"I don't mean to upset you. I only hate to see a good soul in so much suffering."

"A good soul? Buddy, I've killed more people than I can

count."

"For Torrence. I don't pass judgment, Wesley. Like you said, I understand you."

"Yeah, well, you never kill people." He turned there on the hill and sat back down, wiping his wrist across his face. "You save their souls in the streets. And she still likes you better."

"I'm banished, remember?" War moved to sit beside him.

"Yeah, and I'm stuck with you." He looked over to the angel, sniffling but smiling, embarrassed of his outburst. What was regulating emotion these days if one didn't have a violent outlet readily available? He was happy he hadn't tried to shoot the angel. What a thought, what a thing by which to be relieved. Who had Wesley become here? He hadn't the slightest idea anymore.

"You didn't have to bring me here. But you did." War looked about at grass and the sun and the things he never thought he'd see again, not in this plane. "I think you desire something beautiful. Something good. I don't think the world Torrence wishes to rule is the world you'd live in. Not if you had the choice to enter another one."

"Well, I don't have that choice." A pursing of the lips accompanied his sharp but even-toned voice. He opened his hands briefly, then let them hang between his legs.

"You always have a choice. It's the beauty of being human."

"A choice to just swap worlds?" He snorted.

"To change this one, maybe."

"Yeah, okay."

"I mean, we could do it."

"Do what?"

"Change things." He exhaled. "Torrence tells me she's exerting a lot of energy on…infants."

Wesley squirmed. He tried to hide it, but War saw. "Prophecy," Wesley said. "It's survival."

"Right. But what if we found the child first?"

"We can't do that."

"Why not?"

Wesley's eyes darted sharply to War. "I need to say it?" He huffed when War said nothing.

"The prophecy is that this soul will end the apocalypse."

"Yeah, it'll stop the forty-year reign of the antichrist. Guess it has to grow up first."

"So we could—."

"No."

"But, Wesley, think on it—."

"I don't need to think about shit." Wesley rose and walked into the field.

He took great care to focus upon the trees, the leaves, consciously describing their colors so that any perceptible thoughts inside him might only be the insignificant ones he controlled here.

It was no use. The mind prevailed, as it always had. Regardless of what consciousness told it to consider, memories sparked at random, emotions rushed the body and overtook awareness. Opposing thoughts, disloyal thoughts, thoughts of Torrence as simply Torrence, and thoughts of how wonderful a life with her in this way might have been painted lovely visions of a home and a bed and a career into the foreground of his consideration, whether he wanted to focus upon them or not.

In honesty, the thoughts were painful. He felt like he was betraying Torrence, which was bad enough, but if he decided to be truthful with himself, well, he'd probably snatch her from Hell and run away into that parallel world with her, if such a thing were possible.

But it wasn't possible. Was it?

Even if he could do it, he thought, Would Torrence still be Torrence? He couldn't imagine her falling into what she considered the mundanity, the obscurity of everyday life. Would she, in any world, have found excitement or fulfillment in finding a career, succeeding in it, and coming home at night to a man who adored her?

Wesley figured that type of adoration was too small-scaled. What did his affections mean if the rest of the world did not worship Torrence, if the world didn't even know she existed?

He wondered, if he could've turned back the hands of time, if he might've been able to convince her to write a book or run for political office—do something that might bring some sense of notoriety. He scoffed. What a joke these thoughts were.

"Wesley," War said gently, "you brought me here because it's open and bright. It's freedom from the chaos occurring beneath the ever-ripping sky. You don't want that. You don't want this path you've taken. I'm not one to lie to. I mean only that you don't need to lie to me."

"You can see what I want anyway, right?"

"In a sense. Even if I can't see what's in your mind or in your heart, there is no reason to hide these things from me. There is no punishment for desiring the triumph of good over evil—."

"Over Torrence."

"No, that's not what I said."

"It's what you imply."

"You want a return to the old ways, do you not? To you and Torrence as people? People in…in cemeteries…in carnal passion?"

"A return to the old ways, yeah, but that can't happen if you kill her."

"Kill her?"

"That's what you mean, that's what you're talking about. Find the thing that kills her so she can't kill it, then it can kill her when the time is right."

"It's not a thing, Wesley, it's a person, and I don't want to find this soul so they can grow to kill her. I don't want her dead. Look at me. Look at all I do."

"Then what?"

"Then we watch this soul, we help raise it. I'm an angel. Who doesn't want their child guided by an angel?"

"You wanna make it evil?"

"I just want to steer them away from her, but I don't want them dead. We find some way to slow the destruction, we use their abilities to fight hell fire with holy goodness and slow things down. We distract her until we find them. Then we figure out how to use them. Maybe we can…I don't know…Angels become demons, angels become humans, why can't it work the other way?"

"You want to humanize her?"

"I don't know. That, if possible. If she becomes human, I could fall from divinity too. The three of us, we could have a life together."

"Three of us?"

War shrugged shyly, uncertainly. "I don't know. I'm not good at planning. I'm built to follow orders, not give them."

"So, you don't have a plan for this, then? It's just bullshit talk."

"No. I think we need to find the soul who will stop her before she does. We stop the slaughter of these infants. She doesn't even enjoy it, you know? She doesn't want to waste her time with it."

"Yeah, I know Torrence. I'm actually on her side."

"Are you?"

Wesley shook his head, exhaling loudly. "Look, if we're going off on our own little mission, she can't know about it. And I promise you, if I'm missing from Hell, from my brothers, she's gonna know."

"So, we need to distract her from you."

"That means distracting her from our missions, from the takeovers, from the Sun States when they darken. That's a lot to have her lose focus on, especially when it's all tied up together around finding this great enemy of hers."

War closed his eyes, let his mind run through his memories of Torrence, let his spirit read the sensations in those moments he'd been too afraid to define.

The fact was—while she had played audio recordings of Conrad's rituals and music with War in her house, and while she'd attempted to reveal their true purpose to him—Torrence hadn't explained much of anything to War. She hadn't spent time trying to recruit him or convert him. While she was a dominant personality and made no attempts to hide this from him, she hadn't done much to assert herself as his ruler, his leader.

It seemed to War, as he sat here in this lush field with the rays of the warming sun upon his human-esque skin, that in his recollection of their time together, Torrence spent most of it in affection or some sort of loving adoration.

Oh, she had offered him embraces, gentle pets. They'd grown into the entanglement of their limbs, their bodies intertwined on couches, then in beds, and from there came soft, careful kisses to his cheek, to his jaw, to his hesitant lips.

She hadn't pressed, not at first, but allowed the very natural progression of human lust. When paired with the unnatural experience of such things to a being such as War, however, she'd grown a bit impatient, but even in her urges, she was not a great leader of violent men; she was only Torrence.

War opened his eyes. He looked over to Wesley. "The goodness."

"What?"

"I wonder if we find the source of the goodness I felt between—."

"Goodness? What?"

"One like you or like me. One that isn't all bad, but one that she likes…to be a bit closer. The goodness between her and her old friend, maybe."

Wesley snorted. "Yeah, we'll find one of those. We'll pick it for her. You know how many men have come in and out of our gang? How many we've met in efforts to recruit? She has a specific taste, but it takes more than shyness or insecurity or whatever."

"It's goodness." War's eyes widened.

"What?"

"That's what Conrad was saying."

"You spoke to Conrad?"

"She likes goodness. Think about it."

"That doesn't make sense—." Wesley paused as he'd considered it. What was the appeal he'd first had to Torrence? He hadn't been violent back then. Hadn't wanted anything from her, no power or women or money. He'd wanted love, yes, but Torrence rarely offered such a thing to anyone except him and, well, War, an innately good being by way of angelic naivety. He stared at War in consideration of this. "What if she does? Couldn't one of us distract her—couldn't you?" He smiled sadly. Tried to mask the hurt this idea caused him.

War shook his head. "Banished."

"Right. I'm old news, so…" He exhaled. "I don't know why I've always had a thing for the bad girls. You'd think I'd learn from the past, huh? Never did though."

"Maybe that's the answer." War said, trying to hide his delight at this. He'd wanted to peak inside the past since he'd felt that goodness radiating between Torrence and Todd, and now Wesley had given him an opening.

"What is?"

"Torrence's past."

"She's never given me much."

"She doesn't have to," War said, raising his hand to Wesley, the sparks of his divinity already chiming forth from his palm.

"Hey, whoa," Wesley said, pushing at War's wrist and recoiling from it. "What are you doing?"

"Sending you back."

"Sending me what? Back where?"

"To Torrence's past."

"Time travel. Are you fucking kidding me?"

War's hand upturned. His shoulders fell as he tilted his head.

"Sorry. Didn't mean to swear at yah." Wesley smiled. "Just…Time travel? What kind of universe are we in now?"

"The same one that's always been. Why is this so difficult?"

"Are you serious?" He scoffed. "Angels. We don't just travel back in time, you know?"

"You don't do a lot of things." War shrugged. "It will not be like it is in the movies."

"Oh, you know movies?"

"The ones I've seen with Torrence, yes. You will not have a body there. Your body remains with me, here. It's only your soul I send into this memory, much like entering another person's mind. You see, 'time travel' is a human concept. Time is a human concept. There really is no time, you have to understand that."

"No time. Right. Explain how this kid has to grow up in forty years—years—to stop the antichrist then."

"This kid is human. Forty years is a concept God's creatures, you, can understand. Time is much different in Heaven and to spirits as it is to those of you with bodies." He shifted, turning his body toward Wesley. "Understand that there is no past, no future. There is only one moment of time. Right now, the present. This consciousness of consciousness. Nothing else is real."

"Say what you want about the future, but the past is real."

"What do you have as proof of the past?"

"Memory."

"Ah, but what is a memory but a vision? What separates a memory from a thought or a visualization? You could conjure in your mind the moving image of Torrence in a wedding gown, walking toward you down the aisle of a church where sun is flowing in through the windows on each side of her, but that does not make it real. That does not mean it happened or that it will happen."

"Memories are stored in a different part of the brain."

"But they are stored in the brain nonetheless. When you die and the brain ceases to function, where would these memories be found? Can the living locate them? Can the living watch them? Or do they become as you have become—invisible, inaudible; little ghosts rising above your body with your soul, perhaps."

Wesley's brows came together as lips parted. A deep intake of air. Studious. Considerate. "All right," he said, his face unraveling in the excitement of his counter. Gingerly he shook his jacket from his shoulders and off of his arms. He turned his body toward War, extending his left arm across his waist so that the angel might regard it. "Scars," he said, his brows jumping as he looked up to War from his lowered head, which had been angled toward a line of plump, somewhat-pink skin there in the blanket of lovely, tan flesh wrapped around his arm. He pointed to it, tapped it with his finger. "Where'd this come from if the memory wasn't real?"

"The memory," War said, politely indulging Wesley as he looked down to the scar. Then came his eyes, their luminescence always catching Wesley off guard when they first lighted upon him. Witnessing the brief widening of Wesley's eyes, War blinked, allowing adjustment to the sun reflecting the ethereal spirit inside the human-esque irises, then he continued. "What is the memory?"

Wesley's mouth opened to speak, but he only exhaled. His eyes looked away as his head turned shyly from War. A sad smile came to his lips; it rendered the remainder of his handsome face saintlike—solemn and still, but very human.

War realized the memory was not a happy one. He considered this pain the product of Torrence, her anger, who knows?

"I don't need specifics…" War's voice trailed off, his own head turning away from Wesley now. He hadn't meant to hurt him.

Pain slipped across Wesley's lips in the form of another small smile. He looked at War now. "No, it's okay. Torrence…She didn't mean it."

"Right." War smiled sadly. "Of course." War lifted his hand

to the scar now. "The memory is a recollection of an injury, correct?"

"Yes."

"But does it hurt?"

Wesley's eyes widened. "The memory?"

"The memory only hurts when you think of it, when you bring it into this moment, which is the only moment of existence. But when you do not consciously remember it, does it hurt?"

"Well…no…"

"And the scar?" War asked.

"Oh." He looked down to the angel's delicate fingers as they brushed very gently over the scar. He cleared his throat. "No."

"Because it doesn't exist here in this moment." A tingling sensation came to Wesley's arm now. Small sparks seemed to dance very fluidly and purposefully in slow bursts from War's fingers. As they moved along the scar, they seemed to absorb it, for it dissipated beneath the touch.

"Wow," Wesley said lowly, looking at his arm. He raised it, touched it, ran his own fingers over the perfect skin there. He looked up to War, smiling genuinely now. "Man, that's incredible."

"No," he said shyly. "You know Torrence can do it."

"Doesn't feel the same when she does it, though." He looked up to the angel.

"That's because hers is a disfigurement of God's Grace where mine is an extension of it. She manipulates the matter, moves it. I simply repair it."

Wesley smiled gently. "What about a memory two people have? Two people remembering the same thing?"

"Fouleux au deux," War replied. "As your psychology catalogs it. Shared delusion. Whether a memory of an imagining, the visions of the mind are comprised of the same spiritual make-up."

Wesley nodded, looking back to the healed skin of his arm. Why argue? "Gotcha."

"May I send you there, to her past?"

"Why don't you go?"

"I'm afraid as part of my retribution I have been bound to this form."

"For how long?"

"I don't know. It is not relevant right now. What matters is this plan, however strange it may seem to you. Do you trust me enough to allow me this? Let me use my power, whatever remains of it, to study Torrence? To learn from the past? To find some key to her distraction or her deviation from this hellish plan of hers?"

"I don't wanna hurt her."

"I don't either."

"Swear to me, man, that whatever we do here, whatever I discover, and whatever we do with it, it's so we can keep her."

"Of course it is. Torrence is not the problem. Her position is. All I mean to take from her is that position. Not her life or her safety or even her comfort."

Wesley exhaled. Scrubbed his hands over his face. "All right," he said, turning to face War. "I'll go."

CHAPTER TEN

"Would you like to lie back?" War asked.

"Dude, don't make it weird."

"Okay, sitting then?"

"Yeah."

"Get comfortable. As I've said, your body will remain here in whatever position you leave it in."

"Oh," Wesley stammered a bit. "Okay." He angled his body toward War now, studying him in curiosity.

"Okay," War said. He turned his body toward Wesley, too. Licking his lips and closing his eyes, War's lips trembled purposefully—small, inaudible whispers of a tongue Wesley couldn't determine, not at first, but the longer War participated in this litany of language, the more distinctive his words became.

His mouth parted further to pronounce the phrases he spoke; his lips pursing and curling more prominently to better form each syllable spoken aloud.

It was Latin, Wesley could recognize that much, but he only understood certain words within the myriad sentences—words like *Deus*, or God in English, and the obvious *humilem servum*, humble servant.

Wesley tried not to roll his eyes, but then, War's were closed. He watched the angel from the corner of his eye, wondering if War could perceive whatever emotional consideration swirled inside Wesley's mind and prompted the eye-roll reaction, but the angel was too focused on his random rosary to react if he did.

Suddenly War's eyes came open, causing Wesley to jump slightly. The iridescent irises had expanded; all of his eyes taking on the radiant colors.

"I will not see," he said, his voice an echoing choir.

"What?" Wesley asked, his voice breathy and awestruck. "You won't—?"

"No," War said, his voice growing in volume and echo and melody. Around him, the air seemed to ripple. The light expanded from his eyes and his hair and his glittering skin in all directions, blinding Wesley briefly.

He raised his arm up, blocking some of the light from his eyes, which remained fixed on the angel.

From behind War came another light, a light which extended out from the crown of his head in an oval of shimmering gold.

His lips parted, the light exiting his mouth now, too. A great shrieking accompanied this light, but nothing of pain or fear or anger, merely sound and melody and high-pitched, glistening power.

The wind was picking up, circling not only around War but around Wesley, too. After a few long moments of this shrill sound and blinding light, this almost-painfully strong wind, War's hands reached out for Wesley.

Fearful, but entirely trapped within this storm of light and air, Wesley remained steadfast in his position there.

War's hand came to Wesley's arm, which still hung in the air between their faces, and then, after a litany of Latin, War's head flew backward.

At this same, precise instant, wings shot out from War's back, six of them. Two expanded outward, in-line with his human-esque shoulders. Two pushed downward, wrapping around War's bent, meditative legs. The final two rushed around his head to shield his eyes.

"I will not see," he said, his voice a singing melody of echoing strength, "but you will."

And in an instant, all sound and light and angelic chaos ceased.

He blinked a few times, and the darkness grew brighter around him until he could perceive his surroundings normally. He was in a high school. In a hallway.

Moving against the row of lockers on his side, Wesley looked about the large corridor. Teenagers were everywhere, moving in all directions.

In a confusion, he looked about for War, but couldn't find the angel anywhere. He didn't know exactly where he was or why…until he saw her.

Walking directly in the center of the hallway, people moving out of her way, parting as if they'd been a biblical sea, Torrence came into sight.

She sauntered down the hallway as one would expect—with eyes forward and seemingly fixed on some point in the distance, avoiding the stares of the boys around her, of the girls. Her shoulders were back, her chin lifted. Her long, black hair flowed down her shoulders in large, loose, seemingly-effortless curls.

She was beautiful, confident, walked with ease and assertion simultaneously, but there was an air about her, rendering the angelic face mischievous and quite troublesome.

She was desired here, but she was intimidating. She kept to herself, yet people knew her. She seemed exactly as she was when Wesley met her—isolated inside her mind, giving away nothing to those around her, but connected to many of them through some type of business-like vice.

Wesley wasn't sure how he knew these things about her, but he knew them. When she moved by him, he leaned back against the row of navy-blue lockers, watching her glide through the crowded hallway in her black platform heels, which tied behind her ankle in a great, silken bow, and her tight black jeans tucked into these bows, and her red, cropped hoodie.

Torrence here in this hallway, eyes on her, boys starting to move toward her then stopping themselves, faltering at her feet just as Wesley did now, well, Torrence was both exactly what he'd imagined she'd have been and none of it.

Moving away from the lockers, Wesley followed behind her, expecting to go into a class or the cafeteria. Instead, she exited the building and headed for her car. When Wesley stepped outside the building, too, he was caught off-guard, blinded by the radiant sun in the sky. He had to blink to adjust to it—it had been so long since he'd seen such a sun, for even the one in the sky above Sun States was still obstructed in some ways by the rifts in the expanse. High school, he thought, wondering what his past-self was doing now, on this day in particular. Nothing extraordinary, he imagined, but perhaps what Torrence was doing hadn't seemed as such either. He exhaled, staring into the sun. I never would've imagined my future as it is now, he thought, closing his eyes as the sun shone down on him.

He felt its warmth, its energy; felt his body, or spiritual equivalent, becoming lost in it. His mind quieted for a long moment of this sensation. He almost forgot where, or when, he was.

Careful not to be absorbed by the memory around him, Wesley has to purposely pull his focus from the sun and sky and place it back onto Torrence, who was entering her car now.

Uncertain if he could slip inside the vehicle with her, Wesley stood at the driver's side door, watching her in awe. This mysterious figure, this woman without a last name, the human-turned-deity was sitting before him now at some time in 2006, a senior at O'Connell Area Public High School.

With his hands in his jean pockets, Wesley looked about at

the parking lot. He saw a few kids eating sandwiches on steel picnic tables, which had been covered in some hard, yet sticky, rubber. A boy, sitting on the sidewalk, chewed his nails as he stared nervously at a textbook. A few girls walked to a car some distance from that of Torrence. A small group tossed around a football while quizzing one another on Don Quixote. Students chatted, laughed, lived their lives during the forty minutes between bells designated for their lunch.

He looked back to Torrence in her car, her left shoe pressed into the seat, her knee bent, right elbow resting atop it. She pushed what looked like a tape into the built-in cassette player, but a cable was attached to it. Wesley followed the length of it until he found its opposite end, stuck inside a bright-pink iPod nano.

Wesley chuckled, struck by the color in Torrence's hand, watching the swirl of black nail polish contrasted against its brightness as Torrence ran her thumb relentlessly around the white circle of buttons beneath the old device's screen.

No one in this building, not the teachers or the principal or the kids studying and eating, could've known what this girl, sitting in her car alone, listening to old emo music, would become some fifteen years in the future. Not a single one of them might have expected that they shared a classroom with the antichrist, but here she was.

She was a mere human here, a girl, one that bore no true difference from any other, save for her assertive nature or even, perhaps, her ethereally-beautiful features.

Wesley desperately wanted to be nearer to her, to sit beside her before she was some violent, manipulative cult leader, so he walked around the car and attempted to take the door handle into his grip.

Unsurprisingly, he could not interact with the objects here, leaving him to question whether he was sent back to this year or if this was all some hallucination of the past called up by angelic grace. Time wasn't time, after all, at least not according to War. He supposed that didn't matter. What mattered was that he could see Torrence as a person, and he slipped inside the vehicle to get a better view.

Through the windshield, Wesley watched a boy with long, greasy hair approach the car.

Without looking up, Torrence tossed the iPod into the console of the car. Her hand slipped over to her ankle, untying the silky bow, withdrawing from a strange, extremely small, sewn-in pocket, a tiny bag.

She raised her hand toward the window, the pill in the baggy pressed between her first two fingers.

This greasy kid took it and replaced it with a tightly-folded-up bill. Wesley couldn't determine its value or what drug she'd just sold, but he marveled at the sale.

Torrence hadn't looked at the boy. She hadn't said a word. Neither had he. Yet she trusted that he'd paid her correctly, that he was who she'd expected.

She tucked the cash into a small wallet that hung on her keychain, then she reached into the silky, untied bow again. This time, silently offering a different drug-of-choice to a pretty boy in a pale-pink button-up.

It was evident to Wesley in the faces of these boys that they were frightened by Torrence, that they wouldn't dare lie to her or pass her the wrong amount of cash.

He wanted desperately to know why.

After a few more customers, when the students started going back inside, a guy came to the passenger door, prompting Wesley to move into the backseat when he opened the door and moved inside.

Scattered across the back seat were crumpled papers, covered in large, red A's. One hundred percent after one hundred percent, Torrence's homework, tests, essays displayed the intelligence her scarily-accurate manipulation often showed, but in a more positive, however strange, manner.

Wesley had often considered that Torrence hadn't gone to school at all, that she didn't have a last name, that she was a manifested demon who began life at eighteen or twenty-five. How strange to see her how he'd always hoped she'd been—a perfectly human person.

"You sure you don't wanna come to the party tomorrow night?" the boy asked, his smile spread across plump lips. Handsome, dark hair, leather jacket. Exactly how he'd expect Torrence's high school companion to look.

"Don't be stupid," she replied.

"Here," he said, offering a small stack of what appeared to be plastic cards to her.

She took them, eyed the first one intently, allowing Wesley to see that it was a driver's license. She shuffled through them—four of them—and he saw that they all were licenses.

When she looked back over to him, he smiled and handed her as many wallets.

She went through them, removing the cash before placing them onto the dashboard. Next to them, she placed the wad of cash.

He smiled, eyes leaving the offerings and presented to her his empty hand now.

She took it and yanked it toward her. From the bow, she now withdrew a small sewing needle and pricked his thumb with it.

Wesley watched as intensely as her companion watched when Torrence raised the boy's hand up to her lips. "There are some binding rules that come with this offering," Torrence said.

"Okay," the boy said. "Like what?"

"Like you keep your mouth shut about me and what I do and what I tell you to do."

"Okay," he said, watching her bring his thumb to her lips and kiss the small, bleeding wound tenderly.

"Devote yourself to me," she said, licking at his thumb now

before taking it into her mouth.

"I'm devoted to you," he said, grinning a bit as he stared at her.

"Good," she said. She looked over to him, a gleam in her narrowed eyes, and released his hand.

Wesley recognized this gleam; it was lustful intent, desire with purpose, weaponized passion.

He wondered why War brought him back here, why this was the day he'd chosen to show Wesley, but then he considered that there were probably very few days in Torrence's life that occurred differently than this one, and maybe that was the point. Maybe all Wesley had hoped to learn from seeing Torrence before she was the lead of a violent band of bad boys was merely that—a hope. Perhaps Torrence had always been what Torrence was; perhaps there had never been anything kind or connected or warm about her.

When Torrence finished conquering her new acquisition, she gave his hand back to him. Leaning back into the driver's seat, Torrence handed her associate, this new liegeman in her court of crime, two twenties from her newly-acquired, impressive stack. "Your finder's fee."

"Thanks," he said joyously.

She tossed the wallets back to him. "Return them. Make sure no one sees you do it."

He nodded, eyes remaining on her, but she took the iPod back into her hand and began to circle the buttons again. Understanding that this was his exit cue, the man left the vehicle, determined to take back the wallets, his intent becoming clear to Wesley, clear the way the year in which he'd been thrown was clear, clear the way Torrence's age was clear, the way reactions to her were clear.

She leaned back into the seat now, a song having been selected, and via the sunroof, Torrence enjoyed the heat of the light.

"Your mom is gonna kill you, Tor," a girl's voice said, chuckling. Wesley looked out the window and saw a lovely, auburn-haired woman there.

"I have a 107% in AP French," Torrence answered without opening her eyes. "So what if I skip a few classes."

"She is not gonna see it that way."

Torrence's eyes opened now and she leaned up from her relaxed position. "Then don't mention it to anyone."

"I won't," she said, her eyes fearful as she swallowed her words down thickly. "I didn't mean I'd tell. Just Miss Frinese—."

"Miss Frinese loves me," Torrence said, rolling up the window without meeting the eyes of this young woman.

After a few songs of heavy drums and poetic lyrics, Torrence opened her eyes. She smiled at nothing, maybe at her thoughts. He wished he knew exactly what those thoughts were.

As he watched her, his attention entirely on her face, her eyes, their serenity, he moved forward unconsciously. A hand held onto the headrest of the passenger seat as he neared her. Flashes of the man who'd sat there only moments ago came into his mind—his name was David, he was twenty years old, he had no family. Torrence found him outside a bar during a small metal show and offered him a sandwich, a wallet full of cash she'd swiped from someone surfing the crowd inside, and a promise of fulfillment in all ways physical and familial.

Pulling back from the flickers of knowledge, Wesley looked at his hand as it jerked instinctively away from the seat. He realized now that he'd obtained War's abilities here, or some of them, anyway. When he touched things in this time or this memory, or whatever it was, much like the lockers of the hallway that told him of the school and the year in which he stood, he absorbed information about them.

He looked up to Torrence, wanting to see her home, as Todd had mentioned it, her parents. Oh, then he considered Todd. Where was he in this reality? How had Torrence come to meet him? In a cemetery, hadn't Todd said?

His vision became blurred suddenly. Rubbing at his eyes, Wesley felt a sharp pain rush through them, spreading out into his forehead, a spiritual sinus headache, worse than any migraine he'd ever experienced. Yet somehow, through all this tension, the image of Todd, of his face as he spoke of Torrence, remained crystal-clear inside Wesley's mind.

What little of Torrence's car he could still see started to fragment. Through the cracks came beams of light. He recognized it immediately as the light which had emitted from War's hands, his eyes and mouth, when the angel had touched Wesley and thrust him into whatever plane he was in now.

Wesley pressed both hands into both eyes, his curling lips exposing his teeth as he hissed at the tension and the light and the erasure, it seemed, of this vision.

A shrill sound came into his ears, ringing out in increasing volumes as the light overtook him. He did not want to leave this world yet. He hadn't found anything worth taking back. He'd only thought of Todd, who couldn't have been the answer. Could he?

In the same instant the searing light dissipated, the shrill stopped. Beneath him was ground, or at least something solid, but to his palms it was softer, almost fluffy. He realized quickly that he was sat upon grass. Damn it, he thought, Back to the fields with War, and with nothing of value to report.

He blinked rapidly as he opened his eyes, but it took some time for his vision to adjust. No sun shone onto the ground now. How long had he been gone?

He stood from his position, the same one he had been in inside Torrence's car, dusting himself off as he looked up into the sky. It was night, yes, but it did not seem like the night sky of the apocalypse, and where was War?

With a creased brow, Wesley looked back to the field before him. Ah, he quickly realized, he had not been sent back to the same field, which must have meant he had not been sent back to his body.

As he walked toward the little path that ran through the open grass, Wesley's vision cleared more and more. He saw, as he approached the path, that it was more a road, though it was gravel. No, it had not been covered by the nature around it. It seemed heavily used.

He stepped onto this small roadway, heading in the direction of the moon in the sky, the full moon, white and gleaming and illuminating all around its glow a solid and complete sky.

He looked around him at the fields on either side of him, noticing only now as he walked off some of the dizzying effects of such unusual, spiritual travel that he was, in fact, in a cemetery.

A wave of consideration gave him pause. A cemetery now, and the thought of Todd and his meeting Torrence within a cemetery having occurred simultaneously with his transport here. Perhaps, it had been, instead, the trigger of it.

Moving off of the pathway, Wesley looked at one of the gravestones. A simple oval-shaped stone with bold, capital letters, the dirt beneath the slab was fresh—disturbed, but compacted to the original space of its replacement.

Wesley looked down to the writing upon the stone. The date of death: 2004. He looked up from it, eyes darting from undefined point to undefined point. He had traveled back further, two more years into the past from where he'd been sitting in Torrence's car. Was she somewhere here to be seen? Surely, at least, Todd was.

He moved more purposefully now as he went back to the path. His destination, once unknown, was now a man, a young man, and his soon-to-be female acquaintance.

After some time wandering this curling, hilly road, Wesley heard movement. There was breathing, labored breathing, sniffling.

He advanced toward it, following it away from the road and into the myriad headstones. This cemetery bearing obvious differences from that of the church of Conrad, Wesley pondered the simplicity of it all. Rounded slabs bearing only names and dates. The occasional "loving mother" or "beloved husband" descriptor accompanied the names and dates.

Rarer still was a stone with an angel carved into it, just above the name. It seemed in Wesley's reading of the stones an adornment saved for infants and young children. He shuddered at this, at the first headstone he found belonging to a child. What would Torrence think of these, here in 2004, as a sixteen-year-old? Surely she wouldn't have given them a thought, and if she had, it might've been only a passing sympathy, for the Torrence he'd known, the pre-antichrist Torrence battling would-be adversaries of her hellish reign, the Torrence he'd met some five or so years after this point in time, hadn't liked the torment or demise of those under eighteen. No kids and no animals. This had always been her rule.

Well, he thought, At least one is still intact.

He frowned as he placed his hand upon the headstone, a flicker of this child in his mother's arms came to him before he quickly refuted it. He did not want to see the child die. He shook his hand as he moved away from the headstone, moving again toward the gentle sobs of a young Todd somewhere in the near area.

When Wesley found him, he was sat before a gravestone, his head hanging between his shoulders, elbows resting on bent knees.

Why did you do this, Perry? Todd was thinking. Why would you do this? Why didn't you call me? Why didn't you call someone? Anyone?

Wesley recalled the story of Perry, however briefly it had been given. He'd completed suicide when he and Todd, his best friend, were sixteen.

Now, before Perry's grave sat the bereaved Todd, alone, it seemed to the sorrowful youth, with no family who understands him and no friends who truly do, either.

Todd had been shy, fearful, hesitant. Perry, who was none of those things, was more than his best friend; Perry had been Todd's idol.

It was Perry who taught Todd poetry, Perry who encouraged Todd not to fear being called on in class. Perry, who dreamt of being a playwright even though his parents had decided he'd go to law school or medical school or something as appropriate, showed Todd passion, even in the dullest places, like the classroom of a private Christian school.

Wesley saw images of Perry, a handsome, tall young man with dark hair and large, innocent eyes. He saw this young man scribbling out scenes of poetry and passion on the backs of graded science exams. He watched Todd scold Perry, asking him what he'd do if his father found these little musings, these little writings no one would ever see, not if Perry was lucky, anyway. But Perry was fearless. He planned to go to an open mic night at the local college campus, and how would his father know of that? How if he said he was spending the night at Todd's house?

Oh, the thought terrified Todd. What if Perry's parents called his? What would Perry do, then? But it was no use. Perry had been introduced to his passion now, a spark he'd had since they were fourteen in English class, emblazoned now to a point of no return.

Wesley wanted to comfort Todd here, wanted to quell any thoughts that he might've somehow prevented his best friend's death, but before he could consider even another syllable, the shuffling of feet upon grass came into the space behind them.

Looking for its source, Wesley focused upon his hearing, noticing now the crickets chirping and the rustling leaves moved by the gentle gusts of wind.

Then came a figure from the darkness, a slim figure, short of stature and shapely; the type of figure Wesley, as a stupid young man of sixteen, might have welcomed, even in the darkness. Oh, but Wesley knew all too well that this was part of the appeal of Torrence—that body and the saunter which carried it as it seemed to glide through the grass, the gravestones and lush trees merely a backdrop of decay and desolation, which allowed her beauty, not only to shine, but to seem a beacon of safety in a world of the dead and the dying.

He knew her well enough to know this was most likely by design, by her design, for if she were coming here now for Todd, there was a reason for it, and anything for which there was a reason in the mind of Torrence also had a plan devised for its conquest at her hands.

This was Todd's conquering. The crying boy had no idea of what was coming for him, what was just feet away from him now, but Wesley did.

He didn't want to be so aware here, didn't want to feel like a part of what was occurring without the ability to interact or alter any of it, and just as the thought of Todd seemed to bring him to Todd, the thought of consciousness and his dislike for it here seemed to dissipate. He watched now. Just that. A voyeur without consideration of what he viewed.

The scene was set perfectly in the mind of Torrence as she approached her target—not the first target, but surely one that would last this time.

Torrence had started her initial search for companionship in bad boys, in the boys who skipped class and frequented detention. Her parents' money made it easy for her to persuade them with drugs or alcohol, but though they held up their ends of their respective bargains with Torrence, she'd found the completion of their tasks dissatisfying.

It was something about the barter system, perhaps. The buying and trading of it. Small-scale capitalism, however illegal, but that was par-for-the-course, too. What system so well governed could be pure? It was laughable. And while illegal activities in general were not frowned upon by Torrence's organization, the fact that it was most easily defined as an organization was distasteful to her.

She did not want to participate in a system. She didn't want to be a seller or a buyer or a dealer. She wanted to be more than that, she quickly realized, and this is why her targets became more personal, why she decided now to target people not with checkered pasts necessarily, but with pasts that would be easy to exploit.

Perry had been an original target, yes, but Todd had never known it. Torrence met the young man at a movie theatre some months prior to this night in the cemetery with Todd. A late night viewing. Some midnight showing of a film marketed mostly to teenaged girls.

Torrence had been a teenaged girl then, yes, but not exactly the movie-going type, not unless going to a movie served some cause, and the night she met Perry, it had.

She'd been walking home from a party one of her parents' friend's sons had thrown. It was all the Junior Ivy League Bullshit, as she called it. Teenagers drinking champagne and doing cocaine, talking about how they'd conquer the world through capitalism. What a joke. Torrence hated it, but she was prowling; new methods for recruitment meant new circles of friends, new places to frequent.

She realized rather quickly that these kids, the attractive ones, the ones who were handed everything were easier targets in some ways than the criminal-types with whom she'd been bartering. Sure, the others were easy, a twenty here or a pint of something there and they'd do just about anything, but these kids at these mansion parties with their real-diamond necklaces and tailored jackets, they were easier in other ways; for Torrence's purposes, more important ways.

These were insecure people, materialistic people, shallow people. Human beings taught that value only exists externally; one was only important so long as others thought they were important.

Beauty was a commodity. Sexuality was one. Money, the thing that gave the most power. And while that may have seemed true to everyone, it was worse here. In this circle, it was the only thing that mattered—appearance over anything else, and that meant the appearance of power, the appearance of control, the appearance of intelligence, the appearance of happiness, even when one possessed none of these things.

Criminals had their codes of conducts and poor folks had their values. The words "educated" and "intelligent" were not synonymous. So, the so-called worse-off people, the ones without expensive cars or fancy clothing may have been more easily bought for an excursion or two, for a singular act, but this was not what Torrence wanted. She wanted full devotion, and people with personalities, with street-smarts, with the love of art or some other defining trait that existed within their minds or hearts or souls, well, those people were less likely to devote their entire life to another, not without some extenuating circumstance. But amongst her "own kind" as her mother would've said, amongst the kids with rich parents or beautiful features or both, Torrence learned the depth of her craft.

Here, Torrence had to be attentive. She had to watch and listen to every small motion and every spoken word. She had to read between the lines of the unspoken comments, to notice expressions even as they were quickly wiped from frowning faces and replaced with smiles. The feigned joy, the fake perfection.

There was no value here or sense of worth. Only the perception of it. She had to determine who was lacking what—who needed a mother-figure because theirs was addicted to martinis and Valium, who needed a dumb, giggling girlfriend because their A-pluses had all been plagiarized and were now living with a false intellectual role so they now felt inferior to their own persona. Who did Torrence need to be for whom?

But it was exhausting being with these people. Even the most determined aspiring gang leader could only take so much, so she'd exited the party early, opting to walk home before hitching a ride with one of these dullards.

It was on her walk home that she'd met Perry, sneaking into a late night movie as the only act of rebellion he could think of performing. Yes, this was an ideal candidate—a young man bound by the aspirations of his parents, a young man who could be free to be himself and pursue his passions only with Torrence. She wouldn't simply become his friend or his drug-dealer or his leader; she'd become freedom itself. Without her, Perry could not be him.

This bond between them was intense for that very reason. Torrence and Perry had small plans, very small. They'd sneak away to concerts together, to poetry readings, then eventually she'd encouraged him to write his own works. Perry could not be free to be himself, to follow his passions, to even admit them, not with anyone but her.

She'd got to him too early, however. Too many years before the magically-adult day he'd turn eighteen because instead of dedicating himself to Torrence completely once she'd given him the life that had always been meant to be his, he'd killed himself.

Something about his father finding his poetry books and "junk novels" and deciding to withdraw him from his private school and send him to a military academy instead.

Torrence was disappointed, of course, but his funeral gave her plenty of new faces to scan and study and potentially take.

This was how she'd first seen Todd. Plenty of boys—with their mothers in expensive two-piece dresses and their fathers in their businessman suits—were saddened by Perry's death. Genuine emotion clung to all their faces, but Todd was different. Todd was shyer, smaller, his shoulders always turned into himself, his head always downcast. He wiped his eyes frequently, visibly crying.

She'd followed him home that day. Followed him to school the next couple. Watched him.

This night had not been the first night Todd had gone to the cemetery, but it would be the last. Torrence would make sure of it. See, Torrence realized now that what Todd needed most wasn't just a replacement friend, but a friend who understood him. And she understood him.

From behind Todd there in the cemetery, Torrence came. He hadn't heard the footsteps, the leaves. He was not even aware of the wind against his ears, howling inside them. Todd was lost to the world. He had been since he was old enough to be self-aware. Perry gave him a sense of life inside the strange existence, but Perry was gone now.

Todd sniffled as Torrence sat down next to him. He'd only glanced over to her briefly with his eyes, his head falling further into his raised shoulders, as if he could make himself smaller still.

It didn't matter how far into himself he shrank, Torrence had seen him. She'd seen him, and she wanted him, and once Torrence wanted someone—something, anything—she obtained it, even if it only lasted a short while or ended with her dissatisfaction.

She raised a hand to Todd, watching him shrink away like a fearful animal. Maybe that was her target-type, fearful animals. Todd would be the first of many, she decided as she pushed his brown hair from his clammy forehead, feeling the sorrow emitting from his tearful eyes as tangible as the wind moving gently about them. She wasn't sure how she felt his emotions, but she knew why. This was where her life's work truly began.

Wesley watched from the scenery as Torrence stroked Todd's hair, brushed her fingers along his cheek. He fell victim, as they all had, to her charm and her beauty and the natural ability she had for seeing directly into a man's soul to the empty space inside it, ready to become whatever that missing element was.

Torrence was completion. She was freedom. She was everything one might want and everything one might want to be.

"It's okay," she said, leaning into him. "You can make it

worthwhile. You can make it mean something. Don't let his death be in vain."

"How? How can I—?" He stammered, looking downward, looking away, hiding as he always hid.

"Don't shy away," she said, bringing his face back toward hers. "You don't have to shy away from me." She straightened her back, smiling slightly, a seductive slant to her brow. "You should be bold. You shouldn't hold back."

"You sound like Perry," Todd mumbled, exhaling through a painful smile. "My friend who died." He nodded, a very small and uncomfortable gesture, toward the dirt upon the fresh grave. "He always said stuff like that."

"That's how you make his death mean something. That's how you keep him alive. You break out of the rules and expectations that define your entire existence now. You yield only to the desires of your own heart, and you rebuke those of anyone else, of any system or school." She took his hand in hers. "It was that bullshit that took your friend from you. He did not leave, you understand that, right? He was killed, murdered by the prospect of existing when he could've lived. These systems, they can't win again. They can't rule us."

"What can we do, though?"

"We use this pain you're feeling," she said, placing her hand on his heart, "and we use it to avenge Perry. We use it as fuel for our fight back."

Oh, a very-conscious dislike flooded Wesley at this scene—a sad young man so manipulated by Torrence, who took his sorrow and twisted it into adornment for her elegant gestures and soft words. What she could be to anyone, he thought, Wow.

He felt the obvious desire to flee from this place, and without understanding how, this desire was all it took for the memory to chip away and disappear.

Wesley emerged from that meeting in the cemetery and found himself again inside the car with Torrence again. Sitting in the original memory he'd been sent to once more, he exhaled, leaning back into the seat and scrubbing his hands over his face.

Maybe there had never been a chance for Torrence to be good and normal, to go to college and get a job, a dog, a family. Maybe some people simply weren't built for it, for being a part of a society, much less a marriage or a family.

Her family. Wesley still hadn't seen them. He wondered if they had some influence on Torrence's desires. But how could they?

The next figure to approach Torrence's car came into view, then. It was Todd—eighteen-year-old Todd now, Todd two years after he'd lost his best friend and gained a new, more dangerous one.

He was dressed in the navy blue jacket of a private school. A golden shield upon the left breast of the jacket read: Calvary Christian Academy.

"Hey, Tor," Todd said, smiling as he leaned down into her opening window.

"Hey," she said, offering Todd the only real warmth Wesley had seen from her in this realm of memory. "How's my baby today?"

"He was okay," Todd said, standing up as Torrence exited the car. Wesley followed suit, watching Torrence as she handed Todd the keys. "He never says much so it's hard to tell, but he didn't eat lunch today. He just sat there, reading."

Torrence nodded. From her stack of newly-obtained wealth, she removed a few bills and gave them to Todd. "Make sure he eats," Torrence said, "and I won't dock your pay next time."

"Tor, I don't even know him. How am I supposed to do that?"

"Make friends."

He smiled through the discomfort of such a thought. The shoulder that was not supporting the weight of his bag raised into a weak, little half-shrug.

"Todd, come on. Recruiting is part of what you're doing. You said you wanted the job."

"Yeah, but I—." His words were clipped by a shaken intake of air. He shook his head as it fell. His eyes stared at his brown leather shoe as he kicked at some gravel.

He looked up to her, his best friend. He wanted the job, yeah. He'd told her that in the cemetery. He'd said he wanted his life to mean something; he wanted to be a part of something—something greater than an alma mater or an already-established institution. He wanted to rise above the status quo, even though his schooling, his extracurriculars, his parents and their wealth and reputation were designed to secure him a spot at the top of the establishment, it wasn't enough. He hated the establishment. He wanted to overturn it, to destroy those who created it, to strike fear in the hearts of those who loved it and benefited from its rigid inequity.

He wanted his life to be a life, not an existence crafted by the wants of his parents, who knew so little about him he wasn't sure they could even name his birthdate without the help of one of their assistants or receptionists.

But he'd never been sure if he could do the job. Well, some parts of it.

Parts like stealthily pick-pocketing movie-goers or the patrons of museums, that was perfect for him. He so desperately did not want to be noticed by anyone during even the most mundane tasks that it made him naturally very sly in this way, and because he was always so nervous of how odd he might appear, he'd learned from a young age to notice the eyes of everyone in a room and ensure they were not in him.

The parts that required speaking to people, making friends, those were more difficult. But he wanted to please Torrence. More than anything. He did not want to lose another friend, another strong, confident idol. He couldn't.

"I just wouldn't know what to say." His features loosening as if he'd asked a question, and indirectly he had.

Torrence smiled. "You have chemistry together, right?"

He nodded.

"Tell him you forgot what the assignment was or something. Pretend you don't get it. I don't know. If he's sitting alone at lunch again, ask him if he's studying for chem, then just sit down when he answers and start talking about it."

"You make it sound easy."

"It's only hard because you're convincing yourself it will be. Stop overthinking every step of it." Torrence hugged him. "Take care of my car."

"Always," he said, getting into the driver's seat. "See you tonight, right?"

"Of course."

Todd smiled as he started the car. Torrence stood and watched him drive away, then she left the school on foot.

Wesley followed, closely watching Torrence, studying her, focusing very intently on even the smallest and most seemingly-insignificant detail like the way she'd run her hand through her hair or readjust the strap of her bag across her chest.

Everything radiated confidence, assertion. Even at eighteen, even at the beginning of her career as a leader of violent, and not-so-violent, men, she seemed very aware of herself, of who she was, and what she intended to become. The process had started, and perhaps some pieces of it weren't yet fleshed out inside her mind, but the end goal was there. It was evident to Wesley, who involuntarily received flickers of her will and her intention and her desire through whatever magic War had gifted him in his visit here.

When she went into a convenient store, Wesley expected to see her steal the items she wanted, but she did not. No crime for the sake of crime, he supposed. Even when they had no direction, they didn't kill or raid at random.

Torrence took two bars of chocolate and a large chocolate

chip cookie to the counter. Used a credit card instead of a bill from her wad of cash. She did not accept a bag when offered, placing the paid-for items into the bag across her chest instead and wishing the employee behind the counter a wonderful day.

When she smiled, she appeared as any woman. The mask of humanity had always clung tightly to her monstrous thoughts, so tightly one could hardly notice it wasn't her face. Torrence knew precisely how to behave; Wesley had seen her acting properly and respectfully on many occasions. The fact of the matter was that she rarely wanted to.

As she left the store, Torrence crossed the street. She glanced at the road, but she did not pause to truly register if a vehicle was traveling the road toward her, opting instead to stare down the traffic as she seemed to purposefully flutter across the road.

The wind took her dark hair when she trotted across at this lively pace. Its loose, black curls flowed over her shoulders and down her back before the air lifted it away from her hoodie.

A vision, Wesley thought, As always. It must have seemed ethereal here, in this time, when nothing magical ever happened, and if someone were to report such an incident, it was typically scoffed at for its lack of logic. But now, in the world of the open sky, if someone were to see Torrence in such a manner as this, they would have surely assumed she was an angel.

Then came the thought again, the thought of the field with War, when the true angel told the human, in kinder words, not to waste his time on such fantasies. They would only cause further harm to his already-breaking heart. Torrence was not angelic. She never was. She never would be.

Still, he didn't think he was too stupid or naive for considering it. After all, weren't demons mutated angels? Ashen wings were still wings. Twisted bones were still bones. How far could one fall from glory if glory is their nature?

He considered himself now, and how far he'd fallen from that good and righteous soul he supposedly had. Maybe there was redemption. But how to achieve it without denouncing the very being who brought him away from it?

Eventually, Wesley followed Torrence into her destination: the public library.

"Good afternoon, Dr. Lanchik," Torrence said to the librarian at the desk. Her tone was bubbly, and it made Wesley uncomfortable.

"Good afternoon, Torrence," she replied, lowering her chin so she could look at the young antichrist above her red, bifocal glass. "Are we looking for books on cults or theology today?"

"Neither," she said. "Thank you for remembering. I just need a quiet place to work, if that's all right."

"Of course. Let me know if you need something."

Torrence nodded and smiled, thanking the woman wholesomely. What a show. But cults and theology. Oh, Torrence may not have known what she'd become, but she had been prepared for it.

She walked into the back of the library, rounding the corner to her left at the end of the myriad rows of great, towering shelves made from dark, ornate wood, and descended the small stairwell there.

Her steps echoed inside the small space. Heel against wood. A perfect likeness, Torrence at eighteen walking down the library staircase surrounded by architectural beauty, to the modern images now of Torrence at thirty-three moving downward into her Hell, surrounded by ornate candelabra and angelic statues. Oh, Wesley could see so many warnings hidden inside the innocuous. But that was the way with anything in life, wasn't it? The blurry present was so sharp and vivid once it had become the past.

At this lower level of the library were four more shelves on either side of a small pathway, which extended out on each side to reveal four small tables—two on either side, in-line with the shelves.

As Torrence stepped onto the level ground, she moved by

the first shelf, tapping on each partition of wood that separated some twenty books from the next shelf of books. She went into the path between rows, her heels still announcing her presence to anyone at the tables beyond, but her tapping would've accomplished this as well. That was probably the point of it.

She emerged from the bookcases and paused. Her head tilted slightly toward her right shoulder as she eyed the boy at the furthest table on her left.

Though the room was dimly-lit, the small desk-lamp with its green, glass shade highlighted the boy's features. Solemn, naturally solemn, this young man, his handsome face revealed an innocence too pure to be considered anything but beautiful.

Beneath brows that lifted only in the center where they came slightly together, pale blue eyes looked up at Torrence. His somewhat-plump lips parted so that he could roll his tongue over them before they sealed once more.

He'd been writing, his pen, still in his hand, hovered over his book now. His fingers gripped it as if he had not stopped his writings to look up, but he had.

The boy wore a white button-up. A tie had been loosened but still hung around his neck. Settled over the back of the chair on which he sat was a navy-blue jacket with the same golden shield as the one adorning Todd's jacket.

He swallowed as he looked back down to his notes. His hand finally let loose the pen. It twisted slowly in his palm before he sat it down onto the notebook.

He sat up from where he'd been hunched over his work, eyes looking back up at Torrence as she approached him now.

"Hello, Alex," she said.

"Hey, Tor."

CHAPTER ELEVEN

"We have to stop meeting like this," she said, pulling out the chair next to him. Her body did not sit in the chair as designed. She angled herself to face him, an arm slung over its back, the other resting upon the table. Her knees, always spaced away from each other, took up the small space between their chairs. "People are going to talk."

"Yeah, Dr. Lanchik loves gossip, especially about high school students." He smiled playfully and she chuckled in response.

Reaching between her legs for the seat of the chair, Torrence raised herself away from it slightly to pull it into the table more closely. Then she leaned into Alex, reaching around his body with one arm, resting it now on the back of his chair and using her other to take his pen into her fingers.

He let his arm fall away from the table, no longer acting as a blockade of sorts, and looked over to her. "Geometry," he said.

"I remember this," Torrence replied, tracing the convex polygon Alex had drawn onto the page as his answer for question seven. "I hate math."

"You had a ninety-six on your last report card."

"I didn't say I was bad at it. I said I hated it." She grinned.

"You're not bad at anything," he said, grinning back. "It's really annoying sometimes."

"Shut up. You love me."

"Yeah," he said, the word floating through the air on a small, light-hearted laugh. Then his features leveled. Became more serious. "Yeah, I do."

She smiled, a genuine happiness radiating from her eyes as they moved away from the paper and onto Alex, onto his eyes. Closing the small gap between them, Torrence pressed her lips against his; a soft embrace, easy and light.

Stoic in the seat, only Alex's chin moved as he returned this small affection to properly angle himself for the parting of lips and reclaiming of one mouth by another, but after a moment, he smiled and dropped his head.

"Torrey." He exhaled. Roses bloomed upon his cheeks.

"I know, I know," she said, moving away from him, looking back to the paper. "Studying."

"At least enough that I'm not lying to my parents when they ask what I did after school." An uneasy smile. He felt like a child, but was he technically an adult yet? Not until July in terms of the law, but what about to Torrence?

Torrence was eighteen. She was a year ahead of him in school and about to graduate a semester early. She hadn't selected a college yet, much less a major, and didn't seem to have much direction in terms of a trade, either. But he supposed with a family like hers, a trust fund might kick in soon, if it hadn't since her eighteenth birthday, so she probably had time to decide.

Either way, Torrence would be entering adulthood, the first true steps of it, anyway, and he'd still be in school. It was only for another year, but what would that year be like with Torrence, for Torrence?

No longer would the two have the same daily schedule or routine. Their complaints would not even be the same anymore. Alex would still be very much inside the world Torrence would leave behind in May, and how childish he would surely seem, more so even than now, when he spoke of things like curfews and lying to his parents.

He hoped she would not tire of him, would not grow out of him. Alex saw in Torrence all the things he'd ever desired and all the things he did not know he wanted, but now, having experienced them, could not live without.

He planned to go to college after he graduated from Calvary, and the degree he intended to pursue would require the next four years of his time, but after that, after obtaining a job in some field pertaining to his studies, Alex hoped to marry Torrence.

He wasn't sure she'd go for the idea. One of Torrence's many appeals to Alex, the shy, somewhat-sheltered son of a pastor, was her dislike of anything traditional. While he admired very greatly her refusal to participate in any ideology or institution that might suggest her sex was lesser to his in some way, he was dismayed at the consideration that marriage was most likely among those off-limit endeavors. He loved Torrence. Torrence loved him and unconditionally.

It did not matter to Torrence if he was a perfect student or a perfect son. She didn't care if his morality slipped occasionally, like it had on the night of his seventeenth birthday when she'd snuck into his window at midnight with a cupcake and his eyes raked over her body, which had been dressed in only corduroy shorts and a black tank top. The bare skin of her stomach and her chest were so appealing. He'd apologized to her for the brief fixation of his eyes, and he apologized to God for it, for the way he felt afterward when she straddled him on his chair and chuckled at his confession. Torrence didn't care if Alex had flaws. She loved him as deeply in those moments of B- papers and sinful considerations as she had when he wrote perfect essays and prayed over his meals.

Beyond this, Torrence had a natural strength Alex could only dream of. She was unapologetically herself and she did not care if what she desired was deemed appropriate by her friends, her parents, or society at large. Alex wished he could be that free.

He was not sure what it was about him that she loved, but he was thankful for it, and through that gratitude, he learned to appreciate himself. After all, if he had been different from how he was—even in the ways he'd spent much of his life wishing he could change—she might not feel for him in the way she did now.

In the silence of his contemplations, Torrence moved. She threw her bag onto the table and withdrew from it the chocolate bars.

Breaking off only one of the eighteen pieces of the large bar, Torrence pushed the chocolate toward Alex. "It'll make the math go down easier," she said.

"Thanks," he replied, taking one of the squares.

"Take the whole thing," she said, knowing he wouldn't unless she added, "I've got another here." Then she pulled out the cookie. "This is more substantial though."

"Substantial?" He chuckled.

"Yeah. It'll make you strong." She tapped on his slim arm playfully. "Anyway, it won't hurt. Did you have a big lunch?"

"No."

"Then it definitely won't hurt."

She smiled, offering him the pastry. When he took it, she felt accomplished.

"Thanks, Torrey," he said, his empty stomach appreciative of her, too. He wondered how she always seemed to remedy any problem, no matter how big or how small. He hoped if he couldn't figure a solution to their next year, she would.

In Torrence's mind, there were mere hurdles between the Torrence and Alex who sat in this library eating chocolate over homework and the Torrence and Alex who would head an empire. She wasn't sure what that empire might be, of whom it might be comprised, but she knew it would be a force upon this earth and one that she controlled.

She didn't expect Alex would be king to her queen or some equal title or rank, no. Instead, Torrence would be the figurehead of whatever institution she was building, and Alex would be her consort, respected by the army of followers at her command, but not controlled by him.

Of course, Alex was an unaware of Torrence's plans for a gang of anarchists as she was of his plan for wedding bells, and maybe this ignorance or the inner-workings of one another was part of what kept them so close. After all, Torrence knew it would be most difficult to persuade someone with the moral compass of Alex to suddenly be okay with breaking the law, which was an additional reason for deciding he shouldn't participate in the gang, but merely preside in some small, inconsequential fashion over it.

Neither concern was perhaps the typical worry of someone of their ages—marriage or world domination—but both were committed to the idea that they should remain together, no matter if Torrence disliked weddings or Alex disliked crime.

Together. This was the key point of each imagined future.

Torrence's forearms were on the table, crossed before her. Her body leaned against them, against the table. Her head angled toward the book as Alex wrote, but her eyes fixated unblinkingly to the watch upon Alex's wrist now. A motion of the second hand swift as it circled the face of time with each thud of its minuscule, yet extremely powerful, step. Seconds became minutes, which turned into hours, days, months.

"Do you ever think about it?" Torrence asked lowly, unaware really that she had spoken at all.

Alex looked over to her, his lips parting gently when he saw the fixated stare on her dreamily-absent face. His brows lowered from their rising intrigue at hearing a voice to the understanding that this comment carried weight. "Think about what?" His voice was low and easy, comforting. He released the pencil from his grip and placed his hand on hers.

"Time." Her eyes stared at the watch still, following the

thudding mark of seconds passed. "If we didn't have watches or clocks, calendars to tell us how many days have passed, do you think we'd place such time-constraints on our expectations?"

"We'd still track how many times we watched the sun become the moon, right, even if we didn't have a defined system for doing so. So, we'd probably figure out how many of them meant we were old enough to speak, to learn, to have children, to die." He shrugged, but the gesture was small. He only meant to signify that expectation and age were interlinked regardless of human awareness of them, that the subconscious would piece these things together and compare what one had accomplished to what others of the same seeming-age—for without calendars who could know for certain of ages?—had also done.

Alex exhaled frustration at himself. He wasn't sure he should communicate all these thoughts; he was never certain if he should speak his mind, even in class when he knew the answer to his teachers' questions. It plagued him, this fear of speaking. Torrence feared nothing, but he didn't envy her for it. He adored her.

"Yeah," she said, an unconscious agreement, then she came out of her stupor, and looked up to him. "What if we didn't, though? What if we just let ourselves unfurl into who we're meant to be at our own pace? Regardless of what others were doing, too."

He stared into her eyes longingly for a moment, his face revealing the warmth of his soul and the worry it experienced for such a talk. He looked back to the book briefly, furrowing his brow and tightening his lips. "Is this because you're graduating a semester early?" He looked up to her. "Are you worried about your future?"

"I'm worried about you remaining in it," she said simply.

He licked his lips. A slight nod. "I won't go anywhere if you won't. Metaphorically, I mean. I don't mean stay here if what you want is elsewhere."

As the couple sat over homework, both trying to work but distracted by the proximity of one another, stealing small brushes of fingertips against the backs of hands and sharing endearing looks between the great questions posed and their conjectures, Wesley drew nearer to them.

He was starting to obtain a better understanding of his abilities here, of his consciousness within this moment that was both eternity and nothing—a memory that had passed and therefore could never be real or tangible or provable again.

He could slip in and out of awareness here. He could become focused upon a person or a thought and in that focus become aware of himself, or he could choose to slip inside the memory without consciousness to it and absorb.

Alex took his focus and brought him from the obscurity of scenery. He wanted to know more about this boy, and when he neared him, touching him with his spiritual energy, a shiver ran down the boy's spine.

Torrence chuckled. "Cold?"

"No," he said, slightly embarrassed, then he drew nearer to her. "Maybe. Yes is probably the better answer."

"Agreed," she said, bringing a hand to his back and massaging it gently, as if to keep him warm, but she was enjoying the feel of his body beneath her hand, his humming all because of her and her ministrations. It was a power to provide physical pleasure, was it not? To be the cause of the sensual enjoyment of another. Torrence liked that, especially with Alex.

The boy's focus on her touches allowed Wesley another attempt at his own, and when his hand connected to Alex's shoulder, an array of images and words cascaded before Wesley's eyes and into his ears as one gigantic download in orchestral form.

Alex had been born in July. Alexander Milton. Seventeen. A student at Calvary Christian Academy, an excellent student. His father was a preacher, and his mother a housewife. Alex had no siblings, no cousins. He was expected to follow the laws of God, the rules of his father, and when he did not live up to either expectation, a darkness seemed to overtake the sensations pulled from him here. Guilt-ridden, he seemed, at almost all times. If a paper did not come to him with ease or if he spent too much time on a particular math problem, Alex chastised himself for his stupidity, and when he spent too much time with Torrence, he told himself he was too distracted by lustful intent, even though he rarely considered her in such physical manners.

Alex met Torrence here at the library; a meeting no doubt orchestrated by Torrence, perhaps through Todd somehow, but the desire to see that memory was absent in Wesley, who could not help the tinge of jealous he'd already felt for Alex, and the for the way Torrence seemed to genuinely adore him.

But that was not the way of reality—not in the present time Wesley knew and certainly not in this fluid past. The mind was its own master, not the servant or even partner to the personality. Regardless of how intensely the conscious mind pushed at particular thought or memory or imagined scenario, what laid beneath the surface rose up from the recesses of the subconscious to torment the personality, the soul, the ego; it didn't care for what turmoil it caused, if it wanted to be seen or considered, it forced itself into existence by sharply entering awareness.

Like bursts of lightning came these visions now, obscuring the moving tableau of Torrence and Alex as they spoke about the chaos of time and the inability to truly control one's future.

Wesley sat back into the scenery, absorbed by the mundanity of it, of Torrence studying, of her as a youth, of her as anything but a fearsome leader of men.

He was amazed. Here she was, capable of being, or at least pretending to be, everything he'd wanted her to be with him—a regular person, a partner.

After an hour or so of geometry and world history, Alex shut his books. He looked at Torrence lovingly, admiring her beauty as the physical representation of her soul, of the heart that loved him, calmed him, took care of him without even realizing it.

Torrence, when she returned the admiring gaze, noticed Alex's physicality in less-pure ways, loving the person inside the delicate flesh, yes, but wanting desperately to experience the sensations of his skin upon hers as well.

She was running out of time, honestly. She'd expected for him to have given in to carnal sin by now. They'd been together for over a year. If he wouldn't give in to the most basic, natural, so-called sin, how could she ease him into greater ones? Greater crimes?

He couldn't know that she was involved with what the media—her father included—referred to as License Larceny, especially when her gang of bad boys began the next step of the crimes, which had been so confusing to everyone. What was the point? Why take licenses? Why return wallets? Why had some wallets still contained the victim's license while some hadn't? But the next step would be an escalation, one Torrence knew Alex would not be okay with. In honesty, she wasn't sure if he'd be okay with it after she'd eased him into sin and guilt and illegal activity, but she was certain he wouldn't be now.

She didn't want to go to college or pursue a trade; she wanted this, the true beginning of her life as a leader of violent men. When she graduated, their crimes would graduate. All would intensify. But how could she do this without Alex? She wasn't sure it'd be possible to do it with him, not if he didn't know of it. What a secret to try and keep.

Wesley wondered if he'd dismissed Torrence at some point in their short lives, if she'd revealed all to him and he'd denounced her crimes and her aspirations, or if she'd merely given up on Alex as she seemed to have given up on Wesley. Was there always some innocent soul wrapped in flesh too pretty to destroy? Was creamy skin draped over a pleasing bone structure really the savior of purity when the face of evil gazed into it?

Wesley had met Torrence some years after this moment in her past, and he wondered if there had been another between them now that he realized Todd had been a Jason and a Michael, not a Wesley or a War.

And oh, the thought of War. How his replacement, an angel, somehow made sense now.

"It's five," he said, smiling sadly.

"You okay to walk home?"

"Yeah. Are you?"

"Why wouldn't I be?" She grinned. If he only knew.

He shook his head a bit as he put his books into his bag. "I'll try to text you."

"At least let me know when you make it home."

"Okay," he said, rising from his chair before offering his hand to her. Both knew she didn't need assistance, but both enjoyed the gesture. She took his hand and rose from her chair, stepping aside so that he could push it into the table with his free hand. "Are you hanging out with Todd and the guys tonight?"

She shrugged. "Haven't decided. Blake is back from New York on break. If his parents are drunk, it's so worth a trip to his house. If not, they're, like, the most boring people ever."

Alex nodded. His lips thinned though he tried to smile. "Just be careful wherever you go. You know more robberies have been happening later at night."

"Aw, don't you worry about little old me," she said, leaning in to kiss his cheek. It wasn't Torrence who needed to fear the darkness, but anyone who passed her on the street beneath its concealment who should be afraid of her.

CHAPTER TWELVE

When she parted ways with Alex a few blocks from the library, Wesley followed her home, wondering why she'd given her car to Todd back at her school. He came to understand quickly that her parents were not aware of her car—not of this one, anyway.

They'd gifted her a bright pink Volkswagen, a Bug, and she'd smiled in their faces on her sixteenth birthday, thanking them for it. As he touched the hood of this small car, however, he could see inside Torrence's mind, as well.

She'd hated this car, fucking hated it, who did her parents think she was? Oh, a burst of joy inside the hatred though, for Torrence fooled them as easily as her teachers and the students who overpaid her for drugs, and the men in papers who enacted violence on her behalf, and the men in her bed, and her so-called friends.

Torrence was a master not only of manipulation but of disguising it, too.

Entering the lovely two-story home through a bright red door which had been placed elegantly between four white, Roman pillars, Wesley marveled at this life of hers. It was nothing he'd imagined it to be, though, considering it now, he didn't really know what exactly he'd expected.

"Hi, Torrence," called an elegant, feminine voice from somewhere beyond the grand foyer in which Wesley stood with Torrence.

As she removed her shoes, she rolled her eyes. Scoffing, she exhaled the words, "fuck me," then headed for the room.

Wesley followed the young antichrist into the kitchen, exhaling a small chuckle when Torrence's trodding steps became bounces and the annoyance in her voice turned bubbly.

"Hey, Mom," Torrence said, smiling at the blonde woman.

Wesley regarded her as she chatted with Torrence, listening to the young woman regale her parent with lies of her studious endeavors at school while obviously omitting the truth of her nefarious deals.

The lying made sense, even the change in demeanor, but the concept in itself, that she should have a mother seemed bizarre.

Torrence had been this enigmatic figure in her human life, a controller of everyone and everything around her, and now she was the Son of Lucifer; how could she have had a mother? Strange, but here she was.

She was an attractive woman, blonde and lean. Her breasts seemed unnatural, as did areas of her lovely face, and she wore delicate make-up, a navy dress, and a pearl necklace.

The necklace gave Wesley pause. The single pearl. He reached for it, feeling about its smooth, natural surface, and to his knowledge came its origin. Purchased by Torrence's paternal great-great-grandfather, it had been passed down through sons and daughters on the eve of their respective weddings.

It had been a point of contention for Torrence, who argued against the institution of marriage, suggesting the expensive piece of jewelry should be hers, not in celebration of some man, but in celebration of her 4.0 grade average and full-ride to any college she chose.

It seemed her father took issue with this merely for the fact that Torrence had not chosen a college. Yes, her grades were excellent. Yes, she was intelligent and accomplished. But she was wasting her gifts, or so he believed.

Wesley saw the family of three sitting around an ornately carved table in a dining room, discussing this. Torrence, her hair fallen around her face from a part above her right eye, looked upward through the frame of shining blackness toward her father. The rage within her as evident in her visage as in the feel of her, the feel gifted to Wesley through War's abilities; he did not want to return to the present without it now. It provided what he'd always wanted—a truthful understanding of her, her thoughts, and her concerns.

She swept the look of contempt from her face when her mother glanced over to her. Sitting up more straightly, Torrence lifted her chin and relaxed her expression. Her mother was none the wiser to the change.

Torrence did not want to sit at this dinner table. She complained internally about the festivities of the season—the coming December parties, filling her home with gigantic pine trees and red, velvet bows on every fireplace.

She didn't mind these events, not usually, for they were often filled with businessmen and women of distinction, all of whom praised the blossoming Torrence for her beauty, her wit, her politeness, her accomplishments.

Now it filled her with contempt. She realized, now that it was her final year of high school, and she had no solid plans—none that she could share, anyway—that all their talk, no matter how eloquent or seemingly-intellectual the topic, was surface-level. Topical conversation, sure. Historical talks, yes. But who there wanted to change the world? Who wanted to conquer it?

The one saving grace of this dullness has one been the handsome sons of Torrence's parents' wealthy friends and partners. She'd enjoyed taking them into the bathroom and stripping them down while their parents toasted to their high marks and higher morale. She hadn't liked them, however. She liked witnessing their moral weakness, causing it, all while knowing how principled and honorable their parents downstairs considered them.

Now she only wanted Alex. She'd become entirely enamored with him, this innocent boy of meager means, who denied her advances even as he spoke of his great love for her. A spiritual connection, yes. Not a physical one.

Wesley wanted desperately to meet this Alex, at least to see him—not as a spiritual visitor to him in the year 2006, but in the present as a grown man.

Maybe he could bring Alex back to War when he emerged from the memory realms here. Maybe he could convince War that Alex was the key to Torrence's distraction, and genuinely maybe he was.

But Wesley couldn't meet Alex until he left this realm, if Alex survived the open sky, and how would he even find him in a world with limited technology and half the map wiped out?

He couldn't use Torrence's phone or laptop here in 2006 to find Alex's address and go there in the present. He was a voyeur here. Barely even conscious to it. He seemed to blend in with the surroundings of the place, a human spirit in the same positioning as a lamp in the far-off corner of a room or a photo upon the wall opposite the people within the room.

He wondered how Torrence had come to meet Alex, this shy, Christian boy, who did not even go to the same school as she did, but War's powers seemed to pull the answer from the atmosphere of this realm, and a single word came into his mind: Todd.

Todd introduced them? He thought they did not know one another from what he'd said earlier. Wesley's unintentional focus pushed his vision to a place beyond this one, but only for a brief moment. His features, ornamented with the pensive expression of his considerations and his confusion, twisted as he looked about the dining room. It was before him now, yes, but he was not inside it. It started to blur somewhat now, the edges of reality seeming to peel back so that the room in which he stood seemed to flicker.

Chaotic visions replaced at random the room—images of Todd in various positions, a smile as he looked over his shoulder or a nervous shaking of the head as he fiddled with his shoestring. Then the images began to move. They were not full memories, but instances within the memories, small glimpses into already-discovered pasts, like Torrence in the cemetery with him when they'd first met, but now he was lying on the ground, his brown hair falling into the dirt upon his best friend's recently-dug grave as Torrence offered her body in comfort to her new, bereaved friend. As she moved against him, she leaned down, her tongue swiping over her teeth then her lips, her hand taking fistfuls of the fresh dirt of the grave-site.

So Wesley had not been the only one with whom shed shared such disturbing intimacies, but at least he recognized through energetic waves within the fleeting vision that Torrence only offered Todd friendship here, that this coming together was one of manipulation, of gain. It ensured Todd would always associate Torrence with Perry, the best friend and his replacement, but in a far more intimate manner, rending this new companionship by nature of its opening night the closer one. At least in the mind of a naive and lonely young man.

Another flash of memory, a flash of vision or of reality, Wesley was unsure, and he was standing again in the home of young Torrence, only now she moved away from the dining table.

Oh, just when he'd thought he'd figured out these abilities here, he seemed to know nothing of them. But his focus, he realized, his intention was what crafted reality here.

Could he see Alex? Future Alex, he meant. Present Alex, whatever. Focus.

His mind seemed to vibrate at this. He looked up, and the corners of the room peeled back, it flickered to and from one memory to another, the dance of a candle flame as it moved from golden glow to reddened one, until it became more fully a parking lot.

Torrence sat in the parking lot of the Christian Academy in her black car, awaiting Todd.

She eyed the boys who left the building and made their way toward the buses, which were lined up in three rows perpendicular to where the cars, along with that of Torrence, sat in waiting.

Torrence always went to the schools or hang-outs of her followers early. Was always looking for the next potential gang-member, the next lost soul in need of a savior.

Instead, she saw Alex.

There were plenty of boys here, boys who had been indoctrinated and needed only a replacement of ideals to be devoted to Torrence, boys who, like Perry, wanted things their parents didn't want for them, things Torrence would allow them to have or experience or be. But Alex, he shone through the others for no reason in particular.

His head was down, eyes fixated onto a small book, too small to be a textbook. Nothing exceptional about his stride, which was somewhat faster than necessary, but not rushed or worried.

From this distance, Torrence could not see the level of his beauty, but knew through the magnetism of his simple existence here that it had to have been immense.

Where the sun merely shone upon the other boys, it reflected off of him, illuminating the golden undertones of his dirty-blond hair. It was as if the clouds had opened just above him, a beacon shining upon him, or perhaps from him. Maybe, Torrence considered as she watched in awe of his little steps and ignorance to all those around him, he was the source of the illumination, not the subject of it.

As Todd opened the door to Torrence's car and slipped into its passenger's seat, Torrence stared out the windshield.

"Hey," he said, as he closed the door.

"Who is that?" came her reply.

"Which one?"

"The one in the jacket," Torrence said, rolling her eyes and chuckling. "Dirty-blond hair. In front of the guy in the sunglasses."

Todd lifted his chin, eyeing carefully the boys were loading onto the front bus in the middle row. "You don't mean Alex, do you?" He looked over to her, amusement dancing throughout his features. "The one reading the Bible?"

Torrence looked back toward the boys, watching Alex as he climbed the stairs onto the bus, gripping the railing with one hand, the other still holding the open book.

"Is that what that is?" She raised a brow, looking back to Todd.

"You can't get Alex," he said.

"Is that so?" A challenge. She liked that.

"No, you don't get it," he said, chuckling as Torrence turned on her car and began to drive. "His dad's Pastor Milton over at the Baptist church on Second. Really strict religious upbringing. Like, strict. He's reading the Bible on his ride home." Todd laughed now. "He doesn't really have friends. I don't know if he's allowed to."

"Hmm."

"Good luck," Todd said, smiling as he shook his head and looked out the window.

Wesley watched them drive away, left standing in the parking lot. He looked over to the buses and watched the one with Alex pull away when the final bus of the first row had left the school.

So this was how Torrence became aware of Alex, of his name. But it was not how she met him.

That happened twelve days later—her desire for the boy growing each day she spent in watch, studying him—that she did not take the time she typically assigned to her recon.

She and Todd followed Alex's bus that day, locating easily his home in this manner, then she did the same the next day, and the next.

After a week, she deduced that Tuesdays and Wednesdays were library days after school, Saturday mornings were given to physical fitness while the afternoons were filled with Bible studies—taught by Alex to the children of the his father's parishioners—and Sundays of course, were assigned to his father's church.

Alex helped repair the ceiling when the boards splintered or rotted. He painted the siding when needed, cleaned the steps and the handrails. Ensured the four small windows were perfectly clean.

Torrence watched Alex during his father's sermon. Alex, sitting in the front row on the left, followed along in the Bible when his father quoted from it. Though he slouched over the book, he sat in pristine solemnity. The swoop of his hair as the slight curl of it rolled across his forehead and toward his left ear, the height of his cheekbone revealed by the sun shining through his perfectly-cleaned windows, slowly-blinking lashes concealing then revealing the lovely hue of teal in his irises, and the white, pin-striped button-up with its sleeves rolled just beneath his elbows, his fingers gently pressing into the lines of verse as he read them, heard them, felt them.

What a vision.

Torrence, who sat across the aisle two pews back, wore a slim black dress that fit her form perfectly until it reached her hips, where it flowed loosely outward to her knees. A small cork board heel with black, satin ties adorned her ankles with lovely bows. Her mother's pearl around her neck along with her usual strand of diamonds. Only her bangs fell into her face, curled slightly, the fronts of her hair, which had been parted on the left side, were pinned back elegantly by bobby-pins that matched the color of her hair.

She knew she was attractive, and she knew how to don the mask and costume of a refined young lady. And she knew this would be important to become close to Alex, who didn't seem to seek the rebellion so many of his classmates desired.

She couldn't wait any longer. She had to have him, his purity, his commitment to his God, his parents, his faith. She wanted that dedication. She needed it.

Removing himself from the obscurity of the back row, Wesley moved down the center aisle toward Torrence when the sermon concluded.

She stood, exiting the pew but not turning toward the door. Instead, she moved forward, her eyes on Alex as he remained there in the first row, a pen now in his hand, taking notes on a small pad as he read from the Bible.

He didn't look up from his work, even as Torrence's small heels clicked against the wooden floor of the humble church. Nearing him, Torrence removed her eyes from him, a plan in this, of course, but what?

When she neared the front row, she placed her hand on the curving back of the pew, prompting, finally, Alex's eyes to leave the book and glance up to her. A double-take. The glance became a gaze. He stared up to Torrence in awe, as everyone around her seemed to, for she was beautiful, yes, but elegant in a way the girls and parishioners of this small church were not.

She carried herself the way some of the boys at his school carried themselves—the boys dubbed Elites for the wealth of their families. Her chin was almost parallel to the floor, only lifted too far to be straightforward. Shoulders back, long dark hair spilling into the long dark sleeves.

Alex's lips parted as she approached the podium, her hands came together then, folding into themselves.

"Pastor Milton?" she spoke gently.

"Yes?" He turned, head tilting slightly. "Oh. You're the journalist's child, aren't you? Breslin?"

She nodded. "Yes, sir. I'm Torrence."

"Hello, Torrence," he said, extending his hand to her. As she shook it, he introduced his wife, Alex's mother, and the women shook hands, too. "What can we do for you?"

"I, um, honestly am having a crisis of faith, perhaps. I can't go to priests at our church…It's because of our church, I suppose."

"You're catholic?" he asked, noticing the word 'priest'.

She nodded, aware of the difference between the sects of Christianity, specifically the spectacle of Catholicism, their stained-glass windows and body of Christs, and the desire for those who had initially broken away from the religion to become Baptists and the like to turn away from the supposed idolatry of such things and focus instead on the word of God, instead of the materialism of alters and grand cathedrals.

"I worry that I'm sinning by giving confession. That we should not pray but to God through Christ. So why am I coming to a man to ask his forgiveness? Why am I praying to Mary or to Saints? I shouldn't, right? I look around the church at the windows and the red carpeting, the ornate robes of the priest, the display of it all, and I think of the golden calf. If I am to celebrate God, why am I participating in so much excess, and supposedly in the celebration of Him?"

From her peripheral, Torrence noticed Alex's hands, the Bible closing within them, his focus palpable upon her now.

"We all celebrate God in our own ways," Pastor Milton said, trying to remain respectful. "But I agree with your concerns, as a Baptist, of course, which is why we honor God the way we do. You'll notice no grandeur here," he said, eyeing her necklaces briefly, "save for the glory of the word, of course."

"Of course," she agreed.

"You are welcome here," he said, "if Sundays seem better spent in our humble church than in a more fantastical one."

"Thank you," she said, smiling. "Thank you for your time,

too."

"Of course. It's why I'm here."

She nodded, then smiled to Mrs. Milton. As she turned, she was sure to connect to Alex, to gaze directly into his eyes and offer him a gentle smile, too, which he returned.

She made her way to the exit, then. Two more days. Two days, then Alex would walk from Calvary Academy to the public library. And Torrence, well, she would be there, too.

The next day, Torrence took Todd and two other boys into the woods. Through overgrown bushes and falling trees they moved on barely-visible paths. Eventually the came to an old building, run-down and moss-covered. Climbing the stairs that led to its door, Todd went first, opening the door for Torrence, then the others followed these two.

The Hideout, they called this place, found by Torrence and Perry some time ago when they slipped away into the woods to find some poetic inspiration away from the bustling towns and strict, stuffy nature of the place, filled with its academies and churches and tall, towering buildings.

Clean inside, it appeared the old wooden floors had been scrubbed and shined. Long, red rugs had been strategically placed upon the refreshed wood so that only an outline of the floor was visible near the walls and surrounding the coffee table.

So, Wesley thought, She has always blended this lush velvet and smooth silk or satin with the most unsavory of places—whether it be Hell or some old, abandoned home.

Todd thrust himself playfully upon a couch against the back wall, pulling into him one of the pillows, which were various shades of red and black.

Wesley moved against the couch, placing his hand upon it and asking War's abilities to explain how the hell she'd gotten this place.

The answer was simple enough: She stumbled onto it during

a walk through the woods with Perry, a walk of poetics and nature, of taking their shoes off and running through the small, rocky stream barefoot.

In her encouragement of Perry's personal pursuits, Torrence had meant to create a devotee. But too much self-esteem, she learned upon his death, was not good for a follower. It was ultimately what made her pursue shyer targets if the objects of her intrigue were not easily won by promises of power or violence, beneath that of her own, of course.

When the pair of newfound friends stumbled upon the home, both felt an overwhelming desire for it. It represented to each of them a manifestation of their greatest desires—for Torrence, it was a hideout, a place to bring her boys for parties and drug induced blood oaths before turning it into a house of more horrific endeavors, and for Perry, it was the home he'd never had; the home where he could lie down with his books and be free to explore them for pleasure instead of merely for knowledge of engineering or geometry.

Each of them—just sixteen at the time—used their substantial allowances to clean and furnish the home, eventually buying a futon to be assembled within the home, after dragging the contents of its box piece-by-piece through the woods, and covering it with a great, velvet couch-shaped cover.

Coming back to the room where Torrence and her first gang piled into the living room, Wesley looked at Todd upon the couch, wondering if the young man knew of his best friend's parts in creating the atmosphere of the room in which he sat so comfortably. He assumed, however, that he did not.

An additional young man came into the house, then. The other boys greeted him warmly and by name. Blake.

A tall, somewhat-thin boy, Blake had blond hair, gelled back and fixed but in some way that seemed effortless and not-on-purpose. A singular curl always seemed to plague him, falling onto his forehead though he constantly pushed it back, and his ears—his right ear in particular—seemed too large for his head, but only at certain angles. His muscles were firm but not too large to command attention away from his face, which was lined by a strong jawline and adorned with an utterly dazzling smile.

With his impressive form came an equally impressive aura; there was something about him that separated him from the others here in this strange little home of Torrence and company. A confidence, perhaps, not often seen in the men of Torrence, both past and present, for they were either clean and submissive or dirty and unruly. He seemed to be both somehow and neither.

As he entered the room, he put his hands into the pockets of gray slacks. The pants were not anything exceptional or fancy, but he did not seem ordinary enough for jeans.

When Torrence emerged from beneath an archway in the back, left corner of the room, Blake's handsome, stoic and controlled face lightened. A goofiness seemed to enter into his features as he smiled fondly at her.

"Mistress," he said, chuckling a bit. The small laugh like honey rolling from lips more so than a breath expelled from them.

"Young Master Blake," she replied as playfully, moving toward a tall, rectangular stand against the wall and placing a black lockbox upon it.

He moved behind her as she opened it, wrapping his arms around her waist and resting his chin upon her shoulder. "What presents today?"

"I should ask you the same."

"Oh, you don't receive gifts," he replied as he moved away from her. Taking his wallet from his pocket, he withdrew two small cards—school IDs from a private school, but not a Christian one. He repositioned himself against Torrence and placed the IDs before her. "Only offerings."

She eyed them briefly, then nodded to the wall before them. Above the table were similar ID cards. One was Todd's. Another belonged to one of the boys who'd entered with Torrence, a boy named Daniel. Another was a license belonging to another in the room, Don. But these cards were on the left side of red string. Four others were on the right of it.

Blake moved away from Torrence and pinned these two above the string in its center.

Pulling a few baggies from the box, Torrence never looked up to the IDs. "What do we have there?"

"Well, David's the first one. He graduated last year, so he's out of school. His parents disowned him. He works out at the factory on 51. We can expand with him." Blake's hands went back into his pockets. Nothing psychological. Nothing hidden. It was just the way he stood, to be positioned aesthetically, it seemed, as he spoke, staging his body as only a model knew how. "He wants to join up. He's got a record, so I don't think much will be a shock if we bring him straight in. He asked me about you after the Halloween party at Mipsy's. I told him you weren't the type of girl who was interested in much except conquering the world one day, and he liked that. I made it clear relationships aren't your thing when it comes to the guys who hang out here."

Todd laughed, and Blake and Torrence looked back to him. "She's got her eye on a preacher's son," Todd explained. "I've never seen her look at any of us the way she looks at him."

"Well, you might want to keep that quiet," Blake said to Torrence. "You know most of what gets guys into the game is how they worship you. A boyfriend could deter some of that."

"I think you guys are getting ahead of yourselves," Torrence said. Finally she looked up to IDs, so Wesley followed suit. He recognized David in his ID photo as the boy who entered Torrence's car some year or so into the future from this moment—the one who'd committed himself to her in blood. Whatever test Torrence gave these men, he must have passed it. "Who's the other one?"

"Ah, you'll like this. His name is Tom. He graduates this year, too, but his mother is a pharmacist." Blake's brow arched over a gleaming eye.

"He's in for sure," Torrence said. "What's he like?"

"Typical rich kid," Blake said.

"So he's like you." She teased.

"Funny."

Torrence turned him and put her arms around his waist, resting her head against his chest and listening purposefully to his beating heart. "What am I going to do without you next year?"

"We'll still see each other during breaks, and you can always come visit me on the weekends. I'm sure New York's got plenty of people we can recruit. Think about it. You'll graduate next year, building your boys here up, starting the groundwork for more up there with me. If you want to expand, if you really want to fight the pretension of our lives, we can do it everywhere. Not just here."

Torrence grinned as she released Blake. Of course she'd do it everywhere. Of course that had always been the plan with Blake as soon as she realized the prior spring that he planned to go to the same college in a different state that his mother had attended. But she knew with people like Blake that it was better to allow them their egos; he had to think expanding her vision was his idea to keep him fully committed to the ideal, especially when she wouldn't be so near to him to keep him reminded of it.

Todd smiled up to her when she released Blake, winking at her second-in-command there on the couch. Oh, Wesley realized, when he gets back to the present, Todd will be his greatest rival for position in the hierarchy, for both men enjoy comfortably their title as Torrence's favorite.

Torrence handed a few of the baggies each to her boys, save for Todd. She instructed them to spend the remainder of the week making friends, connections, go to parties on the weekend, sell the drugs if no potentials arise, give them out to promising recruits while praising this enigmatic figurehead, Torrence, as they told tales of stealing from the rich, rebelling against parents and teachers, and any other such intrigues to the immature minds who needed a passion and a purpose.

When the gang dispersed, Torrence, Todd, and Blake remained. They shared a bottle of wine and listened to heavy music, discussing their intentions and how they aligned or did not align with the life their families had always planned for them.

It was here Torrence first revealed the true purpose of her plans. She rolled the wine about the pristine glass, staring at it as it settled and commenting on its legs. Her eyes moved up to the boys now, who sat across from her in their small, somewhat-triangle upon the plush rugs. She wanted power. She did not know precisely why. But she liked being the boss of these men, these boys. She liked that their physical strength was superior to hers, but that her superior wit conquered. The idea that brains mattered more than brawn, she liked that, too. She wanted to rule a world of ideas and conceptualists. She wanted an army, yes, but not a mindless one.

She didn't mind destroying those without faith in her—when that time came. She realized that this would not happen for her as a seventeen-year-old, as a twenty-year-old, as a twenty-five-year old. She knew she needed experience, the knowledge that came from practicality when one had only big ideas, and control over herself was necessary before true control over others could be accomplished.

And where did they fit into this plan, both boys wondered. But Torrence assured them both that no matter how many came and went, her commitment to them was as great as theirs to her.

But what of Alex, Todd wanted to know. Torrence quelled the worry. Alex was not a part of this. Alex was not a part of a plan. Alex was a desire not of Torrence the Leader, but of Torrence the person. She hadn't realized then that some time in the future, these two pieces of her—the persona and the personality—would become one and the same.

The following day was a day for the library for young Alex.

Alex, who was just sixteen at this time, left the safety of Calvary for the safety of the library. Both places—places of study—offered very little opportunity for temptation. Or at least they should not have.

When he entered the library, he and Dr. Lanchik shared the same warm greeting they always had on Tuesdays and Wednesdays. It had been a simple walk to this simple place, a simple interaction. Planned ahead was a simple afternoon among his books. But Alex desired very little beyond this simplicity. He hadn't been exposed to much else, and thusly was content with the manner of his existence. Go to school, pray, learn. What else was there? What else could there be?

He went downstairs to the desks positioned behind the rows of nonfiction and history, though Alex had always considered history as fictional as it was real. Yes, events happened. Certain, undeniable outcomes occurred. But the sources of the information—the authors, the books, the historians, the eye-witnesses—well, they had all been human.

Alex learned very early on, most obviously in his English classes, that personal experience and even preference altered one's perception not only of another person, but of their intentions. How could he have read the same thirty-two pages of a novel and come to class the next day with an entirely different understanding of what the author had meant within the text than any of the other boys in class who were brave enough to raise their hands and express to their teacher, in front of the others, their own analyzation of the text?

Some of the boys picked up on things—relationship matters, mostly—that Alex would have never considered. Most of it had been implied, but what did that matter? Everything a person did or thought or believed came from some implication about their past or their experience if they didn't offer freely their reasonings.

The same could be said for the men who wrote history, could it not?

Entire armies had believed in a singular notion that waged war upon the world, so Alex saw no difference in the small-scale biases of his reading a text and the vastly expansive biases of powerful leaders, especially when their ego was stroked by what they'd deemed a triumph over others.

This concept, exerting one's will over another, had always baffled Alex. Its purpose alluded him, no matter how much time he spent contemplating it. He often wondered what it was within his own experience that swayed his views in such a way, and what could have happened to him instead that might have made violent takeovers seem logical.

He couldn't imagine the cruelty that must have been made to seem so ordinary in order to convince someone that another's will or safety or even life did not matter more than one's ideal. Strange, yes, but very sad, too.

When he rounded the last row of the grand bookcases, Alex paused. Another person was in the downstairs area of the library with him today, which was unusual. She didn't turn to look at him, even though his dress-shoes clacked against the floor with each step. Surely, she'd heard him pause there when her mere presence startled him, but she still made no movement, not save for her finger, which continued to trace across the bottom of the textbooks.

Pulled from his contemplations, Alex moved to the right-hand seat at the far left table in an unusual manner. His eyes were fixed to a point here in reality, his mind no longer contemplating broader concepts of the human condition, but now seeking the answers to much more specific questions. Silly ones, he told him, for this girl had long, black hair and painted nails, just as the girl he'd seen in his father's church had. Could it be the same girl? Surely a lot of girls wore their in this manner and with this same color, and no doubt plenty of girls, though not many in his father's congregation, painted their nails.

Television was not something Alex was afforded often, not since he'd outgrown those line-ups about wholesome families and teenaged witches on ABC's TGIF Friday nights in the 90's, but sometimes he used computer programs he really didn't understand beyond their basic use to download bootlegged versions of other programs, movies. They were fuzzy sometimes. Most of the time they shook within the screen and gave him quite the headache. Other times, the viewer of these downloads might see a tiny silhouette emerge from the blackness beneath the recorded film, a movie patron leaving his or her seat to use the restroom or grab a refill of their pop, and the person recording this film on a small, handheld camera could not avoid capturing their exit without obscuring further the film. It always gave Alex a chuckle, though it did break the experience of whatever story he was watching.

The point of this consideration, this small array of memory, was that this girl reminded him of those girls, of those women, the ones on the screen. She looked like Sandra Bullock in Miss Congeniality with her dark hair and makeup, and there was a confidence within her stance, her walk that made her seem as Kristie Swanson did in Buffy the Vampire Slayer; a movie he always enjoyed more than its television counterpart, though he'd only been able to download a few of its episodes.

He made a mental note not to mention any of this to her, should they ever find occasion to speak. He realized the boys at his school, even the ones sent there for religious purposes instead of prestigious ones, had a much more practical experience with the opposite gender than he had. He knew enough of their lives to know this made him somewhat odd, and the last thing he wanted this girl to think about him was that he was strange, though he did not know why.

Carefully he placed his bag upon the table, not wanting to create a sound that might startle her. He removed his books as cautiously, placing them down before his seat slowly, his eyes still on her as her fingers paused.

Her pointer finger tapped at the base of one of the old books, its light-blue binding frayed into strings of uneven lengths. When she removed it from the shelf, she turned. Her eyes finally lit onto him, but with the ease of someone who'd known him, who'd been expecting him. It was somewhat disconcerting, but he controlled his expression enough that his reaction was only a slight turn of his head.

"Oh," she said, shifting as if she'd meant to take a step but decided against it. "Hi." She smiled.

"Hi," he replied shyly then considered it too curt. He added, "How are you?"

Her brows knitted slightly. "Haven't I seen you…?"

"At church, yes." He looked away bashfully as soon as the confirmation left his mouth. How eager he must have seemed, and how ridiculous for remembering so clearly.

Torrence smiled at this, her eyes falling to his jacket and nodding toward it. "You go to Calvary?"

Alex looked down to the gold shield on his jacket, then back up to her. He smiled and nodded. "Yes."

"I knew a boy who went there," she said, walking to the same desk and setting the book down at the seat across from the one he seemed to have selected as his own.

"Knew?" Alex asked without thinking, his eyes looking at the book she'd chosen, Histories of the World's Religions, as she opened it. He looked back up to her.

"He died," she said, her eyes on the pages of the book.

"Oh," he said, embarrassed now. "I'm sorry. I didn't think—. I'm so sorry."

"It's okay," she said, sitting down in the seat when she found the chapter she wanted.

Silently, and in embarrassment, he sat down now, too. His eyes stole teeny glances of her, scanning her features for signs of her discomfort. He felt guilty for any, perceptible or not, he might have caused, but he did not know what to say to ease it.

When he settled into the chair, she looked up to him from her downcast head. "Did you know Perry Wesberg?"

"Yeah," he said, a bit dazed by the connection of their eyes—hers, enigmatic; so ordinary, they were eyes shaped and colored as anyone's eyes, but something different dwelled within them, within her, exuding itself accidentally through these portals through which her mind absorbed and understood the world around her. Deep and pensive, but revealing nothing. "I mean, no, not really." He shook his head slightly, correcting himself. "I mean, everyone knew Perry. He just had that personality, you know? He always spoke up in class, especially in English class. His loss is obvious even for those of us who only knew him from afar. I can't imagine what it must be like for someone who knew him more closely."

"He had a lot of plans," she said. "He would've done great things. Certainly would've been a part of something great."

"Yeah, he was charming and really intelligent. Could've been a doctor or something easily."

"That's not what I meant," she said, looking up to him and smiling a bit.

"Then…what did you mean?"

"I don't know what it is yet," she said, looking back to the book. "I only know it will change the world."

"So it's something that doesn't exist yet?"

"Oh, it exists. Just not in its final form."

"Which is…?"

"You have to be initiated to find out," she said.

"You're messing with me, aren't you?"

She shrugged, smiling a bit. "You all-boys boys can be fun to play with sometimes."

He nodded, smiling in return though he wasn't sure what she meant. He didn't figure he was supposed to. "Did you…" he exhaled a nervous half-laugh. "Never mind. I'm sorry."

"Go ahead. Ask." She looked up completely now, not just with her eyes, but with her head and face too.

"People said he had a…a girlfriend. He wouldn't show up to newspaper meetings or yearbook. He started writing his own poetry, and it was beautiful but it was…odd, too. Like he was talking about a person who wasn't exactly a person. She seemed more like an idea. I always think ideas are as real to the one who thinks them as their arms are real, but to everyone else, an idea is just that; it's intangible and unseen and unheard, and unless the thinker does a tremendous job of explaining it, it remains unfelt as well. But I could feel the things he wrote. He was great at expressing them." He looked down, his fingers coming to his eyebrow and rubbing at it slightly. "I wish I had told him that. I don't know."

Torrence allowed him a moment of contemplation at this. After some time, his knitted brows loosened and the thin grimace upon his lips leveled out. He looked back up to her. "Were you that girl? The girlfriend? The one he was writing about?"

"No," she said. "I wasn't his girlfriend."

"But…you were the one he wrote about?"

She blinked up to him, her lids lifting slowly to reveal her eyes, the assertion that naturally resided within their blue irises. A fleeting second of this knowing expression, this darkness that took her lovely face from beautiful to awe-inspiring. Powerful. Radiant, yes, but not delicate.

"I don't know," she said, this authority slipping from her face, replaced by a looser expression, though it remained phlegmatic. "I never read his poetry." Her eyes went back to the book.

Alex drew his lower lip into his teeth. He picked up one of his pencils and began to write in his notebook.

Torrence blinked up enough to notice the action, but did not want to linger. She had to know what he was doing, but couldn't let him see her intrigue. Not yet.

When he finished, he ripped the paper from his notebook. He folded it, took it into his finger and thumb and offered it to her.

She looked up at it, then to him.

"It's one of them."

"You memorized it?"

"Not on purpose," he said. "I liked it more than the others, so I read it a few times."

"A few." She chuckled, reaching for the paper. He moved his hand closer to meet her hand; his wrist, in the extension of his arm, slipped out of the jacket and out of his shirt-sleeve.

Her brows furrowed at his skin there. In his father's church, it had been the same delicious shade of flesh as that of his hand, his face, his neck. Now it appeared somewhat discolored. Dirty, perhaps.

When Alex's eyes followed the path of hers, he withdrew. "I didn't mean to overstep," he said. "I just don't think I've ever seen someone who could've made the subject of his poetry seem real before."

She eyed him now, looking back to the piece of paper. "You're saying I seem like the person he's describing."

Alex hadn't realized this implication of his words, not until she'd made it clear. Blood rushed to his cheeks, but why go back now? What could be said that would undo it?

"You seem like the idea," he said. "Yes."

"Well, I'm not an idea," she said, reaching across the table to take the piece of paper. Unfolding it, she looked up to Alex from behind it. "I'm Torrence."

He smiled. "Alex."

She nodded, then looked down to the paper, pretending this was the first time she'd ever read Perry's words, pretending she'd never before heard herself referred to as a concept, a symbol, or by the term Most Feverish Fantasy of Unlawful Freedom.

CHAPTER THIRTEEN

Wesley watched Torrence spend more time with Alex at the library. She'd become his study-buddy, this girl with varying course-loads from his own. He thought the idea of learning things at a grade-level above his was wise, and that learning the works of another school, the works he may not learn in his own junior year because of the differing curriculums, would only enhance his knowledge base. It might also broaden his horizons, he thought. See, he told himself, There are plenty of reasons to want to spend time with her, reasons that extend far beyond 'she's smart' and 'she's pretty' and 'she is perfect'.

Torrence held similar opinions of Alex. He was undeniably handsome. He was a thinker, deep and curious. So smart. So attractive in body and in mind. His capacity for devotion to another—God, sure. His parents, why not?—and his submission to whatever their respective, though supposedly-aligned, will were among his most attractive qualities.

The difference between their opinions was most evident, however, in the denial of their source.

Torrence had no problem admitting to herself that she desired Alex. She did not care that some of those desires could've been deemed sinful. To whom should she answer? Her parents? That was laughable. God? Funnier, still.

Eventually she had no issue revealing her desires to Alex himself, catching him off-guard, of course, in her boldness, but ultimately the obvious confession brought him great joy.

He wanted her, too. He felt silly saying it out loud that way. Surely there was a better way to have worded it, but he didn't consider his speech before he'd spoken it.

It was one of his favorite things about being with Torrence—she made him into someone else, someone less careful or less pensive, someone who simply felt things and had no issues in expressing those feelings. Torrence did not judge him, no matter what he said.

As the weeks seemed to rush by Wesley in fits of consciousness. With no rhyme or reason, at least one that he could deter, some memories flickered in-and-out of his mind like bursts of lightning while others unfurled in real-time, as blooming flowers facing the end of summer might attempt to rush to the end of its season in vain; trapped by the constructs of existence, of life, of the evolution of an ever-turning world.

There were glimpses into Alex's experience with Torrence, his getting to know her. There were flickers of memories Torrence hadn't been a part of, but was mentioned within.

When Alex told his parents that he had met a girl at the library, that in their studying together, he'd developed a very deep, but very spiritual affection for her, Wesley saw the worry on their faces, a worry that deepened when he'd told them it was Torrence, the girl who'd come into their church for guidance only a month prior, the girl who seemed placed by divine will before Alex over and over again.

Wesley chuckled at the accuracy of young Alex. A divine will had set her before him, yes. But not the one he'd thought.

Regardless of the length of these passing moments, one thing was always evident within them: Torrence and Alex shared an undeniable love for one another. Even when they disagreed on philosophy or its practice, a respect of intellect and emotion superseded any thoughts that might paint the other negatively.

Torrence did not lash out at Alex as she often did with Wesley. Never once did he see her lay a hand on him in the expression of anything but care.

She'd pet his hair when she pushed it from his forehead, run her fingers along his cheekbone before kissing it. Wesley had never seen such tenderness from Torrence, even when she was pursuing carnal pleasures, even when she was hoping to achieve that great, physical enjoyment with Alex.

Though she'd teasingly called him a prude when he refused to deepen their kisses or playfully rolled her eyes when his explanations bordered on Biblical sermons, Alex exuded love for Torrence. It was obvious in every small memory Wesley saw of him, even the ones where he'd only been thinking of Torrence.

She seemed another person with Alex, but Wesley knew how Torrence was. If sweetness and purity would win Alex, Torrence would embody that. At least at first.

She'd been sweet to Wesley at the start, hadn't she? But Wesley had been introduced to violent Torrence. There was no need for an adjustment period. No time for naive musings about futures and marriage.

He realized then, as he sat himself down inside a memory, slowing it merely by focusing upon it, that he enjoyed these glimpses into Torrence's past as much as he hated them. He could watch Torrence as she spoke sweetly to Alex, innocent Alex who did not have to sleep with Torrence or kill for her to win her trust and her affection, and imagine what it might have been like to be him in those moments. But quickly came the reminder that he was not Alex, and the vicarious enjoyment turned into intense hatred.

Wesley purposely searched their life together for signs of disagreement and found only a few, most of the same nature, one outstanding.

An evening slowed before him in a hotel room, the flickering light outside the dingy window painted Torrence's features in red. A celebration, their year anniversary. An offered sip of champagne taken after multiple attempts. Passionate kisses deepening further than any embrace shared between them before.

Alex wanted to give in. The animalism that existed inside all humans was, of course, present within him. But logic was there, too, was it not? And it had to conquer by its nature the very nature of man.

He wanted her, yes. He could admit that finally without feeling guilty, for it had been Torrence who quelled his worry when he presented it, assuring him that God would not punish him for his body's desire to procreate. She wanted to roll her eyes at her words, but she knew they were what Alex needed, and she loved being the one to provide to Alex what he needed.

A need for him and his affection is what she said burned within her. A need for his love, yes, his kisses, his hands upon her in a way he'd never laid them on anyone. She needed it.

He did not return the sentiment entirely. 'Need' was one word. 'Want' was something different, and Alex wanted Torrence in this way, as shameful as it was, but not necessarily for how it might feel; it was what the act might represent.

To the congregation, intercourse was an act shared only by husband and wife and only for procreation. To the boys at school, getting laid was the ultimate goal of any relationship, however short or long, with a girl. But to Torrence, carnal passion was the manifestation of spiritual bond—the intangible concept of love made physical.

Alex liked that. He liked the idea of expressing in a very provable manner his affections for her. He loved her. He wanted to express that love for her in this way, for it was the only way he hadn't yet.

But wanting something did not make it right.

The odd instance of a fight began in this same fashion. Torrence atop him, her hands running over any exposed flesh—that of his face, his neck, his hands—pushing with her touch when her hips had been blocked by his hands and their gentle urging away from his groin.

He moved to stand, to leave as always when their desires did not align. As he threw his jacket around his back to slip on the sleeves, the raising of his arms pulled at his shirt, revealing the flesh Torrence so desired, even this small glance.

Her brows furrowed at the sight of it, however, for a flash of a red seemed visible before his jacket was on and the white shirt covered his back again.

She moved against him quickly, grabbing at his shirt and attempting to push it upward.

"Tor," he said in a shock, turning toward her, his head and eyes falling to his back and his coat before he looked up to her. "What are you doing?"

"What is that?" she asked quickly.

"What?" he asked, jerking his right shoulder backward as she reached for that side of his shirt. "Stop. What are you doing?"

"What is on your back, Alex?"

"Nothing." He made for the door, but it was a difficult task, for he'd have to turn his back to her, unguarded. "Stop, Torrey. Please."

"Did you get into a fight?"

"No," he said, taking her wrists gently into his hands as she reached again for him.

"Did someone beat you up, then? What happened?"

"It's nothing. It's fine. I'm okay, okay?"

She stared into his eyes, felt their pleading as much as she'd seen it. "I won't let anyone hurt you," she said. "Tell me who did it, and I'll—."

"Thank you, Torrey," he said, bowing to kiss her knuckles as he raised her hands. "But I promise you it's okay. Can we please forget it? Please."

She nodded, but it wasn't forgotten.

As he left the memories, Wesley found himself again in 2006 in Torrence's home. Scrubbing his hands over his face, he sat back into a chair that belonged to her vanity—a grand, wooden piece of furniture with a body-length mirror between its drawers.

He watched Torrence as she laid on her bed. Propped up on her elbows, she read through an old book, a hand holding a highlighter, the other twisting her hair between her fingers.

She appeared here as any eighteen-year-old, sitting in her room, studying quietly. But Torrence harbored many secrets, dark ones. She was anything but an ordinary teenager.

CHAPTER FOURTEEN

Wesley did not realize that the spirit slept, but suddenly he found himself awakening. He was not slowed or sluggish as he swept off sleep, for this had not been a physical rest.

He realized then that he was not within his body as he was used to being, that he was still within the past, still thrust back in time by War and whatever angelic ability remained within him.

He wondered why. Why should he remain here? He'd seen Torrence, and he saw her innocent boyfriend. He saw glimpses of men who obeyed her every command. Fine, War, he thought, She's always been bad. But this was no use. Whatever the angel had wanted him to learn from this, whatever the angel had wanted to learn for himself, Wesley understood that he had not yet seen it or   heard it or in any way discovered it.

As he rose, he felt a sickness overtake him. It seemed centralized in his gut, but he wasn't sure what that meant here. He wasn't physical. How could he feel pain?

Perhaps this wasn't some ailment but of the body. Perhaps, he considered, this was instinct. Ah, yes, instinct. Something more spiritual than anyone had realized, was instinct not the acknowledgment of something unseen and unheard and untouched?

He looked about the room to get his bearings. It was a large room with ornate fixtures and a large, opulent bed. On the far wall opposite this great bed stood a vanity between two large windows. Upon its mirror were photographs of a young woman with beautiful features and shining black hair, a young woman who seemed to smirk even as her friends were smiling. It was Torrence in her youth, and this suggested to Wesley that he was inside her bedroom now.

It looked different in the light and without her darkness. He wondered where she was.

As became more aware of his surroundings now, he began to hear the noise coming from downstairs, the sounds of music and of laughter and of chatter.

He moved to the ground level of the home, following the sounds throughout the expanse of ostentatiously-decorated hallways until he found what appeared to be some sort of ballroom.

He scoffed, somewhat laughing, as he looked around. "No wonder she turned Hell into a fucking mansion." But where was she?

Moving through the party guests, all dressed in fine clothing and sparkling with flamboyant jewels, Wesley couldn't believe people existed in this fashion, at least not as recently as 2006 or 2007. He wondered briefly if he could hitchhike his way to his hometown and check in on his younger-self. Maybe warn him about college, about the beautiful girl who'd break his heart, and the even more beautiful girl who'd kill her for him.

Another scoff left his body, and he found himself nearing the one person in the room he recognized—Torrence's father.

"Mr. Breslin, your piece, The Larceny of the Licenses, was exquisite. But have you heard that the first victim of this string of petty crimes has now fallen pray to a worse criminal?"

"I have. I'm inclined to believe this worse criminal is, in fact, the same man."

"Really? What cause?"

"I should insist you await the latest article, but we're among friends, yes?"

All in the little group of guests agreed.

"The woman was found with the license of the second victim in her wallet."

Gasps came.

"Do you think it will escalate again? From theft to assault to—. Oh, I shudder to even consider."

"Well, I worry for our Torrence," he said, bringing his hand to his wife's back in a gesture of comforting solidarity. "As you know, she's quite the scholar, quite social. An array of various intelligences reside within our one and only child. But, she is our one and only, and perhaps that leads to a bit more worry than we should experience over the matter." He looked to his wife, then back to his small audience. His chin lifted slightly, subtly. His shoulders squared even further than they were in their natural, confident position. "It isn't as if this mad man is targeting young women exclusively, and he seems to have already selected his targets." He raised his brows, his lips pursing slightly. "You just never know what a madman will do next, when he might see someone new and decide to add them to his collection. We can't say what his MO is, not with such varying victims and almost nothing to go on."

"Onto a lighter topic," a woman in the group exclaimed.

"Yes, Mrs. Denton?" Torrence's mother asked with an eager smile.

"Where is that daughter of yours? I've been wanting her to meet my Austin for months now."

"Ah, she's around here somewhere," Mr. Breslin said. "She is spoken for, I might add."

"Yes," Mrs. Breslin added, taking a sip of her martini, "by a preacher's son. He must spend all of the family's money on the boy's tuition to Calvary Baptist Academy."

"He has scholarships, Delia. I swear, she doesn't listen to a thing that poor kid says."

"Poor kid," she said. "Exactly. Poor."

Wesley's nostrils flared at this. He understood more and more Torrence's resentment for these people. But more importantly, he'd learned from this interaction that Torrence was in the room, or at least in the home, and he intended to find her.

After some searching, he found her at the back of the room, standing by a large table of hors d'oeuvres and champagne glasses.

He felt himself sink into the scenery behind her, all focus on her and her movement and her words until there was nothing left of his awareness but his voyerism.

Dressed in a lovely black gown, Torrence appeared as elegant as anyone in the room. Next to her stood Alex in a button-up and black suit jacket.

At Torrence's insistence, he wore his glasses this night. She liked the way the thin, golden frames enhanced the natural tone of intellect his handsome but subtle features housed.

The pair looked more attractive together than Wesley liked admitting, but there was a glow about each of them, a very separate, distinctive glow from the other, that could not be denied.

Still, Torrence refused to be the socialite, even when she had to play the part here.

"Tor, stop," Alex said, placing his hand over hers as she dropped a white pill into a glass of champagne.

"Alex, this is science," she said. "Let's see which mixture," she continued, dropping a blue pill into another glass, "causes the most chaos."

"What if you kill someone? What even are these?"

"Oh, God—."

"You shouldn't—."

"Oh, goodness," she deadpanned, rolling her eyes up at him. "It's nothing lethal." She raised a pill to him. "This one's just viagra." She dropped it into another glass. Sure, others were stronger than this. They'd have more intense reactions. But in a room for wealthy assholes who spent as much time drunk at parties as they did in their offices, well, Torrence didn't think anyone would really notice. Alex, maybe, but in his nativity Torrence could write off any reaction anyone had to the oxycodone or ecstasy they'd unknowingly taken as 'just the way drunk people act.' She chuckled. "Where would I even get illegal drugs, Alex?"

He exhaled a nervous laugh that eventually became more humored. "I don't know." His chin lowered and his fingers scratched at the back of his head. "Where'd you get…viagra?"

"From your bathroom." Mischief embellished her already-delightful features as she looked to him. A brow raised playfully over her eye. "Your mom and dad were probably counting down the minutes until you left for the party."

"You did not."

She grinned, her tongue rolling over her teeth deviously before she spoke. "No, I didn't," she confirmed, chuckling. "But I bet they are excited for some alone time."

"Stop," he groaned, nose scrunching. "That's so gross."

"It's not gross," she said, dropping one final pill into a glass, and then turning to him. Her arms raised slowly, connecting with his button-up on either side of his bellybutton. Her palms flattened there. As she stepped closer, her hands slipped around his sides beneath his jacket. "It's natural to want to be close to the person you love."

Alex's shoulders rose slightly, his chin lowered. Though he was six inches taller than Torrence, this angling of his body required him to look up to her.

Oh, she liked that.

"Torrence." He brought his hands to her forearms, his palms clammy and unsteady.

"You're safe," she said, lifting herself onto her toes so she might reach his lips with hers. "Can't do much in a room full of old stiffs."

He closed his eyes when she kissed him, but pulled away when the connection lasted more than a few seconds. He exhaled through his uneasy smile, looking away as a faint blush crept into his cheeks. "Torrey," he said, looking up to her again, nodding somewhere indistinct but to his left. "Your parents."

"Yeah, they're so focused on us," she said, rolling her eyes playfully.

"Hello, Miss Breslin," came a voice on their side, accompanied by the clicking of dress shoes on the marble floor. "This must be the young Mr. Milton."

"Yes, sir," Torrence said as Alex took the man's offered hand.

"Good to meet you, son," the man said, introducing himself as Torrence's father's editor. "Will you be following Torrence off to college this fall?"

"No, sir," Alex said gently, nervously. "I'm a junior, so—."

"Ah, next fall then?"

He smiled. "Hopefully we end up somewhere close to one another."

"Hopefully. Well, enjoy the party. Torrence, behave yourself."

"Of course." She smiled as he walked away.

Alex looked over to her immediately. "You're going to school now? When were you gonna tell me? It's great, Torrey. We could've celebrated."

"I got a few acceptance letters." Torrence shrugged. "I forget which I told them I replied to."

"So you're…not going?"

"Nah. Not in the cards for me."

"You keep saying that, but what does it even mean?"

"It means I've got a plan, and college isn't part of it."

"But you haven't chosen a job—."

"Alex," she said curtly, then she inhaled a deep, calming breath and released it slowly. She looked around the party, the little suit jackets, the shimmering dresses. "It's so dull here, isn't it? So impersonal." Her lips pouted as she looked up to him. "Have you had enough of it?"

He nodded shyly.

She took his hand in hers and led him through the large room.

They moved by bankers and politicians, writers and photographers who worked with her father, and the educated women who'd taken time away from their own thriving business endeavors to raise their families.

Torrence has such contempt for all this, and Alex knew it. She'd expressed it time and time again, and though he admired both ideas—providing for and raising a family—he agreed with her that the outdated practice of each sex seemingly assigned to one task over the other was ridiculous.

Alex found himself agreeing with Torrence when she expressed her lack of femininity in these traditional standards, for he could not deny that he was far more sensitive to and considerate of others. He supposed this was part of their attraction to one another, however. They each represented one half of the widely-accepted perfect couple, only it was she who sought authority over others and he who had no trouble in surrendering it to her.

Beyond that, Torrence was intelligent and often carried deeply spiritual conversations with Alex. Though they disagreed, the preacher's son saw her collection of Biblical texts and documentaries, and wrongly assumed that her interest in theology was evidence of faith.

As they moved by her parents, Torrence's mother merely tsked at her early departure from this holiday party, which might've taken Alex by surprise had he not been here so often.

Usually when he followed Torrence through her home, he did so wondering where her parents were, either seeing them in a far-off room hosting elegantly-dressed guests or not seeing them at all.

He'd always marveled over Torrence's ability to come and go as she pleased, to bring guests over, to bring boys over and into her room.

"Torrey," he said as they neared the staircase. "We can't go in your room."

"Why can't we?"

"Your parents. Everyone in there. What will they think?"

"Who cares what they think?"

"Torrence—."

"Alex, please." She rolled her eyes again. "I'm not going over to your house dressed like this. It's ridiculous."

"Then I should wait downstairs if you're changing. What if your parents…" he exhaled instead of finishing the sentence.

"Talk about ridiculous, huh?" She chuckled, and he gave in to her, smiling with her and following her still.

Though he stood by the door, refusing to go into her closet with her, Alex wished he had less resolve, less faith, less ideology. He wished he had less worry or fear.

Without his commitment to God, Alex might have experienced all aspects of love with Torrence, and without his concern for misbehavior, he might have sat upon her bed without caring who might open the door and catch him there.

"You're really overthinking this," Torrence said from the closet.

"What else is new?" he said back, chuckling slightly.

She emerged from the closet in a simple gray dress. It was skin-tight so she knew it would not be well-received by Alex's parents, but she didn't own any looser dresses that were not overly fancy, and if she went in pants, that'd be even more offensive.

Alex smiled. "You look beautiful."

"Oh, stop it," she teased, moving against him, pressing him into the wall, and smiling at how he allowed her such control.

Kissing her deeply, he let his hands run her arms, one eventually finding her cheek and caressing it. He was learning from her, learning to act on instinct, learning to touch and to feel good. But still not quickly enough for her preference.

A knock came to her door then, its sound, signifying perhaps her parents, stiffened Alex's muscles. He released her immediately.

"Mistress Breslin?" came the voice on the door's other side. Male and sophisticated, yes, but young.

A gentle laugh came from Torrence as she released Alex, patting his cheek playfully as the worry dissipated from his attractive features.

Moving away from him, she made for the door and opened it, reaching her hand out into the hallway and by his jacket collar pulled in through the small aperture a beautiful man.

"Master Blake," she replied with equal enthusiasm and overdrawn sophistication. Both laughed as Torrence turned and moved to Alex, introducing the pair.

"I've heard a lot about you in the last year or so," Blake said, shaking Alex's hand.

Alex smiled in return, trying not to stare at Blake as he and Torrence spoke about these parties and how nice it was for Blake to be free of so many of them now that he'd moved so far away.

Blake was taller than Alex. Slim still, but firmer, thicker in the correct places. His jawline was sharp. Lips full and long. His eyes were blue, but different than the shade of Alex's eyes. His blond hair, not quite so 'dirty'. He seemed in all ways a different version of Alex, a better one.

"So, this fall," Blake said, "you're coming to New York with me?"

"No school for me," Torrence said.

"You're still on that? What do your parents have to say about it?"

"What can they say?"

"So what are you going to do, then?"

"Oh, the usual," she said, sitting down next to him. "Amass an empire and take over the world."

"High ambitions." Blake and Torrence shared a knowing look, but a few texts and updated MySpace pages hadn't been enough in the last year or so to keep them entirely on the same wavelength.

"Maybe," Torrence said.

"Alex, what about you?"

"Alex is a junior," Torrence answered for him. "We're actually about to leave. Doing Christmas Eve with his family, too."

"Like a real couple," he said, mostly to Torrence, then he looked to Alex. "She never used to be the girlfriend-type. That's all." He chuckled, then he looked back to her. "Is that what you're wearing? It's cotton."

"His family's not like ours," she said. "His dad's a pastor."

"Then that dress is even worse!" He laughed now. "Every curve is accented. You're being an ass on purpose, aren't you?"

"The only ass here is you," she said, hitting his shoulder playfully. She looked over to Alex. "Will a sweater make this more appropriate?"

"No, it's great. I promise."

"He's too polite to say yes," Blake said, chuckling.

She rolled her eyes. Went back into her closet.

"How badly has she corrupted you, church boy?" Blake asked Alex, grabbing his shoulder in camaraderie as he moved by him.

"Not bad in your terms, probably," Alex exhaled a small laugh. "Pretty bad in mine."

He turned as Blake moved, watching him open Torrence's window and sit on its cushioned bay. He lit a cigarette, exhaled the smoke into the wind.

"'Pretty bad' means what then?"

"I don't know," he said, looking down to his shoes. Again, he felt childlike. Torrence and Blake had experienced things he refused to even near.

"You haven't been with her, have you?"

He shook his head.

"Does it bother you that she's been with other people?"

Again, his head shook.

"Well, that's good. I mean, you can love a person without participating in their shit, you know?"

"Yeah," Alex said lowly, not realizing the extent of Blake's statement.

Sure, it applied to physical pleasure, but it applied to violence, too. Another basic animal instinct, one the so-called evolved mind tried to suppress. Was it different from desire, though? From the expression of it? Both began in the mind, in the spirit, in the unseen, and both were expelled into the perceivable reality through tangible acts. Sexual activity. Acts of violence. All sinful, improper, but done behind closed doors. Rebuke it aloud, but give in privately. Have an affair. Steal the candy bar. Hit the man sleeping with your wife. Sleep with his. It was all the same—instinct. But wrath, though just as appealing as lust, was tougher to justify. This was why murderers got life sentences but adulterers were no longer stoned. Maybe in another century, Blake thought, We'll be more accepting of our other, most-ignored instincts.

He inhaled a long drag of his cigarette, held the mentholated smoke inside his lungs as he considered the boy before him, then he let it go. "You think you'd love Torrence through anything, then? Any sin?"

"We hate the sin, not the sinner, right? So, of course."

Alex watched Blake as he lifted the cigarette, pressed against the webbing of his first two fingers, to his full, perfectly-shaped lips. He wondered if Torrence had ever dated Blake, if one of the people she'd been with had been him.

She'd told him about Todd, after all, by name, but maybe that was because he went to school with him. The others on her list weren't given names. Only numbers.

A sad smile thinned Alex's lips. He didn't usually feel so inferior, not to a person, anyway. Usually when he felt badly, it was because he could not live up to his own expectations of himself, or to his parents expectations of him. It was embarrassment before an idea, not in comparison to another person.

Now, he stood before a man with more money, more education. An older man. An almost-supernaturally attractive man, and one who had physical traits so similar to his own that not comparing himself to Blake was nearly impossible.

"What if she went to jail?" Blake asked, exhaling more smoke out of the window. "Would you stay with her through it?"

"Yes," Alex said without thinking, then he considered it further. "I'd think she'd be remorseful. I'd be a total hypocrite if I didn't forgive her, right?"

"Are you asking me or telling me?"

"Telling," he said. "Sorry."

Blake grinned. Alex was sweet, wasn't he? And undeniably adorable. "What if she wasn't remorseful? What if she said, 'Yeah, I'll do it again'?"

"Then I guess I'd try to help her. I don't know."

"You'd break up, though."

"No," he said. "I mean, I don't know." He stared at Blake with obvious confusion.

"I'm just trying to see how committed you are," Blake said. "That's all."

"I'm very committed," he replied. "I suppose I think of it in terms of the future more than unlikely what-ifs."

"Eh, the future is always unlikely until it's the present. We can't ever know what's coming for us. Most of us don't even know what we've already got. Not until it's too late to go back from it."

"I'm not sure what you mean—."

"He doesn't mean anything," Torrence said, emerging from the closet with a black sweater over her dress. "He declares a philosophy major and suddenly everything is a debate." She laughed and pushed at him again.

"Yeah, well, some questions don't have answers until we're face to face with them, not as words but as actions and choices. The choice to act. The choice not to." He hugged Torrence, then shook Alex's hand. "I'll leave you to your Christmas Eve plans. Gotta go back to the party anyway. Tor, I'll see you tomorrow maybe? Lunch on me?"

"Sounds good," she said.

Alex tried to hide his jealousy of Blake, but he couldn't contain it. When the door closed, he looked at Torrence and immediately asked if she had dated him.

"Why?"

"He's really attractive," Alex said. "I don't know. I'm sorry."

"You don't have to be sorry for asking a question."

"You just know so many people."

"I know a lot of people, yeah." She went to him, settling her arms around his neck, pressing her body into his; so natural, as if they were magnetic, as if they always had been, but only to one another. "But you are my only friend."

CHAPTER FIFTEEN

Though she didn't care much for his parents, Torrence enjoyed the event's celebration more at Alex's home than her own.

Though his father was a preacher and his mother disapproved of her son dating a woman who wore pants, their home was smaller and more intimate. Their guests fewer in number but more closely related. The feeling of fidelity amongst this small group was one that appealed to Torrence—a family, not necessarily by blood, but by devotion.

As they all exchanged hits, faces lit up. Gratitude seemed abundant. It was too Stepford to be true, but they feigned perfection for fear of displeasing their God, who Torrence realized at that moment was perhaps the greatest cult leader anyone had heard of. She should've been studying Him when she was reading about Jonestown, she thought.

There was an order to things, too. A hierarchy, yes. Women in the dining room having tea. Men watching football in the living room. And children, including anyone in high school, were sent to basement, which acted as a playroom of sorts.

Torrence and Alex sat on the couch, watching A Christmas

Story with a few other teenagers while the younger ones played with stuffed animals and read from a tattered Mother Goose book.

"So, I got you something else," Alex said to her. "I wasn't sure if I should give it to you."

"Why?"

"It's not…anything special. I don't know."

"If you got it, I'm sure it is," she said. "I want it." She smiled playfully.

"It's in my room," he said, standing. "I'll be right back."

"Oh, no." She stood now, too. "You're not leaving me here with these kids."

He chuckled, brows raising as he looked up to the staircase. "Okay."

It was cute to Torrence how Alex had to sneak her into his own room. Something endearing about him, about his innocence, his desires.

She had far more sinister wants, far less pure intentions, therefore everyone she knew seemed very much the same. They were attractive, sure, but not beautiful. Nothing but purity could be beautiful.

"Wow," she said, following him into his room. She stood at the door, which he quickly but silently shut, with her hands on her hips. "I can't believe it took me over a year to get in here."

"Well, I hope it meets your expectations," he joked, heading for his dresser as she made her way to his bed. She touched the navy blue comforter, smiling at how neatly the bed had been made. Then her attention was caught by his nightstand, by the book upon it—the Bible, of course—and the discs in transparent but multi-colored cases beneath it, the ones in its lower shelf. She slipped down the edge of the bed to sit on the floor and look at them. "What are these?" she asked, taking the red one into her hands and opening it. A silver disc inside with his handwriting in sharpie. It said only "MC".

"Oh, um, I tell mom and dad they're projects for school, but they're…downloaded films."

"Why, Alex," she said, chuckling, her tone high-pitched and excited. "That is illegal, young man. You absolute rebel!"

He laughed and shook his head. "Yeah, I know. I should've mentioned them to your friend, Blake, with all those questions. He might've liked me more."

"He liked you," Torrence said, putting the disc back. "He just knows how much I like you."

"You like me, huh?"

"I love you."

He chuckled. "I love you, too." Shyly, he turned, having removed a small box from the top drawer. "I, um…" he rubbed at the back of his neck, biting his lower lip. With a small exhale, he attempted a laugh, then he came to sit down by her. "I thought of you. But it's…" He offered her the box. "It's silly, and it's nowhere near as valuable as your diamonds, but I…I just saw it and—."

"Alex, relax." She smiled, taking the box in one hand and stroking his cheek with the other. A serenity came into her features, adoration shimmering in her eyes as she looked into his. "Thank you."

"You're welcome," he said.

"Can I open it now?"

He nodded.

"Oh," she said, a smile spreading across her face and bringing its joy into her features.

"It's…The T is obviously for Torrence, but a T is kind of a cross, and I thought maybe the cross might sort of represent me, too. I don't know. The woman at the store said I should get you an A, but it felt too possessive."

She looked over to him now, and he gazed at her with the same intense affection she'd been casting upon him.

"You're no one's but you're own." His eyes seemed to flicker between her left eye and her right one as if the secret to some great unanswered question resides within their deep blues. Alex was raised by a woman who believed her station in life was beneath her husband, subservient and submissive to his authority, but Alex was not authoritative, and he did not want a partner who silently, blindly followed him. In truth, he wasn't certain he was capable of making tough decisions, life decisions, and if he were capable of it, he'd prefer a second person to confirm it. That is, if the other person wasn't comfortable making the decision for them both. "I think it's my favorite thing about you."

Torrence smiled, she moved onto her knees then threw one over his legs. She settled onto his lap. "Put it on me."

He smiled. "Yeah?"

"Yeah."

He sat up more straightly, taking the necklace from the box and putting it around her neck. He bit his lip as he stared to it.

"What's wrong?"

"Nothing," he said lowly, but the necklace, he couldn't avoid noticing, was undeniably cheap next to her string of diamonds and her mother's pearl.

She reached up to the necklace, searching for it, her fingers reminding her of the other jewelry she wore when they brushed against them. "Oh, Alex, no, don't worry about it, seriously. It's gross, honestly, the amount of money people spend on shit they don't even need. The importance they place on materialism. You're not like that. You're not shallow or selfish. You don't value looks or money. You value ideas and concepts, and even though some of them aren't exactly the ones I'd commit myself to, I admire your commitment to them. You're deep, intelligent."

"Torrence," he whispered, feeling uncomfortable in the attention, the praise.

"Indomitable."

"Yeah." His brows raised.

"Perfect."

He looked up to her. "You're perfect."

She smiled, leaning in to bring their lips together; the connections of the bodies representing the connection of their souls, or at least that's what she'd always tried on him.

"We shouldn't," he said simply.

"Why though? Why shouldn't we?"

"Lust, Torrence," he said, looking up to her now.

"No," she said, "Love. Nonjudgmental love. Unconditional love."

"God's love is unconditional."

"It isn't," she said, her voice delicate and everything delectable to a soft and innocent soul. "Otherwise, you'd not hesitate. If God loved you regardless of conditions, you wouldn't fear disappointment or disapproval in enacting a simple and very-human urge—the urge to express physically what cannot be seen. The merging of spirits connected through the bodies which house them. A thing of beauty, really, and your God would disown the soul he cast into this sensory vessel for seeking out what He designed it to desire? A simple emotion."

"A simple sin."

"Who decides what's sin? What's virtue?"

"God does."

"Okay, then define it."

"Sin is the deterioration of the soul."

"Maybe," she said, "but maybe it's just a manipulation tactic used by your parents and our schools and our so-called leaders to keep us in line."

"Torrence—."

"Face some punishment to do something—anything—in this world that makes you feel good or powerful, anything that brings a touch of excitement and they want to keep it from you."

"Why?" Alex's voice raised to the level of Torrence's only for this one, brief syllable. He inhaled through his plump lips, his eyes falling. His head followed the downcast of his vision, and then it shook very slightly. Another deep intake of air, and then he risked a glance upward to Torrence and her intensity in this moment. "Why, Torrence?" he asked gently, slowly; careful not to sound challenging or aggressive. "Why wouldn't our leaders or our role models want us to enjoy things if they weren't harmful?"

"Oh, they're harmful," Torrence said, her voice softer now but still assertive, confident. "They're harmful to the leaders. The threat of sin, Hell, punishment, a record; this threat is all they have to keep us in line. The insecurity we carry, the burdens of our own thoughts and desires; these things which come naturally to us, and we're made to feel shame and guilt for them. The powerful remain the powerful if those they govern remain blind and stupid. I'm asking you to open your eyes, Alex. I'm asking you to be with me, to love me—."

"I do love you," he said, his voice shaky and uncertain as he looked up to her with his dewy eyes. "But you aren't asking me for that. You have that already. You're asking me for lust, and I would give it to you if I didn't feel such shame for it. You're right, I…I feel such shame for it." He glanced away now, his eyes vibrating between random spots on the floor as his brows furrowed over them. It was as if he'd been given this sight of which Torrence spoke, and that he used it now to read the reality of the world, written here in a simple font upon the beige carpeting of his bedroom. He swallowed thickly these emotions, which had balled up into something tangible and lodged itself inside his throat, then he looked back to her. "If desire is natural, then so is guilt."

"Untrue." Her voice was as certain as her expression. "Desire is natural. Society makes you feel guilty for it."

"That doesn't make sense. How would it even start? One person just decides to make up arbitrary rules? For what?"

"For power. For control. Trust me," she said, a slight grin angling her lips upward, "sometimes it only takes one person."

He shook his head, having no response to this, not yet. And

as he considered her words, Torrence continued her small pets, stroking her fingers along his jaw and down his neck.

"Where is this coming from, Torrence? I've never heard you talk like this before."

"I guess I'm just frustrated," she said, exhaling.

"By me?" He looked lost.

"Yes," she whispered. "I adore you, and it kills me that I can't have you."

"You have me," he said, brows creasing. "I didn't realize how important this is to you."

"It's not that it's important. I just want you in all ways."

His knitted brows loosened in the gentle touches, his eyes fluttering closed to better enjoy the feel of it. When of his head tilted to nestle into her hand, Torrence slipped back into his lap and leaned into him. He allowed this, his focus on the tenderness of her connection, of how pure it seemed, for her fingers merely tickled at his hair and the base of his neck.

Unconsciously his hand moved to her thigh, the other slipped around her waist. He held her as she moved more closely into him, still too distracted by the overt playing with his hair to notice the slippery, slower movements of her hips, her torso, her chest.

She moved against him, pressing their bodies together. He hummed gently, lost in her ministrations, which emboldened her. She leaned in, her cheek against his, then her lips there. Tender still, this innocent connection of lips and flesh, but it was not a solitary act.

Her lips pressed against him a second time there, then a third, then they came to his jaw, lingered there, testing him in this connection. Her eyes, opened and studious, looked upward to his eyes and found them still closed, found his lips parting slightly, found him entranced in her touches.

Further invigorated by his potential succumbing, Torrence lowered her head and pressed her lips against his neck now.

His brows creased at this, but he did not protest. He allowed the delicate kisses, the closeness. Only now becoming aware that his hands were upon her, Alex held more tightly onto Torrence. His hands acting as a silent plea to her. We are here, he thought, We are close. Please do not make it any more than that, not when I've been so open about my discomfort with going further.

But she pressed on. Her kisses became wetter, for she was further parting her lips to consume more of his skin, drawing the reactive flesh into her mouth to suckle it.

A soft groan resounded in her throat for all this; for the taste of him, for the implications of these small acts, and for the adrenaline which rushed at the thought of his surrender. Oh, how Torrence always enjoyed the sensations of someone yielding to her.

But Alex, though meek and submissive, was not one to yield.

"Tor," he said, squirming beneath her. His lips curled, his head straightening away from her caressing fingers. "Come on." He pushed gently at her thighs, suggesting only that she put a small distance between them, not that she remove herself entirely from his lap, but she refused. "Torrence," he said, scoffing. His lips pursed, his teeth pressing his inner-cheek into themselves. A painful acknowledgment of her in this moment, of her disregard for his feelings, or maybe just for him, pulled at his brows as he looked up to her. "I told you I didn't want to."

"No," she said, leaning away from him, while maintaining connection to his neck and jaw. "You told me God doesn't want you to."

"Torrence," he said in discomfort.

"I think you'll come to realize eventually that God doesn't always know what's best."

"That's blasphemy, Torrence. You know you shouldn't—."

"Don't tell me what I should or shouldn't do," she said, a sharp tone suddenly replacing the gentleness of her voice as her hand fell away from him. "I, alone, will decide that."

"And you, alone, will decide what I should and shouldn't do as well?" He scoffed, a dissatisfied smile accompanying the sound so that it rang out almost as a laugh.

"Why not?" she asked.

He looked at her, expecting some sort of anger or even humor in her face, but her features seemed sincere in this question: why shouldn't Torrence decide? Why shouldn't she control all those in her company?

"Because…" he said wearily. "You aren't God."

"Maybe not," she said. "But I know a few people who think otherwise."

Alex's brows creased, a genuine confusion encompassing his thoughts now, encompassing them but not erasing them. Dwelling within the recesses of his mind were still the usual emotions: shame, guilt, worry, fear. But something new to consider—the sources of these sentiments.

Most were obvious.

He felt shame for his lust of Torrence, and the fact that he loved her sincerely prior to its emergence did nothing to assuage its strength.

He felt guilt for his part in her own sin, that he was the focal point of her desire, and therefore a cause of her potential spiritual ruin.

He worried, of course, that he may not be able to deny these desires forever, or even until he could turn eighteen and marry her, for he knew his parents would not give him consent to do so now.

But the fear…The fear of giving into her physically and having her leave him. What would he do, then, with a tainted body?

As always, Torrence took silence for compliance and attempted to lean back into Alex. Slowly she moved, as if she were extending a hand out to a scared puppy.

"It's okay," she said, pressing her lips very carefully against his. "I love you."

"Torrence," Alex whispered. "We can't." He smiled nervously. "Please don't be mad."

"I'm not mad," she said. Her hand brushed through his dirty blond hair, revealing a hint of sweat forming across his forehead. "Don't be nervous."

"I'm not nervous," he said, looking up to her. He swallowed audibly, thickly. "My parents are downstairs."

"We can go back to my house," she said, a playfulness overtaking her expression. "If the party doesn't drown us out, the booze will."

He winced, sitting up and moving her gently away from him. "Stop," he said. "Please."

Rolling her eyes, Torrence moved to his side. She leaned against the bed, running her hand through her hair. Her nostrils flared and she took in a deep, soothing breath through them.

"You don't have to do anything, you know?"

Alex looked over to her, her elbow on her bent knee, her temple pressed against the heel of her hand. "What?"

"You could just sit there," she said, her brows raising, a smirk resting confidently on her lips. "If I'm the only one acting, I'm the only one sinning."

"I don't think that's how it works," he said, eyes scanning her features for any sign of humor. When he found none, he looked down to his hands in his lap. "Even if it was, I'd worry for your soul, too."

Torrence's brows raised at surprise of this, but she should've suspected his worries might fall there. Alex, her lovely little preacher's son, certainly would worry more for a potential and unproven eternity than some physical prison. As her surprise leveled from her face, a serenity came into features. A smile spread slowly across her usually-pouting lips.

She reached for his hand. He turned his palm upward so that she could slip hers inside it. Staring at this small, innocent form of affection, Alex twisted his hair around the fingers of his free hand.

"Can't you just respect me?" he asked.

"I do."

"No," he said, staring at their hands. "You don't."

She exhaled, exasperated with all this, but understanding that tonight would not be night for them.

"Yes, I do." She stared at his knuckles, at her fingertips brushing over them. "I just want to be close to you." She paused, looking up to him now beneath her lashes, rendering the dark, and therefore usually-harsh, makeup about her eyes solemn and somewhat sad. "Is it wrong to want to bring us closer?"

"Torrence," he said gently, turning his body toward hers now and taking into his hands both of hers. "It's our spirits that keep us close, not our bodies."

"Maybe," she said. "But maybe it takes both."

"We can do both," he said, lifting a hand to her cheek. He leaned into her, his lips hesitantly connecting with hers. "Just not as much as you maybe think necessary."

When the small embrace ended, he rested his forehead against her, attempting in his own way to create physical intimacy between them. He felt her hands slip up his arms, felt them move to his neck and wrap around it. Their bent knees, uncomfortable between them now, fell aside, straightening, opening their bodies up to each other.

"Necessary or not," Torrence said, lifting her chin enough to acquire a second brushing together of their lips. "At least admit that it feels good."

"That's never been in question," he said, somehow comfortable with affection so long as there was space between their centers, their torsos; so long as it was slow and thin and unforced.

Purposefully he kissed her, reminding her that attraction and adoration were mutual. He wished she understood that it was only divine law that kept on their clothing in moments like this, in moments of physical sensations and firing nerve-endings, in the rushing of blood, and the carnal urges to enact what should be assigned only to procreation.

Still, only fornication was prohibited. Small embraces, tiny massages, soft kisses were not explicitly forbidden. If Alex felt a vulnerability here in Torrence's words, surely he could convince her of his affection, he could lessen any worry through the envelopment of what was, not bad, but merely morally-gray.

Torrence let this timid pace go on for longer than she wanted, but figured easing Alex into sin was the better option than forcing it upon him. She knew he liked the way she played with his hair and used this innocent act again as a distraction as she slipped nearer and nearer toward her larger goal.

It seemed to be working. She'd been able to move more closely into him again. This time, with both of them on the floor instead of her backside in his lap, and with their legs parting to accommodate one another, the proximity of their cores forced her dress up over her thighs.

She pressed against his khakis, only the thin lace of her panties separating her most tender area from him. The sensation of it elicited a small moan from her, which subsequently urged one from Alex himself.

His hands began to wander, slipping down her body and finding the bare flesh of her thighs. There was no rule against this, was there? Against palms upon legs? Surely legs had no significance in lovemaking, and so long as his hands remained above her clothing, what sin could've been committed?

This was not a moment of passive surrender nor was it unconscious desire. Alex realized only now in this room with Torrence that full abstinence from physical affection would not do, and if he expected her to allow him his chastity, which seemed quite the compromise for her, then he, too, must give in, however slightly, so that he was giving as much as he was taking.

Resolute and strong-willed, he would not offer his virginity to someone to whom he had not pledged his life, but he knew that one day Torrence would be that person for him, so a bit of exploratory touches could not have been so bad.

Torrence hummed at his fingers as they grazed her thighs. She felt the accomplishment already, and let her hips advance again.

"I love you," she whispered to him before reclaiming his lips with her own, hoping this was the final step in his submission, but before he could reply with either word or action, the door to his bedroom swung open.

"I love you, too," he said, before the shock of the door registered.

"Dear Lord," Alex's mother wailed, crying out for her husband as Alex and Torrence broke away from one another.

"Mom," Alex said breathily. He stood frozen between the two women, the two most important women in his life, uncertain of whom to console and how. "Tor," he said, angling himself toward her, reaching for her hand.

"Don't touch her!" His mother shifted as if she were going to insert herself between them but was unable to move.

"What would it hurt now?" Torrence smirked.

"Oh, good God, Alexander," she shrieked, "don't tell me you've defiled your blessed temple—."

"No," he said quickly, his brows furrowing. He reached for Torrence again. "Just wanted to hold her hand."

"Stop that! Stop! The slightest touch is the first step toward—." She turned in the door, her hand rushing to her mouth.

"Alex," Torrence said, moving against him. "We can go to my house—."

"He's not going anywhere," Alex's father said, moving between his wife and the door-frame and entering the room. "Come on, Torrence. It's time to take you home."

"But, sir," she said sweetly, a smirk evident beneath her

raised brows and blinking, sarcastic eyes. "Whatever did we do wrong?"

"Your tricks may work on my son because he's naive and inexperienced, but your charm is no match for the knowledge of godly adults, young lady. Let's go." He reached for her now, his hand almost connecting to her upper arm.

"No, thanks," she said, jerking away from him. "I'll walk." With her squared shoulders and raised chin, Torrence moved by Alex's father, stopping in the doorway to eye his mother. She turned back toward the room. "See you tomorrow, Alex."

His lips parted as if to speak, but his father interrupted.

"I don't think so." He crossed an arm over his torso and brought his hand to his chin. "I think it's better that you associate with those at your own school from now on, Torrence. Alex has friends at Calvary. He'll be spending his time with them going forward."

Defiance gave Torrence's lovely features a harshness as her narrowed eyes moved from this man to his son.

Alex met her gaze with worry and submission, but submission to wrong person in the room. He looked away in shame.

Tension came in Torrence's jaw, and she eyed Alex's father in a display of pure hatred. After a moment, she turned her head to glare into his mother's eyes. "Good night, Mrs. Milton." Slowly, an eerie smile spread across her lips.

"Just leave, Torrence," she replied.

"Of course," she said. "Yes, ma'am."

As she exited, time seemed to slow for Torrence. Already in her mind were thoughts of Alex, of his submission to God, to his parents. She wanted his submission, and she realized with uncertainty that it was his family standing her way. With their new rule now more than ever, but only in the physical. She'd have to acquire his mental devotion before she could control his body or his actions, and she saw precisely how to accomplish this in slow-motion.

She looked back into the room as she began her exit, watching Alex's father as he spoke, his voice caught in the time loop with her, his words vibrating through the air in an echo of fluidity. "'Foolishness is bound up in the heart of a child,'" he quoted the Bible. Torrence recognized it immediately as Proverbs 22:15. Alex's father grabbed at his son, roughly jerking him closer. He raised his free hand to Alex, finishing the passage. "'The rod of correction will drive it far from him.'"

Taking her first step down the staircase, Torrence heard the harsh connection of hand to cheek, one after another; the silence of Alex in these moments of violence as evident as the wailing of his mother as she folded her hands and whispered prayers.

It was a loathsome display of faith, if they truly considered it such. This weeping mother, mourning the corruption of her son at the hands and hips of some vile, public-school temptress and her head-of-household husband, who struck his son as he claimed to save him.

She hated these people. They disgusted her. They were misguided, ill-informed, and infantile, and they would not keep her from Alex.

As she descended the stairs, thoughts of her own family came into her mind—not the family of biology and blood, but the family of mutually assured destruction and deviance and devotion. Perhaps, she considered as she made for the door, that it was time to intensify her work, to test the devotion of her brothers, and to become the one and only power on earth to which Alex could yield.

She turned to the house as she left it, eyeing its exterior carefully, noting the placement of the windows, the proximity to the neighbors, the entryway of the garage.

She watched the silhouettes of Alex and his father in the upstairs, far-left window. Her lips curling and trembling in her contempt. She turned. Slowly walking down the sidewalk in the darkness, the diamond around her neck gleaming in the silvery moonlight, Torrence contemplated this situation with conviction to her cause. Her boots, clicking against the pavement, seemed to act as an anomalous, foreboding metronome in the background of her violent thoughts. A brow arched over a devious eye. Her tongue swept across her teeth. She pulled her phone from her boot and texted Todd, the appointed leader of the boys in her absence, and asked him to meet her at their aqueduct hideaway.

And so it came to pass that Torrence was on her way to orchestrating her first murder.

CHAPTER SIXTEEN

It had been a week since the eruption at Alex's home. Torrence hadn't seen him. His phone had been taken, but he spent his fourth period study halls in the library, using the school's computers to message Torrence through a MySpace account with no photo and a fake name.

He apologized to her. He refused to talk about what his father had done. She worried for the full extent of it, but wouldn't press. She knew comeuppance was close.

I'll come get you tonight, she wrote.

We can't do that, he replied.

It'll be okay. Todd will drive my car.

Todd?

Haskins. You have chemistry together.

You know Todd Haskins?

Yes. We'll come get you. Your dad said you needed to spend time with people from Calvary. It'll be okay.

Okay.

Pack a bag. Spend the night. I love you.

I love you, he wrote.

As Torrence and Todd drove, she texted her boys, instructing them on what drinks to take to the hideout, what music to have loaded onto their iPods, what movies to bring with their laptops.

Alex had never been one for parties, he may have tasted a mere sip of wine in his entire life, and Torrence had spent a year with him in subtle temptation to which he never succumbed, not fully. Small victories like chaste kisses becoming passionate embraces were all she could use to convince herself that this might work, but she couldn't take Alex's family away without providing him a new one. Her gang, her followers, her boys, they would become Alex's brothers.

When she and Todd arrived at Alex's home, Torrence climbed into the back of the car. Todd approached home, as did two others—others named Aaron and Don, Torrence's eldest followers; the eldest brothers—selected for myriad reasons to be the performers of this great act, the first true step in Torrence's destiny.

Firstly, their age. Older, out of their teens, Torrence figured they'd be less impulsive, less arrogant. They'd go in and do their job, plain and simple, and they wouldn't be too reckless to properly clean up.

Secondly, experience. These two weren't rebellious high-school students. They were criminals already. Breaking and entering and assault, and assault with a deadly weapon respectively. They were hardened. There wouldn't be hesitation, second thoughts, or fear to stop them from completing their task.

Thirdly, Torrence wanted boys at the hideout for Alex, at least until he warmed up to the ideas of abandoned homes and under-aged drinking. Baby steps.

She figured he'd feel less intimidated by people his age. More comfortable with someone like Todd, someone from Calvary. Someone he at least knew of.

Todd really had come in handy, she thought as she watched

him walk up to the door.

He stood there, watching his older brothers as they moved around the house, one on each side, toward the back porch where there were sliding glass doors. When they were out of sight, Todd rang the doorbell.

With the use of a compact mirror, Torrence watched as Alex's father opened the door, making small talk with the young man before he okayed his son's leaving with him.

Of course, Todd's mother had already spoken to Mrs. Milton, ensuring it was fine for the boys to spend their night at her home, studying their chemistry and playing a few games of something for the PlayStation 2. By the time Todd left to get Torrence's car, she was passed out on the couch, and Todd's father almost always worked late.

Todd's shyer nature came in handy when speaking with the Miltons—the last thing Torrence would've wanted was for an arrogant, self-assured smartass, someone like herself, to turn up at Alex's house and have the door shut in their face—but it created a perceptible tension between the young men when Alex's father finally called up to him and asked him to come downstairs. Both were slightly awkward, and neither had spoken a word to one another. Ever.

Regardless of what they were saying to each other now, Torrence watched Alex's mother hug him. When she released him, the boys made their way to the car.

It worked. Alex couldn't believe it. He said as much when he got into the passenger's seat, turned to place his bag in the backseat and saw Torrence. She grinned at him. "Everything according to plan," she said.

"Tor's plans always work," Todd said. "Just wait."

"Wait?" he asked Todd as the car approached the street's stop sign. They turned right and Alex's home was out of sight. He looked to Torrence as she sat up. "Wait for what?"

"World domination," she chuckled, leaning up between the

seats and unclasping Alex's seat belt. Grabbing at the collar of his jean jacket, Torrence urged him into the back seat.

It was troubling, climbing around inside a moving vehicle like this, but Alex felt strangely enthralled by it all. Lying to his parents, sneaking out. A friend as a cover for spending the night with his partner. Life, it seemed, mimicked art—all those illegally downloaded rom-coms he'd sneakily enjoyed featured tiny plot-points like this, plot-points he was certain happened so frequently in fiction because they happened so frequently in life.

He was seven month shy of his eighteenth birthday, why not have at least one rebellious teenaged experience?

Torrence chuckled, still tugging on him. "Always thinking, aren't you?"

"Yes," he said, swallowing his nerves. This was not the time to consider being found out, being caught, being punished. After a week away from Torrence, with minuscule contact which could only occur in the same forty-minute window every day and no more, Alex desperately wanted to hold her, to feel her arms around his waist, to kiss her lips.

He climbed into the backseat with her, his body clumsy and awkward, smiling when she giggled and set back into the seat. He tried his best to keep only the right side of his face in her direction, even though he assumed she'd heard, if not seen, the beginnings of his beating. Typically he could hide inside his clothing, the long sleeves of his jackets or the collars of his shirts, and, of course, there was the excuse of his physical exertions every Saturday—a fall from a chin-up, perhaps—but these efforts meant nothing to someone who had seen his punishments.

"Why are you hiding?" She smiled, her hands on his jaw urging him to look at her, and when he complied, his eyes gazed imploringly to her. Don't me me, he thought, I don't want you to see.

Instead of studying his face, which was a work of art she always enjoyed consuming, Torrence leaned into him and brought together their lips.

"Torrey," he said, shying away when she kissed him. He looked over to the back of Todd's head, then into her eyes. A bashful smile came to his lips.

"Todd hardly minds," she said.

He lowered his head, allowing her a better angle, and when she lifted her chin to kiss him, he didn't pull away.

The typical teenage experience. At least once. Why not? And maybe, he considered, maybe Torrence wouldn't grow out of him if he acted less childish, even if it was just for tonight.

After twenty minutes, the car slowed, came to a halt. When Alex moved away from Torrence to look out of the window, he saw only woods. "Where are we?"

"We're going to the hideout," she said, opening the door and exiting.

When he followed suit, he looked up into the sky. The moon was large out here, away from the lights of the city, and the silver of the moonbeams illuminated his face, glistened against his dirty-blond hair, and reflected gray inside the blues of his eyes.

The average-sized lips on this handsome face struck Wesley, for Torrence seemed to have a liking for very luscious ones, or to enjoy the thin, almost-shapeless lips of War. Extremes, it always was with her. But standing here without a uniform or a Bible, Alex seemed so normal.

He wore a plain, black t-shirt under his jean jacket. He wore a band of silver on his left ring finger, and his nails were clipped and very clean. A chain around his neck carried a cross. He was taller than Torrence, perhaps taller than War and Conrad, but shorter than Wesley.

Handsome, yes, but nothing so defined or striking as Conrad, and nothing as humble as War's particular brand of beauty. He had freckles around his eyes, but not beneath them like War's, no. Nothing so gleaming or magical either. Just three small freckles on the side of his eye, shaping a little triangle out from the corner of it.

Wesley was enamored with this boy here in this memory, with an average boy, a preacher's son, who seemed to be the object of all affection Torrence had within her.

He saw flashes, memories materialized before his eyes, of Torrence luring men her own age down through the wooded area behind her home. For miles, he followed them, this silent specter, a ghost of the young woman's future, her follower before she'd even known herself to be a leader.

He realized, as he followed the three into the woods, this vision, framed by the lucid memory in a clearer, more precise angle, was given more attention than the others, perhaps because Torrence had given him more attention in the time. Wesley wasn't certain. But memories of Alex were far more sharp and extensive than the ones of the other boys, the men. He tried not to envy this young man.

As he followed him as he followed Torrence, though, he was careful to notice signs of affection instead of those of violence. It was so odd to see no tightening grips or harsh jerks forward, even when Alex hesitated. Wesley hadn't been afforded things like hesitation or concern, not without sustaining some injury for it.

Eventually, the three friends and their pursuing ghost came to a footpath—a thin, uneven trail of beaten-down brush.

Eerie as the sky purpled in the impending nighttime, the pathway seemed a road into the abyss, into the very inferno Wesley now called home, but Torrence was not afraid of it or of what could be lurking in the darkness around it.

Trees lined this path, extending out into the distance on each side of them and before them, save for this small path of somewhat-clearing. The three had to duck beneath branches, and squeeze between trunks.

"Tor, come on," Alex chuckled, and as he followed Torrence and Todd. "What are we doing out here?"

Wesley reached to Alex, wanting to see more of Torrence from his perspective, unobstructed by the thoughts or emotions or manipulation of the young antichrist.

Though the connection merely registered to Torrence's companion as one brushing leaf or limb of dozens, it illuminated Wesley's knowledge of this boy.

Blurry memories, shifting before Wesley's eyes like flickers of lightning trapped in a slowed loop of time, displayed their affections, their enjoyment of one another; Torrence leading him into the confessional box after he attended church with her family for a wedding, their lips delicately connecting, her hands carefully removing from his slacks the white button-up tucked into them. His hesitance obvious, Wesley perceived this internal battle of Alex's desires, love, hope with his worry, naivety, fear.

"It's a celebration of love," Torrence had told him there. "So it's okay."

"We're in God's house," he replied, his hands moving hers away from his body, his shoulders rising protectively as he moved back against the wall.

Always denying her, Wesley thought, But will you tonight?

"We're almost there," Torrence said, breaking through the visions. Wesley watched them slip away, fading into the visitation of the past as if a drop of water melding into a vast lake. Her voice light and chuckling, Torrence teased Alex in these darkened woods. "Don't be a baby."

"I'm not," he said, shielding his head with his forearm from a branch she'd just crossed under and released without concern of him. He scoffed. "You almost hit me with that."

After trudging over a large rock and under an almost-toppled tree, Alex and Wesley were both surprised to find themselves standing in a large, open field.

"Wow," Alex said.

Torrence turned to him and smiled, giddily grabbing his hand and urging him on. She practically skipped through the clearing, the moon casting her fair skin in a luminous, but uneasy, undertone. She appeared a dancing corpse, grinning through her untimely death.

He supposed if he hadn't known her in the present, in the apocalyptic future young Torrence here surely hadn't even considered, this might seem very frightening to him, but when one resided in Hell after years of unknowingly serving the devil, Wesley supposed one could become numb to mildly creepy situations such as this.

After passing through the clearing and into an area that was wooded still, but not as thickly as the previous area, they came to the hideout.

"Wait," Alex said as Torrence led them toward it. "We aren't going in there."

"What'd you expect when you heard 'the hideout'—a five star resort ?" Todd chuckled, nudging him playfully.

Wesley worried himself now. He worried for Alex and his fate. Alex, who wasn't one of Torrence's buyers, who didn't give in to lustful desire, who carried with him a great love for Torrence, and was about to lose his parents. It seemed unlikely he'd follow whatever dark pursuit his companion was attempting to offer, no matter what that meant for him. But then, Torrence had turned an angel, hadn't she? Who couldn't she conquer?

"It's better inside than it looks," Torrence said, taking him by the hand and following Todd down the hill.

When they walked up the mossy steps onto the porch, Alex tried not to think of things like mold or brown recluse spiders. He tried, but failed, to push from his mind the idea that he might awake to a lot of trouble tomorrow and all he'd have to show for it was poison ivy.

When Todd knocked on the door, however, it opened into a world, it seemed for Alex.

A handsome guy about his age stepped aside, nodding to Todd, who also stepped aside so that Torrence could enter first.

The boy at the door seemed to bow to her more than nod, then he looked at Alex and smiled. "Hey, I'm David."

"Hey." Alex returned the warm gesture.

Secular music was playing rather loudly. Music unlike anything Alex had downloaded and listened to in secret. Whatever Torrence's burned on this particular CD, Alex knew it was not something played on the radio, and because it was merely music, just talent and creativity used to express some emotion or some message outside of God's word, he felt a jolt of excitement at pausing to truly listen to it. A sin? Maybe. But certainly not as serious a sin as becoming drunk or having sex.

Torrence took Alex around the dimly lit room, introducing her to the men she referred to as her brothers as music played. The boys drank, smoked cigarettes. A small table had been turned into a bar. Alex felt like he was at a rave, but he took only a bottle of water when Torrence made herself a drink.

"Brothers in what way?" he asked as he settled onto the couch with Torrence, looking around while Todd removed an old lava lamp from the bag he'd been carrying.

"We're more than friends," she said, watching Todd power the lamp with a battery box. It created a purple glow within the room, a glow that made Alex's eyes seem unearthly. "As you can see, we have our own little world here. No one comes here unless they're initiated."

"Into…?"

She chuckled. "The Brethren," she said, shrugging a bit. "I guess that's what we'll call it."

"Am I initiated now?"

"You will be," she said, looking down his hand, his palm, the place her boys had bled from to devote themselves to her.

"What do I have to do?"

"Hmm," she hummed, looking over to Todd at the bar. She moved against Alex now, her hand on a glass, the fingers of her other urging two black straws toward that lovely, average mouth.

"A drink." She grinned.

"Tor," he said, lowering his head.

"Come on," Torrence said, illuminated by the purples and blues of a flowing lava lamp. "One sip will not kill you. It won't condemn you to Hell, either."

He smiled in response, open-mouthed and light, and he looked into the glass. Raising his hand toward it, he bypassed the offered straws and plucked from the drink a lemon slice, which had been stuck on a plastic toothpick and dropped into glass.

He looked up to Torrence as he brought the fruit to his lips, his brows lifting as he took it into his mouth and bites down. Wesley knew this particular expression all too well, though he supposed he'd never witnessed it before. It was approval-seeking. It was compromise. It was the plea that compromise might somehow be enough.

A thin smile spread across Torrence's lips, and she brought the glass to them then and threw back the entirety of the drink in one swift motion. When she came up from the shot, she tossed the glass off to her left and lowered her other hand to his lap, slipping her fingers inside the fraying holes of his jeans to caress his skin.

Alex stiffened. He squirmed a bit, but made no effort to stop her. He merely eyed her. A concern riddled not only his face but his entire body through its physical language.

"There are people here, Torrence."

"They aren't paying any attention to us," she said, leaning into him as kissing his lips.

He let his eyes close, the joy he felt in their connection after their time apart was too encouraging to stop her.

Her free hand came to his jaw, his cheek. Eventually she slipped it around his neck and used her hold to pull him in more tightly.

She hummed at this, at feeling his resistance fade. He gave in to their affection, surrendering to the little world he'd entered with Torrence and these brothers of hers, and let his own hands wander across the uncharted territory of her body.

As their lips parted to accommodate the deepening passion of their embrace, Alex's felt about her neck, her shoulders. A hand slipped beneath the collar of her shirt and fingertips traced the line of her clavicle.

What could it hurt? It was only kisses to lips he'd already tasted and small pets placed upon platonic areas of skin.

She moved away from his lips then, emboldened by his exploration of her shoulder and decolletage, placing gentle, wet offerings of devotion to him and to his flesh upon his jawline and his neck.

Alex gasped at this, the first connection of moistened lips and swift tongue to the sensitive flesh of his throat. His eyes remained closed as she suckled at it, so swiftly and smoothly and with such precision, she seemed to have breathed him into her. It was tantalizing, yes, but also felt very natural, undeniably natural, so much so that his body began reacting in ways his consciousness had no control of.

In recognition of this physical response to her sensuous devotions, Alex's eyes popped open. He moved his head forward now, obstructing her access to his neck, which caused her to pull back from him.

"What is it?" she asked, seeing concern on his face.

He shifted somewhat away from her, his leg moving away from her leg and lifting partly over the other one.

She looked down to his legs, to their meeting point, to the area of jeans that seemed somewhat tightened now over his groin.

"Oh," she said.

His temperature rose at this, his cheeks reddening.

"Don't worry," she said, rising from the couch. She took his hand into hers. "Come with me."

"Torrence, I—I can't—."

"You can." She leaned down, placing her free hand on his

cheek and brushing her lips against his ear. "This isn't something to be ashamed of. You're not in class or at church. You're with me. And they all know you're with me. We'll go into the next room, and if they notice, what they will assume will only make you seem cooler, understand?"

"Oh," he said, swallowing thickly, then nodding. "Okay. Yeah."

They moved through the room mostly undetected, for the boys were busy with their booze and their tales of Torrence-controlled chaos.

They passed a kitchen that hadn't been given as much attention as the living room, passed a restroom that looked fully restored, and into a bedroom that did not a have a door.

They stood between the door and the bed, Torrence moving in front of Alex, and placing her hands on his hips.

"Don't." The word, breathy and shaken, was punctuated by a half-hearted smile. His eyes would not raise from his embarrassment.

"You're not a child, you know," she said.

His brows raised as he glanced up to her. "You heard that, huh?"

"Doesn't matter," she said. "You're not a child."

"I know that." He smiled, looking back down to his feet. "I think…" he brought a finger to his lip and bit at the nail there nervously. He laughed, and brought his eyes to hers again. "I think I'm gonna get a tattoo."

"We'll get matching ones," she said. "On your birthday."

"Yeah, when I'm a man." A chuckle seemed to fall away from his lips as he shook his head and rolled his eyes.

"An official one."

"I am a man," he said. His hands wrung tentatively at her wrists. "I know what I'm doing. I don't….It's my convictions. My beliefs. Not theirs, you know?"

When he looked up to her now, he'd forgotten to angle his

injuries away from her line-of-sight, and the close, white lights of the candles, without shades of purple and blue to mask the abrasions, only highlighted them.

"I know." She frowned, blinking profusely as she eyed his injuries. "I'm sorry," she said, for what might have been the first and only time in her life with any sincerity. "I'll make it up to you."

"It's not your fault."

"I'm gonna fix it, anyway," she said, coaxing him more tightly against her.

When he complied, she moved onto her toes so she could better reach him. Kissing his cheek, replacing the violent connection that had been thrust there only a week prior with a softer, more protective one, Torrence moved her hand into his hair. She placed gentle embrace after gentle embrace over his bruised and broken skin until there was no spot of his face left untouched by her lips.

"I'm sorry," she said again, her brows furrowing as she stared at him.

He stared back for a long moment. Considering her presence here, her action, which seemed to align with her words—she loved him, hadn't she said it? And doesn't their proximity now prove it? He wondered, in this moment of her tenderness, so physical, and so compared to the aggression of his parents' spiritual salvation, why he'd ever doubted Torrence, why he'd ever feared a future without her.

He looked away, trying to control his emotions, for he did not want to cry before her here, not when her hands massaged his flesh, not when his body was warmed against hers. He exhaled a small laugh and looked up to her. "I'm sorry, too."

She smiled, and, in admiration of her lips in this lovely expression, he pressed his own against them, unaware that his parents were being slaughtered at this very moment in time.

But Torrence was aware.

She took advantage of his embrace by pulling him toward the

bed, toward the foot of it, careful always not to push him too far too fast.

As they sat, he let his hands move over her jawline, down her neck. A hand moved into her long, dark hair and played with it.

Kissing him slowly and tenderly, for he always seemed to allow these embraces longer when they were languid and lazy, Torrence offered gentle, nearly-inaudible moans, hoping they might have connected more to his biology than his awareness.

It seemed to work, for he did not awaken from their affectionate trance as he usually did, and as far as she could tell, their slight conversation about his parents and their abuse only diminished his physical excitement for a minuscule, and easily reinvigorated, space of time.

Still determined to give a bit, and newly inspired by a sense of anger at his father's punishment, Alex decided to press his body against Torrence tightly. He angled himself toward her, lifting one of his legs onto bed to more easily reach her.

She grinned against his lips, knowing that she held him in the same sinful caresses for which his parents banished her as they died at her command.

Two murders occurred this evening, and while the rest of the town went on with life completely unaware of the violence within its community. Two lives were taken by her will. Two men became murderers by her instruction. A modern saint fell further victim to her lust as it had happened.

Never had Torrence felt so powerful, so in control of all around her. Her skin prickled and, beneath it, her blood seemed to vibrate, calling out for more, for another rush of adrenaline, another hit of dopamine. She was God here in this town. She could feel the electricity of the divine within her.

Her hand flowed down his chest. Her destination, that sinful organ that seemed ready finally to be received by her, but when her hand came to his pants, his hand came to her wrist. Again.

"If you want to," he whispered, keeping his eyes closed as he kissed her, "you have to marry me."

She chuckled against his lips, leaning into him as he raised her hand away from his groin and brought it between their chests. He looked down to this connection. Stroked her ring finger. His eyes, rendered fearful by the curve of his brows above them, looked up to hers. "As soon as I turn eighteen," he said, "will you?"

Torrence stared into his eyes. Her brows, her lips, her eyes all level and revealing nothing. Not even the pace of her breathing altered. After a long moment, her lips parted, but before she could speak, they were interrupted by a knock.

Alex looked behind him, over his shoulder and saw a hand tapping its busted knuckles against the wooden door-frame.

"Hey, Tor," he said.

"Hey. This is Alex."

"Don," he said, offering Alex a friendly nod. "This is Aaron."

Alex only smiled. He tried to do so sincerely, but something about the men made him uneasy.

"Can I talk to you?" Don asked. "Privately."

"Yeah," she said, standing, "of course." She looked to Alex. "I'll be right back."

"Torrence, wait," he whispered, taking her wrist into his hand.

"What?" she asked, leaning down slightly.

"Are you sure you should go somewhere alone with them?" He glanced over to the men at the door. "These guys don't seem questionable at best."

"Don't worry." She smiled warmly, leaning down to kiss his cheek, then whispering in his ear. "They'd never question me." When she stood, her chin lifted. A brow arched over an eye. The left side of her mouth curled upward into half a grin.

In the next room, in small whispers, the men recounted the deed to Torrence. It was done. Their bodies were at the church.

They'd taken them in their family car, which was now sinking into the lake. No evidence left, they were certain.

Alex was hers now.

CHAPTER SEVENTEEN

Along with the rest of her brothers, Alex and Torrence spent the night at the hideout. It was the first night they shared together, the first night they'd fallen asleep in each others' arms without having to wake up and part ways.

When Alex awoke, he nestled into her, using his arm, which was hooked loosely around her waist, to pull her tightly into him. He had to get home, though. He taught Bible class at 4 p.m. on Saturdays, and he needed to get to his parents before then.

Todd dropped him off at his house, but they were not home. Neither was their car. He assumed they'd left for the church without him. He was meant to be home sooner than he'd arrived, after all, and what of his physical fitness in the morning? He'd missed it all.

He tried to call his mother but received no answer. The same went for his father. He'd have called the church, but if a sermon was in progress, he did not want to interrupt it.

He counted his losses. Went to take a shower. Spent the next few hours studying, then tried to call again.

With no answer still, he figured he was receiving the silent treatment. He shuddered. If they were this upset, he did not want to imagine what punishment awaited him when they came home. He resigned himself to wrongdoing, guilt, shame, and therefore decided to watch one of his movies instead of continuing his studies.

He'd fallen asleep with his laptop on his knees, the party and the stress of it all not exactly making for a restful night, but the movie was over. It was dark outside his window. It was almost six p.m.

When he sat up, he realized no lights were on in the house, at least not in the hallway or even the bathroom. It was odd.

He left his bed and slowly peered out his door. No light came from downstairs either.

It was too late for his parents to be at church still, but when he looked outside their car was not there.

He picked up the phone, trying each of his parents and then the church one more time. When he still got no response, he called his father's best friend, who informed him that the church had been locked up all day. No sermons and no Bible studies. Alex, then, called Torrence and explained his situation.

"I'm going to walk over there."

"No," she said, not wanting him to find the bodies alone. "I'll come pick you up. We'll go together."

"No, they're not going to like that."

"Who cares? You can't go alone. You can't walk the entire way there in the dark."

"I'll be fine," he said. "Just wanted you to know what's going on in case something happens."

"Alex—."

"I'll talk to you later, Tor," he said, adding before hanging up, "I love you."

Torrence went straight to Todd's house. Blake joined them shortly after she arrived.

She needed guidance. She was debating on what to do, on whether or not to go there. She knew she'd get there before Alex. She didn't know if this would look suspicious. She couldn't have that. But she didn't want him to be alone. He was in no danger, she knew that. The only people in the area participating in crime did so at her instruction, and they'd known for over a year not to harm Alex. What a horrific sight he was walking toward, though. The pain that was surely coming for him. She hoped eventually he'd feel free. No more bruised wrists or backs. No more biblical verses yelled out between blows. He was free from the tyranny of it now. He'd see it eventually, wouldn't he?

As they debated, another call came. This time from an unknown number.

"What?" Torrence gasped as she spoke into the phone. Her brows moved with her emotion, as if she had become the worried, confused girlfriend more than she portrayed it. "Slow down. Alex, wait. Slow."

She looked at Todd and at Blake. A brow arched over her gleaming eyes. She was having fun here, but not at Alex's expense. Instead, it was the sense of control that washed over her, that seeped into her pores as it spread across her skin. Alex was hers. He was undeniably hers now. "Of course, I'll come get you. I'll be right there."

"Torrence," Alex whispered as she arrived on-scene.

"Alex," she said breathily, rushing from her car without shutting off the engine or closing the door.

Her arms opened as she moved, ready to receive him as he shifted slowly; partially paralyzed by what occurred here, by the fact that this was his reality, by the barrage of emotions that seemed to spring forth and explode into nothingness before firing off again. His body, fragile in its humanity, was only flesh and blood, and, because of its mortal makeup, seemed unable to withstand the weight of these internal, spiritual eruptions, much less to carry them across the grass and toward the driveway.

"Tor." He barely spoke the word aloud as he collapsed into her embrace. His hands, hanging by his sides limply, shook as they attempted to rise. Only one hand found her body. Trembling, it settled on Torrence's belt, caught there as it attempted to grip onto her but fell away in weakness.

"What happened?" She wrapped an arm around his body. Her hand held onto his neck tightly, protectively.

He didn't answer. He couldn't. He sobbed, but serenely. No sniffing or gasping. Only labored breath accentuated sporadically with a small whimper.

An officer, who remained outside the scene with Alex until his next-of-kin arrived, approached the young couple, offering Torrence only the necessary information as explanation and asking her if Mr. Breslin would mind taking Alex in for the night.

Torrence ensured him that her parents wouldn't mind, and it took little more than that for the officer, who knew her established family well, to release the all-but-incapacitated boy into her charge.

Alex said nothing on the ride to Torrence's home. He sat with his elbow on the handlebar and his chin in his fingers, staring out the window, watching the driveways of small homes become stone gateways that led the way to mansions.

Torrence glanced over at him, watching him as the occasional stoplight illuminated his face before it was lost inside the darkness of the night once more.

She was pleased to have him so fully now, but could not shake the discomfort pooling in her gut. His handsome face so pale and absent of its typical vitality seemed wrong, even when freeing him of parental bonds was surely the correct action to have taken.

How beautiful were elegant features when touched by sorrow; the loosely furrowed brows of uncertainty angled over glistening eyes and the downward slant of turmoil on shapely, trembling lips.

Of all things in the world, Torrence appreciated beauty, and the idea of draping it in desolation was tragically poetic.

Much like a work of great art, this obvious and all-consuming pain deepened Alex's beauty. No more were the days of shallow smiles and half-hearted passions. Inside the creamy skin and taut frame lingered the same childish inclinations, the dreams and the desires, but now the idealism of such things had passed. Mortality was evident. Emotion was proven physically painful in its manifestations, for his lovely blue irises were wading in rivers of salt and sorrow, which reddened his eyes and filled his sinuses with tension.

All things tangible were acknowledged now as impermanent. All things invisible were verifiable. Nothing had meant what it had before tonight, and everything tomorrow morning would be different.

Depth, Torrence realized, came with great suffering, great pain, and great loss. And nothing was so beautiful as the watering eyes of an innocent spirit.

"Alex," she whispered when they arrived in her parents' garage. Gently she reached for his hand on his lap. "I'm so sorry."

He inhaled deeply, eyes still gazing out the window, as if he might witness his parents' ascent into the heavens if he stared into the stars long enough. He let her slip her hand into his, let her fingers close around his palm.

After a long moment, he turned toward her, but his eyes fixed on their hands. He tried to smile, but with the expulsion of held breath came a torrent of sobs.

Allowing him this suffering, Torrence merely watched him. In awe of his splendor here, this raw emotion, she felt the tingling sensation of undefined thought spread through her body, prickling her skin and increasing the rate of her heart.

There was so much dishonesty in the world, so much

hypocrisy and insincerity, that this display of truth was hard not to admire.

Alex, forlorn and longing, seemed an angel here; his countenance flawless as the emotion encompassed it, his spirit as raw in the expression of his pain as his body's reactions to it.

"Come inside," she said. The minute-hand of arbitrary time turned their late night, in an instant, into early morning. "You need rest. Warmth."

He merely nodded, following her inside.

In eerie silence, he moved through the home with her. His thoughts never circled around her parents or their whereabouts or what their opinions of him, as a man, entering their daughter's room so late at night might have been.

His mind was a blank slate, whittled by turmoil and composed of pain, but nothing so defined as words or thoughts was carved upon the board.

As he ascended the stairs, he did not consider sin. Temptation was not a concern in his mind nor a worry in his heart. He only wanted to sleep, to shut out the world, but Torrence had taken him and she held his hand now and she guided him toward her own desires.

He did not have the strength to fight them. He did not even have the consciousness to consider this battle of wills as such.

He felt darkness encompassing him, and he wanted to be lost to it.

"Are you hungry?"

Briefly his eyes looked up to her, as if the sound of her voice made him suddenly aware of her presence there, then they fell again, and he gently shook his head. He couldn't eat. He couldn't imagine eating.

"Okay," she said, wiping at his silent tears. "Wait here. I'm gonna be right back."

Alex sat on the edge of her bed stupefied. He wanted to pray. He wanted to speak, to talk to Torrence or to God, to get it all out. He didn't know how to control his thoughts or his body enough to do either.

When she returned, she sat beside him on the bed, wrapping around his back her free arm and resting on his shoulder her hand. She brought a bowl of hot water with her and removed a cloth from it.

Torrence was careful to expel the fluid from it before raising it to Alex's face. Pressing it against his cheeks, she wiped at the skin tightened by salt and expanded by dehydration. She used the soft cloth to brush away his tears, to cleanse him of the pain they represented, to warm his skin, which had been chilled by the winter air outside.

Slowly he looked up to her. They gazed at one another solemnly as she pressed the cloth beneath his reddened eyes, warming him, cleaning him, taking care of him.

Suddenly he reached for her; his hand moving to her cheek as his lips pressed frantically against hers.

She moved against him, both unconscious to their position, as their lips and tongues and teeth mingled and clattered. All was passion and intensity. Nothing was so physical as it seemed.

Alex wanted to be absorbed by her, to fall into her caresses and her kisses and be lost to the world around him. All this pain, all this tragedy, he wanted it replaced, all of it, with something pleasant and pleasurable.

He saw his future go up in smoke. The idea that he and Torrence might have a family some day, that his father might marry them, that her father might send them on some extravagant honeymoon where they, among the sandy beaches of some far-off paradise, might come together as husband and wife and create a new life comprised of her blood and of his—this idea was gone. Images of their child at Christmas with both families, gone.

What good was planning now? What good was daydreaming? Was this all it had been, a dream?

Perhaps life did not unfold that way, and perhaps Torrence

was his family now, but only by default, for as badly as he wanted those imaginings, he could never truly see Torrence as someone's bride or as someone's mother.

He wondered if he'd been the reason for his parents' tragic deaths, if they'd died to satisfy his fantasy, if the only way he could have Torrence forever was if she felt responsible for him. She was all he had now, and he knew that she knew it.

With this worry in his mind, he fell back into the bed, pulling her into him. As they repositioned more comfortably, Torrence laid back into the pillows and Alex, whose lips never left hers, pursued.

His breathing grew heavy, heart raced, but he slipped inside the intensity and let it push everything else away from him.

As she repositioned herself, moving her legs so that they pressed against his sides, he settled down between them, leaving no space between them save for the thin layer of their clothing. He felt himself harden, but didn't want to shy away from it this time.

He pressed against her further, hearing her humming reaction, feeling her lips vibrate against his own.

Why was this so wrong? He'd been convinced Torrence was here for life, he knew it; he knew he'd die in love with her, in her arms. Why, then, did it matter if they behaved as husband and wife before the title applied? What if it never came? What if Torrence wanted to spend their lives together without involving the church or the court systems? Then what? They could never cohabitate? They could never procreate? They could never simply touch each other? How long would Torrence, who so often expressed her affections for him physically, tolerate such a thing?

He couldn't lose her, especially not now, but his mind was everywhere and nowhere, focusing on the feel of her skin and the touch of her lips, instead of facing the reality of his turmoil and his loss.

Torrence was lost in him, too. The fact that his parents were murdered was absent from her mind, just as the fact that it was by her doing had been forgotten. All she knew was Alex, her sweet, beautiful Alex, was on top of her, touching her, letting his trembling hands run tentatively across her chest and down her side. Finally, it came to her hip, his fingers slipping beneath her shirt and massaging the skin there.

He didn't know what to do with it. He only knew he was nearer to the act than he had been before.

When she felt his hand move away from her hip, she opened her eyes. She assumed, as what usually happened, that she was losing him.

Instead she looked down, feeling his lips still on her neck, to watch a trembling hand and unskilled fingers fumble with his belt, his button, his zipper.

His lips fell away from her neck, a great exhale of emotion fleeing from them. His hand stopped. His forehead creased as it fell against her neck.

Her hand came to his neck, her fingers petting the base of his hairline. "Alex," she said, shifting a bit so that he came away from her.

He kept his head angled away from her for a long moment of thought. Tension flooded his face as his tears fell in waves again. After a few heavy breaths, he looked up to her, gazing into her eyes, his features tightening. "I don't want to lose you," he said. "Torrence, be honest, will I lose you if I don't have sex with you?"

"What?" The word was a breath. Confusion conquered all emotion within her and shaped her features in its control. It was if she'd never considered such a thing, as if her actions, her insistence should not have suggested this worry. "No," she said, hands moving to his neck, his chest, pressing their weight on him as she crushed him against her so that he felt her sternness, her reality. "No, you won't lose me."

"Torrey," he said, eyes full of tears. "I don't know what to do from here. I don't know where to go. I can't go home."

"You don't have to."

His hands moved to her body now, an attempt at a hug, but it felt wrong. Why should he express such affection? Why should he seek comfort or love here? How could he think of anything but the fact that his parents were gone, taken away? He felt selfish. He was in pain. But he loved Torrence and she was holding him, and while it didn't make anything better, it did feel good, for he wasn't alone and this was a reminder of that fact.

"Alex," she said as they came together, "I've got you. I promise."

"Tor," he whispered, burying his face into her neck, her hair. "I'm sorry. I'm mixed up."

"Of course you are." She pushed his tears away from his eyes, his fingers moving into his hair and rubbing at his head. "Lay down. I'll get something for your head."

"You don't have to—."

"Lay down," she said. "I'll be right back."

Coming into consciousness, Wesley watched Alex closely, seeing him curl up onto the bed, shifting and dismayed. He slipped off his socks and then tried to lay down again, but there was still such discomfort in his face. He looked up to the door to Torrence's bedroom, which she'd closed behind her when she exited, sat up, and after a deep breath, removed his stiff, uncomfortable jeans. Quickly he moved beneath the covers, biting at the inside of his jaw.

When Torrence returned, she brought a glass of water and two small pills.

Wesley moved closer to her, eyeing her hand, wanting to see what she was giving him, fearing what she was giving him. He stood up in surprise as she moved into the bed with him, for she brought him basic aspirin.

He looked helpless, slouching and teary-eyed, as he gazed up to her. She handed him the medication and he took it into his fingers, looking at it, reading the letters printed upon the pills.

After putting one into his mouth, she brought the glass to his lips, petting him as he drank from it. He was hers.

He took the second pill, and then smiled as best as he could at her, lifting his hand to her hand and nestling into it.

"Thank you."

"I'm sorry, Alex."

"For what?" His reddened eyes opened, looking up to her.

"Everything," she said, pushing away another bout of tears.

He hissed when her fingers passed over the bruised skin there, freshly made tender from his sobbing.

"I don't know why this happened," he said after a long moment.

"I know. I wish I could give you some answer that would make it feel okay."

Another attempt at smiling tugged at his gestures, his eyes falling, catching the shimmer of Torrence's necklace, the T he'd given her just a week ago. "You never answered my question," Alex said, eyes moving up to hers. Insecurity creased his forehead, pulled his brows together. He exhaled through his parted lips, the uneasy smile upon them almost made the sound seem a laugh, but it wasn't one.

"Not any time soon," she said, "but maybe someday."

He looked up to her, brows knitting together as a thin frown came to his pursuing lips.

If Alex had been anyone else, she'd have lied to him, she'd have lied and said yes, of course. But Alex was not just a boy, not just a man, just a person, or even just a soul.

Torrence knew it. She saw the radiance in him. She'd seen it the first moment she'd seen his body, slouched over a Bible as he walked onto a school bus.

She didn't know what it was about him, whether the spirit existed truly or not; maybe it was just the structure of his bones and the porcelain quality of his skin. Maybe it was nothing but her hormones. She didn't know, but it didn't matter.

Much like her path here on earth, her destiny, she felt it more than she knew it. It was undeniable, but unclear.

"We don't have to be married to be together," she said. "What we have is deeper than that. We're bonded. Bound together by some force we're too limited to understand. I don't know if we did it, if we created this bond by coming together, or if we came together because it already existed, but either way, it's real. It's a force—an unseen one—but a heavy, powerful one. I can feel it. The way I feel about my future, this uncertainty in terms or language, but a knowledge that what I'm doing is right, it's how I feel about you. Like you're meant to be on this path with me. Like you're part of the destiny."

Alex's watery eyes gazed into hers. His hands came to her face, thumbs brushing over her lips, the lips that not only pressed upon his flesh a great affection, but also articulated it, somehow, perfectly even without the language to define it.

He leaned into her, bringing his lips to those lips, those passageways through which he'd come to know her, her wants, her desires, her opinions, her thoughts. He parted his lips to allow her the deepened kisses she'd always worked toward, understanding now that without the mouth or the tongue, getting to know Torrence—getting to know anyone—would've been exceptionally more difficult.

It was language, he understood, that bound humans to each other. Actions perhaps proved them or disproved them, but it was the word that was convincing, the concepts of the words, what the words represented to the mind which translated their vibrations when the ear merely heard them.

To praise these lips was to honor what they'd spoken. To bring their lips together was an agreement, a requited understanding. Yes, he, too, felt this way, felt this connection, this bond.

They fell back into the bed, Alex refusing to shy away from these physical affections now. The pressure always circling in the pit of his stomach, the worry that this mingling of flesh must end with the lustful friction of entering and exiting in fluid motion had been eradicated.

Torrence loved him—him, not his body. This connection that paired them on the path of destiny was one of the mind and the soul, it was evidence that she wasn't lying when she told him she would not leave him if he did not succumb to mutual desire.

He let her pull his shirt away from his body so she could see his flesh, to recognize it, to trail its lines and contours, but no more than this. He trembled as he brought his hands to her clothing, ready to release her from it, too, but she performed the act for him.

Their bodies pressed against one another, nothing between them save for their undergarments, their flesh against flesh, the spirit closer than ever it had been before.

After some time of this, they laid in silence. On their sides, they faced one another, eyes ignoring the tantalizing forms for the depth of their eyes.

Torrence moved her arm around his waist, holding him. Her fingers running down his back, they paused. They came across small mounds of soft flesh. Her breathing caught there.

"Torrey," he said wearily, knowing she'd found scars.

"I thought I saw cuts here once."

"No. I—." He stopped. No reason to deny it. He remembered the semi-fight they'd had when these scars were opened, scabbing wounds. His tongue slipped from his lips and licked their drying skin, but his mouth was drying, too. "I didn't want you to know."

She kissed him, then brought her fingers to her lips and kissed their tips. Slipping her hand back to his body, she brought the moisture of her gentle affection to his back and pressed her fingers delicately against the scars.

Flowing around his body, her hand came to his wrist next, the memory of the bruise there hidden beneath the sleeve of his button-up when they'd first met. She kissed the area, closing her eyes and caressing it.

"No one will ever hurt you again," she said. "I'll make sure of it."

"They didn't…" Emotion tightened his throat. He could barely breathe, let alone speak. "It wasn't the way you think it was."

"The way it was doesn't matter. Only that it was."

Pressure built in his face as he attempted to withhold these emotions. He didn't want to face them himself, especially now with what had just happened this day, and he detested the thought of Torrence hearing it, knowing, but it seemed she already knew.

"It's okay," she said. She repeated it. She stroked his face, his hair. She continued a litany of small, comforting phrases and delicate pets.

Finally he gave way to his experiences, allowing the memories of righteousness and repercussion, of Biblical verse and broken arm to flow freely into his awareness. He sobbed. A broken thing. Body shaking as the weakened cries fled his trembling lips.

Torrence pulled him into her fiercely. Her arms were all-encompassing and forceful. Protective. Strong. A rock on which to cling when all the world at Alex's feet seemed to crumble and break away.

He felt weak. Stupid. A child here without his parents, abused by his parents. Fearful of every experience they'd told him not to have and hating himself for being so intertwined in one of them now—a weakened man, a man who showed his partner his vulnerability, and why be so near a partner, in her bed with her, when she was not his spouse?

This woman, her almost-bare body pressed against his almost-bare body in this sinful expression of affection, somehow seemed to exude a purer love for him than the strict, godly, authoritative love of his parents, who were good, humble, modest

Christians, and with this in mind, regardless of the pain he felt this night for his great loss, he raised his throbbing head and pressed against her lips his trembling mouth.

He realized the foundations on which his potential and now-lost future, the metaphors of spirituality and their practices were crumbling this night too, for all he had to fear with Torrence hadn't come from Torrence, but had been spoken to him about her in specific and women in general.

"Thou shalt not…" It was all he could hear reverberating in his mind, this great, echoing sermon in the distorted voice of recently-dead father as he laid half-naked in the bed of his lover. Lover, yes, in spirit, but how could he continue resisting the word in physical form, too? How? How when Torrence had shared this experience with other men, with men like Todd, who Alex knew she did not love.

Maybe it did not negate anything between them—the fact that he would not surrender to physical love when others had experienced it with her—but instead only reinforced the fact that love was not physical, and that its physical expression was not important in the way he'd always been told.

After all, if Torrence could have sex with someone she did not love, then it only brought validity to the idea that she could love someone with whom she did not have sex.

It was too much to consider, too broad a spectrum of experience and emotion and individual perceptions to come to some sort of true conclusion, which pained him further.

He either had to lie here in this bed, having lost his parents to a violent and untimely death, with the understanding that eventually this most precious relationship would falter for the belief instilled in him or he had to accept that no matter what he'd lost already, he would not lose this connection regardless of what he withheld from its physicality.

Torrence felt a moisture brush against her lips, and the awareness of this small sensation brought awareness of all others.

Alex's lips, though working desperately against her own, were trembling. His breathing was punctuated, shaken, and the understanding now that what slipped inside the crevices of their conjoining lips had been tears.

She attempted to withdraw from him, but he held her tightly, chasing her lips as she pulled away.

"Alex," she whispered, but he insisted, pressing on.

His brows creased intently. Tears streamed from the corners of his tightly-closed eyes. He tried to steady his shaken breathing, but ultimately faltered.

His head fell away from her, finding rest upon her shoulder as his arms wrapped around her more completely. He crushed her against him, burying himself in her, wanting to shed from their bodies their remaining clothing and to expel from his mind the guilt surrounding such a thing. Closer than he'd ever been now, he wanted closer still. He wanted to know, not to very much believe, that no one was connected to one another the way he was connected to Torrence. And hadn't she already said as much?

"It's okay," she said, her go-to statement. She stroked his hair, kissed his temple.

When he tired of this, when the wells of his eyes ran dry and the heaving of his chest slowed, she urged him onto his back. He sank into the bed, rolling on his side and cradling a pillow.

Torrence moved against him. She wrapped her arms around him as he curled into himself in the middle of her bed. Conforming her body to his, Torrence nestled her face into his neck and placed offerings of tender affection about the flesh there and the flesh of his back, his shoulders.

She whispered reassurance to him. She spoke gently of love and comfort and safety. No one would ever harm Alex. No one who has previously would ever again, including his father.

Torrence was the ruler here. Torrence led men to death and desecration. If she wanted Alex secure, this is all he'd ever be.

CHAPTER EIGHTEEN

Alex spent the following days in a blur. He divided his time between Torrence's home and Todd's home, always feeling out of place in the grandeur of their houses, the lavish rooms filled with expensive artwork and pristine chandeliers.

He'd attempted to go to school, but found it overwhelming. He couldn't go home, it felt empty and somewhat frightening.

He felt like a ghost, a spirit wandering around in flesh that no longer seemed attached to the world around him.

He spent more time at the hideout, though not necessarily with the other boys. This was both by his own choice and by Torrence's design, for he spent much of his time with his books and going over missing homework with Todd while Torrence preferred still that their mission, their activities be unknown to him.

Even when she congregated with the boys in the living room, Alex remained in the bedroom with his books or his laptop. Certain members of his new family still filled him with unease, others made him feel awkward. But the hideout was the only place in which he did not feel as if he were a burden or in some way inferior to everyone within it.

And for all the turmoil felt for the lost lives of his parents, a new concern seeped into his mind—what of his own safety? What if whoever had done this wasn't finished? Because Alex was supposed to be at that church that day.

For the gang and for Torrence, life went on. Torrence made preparations for her brothers and her boyfriend respectively.

It hadn't yet been two weeks since Alex experienced the greatest tragedy of his young life, but he hadn't cried himself to sleep the night prior, as he had all nights since the murder, so Torrence figured it was time to address the new fear, the fear Alex had of this criminal and the fact that they had still been unnamed, uncharged.

She knew it was time to name this great perpetrator, with an omission or two of specific guilt, with the truth bent just a little.

It wasn't that she thought Alex was ready to accept her actions, her plans for her future, or even her position as the leader of a gang of vile men—she'd expected to have more time tempting him at the hideout with parties and wine, commenting to him during horror films and heavy metal on the great power these violent beings held, how Alex could hold it to, or could at least lie next to it and know that it would never exert its will upon him.

But Alex feared his life was in jeopardy, even though it was the most revered in the minds of those violent perpetrators, for they knew Torrence's instructions were to never harm Alex in any way—physical, mental, emotional.

He had to know that now. To calm him. Torrence would reveal all she was and all she controlled prematurely to her plans, which were crafted to benefit her, so that Alex would not feel so much stress.

She worried, of course, that she would lose him, but the worry was easily pushed aside, for Torrence was the ruler of men, the conqueror of their hearts, their minds, and even their spirits. No one denied her. No one.

For his safety, she brought Alex to the hideout. She brought him there alone. No external presences, no threatening faces or unrecognized bodies.

Just them, their love, their intertwined destinies.

When they entered, Torrence lit every one of the myriad candles on the walls and the desk and the tables. She wanted it as bright as possible for Alex, as comfortable as possible.

"I've made some adjustments," she said, opening the door and extending her arm into it.

"Adjustments?" He walked inside, momentarily surprised by all of the light, astonished that so many tiny, flickering, unstable sources could illuminate an entire room, but when he looked at Torrence, he knew things, beings, entities did not have to be large to be powerful.

"Fixed the lighting," she said playfully, her brows jumping as she looked to the candles.

They were everywhere, in candelabra upon the wall and upon shelves there, their red wax melting and rolling down their pillars in unsteady streams.

Across the table, encompassed by the burning candles, were framed photos of Torrence and Alex together, above them on the walls was the red string, the IDs of her brothers on one side of it, the IDs of her victims on the other.

"What is that?" He looked at the string and the IDs and the photos surrounded by candles.

"Offerings," she said, her arms slipping around him.

"To who?"

"Me," she said, smiling as she slipped her hands to the back pockets of his jeans and then removed his wallet.

Stepping toward the altar as she opened his wallet, Torrence plucked from it his license. She turned to face the wall, staring to the card in her hand then up to the offered ones.

Slowly Alex came to her. His hands in his pockets, shoulders slightly risen, he stood behind her, staring at the licenses and school IDs.

"If you were anyone else, I'd tell you to pick a side," she said, her fingers brushing over his smiling face on his license, holding it out and comparing it to his face within their framed memories. "But you're not anyone else."

"A side of what?" He looked up to the string, his brows creasing. "Is that Todd? And Blake. The brothers on the left, huh?"

Smiling as he looked at the ID photos of his new friends, he moved against her, his arms hooking around her waist as his eyes moved to the right side of the string.

For a few seconds, a few scans of strangers' faces, nothing clicked, but then came the serene face of a lovely young man with brown hair and wide eyes, a young man named Joe.

"Wait…" Alex said, his features falling. "I've seen this one." He moved around Torrence now, keeping an open hand at her shoulder as he leaned over the table and the candles and his photos to better see the ID. "Joe Glasser. He was in the paper. He was…"

His head turned sharply to her. She stared up to him from the license in her hand.

"Did you do something to him?"

"No." She handed him back his wallet.

Hesitantly he took it. Tapped it against his fingers a few times. "What is this?"

"Your initiation." She took him by the hand now, guiding him through the hallway and into the bedroom. "It's just us tonight."

He swallowed what seemed a great mass of sand and glass, and then he looked away briefly. Tried to collect himself. Tried to imagine the world he'd been living in—the one of uniforms and faith-fueled sciences, the one he'd begged to leave for something more considerably normal, something like schools on ABC's teenaged-geared television shows on their TGIF line-up.

He'd escaped the rigid world of religious-everything and thought he'd found himself, a handsome boy in a jean jacket, hand-in-hand with the absurdly beautiful young woman who was not only ideal in terms of intelligence and affection, but was also surely his soulmate.

Now he realized all the isolation from the average immorality had done was blind him to the fact that old adages such as "too good to be true" were so cliched because they had been, in fact, too common and too true to be anything except overused.

Oh, an understanding set in now, an acknowledgment of human flaw and frailty. A person as equally intelligent as attractive had only one space of the human condition in which to fall deficient, and that deficit was of the soul.

"Torrence," he whispered.

"It's okay," she said as gently but with much more assurance. Still gripping him tightly, her hand possessive of his, Torrence drew attention to her opposite appendage, raising her free hand to his gaunt face and caressing his cheek tenderly. "No matter what happens," she said genuinely, "I'll never let anyone hurt you. You'll always be safe with me."

Alex hated it, but he felt himself melting into the touch and into the words, closing his eyes and sinking into the promises she spoke. He couldn't conceive of a sensation more pleasurable, especially when he'd felt his body turn so cold so suddenly, than the warmth of her hand, and he noted the same reassuring temperature enveloping his hand where it remained in her grip.

She was strong, yes. Aggressive and untamed in her keen intensity, but she was tender, too. She had been adoring always. Even when he denied her the physical acts of their affection, she loved him still.

Couldn't it be possible, he considered, here in her captive embrace, that she was the indomitable force, too often portrayed as male, that conquered as easily as it existed, but softened only for the one delicate soul that would never challenge it, only love it;

that would never judge it, only embrace it?

Yes, Torrence was vicious, he realized this now in all she had been doing unbeknownst to him, to her father, and to the authorities, but that was part of the force she represented. She was charming and commanding. She was headstrong and self-assured. And while men fell clamoring to her feet, spouting praises of worship and pleading to attend to her every whim, Alex couldn't deny the fact that she only returned such attention to him alone. He liked that especially.

"Tor," he whispered, his voice still slow and uncertain as his eyes came open.

"Don't worry," she said, still stroking his cheek. Stepping toward him now, she used her grip to move his arm around her, instructing his hand to rest at the small of her back. "You are safe with me. No one will ever hurt you. No one will ever hurt you again. I'll make sure of it. Your brothers will make sure of it."

His eyes opened more widely at this, the haze of his comfort with her proximity and their past lifting in the realization. Brothers. Men who worshiped Torrence, who followed her into literal and figurative darkness. She'd adopted them, her brooding and rebellious boys who sought destruction for the institutions which bound them to meaningless, material existences. What Torrence had offered to them was—Alex could not deny—very spiritual. A cause, a purpose, a freedom for which to fight, and when she declared this small but passionate war upon society at large—the great adversary, the devil in this tale of Saint Torrence—she'd painted herself the savior.

Her practices, however frightening or illegal or sinful, were not rooted in religious, regardless of how cerebral or spiritual the cause. It wasn't blasphemy, was it, if Torrence had not declared herself as God, but merely as a ruler here in this rebellion that denounced the things that God denounced; greed, false idols, lack of charity, over-consumption in all forms?

"I can't participate in this—."

"I don't want you to," she said, moving closer to him, decrying her arms in their protective force about his waist. "I want you exactly as you are."

A sharp exhale left his nose. An exhale of relief. The desire came with it to relax into her embrace. This closeness, this mingling of body temperatures in the chilly house of some isolated forest, was comforting in the obvious physical manner, and as Torrence raised her chin and shifted her weight onto her toes, Alex leaned into her as well.

He let her lips brush against his, tentatively for his sake, not for some hesitation within her, and this consideration of his consent, though unexpressed in words, was not only evident to him, but also an incentive to proceed.

The small embrace, unchaste in some regard as the potential first step in a dance of carnal sin, seemed purer here than ever before.

"Tor," he tried again, but she closed her lips around her name on his tongue.

Cooing at the returned intimacy, Alex used his hand at her back to pull their bodies more tightly together. His lips parted when hers did; his mouth mimicking her motions in both the desire to perform well for her benefit, and to continue such pleasurable sensations for his own. Passion in the physical, but the spirit revolted. Robbery. Theft. Assault. These things occurred in his city at his girlfriend's command. How could he experience some comfortable safety with her when she caused so much discomfort in strangers by robbing them of theirs?

He squirmed slightly, stepping back but not releasing her. He couldn't release her. What if he could save her?

He felt the base of the bed against the back of his knees. He hadn't realized he'd moved them this far, but he had. She used it to her loving advantage, urging him downward, and he complied and sat.

She moved atop him as she always did, so familiar and so

warm.

Warmth, heat, Hell. Oh, damnation. He could not bear the thought of Torrence in eternal turmoil. Hell. Torrence in Hell. The very thought caused his guts to tumult and filled his muscles with tension.

When his limbs stiffened, he spoke to soften it for her. "You can't…" the air Alex attempted to draw into his parting lips seemed to shake in response to his trembling body. "If not for the sake of others, then for your own."

"No one will catch me," she said, pulling back, but refusing to release him. "I don't know how I know, but I do. This is what I'm meant to do, though the reasoning is still a little blurred."

"You want to inspire change, Torrence, you don't need to involve these people, these innocents."

"Innocents, no," she said. "There is a method for choosing them. They are either candidates for our mission or they are deemed unworthy. The unworthy are either given back their wallets and never bothered again or they are revisited. The difference is how they live their lives. The last guy—Todd watched him kick his dog, so the boys broke into his house and took the dog to a rescue, but not before kicking his teeth down his throat. An eye for an eye, isn't it?"

"Turn the other cheek doesn't seem to apply to abuse," Alex said, somewhat dejectedly, for assault was bad, yes, but a person who exerted violence upon the most innocent of God's creations, the nonhuman animals, well, that person deserved what he got. Alex couldn't deny it. He only wished there was no abuse and no consequential assault instead of a world that had both or either.

"There is no abuse here." Torrence, in his lap, spoke the softest words in an equally soft tone. She brushed her hands along his cheek, ran her fingers through his hair. "Only devotion. Love. Safety."

"Torrence, what of your safety? If you don't worry about spiritual consequences, what about earthly ones? What about retaliation? Fighting back? What about dying?"

"Aren't we all dying, Alex?" She pressed her lips against his cheek, lingering there, nestling against him, closing her eyes and breathing him in. "Isn't this flesh, this body, a moment closer to decay every moment it lives?"

"Yes, but to hurry the process—."

"I only hurry toward my destiny," Torrence said. "And I die swiftly to think you aren't a part of it." She pulled back slightly, looking into his eyes as she brushed her fingers along his cheek, his neck. "The spirit dies," she said, taking his hand in hers and bringing it to her chest. "The heart beats, but only for you. Otherwise, its chilly nature will surely freeze. It'll crack in the frostbitten absence of your divine heat. It'll break away. Disintegrate. I'll be no more alive, no more human, no more warm than the silvery blade painted red by a physical death. Only my body will continue existing. It'll go on without its soul. You are my sanity, perhaps, but you are certainly my warmth. My conscience. The only being who could fill my heart with life. I don't want to die, Alex. Keep me warm."

CHAPTER NINETEEN

It was difficult for Alex, this paradigm shifting that never seemed to stop.

In less than a month's time he'd had to face the death of his family, the loss of their lives, the potential loss of his own life, the worry for strangers who suffered and were written about by Torrence's father in the Daily Knowledge Pages, and now that his most beloved companion was somehow involved with the tragedies of which her father had written.

Beyond these very material, physical concerns came spiritual ones, emotional ones. He had already been wrestling with the concept of love and affection and the ways in which it was healthy to express these emotions, the ways in which it was sinful to do so, but now he looked at those sacrilegious performances and saw them draped in a new light—the cascading, warm light of sunbeams upon the flesh; how was so much pleasure so wrong for the soul? If the body is the temple of the soul, how can its desires be so separate from the good of the spirit?

But he did not have his father, the preacher, the knower of the word, to help him analyze these considerations and interpret, not only their meaning to God, but their meaning to Alex himself.

It wasn't that he did not trust Torrence with these thoughts, more so that he did not trust himself with them. He was reaching a point of confusion where he felt he might he agree with anything so long as it followed some train of logic, so long as it provided some answer that made sense, where prior he would've been able to understand and follow someone else's logic without conceding to it. But if he did not have his own sense of understanding deeply intact, how could he properly argue some opposing interpretation?

Still, he went to her with it. Torrence, who read the Bible and studied theology, Torrence, with her excellent grades and early graduation, Torrence may not see it from the aspect of faith and rule, but she would see it from the viewpoint of a scholar, and if knowledge was power, then it was also a form of religion.

He knew what Torrence would say, and he'd been mostly correct. Not everything was black-and-white. Life was gray. She scoffed at the cliches but reminded him that cliches become overused because they apply to frequently and with such truth to myriad aspects of human existence.

"The road to Hell is paved with good intentions," he replied. "On the topic of cliches and their truth."

"Maybe you need to talk to the boys," she said, always using the infantilizing term for men who were older than her, and for those of her own age. "I told you to consider them your brothers. They're bonded, especially through the work they do, but not because of it."

"What's at the core of this bond, then?"

"Belief," she said simply. "Belief in a better world."

He licked his lips, bowed his head. His arms rested upon his knees, his hands coming together between them. He'd been picking at the skin near his thumbnail, but stopped. He shifted his hands, opening his fingers, pressing his palms very tentatively together. He thought about praying there. But he wasn't sure if he could.

Instead, he looked over to Torrence, to her lovely face and the genuine love she exuded for him, and felt somewhat at ease in the thought.

After all, he'd spent nights in her loving embrace, days in her shower, her bed, and since their conversation the night of his parents' death, she hadn't pushed for much beyond the deepened kiss or massaging of innocent areas of flesh.

He felt a more complete trust of her since then, since she'd said he would not lose her without this physical aspect of modern relationships, because her actions since seemed to prove it. And since she'd confided in him, her own personal priest, ready to absolve her of all sin through his unshakable love, well, in all honesty, he'd felt safe, and for the first time in a month. Maybe, he truly considered, for the first time in his life.

Though his family loved him, they had believed in a very carnal sense of punishment for sin. Alex had worn the bruises of retribution and had bled, as Christ had bled, for the forgiveness of sin. Now his family could not harm him—they could not love him, support him, teach him—but they could not harm him, either.

And with the knowledge that an entire force of capable and violent men, all dedicated to the desires of his girlfriend, would defend him against whoever killed his parents, well, who did Alex have left to fear?

What he wrestled with now wasn't so much physical as it was spiritual. Was it right? No, of course not, no violence was, but in his youth and his vulnerability, in his loneliness, Alex found it hard to rebuke Torrence's continued presence in his life, especially when she had been there for him through all of it.

So he agreed, reluctant as he was, to talk with the boys, with his brothers.

The conversation was delicate. Everyone knew it. When Torrence took Alex to the hideout for it, she'd reminded everyone of what was appropriate to reveal and what was not. They all knew, all agreed. They loved Torrence and loved all she provided—the sense of family, of power, acceptance with absolutely no judgment or rules save for one: Follow Torrence, respect her at all times. They were more than happy to do so, and always eager to prove it. Tonight was a chance to do both.

Don and Aaron were already at the hideout, but Torrence wanted to wait for Todd, for a peer, before the conversation started, so when the boys sat down on the couch and opened two bottles of beer, she had considered offering one to Alex, hoping the mental influence of the alcohol might make the conversation more appealing to him, but this wouldn't create a lasting viewpoint. It might do the opposite, it might lose the trust she'd been gaining all this time. So she leaned against the table, the high table before the licenses and IDs, which had become an altar of sorts dedicated to Alex and his saintly face within the frames there, all still surrounded by the conglomerated candles; their hardened wax wrapping around them, melted to them, encompassing them in a red blanket of sinewy, strong, affectionate control.

Alex stood awkwardly between Torrence and the door, his hands going into the pockets of dark jeans, head lowered, eyes watching Don and Aaron as the brought the brown glass to their lips and consumed the intoxicants.

These men were three and four years older than he was, and he stared at them not as they were but as what they could be; they could be him. If he stayed here with Torrence, if he succumbed to this cause—her cause—if he simply allowed it, would he be one of these men?

His brows knotted above his weary eyes, but a sense of conviction flooded him suddenly, as if the answers he'd been seeking were answered divinely and with absolute certainty: No. No, Alex would never be these men, he'd never be like them. He was bound to Torrence, their destinies undeniably intertwined, a mingling of the souls in some atmosphere unseen to their eyes, but more important, more defining than anything they could physically experience together; yes, Torrence had been correct with these particular assertions, but no, it was not possible for Alex to ever be a follower of her will.

A sense of relief washed all apprehension from his body then. He didn't think it was God directly communicating with him, but someone or some entity at His instruction did. Of that, Alex was certain.

Maybe his part in all this wasn't to participate, but to enlighten. Maybe he was sent here with God's word to ensure their violence remained on the path of righteousness—no matter how unusual and innately wrong such a claim, that violence and righteous could be linked, might have seemed.

He wasn't sure of the why, but he knew the path, and the similarity of this sentiment, shared with him Torrence of her own destiny, was not lost upon him. If nothing, it made more sense. They were connected—her, the courageous and chaotic upturned of inequity, in love with him, the tentative but truthful conscience who would ensure its purity to the cause.

He moved into the room more fully now, even going as far as taking a seat next to his brothers on the couch.

Don offered him his bottle, but Alex denied it, instead taking the opportunity of connection provided by it.

"Do you ever think about what alcohol does to your mind? How it connects to the spirit?"

He exhaled a semi-scoff, an almost-laugh. "No. Why, do you?"

"I think about a lot of things and how they connect to the spirit, honestly. A lot lately."

"Yeah, the whole gang thing," Aaron said, taking a swig. "Look, I get it. It can seem like what we do is evil, but it's not. Not to us, anyway. Evil is just a concept after all. And I don't think I'm evil for hurting someone who hurts others."

"Do they all hurt others?"

"In some form or another," Aaron said, "yes."

"That feels different than a simple yes."

"Well, it's not a simple thing we do. Torrence isn't simple. The cause isn't. Nothing religious or spiritual is."

"I don't know if that's necessarily true," Alex said, biting the inside of his jaw. "I think the idea is always simple. It's people who complicate things. Especially pure things. We deal with so much secrecy, so many lies, so many hidden things, and half truths that we don't know how to accept something pure for what it is. We're always digging into it, always digging, trying to find some hint of something within it that seeks to hurt us. We do it until we've corrupted it. We dig and press and push until we create the darkness we've been fearing. Then we feel justified. We've found it. But we didn't find anything. We created it."

"Do you think that's what you're doing now?"

Alex blinked, his brows raising. Slight shake of the head. He hadn't thought of it like that, hadn't realized how from experience and emotion he'd been speaking.

"You're looking for something worse here, Alex. Instead of being with Torrence, you're searching for a reason not to."

"That's not true. I'm here because of her, not for any other reason."

"Yeah," Malcolm spoke up now, eyes glaring over at Alex from the side. "We're all here because of her."

"Not like you, though, Alex," Aaron said, placing a hand on his shoulder. "None of us are here the way you are."

"You don't feel like the things you do seep into you somehow? Like the hurt you inflict comes into you, too? That it can hurt you, too?"

"That's the real debate, isn't it? How much of what we do becomes who we are? It's like being with Tor for you, but, I mean, what can really get inside you from your flesh? Isn't your body just a house? If it rains, your carpet doesn't get wet. When it snows, you're not scraping ice off of your TV."

"Sin," Alex said worriedly, "is an infection, an infestation. It's like mold in your analogy. Maybe the rain itself doesn't get into the house, but if the wood is weakened or rotting, its effects can be experienced on the inside, too."

Aaron regarded him for a moment, considering his words. He did not want to mess this up for Torrence, but Alex wasn't as easy as the others.

As he contemplated his next move, his response, the counter-argument, a quick, light knock came to the door, and Todd entered.

"Todd, how do you feel about violence for a purpose? Does it fuck you up because it's violence or does the reason keep it from harming you? How many people die in war supposedly for righteousness, for being on the side of the righteous?"

"War often harms people, even the righteous. Death affects us all."

"But only the mind, right? Isn't death spiritual? Isn't it going to paradise? It's being with God, isn't it?"

A scoff interrupted their conversation, and both looked to Don as he spoke.

"You sound just like that preacher and his wife when we killed—." Don started, but Aaron slapped him roughly, but enough had been said.

Alex's eyes were wide and open, vulnerable in their uncertainty. "What?"

"No, he's just—." Aaron tried, but Alex stood quickly. Aaron followed suit, then Don. Both men stared at Torrence, both upset but only fear was present within Don.

Torrence moved for Alex immediately and with as much vigor as Alex exerted. Emotion was palpable; it radiated from Alex in waves of fear, hurt, worry, shock. Torrence did not like registering any thoughts of her within Alex that were not loving or affectionate.

When he came to her, his hands fell onto her forearms, loose but trying their hardest to close and hold and grip and feel. There was no feeling, though. No grasp on her and therefore onto reality. Another shifting world, another new understanding of it. When would this end?

"Tor," he said weakly, looking up to her. He felt a tingling sensation in the back of his head, just at the base of his neck, that seemed to extend into his head and back in branches of electricity. "What does…what does that mean?"

Her lips parted but the words would not form. Instead, a slight shaking of her head came as response, but it did not satisfy.

"What…" Alex exhaled defeatedly, all color draining from his face. His body seemed limp, his brows came together and raised, his face had fallen in all places that required even the slightest bit of strength to tense or uphold. "What's he saying?"

The words were breathy, sharp. It seemed to take a significant amount of effort to expel them, and to take in new air as replenishment. She blurred in his vision as he stood, but no tears were materializing in his eyes to cause such an obstruction. "Tor," he said again, a searing pain shooting down across his breastbone and down the center of his rib cage. His lungs seemed to shrivel; he could not make them expand enough to nourish his blood, which had gone cold now, or perhaps it was the lack of circulation due to his thumping heart, for he felt numb suddenly, especially in his fingers and his feet.

"Alex," she said. "Wait. Sit down. Just…just breathe."

He tried, but all he could see was his parents, their faces paled and riddled with blue sinews, blood spattered across their cheeks, their mouths, their open eyes. Their dead eyes, oh, how they'd stared up to him, judging him in justified disappointment, for Alex, their only son, spent his night in an abandoned home with his girlfriend and with drunken men, and now his parents were dead. They were dead at the hands of Torrence's men, and their hands only worked when she commanded them to. Had she done this? Had she killed his parents? Had she taken away the only family he had?

He stumbled. The room seemed to shift now, tilting toward the left, toward where he'd staggered. He couldn't right himself, couldn't clear his vision or calm his thoughts. He needed answers, he needed to hear her say it, but no words, much less demands, would rise from his tightening throat.

"Alex," Torrence said, her voice far-off and echoing. Sight was gone. Sound was fleeting. His knees buckled.

Torrence and Todd both reached for him as he fell, but they were not close enough, didn't make it to him in time, and he collapsed.

When he hit the floor, Torrence rushed to him. She looked up to Todd. "He's not eating. The pressures, the pain, and with no nutrients—."

"Tor, I think it's more than that—."

"No, it's not," she yelled now, pulling at Alex and bringing his head into her lap.

"What do we do now?" Todd asked, but there was no response. She sat in silence there on the floor, holding onto Alex and stroking his unconsciousness.

Todd tried to make contact again. "Tor?"

"I tried—." Aaron started, but Torrence shushed him.

After a moment, she placed Alex gently back onto the floor, onto the plush rugs. She stood, thinking. She brought her hand to her head. She rubbed at her eyes and her cheek and jaw, exhaling exasperation and annoyance.

"Now what?" she asked aloud but to herself. "Now what? Now what? Now what?" She exhaled loudly as she tapped her fingers against her head, her eyes staring down to Alex on the floor.

The three men shared looks behind her, wondering if they should move or speak, fearing the same considerations.

Finally, one broke the silence. "Well…" Don started, taking a step toward Torrence, then pausing to look back at the other two.

Todd reared backward, shaking his head warily, but Aaron merely shrugged. Don pressed forward.

"I mean, you know what you usually do to people who know about us and don't join up."

"He never said he wouldn't join up," Todd added, though fearfully. He looked down to Alex, more afraid for him than for himself.

"Okay, well, he's this goody-goody, little church-kid type. Who wants that? Walking around on eggshells, tiptoeing because he's too much like a toddler to hit someone or fuck them. It's more work than it's worth. If you want my opinion." He shrugged.

No sounds or movement came from Torrence. She stood stoically before them, her hip still out, her hand still on her head. He wished he could see her face.

"R-right?" he asked hesitantly.

After a long moment of worry and discomfort occurring behind her in silence, Torrence turned. She glared into the man's face for a few seconds, then she smiled. "What exactly are you suggesting?" she asked sweetly, stepping closer to him.

"Well, you know—."

"Say it."

"Take him out."

"That's what I thought you meant," Torrence said, and in one swift motion, she withdrew from her pocket her favorite weapon, switched it open, and thrust into his stomach its silver blade.

Grunting, grasping at his midsection, her follower fell to his knees before her.

She stared down to him, revealing nothing of her emotional state in her elegant features, as he   collapsed entirely at her feet.

As he groaned, Torrence's eyes darted up to the other two men. "Anyone else have any ideas?"

"No," Aaron said.

"No, Torrence."

"Good," she said, wiping the blade on her jeans then closing it and concealing it again in her back pocket. "That's what I thought."

She turned back to Alex, bloody fingers tapping on her temple again, but her concentration was consistently broken by the dying man's groaning.

"All right," she said sharply through gritted teeth, her arms straightening at her sides as her fingers bent and twisted in the air. "Todd, take Alex to the room."

Silently, but in utter obedience, Todd moved quickly to Alex, more than eager to remove him from harm's way, and hauled him upward.

Torrence moved to them, aiding Todd in his task. She took one of Alex's arms and threw it around her neck.

"His groaning is maddening," she complained, glancing at Don at their feet. She looked to her third follower now. "Finish him off."

Aaron nodded, somewhat uncertain, but he made no hesitation in moving. As he went to the man on the floor, Torrence and Todd carried an unconscious Alex toward the small hallway in their hideout.

"Sorry, Don," Aaron said as he bent down and withdrew from his boot a blade of his own. "But Torrence said—."

"Fuck Torrence," Don gritted, coughing and sweating and bleeding and shaking.

Torrence turned at this, releasing her hold of Alex momentarily to stand in arrogance and judgment. She was law here. She was god.

Her chin lowered, the angle sinister in the dim light of the flickering candles, and she arched a brow.

Aaron nodded to her, then looked at Don, and without pause or apology, slit his throat.

CHAPTER TWENTY

Time became irrelevant.

Alex would come to consciousness only to be knocked out again by the combination of his body's weakness and the emotional turmoil that might have been the worst blow of them all, for Torrence, his protector, had become what she swore she'd never be—a cause of his pain.

She'd sent Todd out for pineapple juice and strawberries and cheesecake. She was there when Alex would become lucid, and tried to fill him with fruits and cream cheese and sugar. Water, yes. Drink lots of water. It'll be okay.

Her voice, like the atmosphere around him, seemed in motion, wavy and distorted. Nothing clear. Very little understood.

When he finally came back to consciousness entirely, Alex awoke a changed being; a being existing in a world of which he was finally aware. Innocence stripped away, wool withdrawn from his eyes. The room, and even the world outside it, seemed darker, shaper. Contrasts were more extreme in this crueler world. Faces distorted, flickered between human and inhumane, while kind words from familiar voices were unsung hymns expressed in growls. Perhaps nothing was ever what he'd thought it'd been.

After all, there had always been the sense with Torrence, especially the idea of her, that there was an entire world of action and experience and understanding that Alex simply wasn't aware of. It was as if he'd been living inside a painting or a television series, as if his perception of life and existence and all that occurred within those very expansive confines had been limited, not only to his personal experience, but the experience he knew about.

Before Torrence, he didn't really know about parties. He knew the word and its definition, but did defining something as a piece of the language give one an understanding of it? Not really.

Vocabulary words were not experience. Definitions were not felt. What could a person have known if they did not experience?

He knew what a woman's naked body looked like in the same way he knew the definition of the word "nude", but he had never seen a naked woman, so how much of being so vulnerable, so without armor, could he understand? None of it until her thigh ran the length of his thigh. Nothing until she sat next to him in only panties and a loosely-fitting top. Knowing something, even conceptualizing it, would never equal knowledge of it.

He knew violence happened, but hadn't felt the weight of it until it burst into his father's church and affected him directly. He knew who Todd was by name and face, but didn't know who Todd was until he conversed with him. Didn't know what Todd was capable of.

He'd been safe inside a bubble not of inexperience, but of naivety. The difference was merely that one was lack of experiencing personally some thing and the other was not even knowing it existed.

He knew what existed here in this world now. He knew he was alive within it, and that all around him, in what had seemed a mundane but very happy existence, was cruel and unlikely. A tragedy made from experience, not crafted by words. It was his life. Maybe it was his destiny.

He emerged from the bedroom that evening with a new sight. His eyes were the same eyes, no change in color or rise of number on a vision-scale, but his mind had opened; expanded by both the knowledge and experience of suffering. Oh, suffering existed. Oh, suffering had been felt. And now, with his mind's interpretation of the sights around him altered so drastically, Alex wasn't sure, as he stepped into the living room of the hideout, that he saw Torrence the same, perceived her the same. He wasn't sure he had ever truly known her.

"Tor?" Alex asked lowly, his throat dry despite all the water she'd left him.

She looked up, an eagerness in her features that seemed to Alex so pure, like she was a child reunited with her lost puppy. It took him by surprise. He blinked rapidly, his lips parting so that a heavy breath expelled from tightening lungs passed through them.

His eyes a deeper hue than usual, contrasted by the sparkling white orbs of flickering candlelight as it reflected in the pools of his welling sorrow, he leveled as best he could for this conversation or confrontation or maybe some composition of both communications.

His brows raised slowly, knitting together in their center. "You…you didn't." His voice was high, questioning, though it was almost too soft and uncertain to be properly registered. "Tell me," he said, pleading with her as he moved against her. "Torrence, please," he whispered, his voice shaken by his tears. He gripped onto her shoulders, taking desperate fistfuls of her shirt into his hands, clinging on with every ounce of mental equilibrium remaining within him to the one constant figure he'd still had. "Tell me you didn't….didn't kill my parents."

She stared into his eyes with her usual strength and conviction as the excitement of his image faded away beneath the remembrance of their shared history. Her lips were steady, strong; their typical stoic expression of poise and power. "I didn't," she said evenly. It was technically true, but what did she care about being honest?

Still, there was something to Alex, whether it was his innocence—his indomitable innocence—and the appeal of his inner-strength that was so opposite her own—less aggressive and less violent, but strength nonetheless—or it was something more personal, Torrence couldn't have been sure.

Perhaps it had been a mixture of the two; an amalgamation of this beautiful man who faltered in frailty but remained steadfast all the same—entirely open and owning every gentle, soft, unusual fragility no matter how much derision, from society at large or individuals in specific, was thrust at him because of it—and the trust he'd given Torrence even when his instinct, his family, his belief systems suggested he shouldn't.

Whether it was one of these realities or both of them, whether it was neither and Torrence had been entirely clueless, was irrelevant. What mattered there, standing in this dark room of deviance, was the look in Alex's eyes, the relief which washed over his heartbroken face when she said the words.

"I didn't."

They resounded in her mind, and she broke. Looked away from him. Taking a deep breath in, Torrence lost her resolve for a split second. She turned her head back to face him, but didn't meet his eyes. Her lips pursed, and the hand that had been planted firmly on his forearm fell limp.

"I mean, not directly," she said lowly.

"Not…directly?" He leaned down, trying to find her eyes, but she rolled them.

Her arms moved to his chest, his neck, feeling about his flesh in tender but very desperate ministrations. "This level of honesty, of trust, and hopefulness is reserved only for you," she said, finally looking into his worried eyes. "You have to understand that all I do is done for you, for our future together, for what I will become and what you can be with me." She exhaled audibly, eyes falling for a long moment before finding his, still full of worry and imploringly gazing beneath furrowed brow to her. "I told them to." She nodded toward the men behind her. "I didn't do it. But they did it. They did it because I wanted them to do it."

"What?" A shaken breath came into Alex's mouth but its path into his lungs seemed obstructed. He turned away from her, angled himself away. His hand came to his falling head and his fingers rushed into his hair. "Why?" The questions seemed directed to no one, certainly not to Torrence. His eyes were no longer attached to his brain. He stared at the floor or the wall, but he saw nothing. His mind couldn't interpret visual cues; it could only focus upon the experience of Torrence's words, their implication. She had killed his parents. Torrence killed them. Took them away. Torrence.

"Torrey," he whispered, a tear slipping from his eye, which was still an unblinking, disconnected part of his body, having no reaction or connection to himself or his spirit.

"Alex, I did it for you."

"For me?" he exhaled the words, not entirely aware of them, then he blinked, came back to reality. His head stayed lowered but he looked to her. His brows knitted. "For me?"

"The day we met I saw those bruises, Alex."

He scoffed, turning away sharply. His back to her, his hand went to his hip, his other rubbed at his mouth, his jaw.

"I know you don't like to think about it or talk about it, but it shouldn't have happened, and it kept happening. I had to protect you." Her hand went to his shoulder. She didn't urge him to turn it to look at her, she knew she probably did not deserve the connection, but she wanted to touch him, to apply pressure there, weight. She was strong, she was constant. She always would be, even in moments of great despair or disagreement. "There was no other way, Alex. What else could I do?"

"You wanted to protect me? By…I can't even say it. Tor." Tears welled in his eyes, threatening to flood his face with grief at a second's notice. "Torrey," he whispered, almost-whining the pet name. His head shook as his features fought the tensing muscles in his chin and jaw. "No, no, no. Please no."

"They were hurting you. They were trapping you. Abusing you. Brainwashing you. They were going to keep us apart. They weren't going to let you see me, and I knew you wouldn't keep sneaking out with me. You knew it."

"That's what it was about, really, wasn't it? Me not coming to parties, not drinking, or having sex."

"I told you that stuff doesn't matter. You matter."

"Then why keep bringing me here? Why not spend time with me at the library or the—."

"Your parents would've put a stop to anywhere but here and you know it."

"So you killed them? You killed them!"

Torrence's nostrils expanded. She felt her jaw stretch, her lower teeth extending beyond her upper ones momentarily. She had to calm herself. She twisted her head a bit to stretch the tension out of her neck. "How were we going to keep—?"

"I thought when I went to college, I could see you. It's only the rest of this year and next, and then we wouldn't have to hide. I wouldn't be at home. I didn't think—."

"That's it," she said, a spark igniting in her eyes, pushing her brows upward. She saw her in, her twist. She was herself again. "You didn't think. Not that far ahead, anyway. But I did."

"Torrence—."

"Alex," she said gently, reaching toward his cheek now, wanting to pet it, to soothe him.

He flinched, jerking his face away and scowling, even as he sobbed, but he stood firm in his position and kept his eyes on hers.

Her nostrils flared, lips tightening, but this expression was brief, and she purposefully replaced it with a softer one.

She'd seen the expressions of empathy and guilt, of worry and fear, and beyond witnessing their physicality, she understood their emotional connections. Further, she knew enough of psychology and body language analysis to remember to match her upper expressions with those of her lower ones; so many times eyes betrayed the liar because the liars often forget to use their foreheads, their eyebrows, their noses. But not Torrence.

She knew how to position her brows so they conveyed sympathy, knew how to glaze her eyes so she appeared pleading even when both knew she was in utter control.

"Alex," she tried again, and this time he allowed her to caress him tenderly. "They were going to keep us apart. After the year ends, after the summer, you'll go into your senior year, and I won't be there with you. You won't see me at all during school. You won't see me after. You won't be allowed. A year of that? You'd—."

"What, Tor? Get bored? Forget you? Forget how I feel for you? No." His tears fell around his lips, which closed sternly and curled in disgust. "What about me makes you think that? What makes you think our physical closeness matters even half as much to me as our emotional closeness? I thought we were perfectly in-sync, even when you told me about this cause of yours, but now I see we've always been separated. You made sure of it."

"Alex—."

"You killed my parents, Torrence." He spoke evenly now, without a hint of accusation or upset. It was a fact, and Alex had to say it aloud, had to re-enforce the concept in his mind, had to understand and accept this as true.

"For you," she said.

Disturbed, he winced. How could she not even attempt to deny this? How could she try, instead, to justify it?

"And I killed one of my most devout for you." Her features loosened. "How often do lovers say, 'I'd die for you' 'I'd kill for you', and how many ever prove it as I have proved it? I don't ask you to kill for me, Alex. I don't ask you to die for me. I only ask that you live with me, for me."

"I have to leave, Tor," he said, eyes brimming with tears.

"No," Torrence said, her teeth gritted together, lips tight and barely moving.

"Torrey," he said, panting heavily, his body shaking and losing strength.

"Don't," she said, but his hand grabbed at the door, at the knob, his other arm fighting to be released from her.

"Stop, Tor," he begged, finally pulling his arm from his jacket as they struggled against the force of each other's wills, and freeing himself of it.

Torrence staggered backward, all of her strength, which had been focused on his arm and his body weight now exerted on a falling piece of fabric.

She gazed at it, momentarily stunned, then looked up to see him opening the door.

She was losing him. She couldn't. She rushed him, grabbing him at the shoulder, and yanking him toward her. He staggered a bit at this force, turning to face her in the momentum and almost falling against her.

One final time, she jerked him around, pulling him into her and trying to hug him.

"Stop," he said, crying. He loved her, he truly loved her, and feeling her comfort was a hard thing to process. He tried to pull away from her, tried to hate her. He did want to think, but not here. He couldn't think here. He couldn't think clearly so close to Torrence, so encompassed by his love for her.

His shoulders shifted, signaling for her arms to fall away from them. She only partly complied, letting him slip away from her, but she gripped at his shirt as he stepped back.

"I can't think, Tor," he said shakily, his brows coming together as they rose.

From behind her came the brothers now, staring at him in distrust, anger, fear. He recognized the fear. Knew it stemmed from the uncertainty of what he might do, for his fear now came from the same dreadful, unsure thoughts. What would they do? What would Torrence do?

His eyes went back to Torrence, who stood in stoic superiority. No movement, no trace of emotion. She regarded him as if watching a drama, a play, as if she couldn't look away from what happened next.

Internally, she raged. She could see Alex slipping away from her, could see him backing away slowly, heading for the door.

"Don't leave," she said.

"I have to," he answered, looking away from her, noting the proximity of her brothers now. Had they moved? When? They were surely closer now.

He shook his head slightly, stepping back again, but when Aaron put his hand into his pocket, clearly taking hold of a weapon, Alex, in one swift motion, turned to the door and fled from it.

"Alex!" Torrence yelled, chasing after him. The men followed. All pursued Alex, who did not know the woods as they knew them.

"I'll get him, boss," Malcolm said, rushing by Torrence, sneering. "Don't you worry. I'll get him."

Torrence watched him remove from his pocket his own blade as he breezed by her. Damn her height, she thought, Damn her short legs.

"Don't you hurt him!" she yelled. "Malcolm!"

"I'll get to him first," Todd said, withdrawing his own weapon now. "I'll stop him before he does anything."

"Shit," Torrence whispered, still rushing through trees, coursing the path Alex had trailed. Leaves had been stepped on, slightly disturbed, but not enough to present to any pursuer a clear direction. What she followed was instinct or gut-feeling; she could feel him somehow, feel his path, knew where he was going.

There was no time to consider it, to consider how, but all she could think of was this undeniable connection she had with Alex, how deeply it ran, how it seemed a product of her very DNA and of his, that somehow they had been born of the same matter, not just the oxygen, carbon, hydrogen, nitrogen, calcium, phosphorus combination that accounted for ninety-nine percent of every human's body. This was something entirely different, something only they shared; it was like divine intervention, soulmates, prophecy.

A cackle echoed through the trees somewhere to her right. Malcolm. She heard Todd yelling, Alex yelling back, Malcolm swearing.

Veering off into the direction, Torrence rushed through trees and around rocks, were grew in size and number the closer she got to the boys.

"Fuck," she heard Todd say as she came to an incline in the woods, rounding a great mass of rock and stone.

"Alex," she said, watching Malcolm yank him nearer to him by the collar of his shirt.

"Stop, stop," Todd was repeating, grabbing at Malcolm, both boys threatening with their knives, but not actively using them. Not yet.

"He doesn't want in. Don was right. You know what we do when people don't want in. What Torrence does."

"She doesn't want this," Todd said, pulling at Malcolm's raising arm.

"Right, we only make exceptions for her, for her little boyfriend. This is bullshit."

"Get off me," Alex was saying behind this conversation, but no one paid him any notice as he struggled against the fighting boys.

"Guys, stop," Torrence called out, her boots slipping as she rushed down the sloping hill. "Stop!"

Still, no one paid her heed, no one but Alex, who tried now to move in her direction. "Tor," he said, suddenly unconscious, it seemed, of his own predicament. "It's slippery. Watch—."

Malcolm heard this, felt Alex pulling away, trying to rush to Torrence, who was switching open her blade now, a look of absolute hatred in her eyes.

"Get off of him," she said to Malcolm, who still held Alex in place, even as he wrestled with Todd, with Todd's fists pounding into him, with Todd's blade. "Shit," Torrence gasped, sliding down the hill, losing her balance, but so near to the fight now.

"Yeah, you want him," Malcolm said, whirling around and shoving Alex in her direction. When he released Alex's shirt, he swung back and punched Todd in the face.

Todd staggered back, but recovered quickly, looking up through watering eyes to seeing Alex knocking into Torrence and Malcolm seeming to dive atop them.

Torrence's hands grabbed at Alex's shirt, an effort to steady them both, her blade slipping from her grasp. Malcolm caught it with his free hand, swung it upward in the chaos of the three staggering, slipping bodies, and felt it press into one of them.

His eyes widened when Alex grunted; they moved to Torrence, whose eyes were fixated on Alex's grimacing face.

Alex's hands reached for his side, his face and head falling slowly in the registering of pain. When he looked down to his side, so did Torrence.

"Alex?" she asked, one hand at the small of his back, the other on his arm. "Alex…Alex…"

He staggered back but she couldn't maintain his weight. Malcolm fled, she heard the sounds of leaves cracking beneath his feet, but merely heard it. It didn't compute. Nothing did. Only Alex.

"Tor," he said softly, knees buckling.

"Oh, God," she gasped, catching him as he slipped away. "Alex. Alex?"

Easing his weakening body down to the ground, Torrence cradled Alex's head, his neck, his shoulders. She pulled him onto her lap, her knees bent and splayed there in the dying leaves and dirt. "Alex, hey, look at me. Hey. You're okay. You're okay."

His eyes fluttered opened, blinking slowly as he seemed to process the pain, the weakness he felt. Dizzying and bright.

"Torrey," he said.

"You're okay," she repeated, looking down the length of his body. When her eyes fell on the handle of her blade, which had been thrust almost entirely into his flank, a sharp intake of air filled her lungs through her parting lips. "It's okay," she said again, swallowing thickly and trying not to cry. "Alex, you're okay."

"I feel dizzy," he said.

"I know, but you're gonna be all right."

His brows came together over glazing eyes. He breathed roughly through his lips, chest rising and falling in harsh, uneven pulses. He blinked, wincing as he tried to lift his head.

"Alex, wait, wait…" she placed a hand onto his chest, trying to steady him, but he wanted to see the source of this searing pain overtaking his body.

As his neck bent, his head rose from her arm, but it seemed to stick to her. She glanced at this connection and saw that blood had gushed from the back of his head all over her forearm.

"Alex," she said, her breathing becoming labored. "Lie back. Please."

"My side," he said, still leaning forward slightly. His vision blurred but he recognized the knife there in his side, saw the staining red spreading out into his t-shirt from it.

"Torrence." He exhaled, his head falling back into her arm, her lap. He licked his lips, swallowed harshly.

"It's okay," she said, staring at the weapon, shaking her head. "We'll call 911. You'll be fine."

Alex winced again. "My head…"

"You'll be fine."

"Tor, he's dying," Todd said from somewhere behind her.

"He's not!" she spat through gritted teeth.

"Torrey," Alex said, gripping onto her forearm where it lay

across his chest, his eyes rolling as he blinked. "I think I can see Heaven."

"No, sweetheart," she said, brushing his dampened hair from his forehead. "No, that's just the sun. It's the stars. You're fine. You're here. You're with me."

He shook his head slightly. "I want to go home," he said weakly.

""I'll take you," Torrence answered, her breath shaking, hand brushing the tears from his eyes. "We'll get you to a doctor then we'll go straight home. I—."

"No," he said. "I can't."

"Yes, you can."

"I don't want to," he said, eyes filling with tears. "I want to go home. I want to go to Heaven." He licked his trembling lips, tried to swallow. His eyes shifted jerkily away from hers, eyes gazing now into the sun. "I want to be with God." He looked down the length of his body, at the switchblade in his stomach, then back to her, his face pleading and in-pain. "I can't accept what you've done," he said, "but I can't live without you, either. I want things the way I thought they were. I can't bear them as they are."

"That's okay," she said, inhaling sharply through her lips, tears brimming in her eyes. "But don't let go. You don't have to stay with me, Alex, but don't leave. Don't go. Not like this. Please."

"I can see paradise," he said, "and I can see it in your eyes. It's not as bright but it shines. Distorted, maybe, but it's there."

"Alex—."

"I'll be with my parents," he said. "I wanna be with my parents."

"No, Alex, please," she whined, tears falling from her eyes. She balled his t-shirt into fist, leaning over him, pulling him into her, kissing his forehead.

He reached for her with his hands, weakly returning the

embrace. "Torrey," he said, "let me go. Help me get to Heaven."

"What?"

"Finish it," he said, nodding toward the blade.

"No," she recoiled. "Alex, no. I can't."

"I don't wanna die at the hands of some stranger," he said. "Please, finish it. Let me go home."

"How can you ask me that? How can you—?" Her lips pressed tightly together, stifling a sob as she held her breath, clipping her words.

Alex groaned, shifting as his body tensed.

"Tor, he's dying," Todd said. "He's suffering."

Blood pooled in the corners of Alex's lips. He brought his trembling hand to her wrist and tried to hold it. He gazed into her eyes, his own fluttering closed as tears fell silently from them. He urged her hand with every bit of his remaining strength toward the knife in his side.

"No," Torrence gasped, inhaling sharply through her lips. "No, no, God, please no. Don't…don't make me."

"Please, Tor," Alex whispered, watching her hand slip away from his.

"I can't." Her head fell as her hand hovered over the blade.

"It's okay," he said. "You're releasing me. Freeing my spirit. You'll join me later. Much, much later. You'll join me." He tried to smile up to her, but both faces were riddled with turmoil.

She inhaled a very deep, very shaken breath, eyes staring over at the blade from beneath her bowed head, her vision almost entirely obstructed by her fallen hair. Closing her eyes, turning her head away, she gripped the handle of the blade. Tears fell along her cheeks from the tightly-shut eyes. A great gasp, almost a wail, came from her quivering lips.

"It's okay," Alex said, sniffling, tears slowly falling from the corners of his eyes. "I forgive you everything," he whispered, brows knitting together. "You know that, don't you?"

"Alex…"

"I forgive you," he said again, trying to smile.

"Don't," she whispered.

"For everything."

"I can't."

"Just make it stop, Tor. Let me go."

"Don't make me."

"I love you, Torrey," he said.

She licked her lips, their muscles tensing. "I love you, too," she said, hissing as she inhaled.

He nodded, their eyes locking, then his pupils widened. His breathing halted. She pressed the blade further into his side, watching the sharpness of the pain slip away from his features. He blinked slowly. A serenity eased into his face as it loosened, as his breathing grew slower, then stopped.

Her arm, still wrapped around his neck, drew his faltering body against her. She felt his fingers loosen and limply fall from her waist.

Torrence gazed at him for quite some time, closing his eyes to this world, then brushing the sweat-soaked hair from his forehead, the tears from his eyes.

She leaned down and pressed her lips to Alex's lips, savoring the warmth within them before it fled forever. As she closed her eyes, she rested her forehead against his, placed her hand where his heart laid in rest.

After a long moment, she stood. Wiping her wrist across her mouth, Torrence stared down to him, to Alex, this corpse which had moments ago been her first love.

From behind her came the weight of a hand upon her shoulder. Todd bent his knees, knelt down beside her. "Tor?"

"Where's Malcolm?"

"He ran," Aaron said gently, compassionate for his leader in her obvious loss. "I tried to chase him, but the woods are so thick."

Her lips curled, her cheeks reddened and wet, eyes bloodshot.

"I'll take care of it," she said.

"Tor, maybe we should—." Todd started, but she shook away the hand he'd placed on her shoulder.

She laid Alex gently onto the ground. Todd stood when she did.

"We'll take him back to his house. They'll find him when he doesn't go to school." She lifted her chin, staring into the woods ahead of her, unsure of where to go from here but listening for any movement, for Malcolm. When she heard leaves rustling off in the distance to her left, she extended her arm toward the remaining boys. "Give me my knife."

CHAPTER TWENTY-ONE

Around Wesley the world seemed to become liquid. He felt he was a drop of water entering a large pool of it, time and reality extending out from him, quivering at his presence, no matter how small he was.

He realized War's abilities were leaving him, his senses were coming back. He was materializing maybe, here against a warping reality that became black. Only a small echo of Torrence's heel against the floor resounded, somewhere far-off, barely audible. Silence then. He thought he felt a breeze touch his face.

A chill shook down the length of Wesley's body.

When he came back to reality or to the present—he wasn't sure which—Wesley was lying on his back in the lush grass. The sun shone down on him, filling him with warmth. The skies above him were solid and very blue.

He sat up and saw War sitting some feet from him. His back was slouched. Arms rested on his bent knees. His iridescent hair shimmered as always.

"What the fuck?" Wesley whispered as he blinked. A dizziness remained in him, as if he wasn't entirely connected to his body yet.

Shyly, War looked over his shoulder to Wesley. "Are you all right?"

"Yeah," he said. "Yeah, I saw a lot. I saw the goodness."

"What is it?"

"Kid named Alex. He's dead, though."

"This is the time of the risen dead."

"Can she bring back a good soul?"

"No."

"Can you?"

"I am not as powerful as she is, but I could try."

For all War's claims of weakness, his powers were extensive. It took him only a few touches to Wesley's forehead before discovering the locations of certain memories—the cemetery where she'd met Todd, the church where Alex's family preached.

The drive took only a few days' time, Wesley communicating with his brothers through new recruits in the towns he passed through. "In Torrence we trust," he would say to them, and have them repeat it back. They'd been instructed to say it to any men who came into their cities, and he knew through the promise of safety that they would.

He hoped that when it got back to Torrence, she'd think only that he'd taken the angel out to conquer, to convert, to do as she'd instructed and discover the motives of War. He'd somewhat accomplished it, he figured.

When they reached her hometown, Wesley was surprised to find that it hadn't been leveled. Not yet.

Wesley wanted to go to her home, to meet her family, to be as near to her humanity as Todd had been, but War told him there was no time. He knew it, too.

Torrence's gang was raging across civilization. They'd heard voices speaking through static as they drove through Sun States, bits and pieces, weather reports, wild fires, babies being stolen from their cribs and their parents hung in the streets.

It hadn't happened here yet, but it would. It would if Wesley and War didn't stop it, didn't distract her, didn't get to the soul before she did.

The idea, which had seemed so perfect at first, now seemed silly. A distraction in the form of some beautiful soul. Resurrecting him. Their lives hanging in the balance as a zombie fought the antichrist by passively lying in her bed.

But if goodness was her weakness when it was housed by handsome flesh, Wesley couldn't see a reason not to try it. After all, War was the chosen partner, even when Torrence denied him. Wesley knew it. He wasn't stupid. If Torrence really thought War was up to something, she'd bind him in Latin-clad iron and break the bones in his human-like form. She'd force the violence of sin upon him, not deny him its pleasures. Seeing Alex confirmed it: Torrence did not want purity to succumb to her, for surrender meant tarnished. Once purity was offered up and handed over, it could not be taken back. The act committed could not be undone.

This was where Wesley had faltered, where he'd messed up. By giving in to Torrence, by giving all she possibly asked for, by trying his damnest to be what she wanted, by pushing through inner-turmoil and the sense of self-destruction to please her, he'd undone his own appeal. Torrence hadn't stopped loving the Wesley she first met. Wesley simply hadn't had the strength to remain that guy.

As they moved into the cemetery behind Alex's church, Wesley scoffed.

"What is it?" War asked, looking over to Wesley as he lugged a shovel over his shoulder.

"I just don't know what this is. It seems simple," he said, thinking of Alex's words. "Maybe too simple. Can anything be simple, though?"

"No," War said, somehow mimicking Torrence now. "Nothing is simple. Especially when it's designed to be."

"Did you design this to be simple?"

"I tried to make it seem easy and very easy to accomplish," War said, "I'm sorry for that. But we can't let this world continue as it is."

They moved through the humble stones, the resting places of souls who hadn't lived to see the end of days. Now they were about to awaken one to it.

"Here it is," War said. "I can feel it. He was truly good."

Wesley approached the headstone slowly, his eyes falling to the name: Alexander Milton. The years inscribed beneath his name and nothing else.

Wesley began to dig. He wasn't sure that what he was doing was right, but in a way he felt he was freeing Alex, that Alex, who seemed so alive, so vivid and real in the flickering memories Wesley had just experienced, was trapped beneath this earth, trapped inside it. He wanted Alex to breathe.

They were only a few feet down, when a gust of wind seemed to come from behind them, a very focused gust. Then came two bursts of lightning.

"What was that?" Wesley asked.

"I don't know," War said, looking around, recognizing the bursts as angelic, but unable to discern whether or not they were distorted. "We have to move quickly."

He bent down, assisting Wesley in the uncovering of Alex, using his hands, his abilities to shake the dirt, to loosen it so that Wesley might more easily shovel it away.

After some time, they came to the casket. Wesley frowned. He did not want to imagine the sweet, delicate Alex inside it, but he wanted to open it immediately, wanted to release Alex from it. War suggested they lift it from the dirt first, and he agreed. Another daunting task.

Thank God, Wesley thought to himself as he wrapped his fingers around the bottom of the coffin and began aiding War in raising it, That Torrence's rituals gave me extra strength. As the box rose, Wesley's bent knees straightening in the effort, he caught a glimpse of War's feet across from his in the dirt. Small, his tennis shoes seemed. Small was his entire body, really. Huh, Wesley thought, Thank God for angelic strength, too.

After hoisting the coffin out of the hole, Wesley emerged, then assisted the smaller-frame angel. The pair knelt before the coffin—War's shins on the ground, bent knees together, and Wesley merely crouching next to him with the spade in the ground and its handle in his fist—examining the sealed box, looking for a way to open it.

The latches were not the only obstacle. This coffin required a large, hexagonal key. This was a more secure, and more expensive, coffin, but with the key it'd be an easy open. They did not, however, have the key.

"Maybe we shouldn't mess with it," Wesley said, rising. "Maybe it's a sign."

"A sign?" War looked up to him, unamused. "I'm an angel of God. From whom would we be given a sign? The universe? Look into my eyes, look at the fingerprints on my shoulder. I am the universe. And so are you, so is this young man." He looked down to the coffin, placed a hand on it. He considered using his most glorious power here to blow open a box full of bones, but it not only felt disgraceful, for it would also be a waste of what energy might be fleeting. "Use the shovel."

"Man, this feels wrong," Wesley said, loosening his grip of the handle and flicking his wrist so it moved upward in his hand.

"If defiling your spiritual temple through carnal intimacy atop graves was fine," War said, flicking his eyes up to Wesley's, "I can't see where merely opening a coffin presents a problem."

"Okay," Wesley said, shaking his head as he raised the shovel. "You don't have to be a dick."

"We are running out of time," War said, thinking on the bursts of lightning they witnessed and how quickly whatever being caused them could move. "I'm sorry."

"Yeah," Wesley said. "It's all good."

War offered him a smile of thanks then bowed his head before the coffin. "Dear Lord," he said, closing his eyes beneath his ever-worried brow. "Forgive us this trespass." He looked up to Wesley and nodded.

With great force, Wesley shoved the point of his tool into the seal of the coffin, attempting to pry it open this way. It took more time and effort than expected, for he assumed the rotting wood would be fragile, but it wasn't. He wondered if some type of of spiritual magic seeped into it, some power of good souls and their God, that meant to protect this righteous one from an act such as this—defilement from the devil, from her tainted-souled boy-toy and her almost-fallen angel.

After some trial-and-error, some sweat and sickened feeling, Wesley made a just-right connection between box and blade and the coffin finally opened. Sticky bones laid inside a musky, black suit. Traces of dirty blond hair remained, but only traces.

"Oh, God," Wesley gasped, turning away from the body. His wrist came to his mouth.

"Don't blaspheme," War said, stepping closer to the body. "It is so easy to pick up your speech patterns."

"Just do something." He looked to War. "Please. Hurry."

War bent down over the corpse, the skeletal remains of what had once been a corpse, seemingly unaffected by it. He stared down to the bones as if he could see the flesh that had once wrapped over them, as if what laid before wasn't death, but life; then again, it was rebirth, wasn't it?

War's hand stroked Alex's skull, the material that housed his mind, his emotions, his thoughts. Wesley found it strange that bones didn't fade from existence like flesh did. What did that say about them? About their role in who were are? Are we not our flesh? Skin and bones. But we are the bone? The structure. The strength. He wasn't sure.

But those sparks began to ignite in War's palm, bursting over the bone as he petted it. This glory rang out into the silence of the night, filling the air with great, ominous tolling bells and smaller, gentler, chiming ones. Here and there the bones shifted, absorbing the sparks, but little else occurred from this expression of ultimate divinity.

War trembled, his face tightening in his effort. Sweat began to form across his forehead, then a clear, somewhat-reddish liquid slipped from his nostril.

Finally, he released a breath Wesley hadn't realized he'd been holding. In time with this, the bells stopped tolling and chiming and ringing out and the light vanished, leaving them alone with a box full of bones in a silent, dark cemetery.

"I can't…" War whispered, opening his palms and looking down to them. "I don't know what's wrong with me. I can't tell if I'm an angel or I'm not, and I—."

"Armideus," came a deep, loving voice behind them.

War looked up from the casket. Wesley turned his head toward the voice. Walking toward them, blinding as the moon shone onto to him, his glistening skin, his armor, was a heavenly spirit, a warrior son.

"Angels," Wesley said, looking over to War as he stood. "That was the lightning, huh?"

He offered only a sad smile in return.

"Grave desecration does not become a Son of God." He eyed War with contempt, ignoring Wesley entirely, as he stood in glorious conviction before the pair and the body at their feet. "We saw the energy, but nothing seemed to happen," he said, his head tilting as he studied the angel, who was clad only in the thin synthetics of man, instead of the spiritual shields of God. "Perhaps the clothes do make the man. You are a man now, aren't you, War?" The self-given name left Mecial's mouth in a hiss of disdain.

"All right, whoa," Wesley said, voice practically a growl as he put his right arm out before War, a small barricade between his angelic companion and the armored one approaching. "Who the hell are you?"

"Mecial," War said lowly to Wesley, then reluctantly looked to his brother and all his heavenly trappings. "You look well."

"Well enough. I cannot say the same for you."

War watched the angel's eyes fall to War's clothing, the t-shirt, the jeans, then they fixated upon the spot on War's side where The Great Sword had pierced him. War's hand went to the spot. "I am recovering."

"Quite the opposite, I would say," Mecial said. "Instead of learning from your punishments, you continue to sin. And with the most unholy of souls. You lie in hot baths with her. You touch her, kiss her lips. You are as sinful as the fallen Lucifer, yet your essence is that of God."

"Hot baths," Wesley muttered, looking away, brows raising. A hand came to his face, scrubbed across his jaw and lips. "Wow." He fought the urge to ask the angel as plainly the question he'd asked Torrence, but knew that this was not the time for it. Besides, he'd seen two bursts of lightning. Where was the other angel?

"Clever little deviant," Mecial said. "My brother is approaching."

From the distance came the other angel, his blond hair shimmering in the moonlight, face pristine and powerful.

"Virtutdeus," War exclaimed. "I thought you'd succumbed."

"No," he said solemnly, "only you have." He smiled sadly to his brother, then he looked to Wesley. "What are you doing here, child?" He looked over to War. "What are you doing, Brother?"

"We don't need to explain ourselves to you," Wesley said defiantly.

"Then we shall smite you," Mecial said.

"I felt goodness here," War said quickly. He looked over to Wesley, a plea in his eyes, silent communication concealed in the human's mind, hidden from the others. I am weak, War seemed to say, We must have their assistance. He looked back to his brothers. "No doubt you feel it, too."

"So you desecrate a grave? A holy grave, at that. Because you feel its goodness." Mecial glanced to Virtutdeus, carefully selecting his words, for he did not trust his brother, Armideus. He looked back to Wesley. "Why? Do you mean to destroy it?"

"Destroy it?" War asked, taken aback.

"You play with the devil's aid here, do you not? He was with the antichrist before her power was restored. They destroyed good souls, virtuous ones. No doubt his intentions remain the same, and I cannot allow it. Not with this one."

"This one?" War's brows furrowed.

"It ends now," Mecial said, stepping closer to them. "This man you befriend beat one of our Brothers with his fists, with weaponry that slips over the fingers and worsens those human blows. He—."

"Mecial, please, reconsider. This human, he is merely that. They are flawed, you know this. Emotion clouds reason, judgement. He does is out of human flaw and insecurity." War looked down, realizing the truth of his words, and placed a comforting hand upon Wesley's shoulder. Frowning when he saw the pained expression twisting the handsome features of Wesley's face into a horrific beauty, War inhaled deeply through his lips and offered a sympathetic smile. Above this half-hearted curl of the thin lips Wesley had already grown to enjoy so thoroughly were the gleaming eyes of angelic grace, but they performed a very human act now—a widening gesture suggesting Wesley agree with whatever ruse War was about to work them into.

War looked back to the opposing angel. "He has never felt worthy of affection. Humans, their psyches suffer at the hands of others. His parents displayed their care for him through material items—necessities like food and clothing, yes, but unnecessary ones as well. They paid little attention to his thoughts and feelings. Hearing him when he spoke but never listening to what he said."

He tightened his hand on Wesley's shoulder, looking over to the human and seeing a stunned and sorrowful gleam in his eyes.

"He found friends and romantic partners who mirrored this dynamic. Unconsciously, of course, and when he found Torrence…I think he believes he deserves the type of love she provides."

War's hand slipped down Wesley's arm now. He took his hand into his own and pushed up the sleeve of his hunter-green jacket.

"See the bruises?" War asked the angel, looking up to him now. "This human suffers. Take him into God's light. See his soul. It is good."

"We have no use for such methods. Neither should you," Mecial said. He looked to Wesley, raising a hand to him. Sparks ignited there. A few at first, then the number doubled, tripled, tripled again. Before Wesley could register that this power was the same he'd seen in War and defend the almost-fallen angel to his vengeful brothers, for no, War was not human, not yet anyway, a great light encompassed Wesley's vision.

When the light dissipated, Mecial nodded. "A very troubled soul, indeed. Tarnished with carnal pleasures, spiked by bloodshed. Wrath swirls inside him. He covets. He lusts. He envies." Mecial looked to War. "He envies you."

War looked over to Wesley, the apology he could not muster from breath or find the proper words to speak existed silently inside his iridescent eyes.

"So, what is your purpose, then?"

"Merely distraction," War said. "We was to use this soul. Resurrection shouldn't be the issue it might have been prior to the open sky, especially with you two here to assist me."

"Use him?" Virtutdeus asked, stepping closer to the open coffin, the resting corpse inside it. "Use a child of God?"

"It's always semantics," War said. "I mean that he was righteous in life and should want to work with us to save God's creation. We'd like to send him into Hell with the Son of the Devil, for she'd loved him once."

Mecial scoffed. "Devils do no love." His narrowed onto War. "Neither do angels."

"She was human, then. They shared great affections. Wesley saw it. I sent him into the moments."

"And what will this resurrected human do in Hell?" Mecial eyed War, signaling in his own stream of silent thought to Virtutdeus that they should pay close attention to this answer, for he did not know if the coy angel knew what they knew.

"Distract her, as I've said. She seeks the soul of the prophecy. The one who will grow into adulthood in some forty years and destroy her."

"Ah, yes," Mecial said. "Born beneath the broken skies." His eyes glanced up to the atmosphere around him, which had been solid before he'd entered it. "Wasn't your task to find the soul?"

"Oh, it was?" Wesley asked. "Your task?" He scoffed.

"I manifested originally to find the soul who would begin the apocalypse. When I cam back, after enduring great punishments for my confused identification, I assumed God wanted redemption from me. He is so eager to practice forgiveness, you know. I suppose…it makes sense if I find the one who stops it as redemption for not stopping the soul who started it." He looked up to Wesley.

"You promised me ."

War's eyes widened at him. Stop, he whispered to Wesley's mind. Let them think what they must, for we need them now.

He looked back to the angels. "We wish to find this child before she does." He glanced to Wesley, begging him through a widening of his eyes to remain silent at this next bit. "For obvious reasons."

"And there is no way to distract her but this one?" Mecial asked, still so unable to trust War, to believe the simplicity of it. This plan was not much of a plan. Resurrect an old boyfriend, send him into Hell in the hopes that the Son of Lucifer would fall back into some old, human romance with him. It was ridiculous. And Mecial knew better. But did War? He could not tell. He had to inquire further. "We cannot do something that does not require disturbing the slumber of a soul in paradise?"

"Torrence is smart, manipulative, methodical. There is not much that would distract her, save for her affections, of which there are few. Wesley, myself, we seemed to have outlived her favor. But this soul did not. She loved him when he died. She will love him still. Nothing but a good soul in a beautiful body seems to take her attention away from her violence."

"And you have no solid plans for this soul once he enters the kingdom of Hell? You simply mean to toss him to the devil?"

"We do not believe she is a threat to him, so no, nothing further but reunion. He died in her arms. He loved her. He will want to see her again."

"And you're telling him he's a distraction?" Mecial asked, knowing he was more than this.

War hesitated, looking away as he considered it.

"No," Wesley said sternly, clearing his throat. When all three angels stared to him, he elaborated. "Look, I'm human, okay? I'm a person. Whatever you wanna say about humanity, I'll tell yah that witnessing it ain't nothing like experiencing it. When you love someone, especially when you don't love yourself, the worst thing that could happen is complicating it. The more you know, the worse it is. It's better to let him have his understanding of her. Don't complicate it. Don't tarnish it, not any more than she's already done. He's gonna have a lot to deal with as it is. The world he died in was nothing like this one, even before the apocalypse shit started. Beyond that, he has to deal with the shit that happened between him and Torrence that he never got to process before he died. Just tell him he's resurrected because it's the end of days, there's a battle between good and evil, and the risen dead are all a part of it, just like the Bible says. We're taking him to Torrence as her brothers, her followers. The kid's not gonna be good at lying or fighting or defending himself. He's too naive."

"Help me resurrect him, my brothers. I cannot do it alone," War said.

"One condition," Wesley interjected. "You," he glanced over to War, "all of you, let me talk to him. I'm a person. You're all gonna just freak him out or get all Biblical. He's a kid. A pre-apocalypse kid. Let me re-introduce him to the world."

"Okay," Virtutdeus said. "We will assist you."

"With our own condition," Mecial said. "We will witness your introduction. We shall ensure his safety."

"Why would we hurt him?" Wesley glared at these angels. "Bring him back to life just to kill him again? At least make some kind of sense if you're gonna be dicks."

They are ignorant, Virtutdeus communicated privately to Mecial, Stop before they become the inquisitors.

"Anyway," Wesley continued, not realizing they angels were conversing privately, "You two shouldn't be there when we take him to her. You can't go into Hell without setting off alarms. We don't want her suspicious of him. She can't know you two have anything to do with it. I don't even think she should know me and him are involved."

"We will ensure he is safe," Mecial said. "Then we will leave you to his reintroduction."

All nodded, sharing uncomfortable eye contact in an effort to make an agreement.

Slowly, Virtutdeus went to his nearly-disowned brother and the tainted human, bending down over the bones and the box in reverence. "God forgive us," he said, "if what we do is wrong." He knew it wasn't, though. He knew.

He rubbed his hands together, warming them, looking to the remains. His eyes moved up to War's, the heavenly brothers taking their positions over the remnants of a saintly soul's earthly incarnation. After sharing a long, understanding look with War, Virtutdeus closed his eyes. He reached for the body when War did, using his hands in the same fashion as War, sparking power and flame upon the bones, which had started to shift in the shared spiritual force.

Here and there, in spots at random, small lines began to form around the bones, lines that grew and thickened into ropes, which wrapped around the bones and seemed to pulsate upon them.

They filled with blood, Wesley could see it. It spilled over the bones in spots that hadn't formed muscles yet, seeping into the lovely, white, satin lining of the casket. But in other spots, it filled the rope, expanding them. He watched muscle birthed from these ropes. Watched tissue and marrow and organs grow from nothing there.

A muscular form laid before him, and small pools of flesh grew in rippling spots all over. He blinked, staggered backward, finding himself caught against the wall of dirt behind him. No matter what he experienced with the antichrist or the angel, nothing so unrealizable ever seemed real.

Before his eyes, Alex's body was returned in full bloom. He'd witnessed a melting in reverse. He was whole again. A beautiful man lying in a funeral suit with his long lashes on his loosely-closed eyes and his pillowy lips closed without tension. He looked so at-rest. It was wonderful, but he was dead. Not for much longer.

The sparks from the angels' hands seemed into the flesh now, giving the porcelain skin back its pores and its lines and its life.

A shifting happened behind Alex's eyelids. His fingers twitched. Then, all at once, his eyes came open. He coughed, sniffled, cried out. Tremors ran through his body, fits of muscular cramps seized him, his legs, his feet, his arms. His back arched. He screamed, but his vocal chords were not used to such effort, such strain, which only caused the screams to continue on in number. Tears streamed from his eyes. He reached a jerking hand to his side, to his stomach. Gripping onto the very spot where a dying wound had been inflicted, Alex wailed.

The angels seized Alex, using the beams of their glory and their power to calm him somehow. His back lowered, his muscles released. He laid back into the coffin and turned his head on the pillow there, nestling into the satin. After a moment, his labored breathing steadied, and they withdrew him from the coffin.

CHAPTER TWENTY-TWO

When Alex awoke, he was in bed. The pillow was plush, comfortable, but the comforter was dense, scratching against him. It felt almost like plastic.

His eyes blinked open they were still so sore and so raw the light burned them it was hard to adjust he realized quickly that he hadn't just awoken from any old sleep.

Flashes of his memory came. A childhood swing. His ninth-grade social studies textbook. Torrence.

He wondered if he'd been in a coma. But he knew he was not in the hospital.

"Hey," a calm voice came on his left side.

He sat up quickly, wincing in the pain of such motions. He grabbed at his shoulder, his stomach, hunching over and looking at Wesley.

"You okay?" he asked. "I'm Wesley. I'm, uh, I'm a friend of Torrence."

"Torrence?" Alex gasped, the effort it was taking these muscles and chords and organs to simply work was almost incapacitating. He was a seventeen-year-old mind inside newborn skin, held up by thirty-two-year-old bones. What a creature,

Wesley considered.

"Yeah."

"How do you know Torrence?"

"We, uh, work together. We—."

"Are you in her gang or whatever it is?"

"Yeah," he breathed the word, shaking his head a bit. "It's not how you remember it."

"How I remember it?" His brows furrowed and he blinked around at the room. "What happened to me? I don't feel right."

"You…you died." Wesley exhaled an odd laugh, worried about the absurdity of it all. Wesley could easily process the idea of angels, of the apocalypse, of the risen dead because he'd been here when it started; he helped to start it. But Alex, Alex left a normal world, one without magic or glory or parting skies.

"If I died…" Flashes of memory came back, the hideout, the brothers, Torrence's eyes, the leaves.

"Angels," Wesley said.

"Angels?" His brows jumped, eyes fell to the indistinct pattern of pink over green on the uncomfortable bed.

"They're in the next room. I thought it'd be better if your first interaction in fifteen years was with a person."

"Fifteen? What—?"

"You died back in 2006. I figured you'd want some proof of what year it is now, so I got this for you," Wesley said, turning to the nightstand and grabbing a newspaper from it. "A lot's changed. It's not just the years you've slept through, but what's happened in the last couple."

Taking the offering with an unsteady hand, Alex stared with great concentration onto the paper, at the words. The little symbols seemed to elude him, even as they came into focus. "That…" he winced, head turning as his body folded in on itself. Suddenly his mind was filled with shifting images of open books—novels, the Bible, textbooks of anatomy and astronomy—then came handwritten notes, then giant, cursive letters on a chalkboard.

After a few heavy breaths, he swallowed. Releasing the breath in a concentrated effort, he felt the sparks of memory dissipate again. He blinked, opening his eyes carefully. When the sharp pain seemed dulled, he straightened his head. Looked to the paper again. Ah, words. Numbers. Dates. He remembered now.

He stared to the date on today's newspaper, his eyes fixated on the year. Brows furrowed deeply. After a moment, he looked up to Wesley. "How old am I?"

Wesley exhaled another uneasy laugh. "Depends on which part of you we're talking about, I guess."

Alex's face was tight with pain and confusion, but he didn't press on. He wasn't sure he wanted to know. "These angels…Why did they resurrect me?"

"You're a good soul. Angels like those, and there aren't many left these days."

"These days as in…" His eyes moved again to the newspaper, which trembled in his hand. Photographs, grainy and out-of-focus, almost vintage-looking, displayed fires, vacant cities, floods, reports of chaotic weather, and this was only the front page.

"As in the end of days," Wesley said, his eyes flashing down to the paper then back to Alex. "It's hard to understand if you aren't in it." A small, tense laugh. "It's hard to explain if you are." He brought a hand to the back of his neck and rubbed the area in contemplation. "There are places in the world—in the country, too—that haven't been wrecked. Tor…uh…the whole angels and demons thing, the divine stuff, it interferes with technology, so the places angels manifest, the places demon rise into, the computers and radios and phone service all basically get wiped out. Phones are so much different than how you remember," Wesley said, pulling his phone from his pocket and tossing it to Alex, who barely had the strength in his fingers to clasp it properly. "I don't think commercially-available smartphones were a thing until, like, 2008." Wesley chuckled. What a way for his technology-nerd title to come in handy. "So you've got the internet on there. Social media—stuff like MySpace, which isn't really a thing anymore—it's on there. Calls, texts, video chat, calculator, weather, everything. And you don't even have to wait for 9 p.m. for it to be free. Minutes aren't really a thing. Just monthly plans. No wires needed for internet. No landlines. No landlines, really, at all."

"Wait," Alex said, looking at the phone in his hand. "This is…It's all screen."

"Yeah, great for watching videos in the Sun States." Wesley leaned forward and pushed a button on the side of the phone. The black screen became a photo—Wesley near the camera, holding it with one hand apparently, his body angled away from it, opposite arm around a woman…Torrence.

Alex's lips parted at the image of her. He hadn't seen her in fifteen years, but it somehow felt like both a millennia ago and just yesterday that they'd been in the woods together. Now, here she was, curled into this stranger, her arm against his chest and bent, hand placed almost-shyly beneath her closed but smiling lips. Her forehead against his cheek. Their embrace. Their joy.

"Oh," Alex exhaled the word, his eyes clamoring about the image, her face, her closeness to Wesley.

"Oh, that…" Wesley's eyes widened when he realized. "That was years ago, honestly. I was, like, 24 or 25. We used to be closer than we are now. Maybe not closer. Just…different."

Alex licked his lower lip into his mouth, nostrils flaring slightly beneath lightly-creasing brows. He nodded.

"The, uh, the date's on there, too," Wesley said, trying to ease any tension. "A little mini computer."

Alex attempted a smile of understanding; the gesture very slight at first while he adjusted to the information before him, not just that Torrence went on living after he died, but that she went on with other people, with other men. He tried not to make it a big deal. He'd wanted to die, hadn't he? He closed his eyes, wincing again, more of the memories igniting inside his brain.

"You, uh…" He bit his lip, fighting the pain of the emerging memories. Pushing through it, he opened his eyes, looked up to Wesley instead of the phone. "You said you don't need a phone for the internet?"

"No, there are towers. No more dial-up." He smiled awkwardly.

"And a Sun State is…?"

"It's a place unaffected by the divine," he said, trying to be evasive.

"They still have technology, then?"

"Yeah, radio stations, TV. Papers." He looked away, scrubbing a hand over his face. "So the end of days is really Biblical in some places. Kind of the same, just with crappy service and bad weather in others."

"How long since it started?"

"February 17 of last year."

"Has an antichrist risen, then?"

"Yeah."

"Forty years, then." Alex looked down to the newspaper. "Thirty-nine." He looked back to Wesley now. "Why was I brought back? What role does Torrence have in all this? I mean, she always says—always said—she was destined for something great. Is she a prophet?" His mind raced. Torrence had said they worked for a cause, hadn't she? Had he been wrong to deny it? To deny her? Was her work praised by the angels? How could it be? She killed his parents. Oh, God. He winced. His parents.

"No," Wesley said, smiling sadly.

"She's…I mean, the angels with you, they're with her, too, right? She's not…She isn't with the antichrist…"

"She's not *with* the antichrist," Wesley said, his brows raising, "no."

"Where is she?"

"We, um, we can take you to her."

"You and the angels?"

"One of them, yeah."

"Not the others?"

"I'm not sure I trust them."

Alex's brows creased at this.

"Look," Wesley said, "I don't know them very well, but the one, he's okay."

"Okay?" His lips thinned, curling at their corners. He hunched over further, wrapping his arms around his stomach and waist.

"I don't know. They're not like people so how can you say?"

"Can I meet them?

"Yeah," Wesley said, nodding as he stood from the bed opposite Alex. "Yeah, of course."

When he exited the room, Alex closed his eyes. He considered running, escaping, but he wasn't sure if he was even captive. He did remember fleeing, though, or trying to. He remembered Torrence and holding onto her as the pain in his side stretched upward and then consumed his entire body.

He felt confusion, not only at his place here in this hotel, but centering around Torrence. He loved Torrence, he couldn't wait to see her, but he felt such fear at the thought of sharing a space with her. What if she didn't want him anymore after so long? Wesley was undeniably attractive, after all, and bigger, toned and obviously-strong. And what of these angels, the antichrist, her position in it all?

He gasped as he opened his eyes. Sniffled. Wiped a wrist across his mouth. Everything so familiar, like breathing or thinking, felt difficult and foreign. He didn't know why.

A knock came to the door then, and it opened. Wesley came in with three men—or three beings who looked like men, though perfected, it seemed.

Their skin was porcelain and bright. Their hair and eyes seemed to shimmer. The first one was of average height, average build. The second was as tall but firmed. The third, the only one to enter with his eyes downcast, was smaller, shorter. He seemed the most beautiful, though. The lamb here with two lions, two warriors of God and a cherub.

"Hello, Alex. I'm Virtutdeus. This is Mecial. Behind us is Armideus, but humans call him 'War'."

"War?"

"Don't worry," War said, his mannerisms more human than that of Virtutdeus. "I don't represent the loathsome concept."

Mecial laughed. "No, you only allowed the greatest war of eternity to be unleashed into the world. You represent nothing but kindness, though."

"I didn't know," he said lowly through grating teeth, his face only angling slightly toward this angry angel.

Alex sat in awe of these beings, though the small conversation confused him. He supposed much would be confusing here, for this was a time not only far different from his own, but also of the apocalypse.

His eyes, moving from angel to angel, grew tearful. Before him stood Sons of God, proof of his faith. He remembered angels in Heaven, he thought so, anyway, but they hadn't bodies there, or had they?

"It is the end of days," Virtutdeus said, his voice gentle but inhuman.

"Yes," Alex said.

"I'm sorry for what we must ask you to do."

"Easy," Wesley interrupted, walking toward the bed now. He sat on its edge.

"What? What is it?" Alex asked him, his eyes darting to the angels but finding focus on Wesley again.

"They're not asking shit of you," Wesley said, looking up to them.

"It is nothing," Mecial said, stepping closer after shooting Virtutdeus a glare. "They mean to take you to Torrence. Would you like that?"

"Yes," Alex answered, eyes full of wonderment and sorrow.

"Then we entrust our brother to deliver you there unharmed." He looked to War.

Unharmed. Alex wasn't unharmed. That pain he remembered, the intense pain in his side.

"We've been over this," Wesley said, sneering. "If you two don't lay off us——."

"Lay off you?" Virtutdeus seemed confused by the expression.

"He means that we've already discussed this," War clarified, looking to both angels before focusing upon Virtutdeus. "Do you not trust me, brother?"

"I wish that I could," he said. "It is so very confusing here, in flesh."

"Trust me," War said softly, "I know."

"It is confusing," Mecial chimed in, "but not tempting. Bear that in mind, brother."

"Tempting?" Alex asked. Oh, temptation. The word sparked another onset of memory; Torrence seated in his lap, Torrence's lips against his own, his hands running along her thighs, along her jaw, pulling her into him. He winced.

"Are you all right?" Wesley asked, a hand coming to Alex's hunching back.

"When I died…" Alex breathed the words more than he spoke them, his head falling, eyes seemingly magnetized to the fabric over his navel. His hands went to the spot, gripping at his shirt. The pain of the old wound measurable now that the rotted flesh was manifesting anew and alive. Fresh tears formed in his eyes, this time issuing from some intangible source within his gut—the metaphorical heart. "She wept," he said, gripping his side. "I remember seeing such pain in her eyes, but it's all so unclear." He looked up to Wesley, to the angels. "Why can't I remember?"

"You've just manifested," War said, stepping nearer to him, his radiance enrapturing Alex, as it was as evident in his motions as his voice. "Your spirit is still attaching itself to your brain. All humans undergo this process when their souls become flesh. Parts of you will feel confused, lost, unsure. It is a tiring process, so like all newborn spirits, you'll require a lot of sleep as you reattach. You are much like an infant. But because you are reborn here, not merely born, the circumstance is vastly different. What typically takes the spirit years to fully form should take days, weeks. By the time you reach Torrence, I'm sure much will have returned, though not all of it."

Alex nodded. Torrence. He pressed the button on Wesley's phone and looked at the photo of her there. "You think, after all this time, after everything that's happened, she'll want to see me?"

"I know she will," Wesley said. "I realized…you're the guy she was looking for in us, in everyone she meets, probably, but none of us, not even an angel, can measure up."

"Why didn't she come, then? Why isn't she here?" Alex's eyes shot quickly to Wesley's eyes, stunning the man with this new, too-visible display of emotion. The reddening sclera of his newly-restored eyes, the pull of his brow above them, the moisture rising up within them and falling from them in rapid, turbulent rivers.

"She is in Hell," Mecial said.

"She's what?" He gasped in confusion and disbelief.

"The world—." War started but was interrupted.

"In Hell," Mecial said, his tone, always more forceful than War's, and his niceties always far less present.

A worried confusion plagued Alex's face. "She's in Hell? How did she end up in Hell? She's alive, isn't she? Don't tell me she—."

"No, no," Wesley said, "she's okay. She's—."

"The world is Hell," War interjected now, seeing an opportunity to calm the newly-resurrected man without being entirely honest about his beloved's position here. "The end of days. That's all."

He looked to Mecial, who sent him a silent communication: This is the end of days and within it she is the antichrist; she is god here.

War sent him a warning at this blasphemy, his eyes narrowed and fearful.

Oh, don't play the idiot with me, War, Mecial responded, sneering at the earthly name of his brother, Armideus, before continuing, The spirit does not reign on earth. Flesh does. He stared at War with accusation, finishing his thoughts, You know that better than anyone.

"Oh, that my brother should forget his angelic spirit," Mecial said aloud now. "He becomes distracted by——."

"Everything," Wesley interrupted, offering War an empathetic look. "Imagine not having a body for millennia then suddenly you can see shit. Touch it. Smell it."

Mecial scoffed, but he didn't argue or lecture. Now wasn't the time. He knew it. "My brother and I must leave you," he said to Alex. "Be vigilant. Remain righteous. The world is tempting, all is flesh and blood and chaos, but much of it is still disguised by beauty. Do not succumb to it."

"He will be fine," War said. "I will be with him."

"Comforting," Mecial said, sneering. "An angel who cannot resist temptation becomes the devil, you know. Becomes a demon."

"Hey, man, just back off him for a minute, okay?" Wesley scoffed. "He did whatever he did, but we're here now, and we got bigger shit to do than guilt-trip War over choices he can't change now. All right?"

"You are in no position to preach, boy," Mecial said through gritted teeth. "The trespasses you've committed. The blood on your hands."

"Yeah, and again it's too little too late. We can't change the past, but we have right now, and we have the next forty years—if we're lucky. So let's shut the fuck up about how wrong everyone is, and get back to the matter at hand. You guys have stuff to do. You gotta find the soul and all, remember? We're not gonna let anything happen to Alex, to any righteous soul ever again. You trusted us this far. Have a little faith."

"Faith, yes," Mecial said, eyeing Alex studiously. He looked to Virtutdeus. "Have you faith, brother?"

He nodded with conviction, looking to Alex. "The pains will subside. Take care until they do. We shall see you again." He looked to Wesley and then to War. "We ensure it."

"Yeah, yeah," Wesley said, flicking his hand at them. "So do we."

"I have had enough of your disrespect," Mecial said to Wesley. "I should send you back to Hell—."

"Send yourself back. You aren't any help here. You've been a dick. Causing confusion and chastising everyone. I mean, what are you even doing here? We didn't call out for any help."

"Brother," War said, eyeing him curiously now. "How *did* you find us?"

"With this," Mecial raised his hand, a glittering string hung from his clasp, at its base dangled a glittering T.

All three men—Wesley, Alex, and War—stared at the necklace, the faux stones dulled and its metal tarnished. Each of the men, each of Torrence's own trinity, so affected by it, by what the little, inexpensive object had meant to each of them. "It was found on the floors of Heaven. Dropped, was it? Oh, no, ripped away." His eyes flicked to War's side. "You remember that day, don't you, Armideus?"

"Heaven?" Alex asked.

"Torrence gave it to me," War said.

"I gave it to her," Alex answered.

"You can take it back to her," Wesley said, snatching it from Mecial. "Here."

Looking up to the offering, Alex took it. He brought it into his fingers and stared at it. After a long moment, he exhaled, looked up to the angels and to Wesley.

"Mecial," Virtutdeus said gently, understanding the fragility of humans and their psyches, especially one is such an unusual position as this Alex. "Enough. Please, brother. Allow this boy to readjust to the world." Silently, he finished this thought, sharing it only with Mecial, *Before you place its survival upon his shoulders.*

"You two go find the kid," Wesley said. "Alex is good with us. I promise."

Virtutdeus nodded, sharing a look, perhaps of mutual understanding, with each of them.

"Be well," Mecial said to War as he moved to the door with Virtutdeus. His eyes narrowed, a curl shaped his lips. "Brother."

When they exited, Wesley looked to Alex. "See what I mean about those ones?"

"Yeah," Alex replied breathily, trying to smile. His features leveled after a moment. Pained memories flooding him again. "I feel so tired," he said. "I hurt. I'm hungry, but even the thought of food makes me sick." He frowned. "You think she still cares about me? For real?"

"Yeah," Wesley almost whispered the word. He cleared his throat, tried to shake off the lingering pains of the old vision he'd been inside, the jealousy he'd felt for this man, even as he watched him die, for he saw the tears in Torrence's eyes and watched the way her brows, her lips, her nose all synced with the sorrow of it. She'd loved Alex then. Wesley knew it. And he knew she'd love him now; she'd love him more than she could've ever loved Wesley. It killed him. Maybe that's why he wanted to kill her. "Yeah," he said more audibly, more evenly. He looked at War, recognizing the similarities in an angel and a devout human. "Yeah, I know she does." A feigned smile. Feigned reassurance. Feigned fellowship.

So much of Wesley's spirit had become an enigma to himself.

So much was push and pull, stagnant in the dance of uncertainty; this hatred for all he loved and this love for all he hated.

He wasn't sure what he hoped would come of this. He loved Torrence, and he wanted her, and even the consideration of her death tightened his chest and shook his spine. But in the idea of her absence, he felt the potential of freedom; an escape. He'd no longer be tied to her by the uncut table rope of his affections. He could pursue a life, a career, if those things could exist in an after-antichrist world, and if they couldn't, he considered as he glanced discreetly to War, then perhaps he could pursue something entirely new.

Alex looked down to the T in his hand, to its aged appearance. Something more was there, however. Something attached to it, carried with it through the years. Something old, a feeling or a thought. A memory, maybe.

"I remember seeing her cry," he said, studious expression upon his features as he came to understand these flickers of liquefied, pulsating memory. He looked down at his side, brows creasing and stern, eyes lighting on his fists and their grip of his shirt, his flank. Unclenching his hands, the fingers spreading open and trembling, Alex removed the pressure he'd been holding upon the still-open wound. Still open after fifteen years. Swallowing harshly, concentrating, he brought a hand to the silken shirt, shakily grasping it at the side, lifting it. There in his creamy, restored flesh was a great aperture, a slit in his skin, wide and blackened and festering. "I remember her killing me."

"I'm sorry," Wesley said sincerely, gazing at the wound. "Everything's back? Or pieces."

"Pieces," Alex said. "I...I remember seeing her after she did it, seeing my body." His lips shook, tears welling in his eyes. "I hated seeing her cry. I never...I never saw Torrence...hurting." He looked up to Wesley, then over to War. "Does God know how sorry I am for that? For causing her so much pain?"

Lips parting, War could only inhale, couldn't speak. After a moment, he collected himself. "Of course," he choked out.

"You remember seeing her after you died?" Wesley asked. He looked to War. "That's possible?"

"The spirit is far greater than what fits into these earthly bodies. It's everywhere, the full-self, all around you at all times. Here on earth, in the air, and also out in the expanse. Always. Both. Everywhere. When you die, it doesn't die. Only the consciousness dies. The spirit held inside your body is released, then, and can rejoin the unattached, eternal part. It doesn't remain on earth for an exceptionally long time before finding its way into whichever eternity awaits it, but the consciousness, the humanity doesn't shut down the way the flesh does. It isn't as immediate. It merely fades. It fades into the soul. Once rejoined, it slips into the heavenly plane. Or the hellish one."

Alex nodded. "It wasn't clear. It wasn't like seeing things before. Even now, everything's kind of blurry, but this is much sharper—more defined, I mean—than that."

"So you saw Torrence after? You saw your body?"

"Yeah, I mean, I'm not sure I recognized it as mine, but I saw it, and I knew it was significant to me. But Torrence, she was more significant. It's hard to explain. I felt disconnected—or maybe I just was disconnected. I'm not sure I felt anything, not very deeply anyway, except the guilt. I don't think I knew it was guilt then, but I recognize it now. I didn't want to leave because of it. I wanted to stay with her, with Torrence. I think I wanted to comfort her, if I could. I realize how selfish I'd been, what I asked her to do..." his brows creased tightly, eyes falling and full of glassy emotion. He winced, lips tightening as he looked up to Wesley. "Emotions aren't like this when you're just a soul. They've got to be physical somehow. I always thought they weren't, that they were the true connection. Now I...I don't know what's real and what our minds make up."

"It's okay. We all ask things we shouldn't of the people we love especially."

"But I asked her to kill me. Who does that?" He exhaled. "I saw her right after. I saw her holding me, crying. I saw her stand away from me. Saw Todd take the knife out of my side and put it in her hand. She stood there for a long time, quiet, just listening. The guys stood behind her, watching her, saying nothing. Just waiting. Just waiting to see what she'd do or say." He looked to War now. "Can people have abilities they shouldn't have? She...she found the one who caused the fight, the one who ran. He'd run away immediately. Before I died. I remember seeing his boots in the leaves, seeing them with my eyes. But she stood there after I died, listening for him, and she figured out which way he went. How did she do that?"

"How do you know she found him?" Wesley asked. "Maybe she didn't."

"She did. I saw it. I was slipping away from my body, from the ground. I felt like I was expanding and I was rising, but I could see more. I could see a greater space. I saw my body in the leaves, and I saw Torrence walking slowly through the trees, toward Malcolm. I remember trying to get nearer to her, trying to talk to her, to tell her it wasn't worth her soul to take revenge on him, but I couldn't communicate. I couldn't speak. But I could hear her suddenly. Maybe it was how focused I was on her, I don't know, but I heard her thoughts or her feelings. They were fuzzy, broken, but I understood the gist of it." He looked up to the angel then to the human, his lips trembling, eyes fearful. "She didn't want to stab someone else with the same blade that had been inside of me. Not when my blood was on it. She didn't want my blood mingling with anyone else's. She was thinking about how much blood she'd taken from people, from her brothers, and she was sad that she never got to have mine. She was thinking how it would've been mutual. How she would've cut her own hand for me, if I had wanted it. She didn't do that for anyone else. She...she didn't want to wipe my blood away. She didn't want to treat it like it was dirt or mud or secretion. I think she..." his brows furrowed tightly. "It felt like reverence when she looked at the blade, at my blood on it. She put it into her palm, closed her fist around it, and dragged it across her skin. She cut herself open. She mixed our blood together. I remember—I see so clearly—how intensely she was staring at her wound. She wanted to make sure that my blood went into her. She thought it did. But she needed to be sure, so she brought the blade to her lips and cleaned it of our mixed blood. I watched her.

"I kept watching. She was satisfied with the blade now, ready to use it on him. She moved faster. Started running. I watched gain on him. Watched her get to him. She dove at him, jumped on his back. She she stabbed him so many times." Alex's voice broke. He brought a hand to his face, his temple, trying to hide the forming tears. Oh, the tears. How they burned his newly-manifested eyes.

Wesley got up from the bed opposite. He sat next to Alex and placed a hand on his shoulder. "I'm sorry you had to see all that."

"It wasn't all bad, you know?" He looked over to Wesley, head downcast but eyes lifted. Above their glistening depth were creased brows, raising in the center, rendering what might've been a sudden face entirely heartbroken. "She had the guys take me back to my house. She laid me in my bed. Took off my shoes and my socks and my jeans. She took the bloody shirt away from me. She wiped the dirt from me. Dressed me in pajama bottoms and a fresh t-shirt. She brushed my hair from my eyes and told me she loved me." He paused. "How has she never been caught? She killed that guy. She had my parents..." His lips rolled into his mouth as he winced. "Is she protected somehow?" He looked to War. "Are angels watching over her? Is all this violence somehow good?"

War shook his head, a sadness overtaking his pristine features. "No," he said. "Violence is never good."

"I want to see her," Alex said. "I just…I want to see

someone I know."

"All right," Wesley said. "How about you get some sleep in the car? We should get going, anyway."

"Wait," Alex said, looking down at his body. "Can I go home?" When Wesley's lips parted, Alex added quickly, "Just long enough to change, I mean."

"Well…" Wesley's head tilted away briefly. His eyes came up to Alex's from within a concerned, almost-parental brow. "It's been a while. It won't be at all like you remember. Probably someone else lives there now."

"Right." Alex exhaled. He looked down to his dusty suit, his crumpled, red tie, the outfit in which he'd been dressed for his funeral. He raised the tarnished, but still glittering, T in his hand and looked to War, who silently felt so like the thing—so small, so fragile, so dulled. Alex smiled. "Do you want this back? She gave it to you."

"No," War said. "It's yours, isn't it?"

"I thought it was Torrence's."

"She didn't give it away because it didn't matter to her," Wesley said. He looked over at War, trying to quell his jealousy, then his eyes connected very steadily, very sternly to those of Alex. "She loved you so much, it took an angel to even come close."

Alex nodded. He brought the T to his chest and secured it around his neck. It fell against the cross hanging there, against the red tie. "So," he said, looking up to Wesley, "we're just…leaving."

"Yeah. I'm sorry."

"It's okay," he said, shrugging slightly. He wanted to understand the present moment for all of its reality, not just his personally; tried considering the world now, how much time had passed since he died, the concept of the ending of the world in more literal terms than the ones in which he'd always considered it. "I guess without Torrence I wouldn't have had much here anyway." He tried to smile.

"We can try to catch up on the way back," Wesley said.

"We'll find a store or something in one of the Sun States—."

"Sun States," Alex repeated in disbelief as they exited the hotel room.

"Yeah," Wesley said, looking up to the rising sun. "Don't look up, not unless we're somewhere the sky hasn't broken yet."

When he stepped outside, Alex paused. He was overtaken by sensation—the warmth on his face, the crisp coolness of a breeze, the smell of grass just after it had rained. He let his eyes close so he could absorb it. Was it really possible that these things only existed in certain places now?

"Don't get too used to it, though," Wesley said, placing a hand on his shoulder. "There isn't much sun where we're going."

"Are there many people left?" Alex asked, moving toward the SUV with Wesley and War. He stared at it, blinking as he drank in the design of this vehicle. It was recognizable, of course, but it was not like the SUVs in 2006, that was for sure. It was sleeker in design, futuristic without seeming out-of-place or out-of-touch. He liked it. He wondered if it drove the same.

"A lot," Wesley said as he got into the driver's seat. War went to the passenger's side but hesitated. He stepped back toward the back door on the same side.

"Go ahead," War said, nodding toward the front seat. "You should see everything as it comes to you, not as it passes."

Alex smiled thinly. "Thank you," he said, looking down at the sidewalk as he stepped away from it.

He stared at the blackened, flattened misshapen circles that had once been the bright pinks and baby blues of bubble gum, spat out by passers-by then trampled by the dirty, grimy feet of all who walked the path of this concrete desert.

"A lot of people in the end of days, huh?" He looked up to the car. "You'd think at least they'd stop littering."

As they drove, Alex slept. When he awoke sporadically Wesley tried to fill him in on the world. Most shocking to Alex was not the evolution of phones, or even the slight advances of societal norms, or the break-throughs in science, but the idea of a push-button engine ignition. Keyless entry. An entire computer—a touchscreen computer!—where a radio used to go. He wowed at it.

He wondered if everything so common as starting a car had changed. Obviously phones had.

Wesley wished he could've brought Alex back before all this; could've shown him the world of reality television, social media sensations, and meme culture. He wanted to take Alex to science museums and rock concerts. He wanted him to experience a full life before he delivered him quite literally into the belly of the beast.

They spent the night in a Sun State hotel, stopping off well before necessary for this purpose, not only for its safety but for its claim that televisions still worked here.

Of course, even in Sun States, cable wasn't what it had been, neither was satellite television. But there were DVDs and old gaming systems, and Wesley at least wanted Alex to experience a bit of modern, pre-apocalypse life before taking him into the broken skies of half the world.

"It's good that you're seeing this," Wesley said when they first crossed into a darkened place, a place of burnt-down buildings and rampant burglary. "It'll prepare your for the manor."

"I think it's best," War said, "if I assist with that. I will enter Hell with you, shield you from its horrors. Torrence wouldn't want you to bear witness, not if what Wesley describes is true."

"What he describes?"

"You know, with dating her," Wesley said, covering for the angel as his eyes connected with War's in the rear-view mirror. "She wouldn't want you to see it, though. That's true."

"Then I'll sneak Alex in," War said.

All agreed.

CHAPTER TWENTY-THREE

"How did the angel escape?" Torrence asked, slamming a knife onto a metal table riddled with weaponry.

"I do not know," gasped a heavenly warrior, his glistening skin clammy and sweat-covered.

"He was in the tunnel. War released him. But he was captured again, and War hasn't been home in days."

"Your Hell is not a home."

She backhanded him. "Who released him?"

"I would not tell you if I knew." The angel spat a blood-like substance onto the floor—a clear liquid, not deeply-colored or able to coagulate, but it was more than what an angel should produce. He was weakening. The turmoil here smashed his spirit, and now Torrence would break his body, too. She'd crush his bones, tear his muscles from them, rip apart the tendons which connected them, then, for a final flourish, she'd split open his remaining flesh.

"You know what happened the last time I, personally, strung an angel up?" She stepped against him now, no weapon in her lovely hands. Speckled with blood-like, faintly-pink secretion and adorned with long, sharp nails, her fingers came to his cheek. Stroked him. "He's since become a father."

"You will not defile me," he said through grated teeth.

"I, of course, will not. We have women specifically assigned for it." She grinned.

"Your monsters do not even live long enough to know their parents." He chuckled now, coughing through the pain of it. "You cannot recreate Nephilim as they were. Watchers were a different breed from us. They were willing."

"Oh, I think you'll find angels a lot more willing than you realize." She moved back to the table now, ready to inflict a worse pain upon him than he'd ever imagined, than she'd ever imagined. Insulting her great plans. He would pay.

As she stared to the devices, the knives, yes, and the chains, the brass knuckles, the pear of anguish, spiked collars, crocodile shears, Torrence's eyes, blazing red, lit up. Oh, the things she could do to him. She could string him up in a Judas Cradle or throw him onto a Spanish Donkey with weights tied at his ankles. Angels could not die as humans could! Oh, what fun could be had. She laughed as she imagined it.

But something broke through her musings. A calling out to her. Soft. Unangelic. Afraid.

She turned slightly, looking at the angel. She could tell in his face that he'd heard it; perhaps that he could see it, even though she could not.

It came again, this time audible enough to understand. "Torrence?" it asked.

Her eyes narrowed. Had she heard it correctly?

As she turned back to her table, the small, weary voice came into the chamber now; its gentle tone masked inside the unending torrent of screams and crying, crackling fire and snapping bones.

Her head moved slowly. Had she heard a voice? A human on? Her jaw clenched as she looked back to the table, to the weaponry, to blood dripping from the blade there. She cracked her neck.

It came again, she thought. Turning, she narrowed her eyes on the direction of this sound. Recognizing the voice as human, though nothing of its tone or timbre broke through the harrowing sounds of Hell, she slipped the brass knuckles onto her hand. She sneered, ready for a good, old-fashioned, physical fight.

Her chin lifted as she stepped toward the darkness of the doorway. Her eyes flickered as she illuminated all with the flames of Hell around her.

"Tor?" it asked, so near to her now that it became recognizable. She stiffened, stopping dead in her tracks. Impossible.

"Torrence?" it called out, pressing against her now, caressing her, throwing its weight upon her, weakening her knees.

"Alex?" she whispered in confusion, eyes scanning the archway for movement. Only footsteps seemed to come through it now.

Her breathing shook, shoulders rising as she stared into the darkness of that great entry-way.

"Tor?" he said again, softly, and after a long moment of silence, finally, he stepped into view. "Torrence?"

"Oh, my God," she whispered, staring at him as he entered the room, his blond hair and blue eyes brightly shining even in the pits of great despair. Beneath them were lovely, pink lips. Lower still, a small frame dressed in a dirty button-up and dress slacks.

Torrence froze in recognition of this body, this face. Her lips parted, eyes widened beneath her lifting brows. She stumbled backward before she caught her balance and regained composure. Her eyes ravaged over him, consuming all of what she never thought she'd see again. She swallowed thickly, then took a deep breath of the air around her. He was human, the scents in the room confirmed this, but Alex was dead. He could not be here now, not as anything but spirit, and she smelled the salt of sweat and the iron of his blood.

"Tor?" he asked tentatively, stepping further into the room, looking about. Then he saw her. "Torrence," he said, an exhale of relief washing over him as he came at her.

"Alex?" she said, standing in shock as he wrapped his arms around her. Her lips parted at this sudden connection. Her arms moved instinctively to accept his body, to hold onto him, to pull him in. "Oh, my God," she said again, a burning sensation rising into her sinus now, as tears filled her eyes. "It…it can't be."

"I know why you'd think that," he said slowly, his voice shaken in the start of his own tears. He gripped on her more tightly, burying his face into the crook of her neck and smelling her hair. "But it's me. Torrey, it's me."

"How?" she asked, her own hands clasping at him now. She nestled her face against his, ignoring the smells of rot and decay and must upon him. "How can you be here? How can you…How…?"

"Good souls, I guess," he said, pulling back slightly. He stared into her eyes, which she quickly hid away from him.

Blinking rapidly as she looked away, Torrence brought blue back into the red irises, humanizing them, humanizing herself for him.

"Tor, you okay?" he asked.

She returned her gaze to him. His eyes were wandering across her body, her shoulders, her hair. His brow furrowed in that familiar way; that very Alex expression that would've painted anyone else's face in confusion, but instead rendered him scholarly.

Perhaps he didn't understand whatever caused this curling of his brow, but in his features was evidence of his ever-working mind. He looked up to her with this expression, and she reared back in its familiarity.

"No," he said when he saw her react to him. "Please, don't be…I don't know what you are. I can see you're not afraid. You've never been afraid. It's me, though. I don't really understand the physics of it, but I'm here again and whole."

"You can't be…There's no way you're…" Her jaw clenched.

"It's me," he said. "Torrey, it's me."

Her head shifted slightly, her lips parting. Her brows came together as swiftly as they raised, then settled again

A person with less control of themselves might have fallen in him, might have flung her arms around him, might have used her demonic strength to enrapture him with the embraces of a time long past its prime.

But Torrence was in control. Certainly of herself. She eyed him cautiously, her mind filtering through possibilities. Nothing came to her. No waves of deception or of divinity. Purity issued from him, but this was warm and alive.

"You…" Alex paused, his face shifting instinctively away from the incarnate evil about which he'd so often heard his father preach theoretically. His eyes narrowed beneath his troubled brows—troubled but not fearful, merely conscious, for the first time in his life, to the reality of all he'd ever been made to believe. "I missed you," he said.

Torrence exhaled a subtle breath of astonishment, disbelief, affection, and concern. An amalgamation of emotion long-since lost to the fragile eighteen-year-old who had believed herself so strong by the pride of youth of the arrogance of petty crimes unpunished.

How different Torrence at twenty, at twenty-five, at thirty had been from that child Alex had known; how her passions grew in intensity and in number. How her violence took on new forms. How she rendered the past versions of herself with every new offense somehow weakened, even in their strengths, with the growth and evolution of her evil.

How innocent Alex had been as the gentle and compassionate lamb of a preacher's son at age seventeen. A beacon of purity, of virginity, of devotion to his father, his mother, and their faith and all the practices thereby that denied Torrence every desire she'd asked of him, every desire for which she needn't ask but tried to take.

Here he stood, entirely the same. It was not merely the color of his hair or the style of his dress. His skin hadn't changed. His voice hadn't. Lines had not creased the fragile skin around his eyes. Hair had not surrounded his lips. Nothing issuing from his spirit provided any sign of maturing or of aging.

"You are exactly as I remember," Torrence said, her voice low and easy, careful not to startle the risen, delicate man. "Not a scratch or a scar."

"Maybe one," he said, looking toward his intestines, remembering, of all things from that former life, the white-hot sensation of a forceful blade thrusting through them. His hands moved toward his center, his fingers taking gently into his hands the black cotton fabric there. "It hurts," he said. "The last piece of me to become whole again. So I'm told, anyway." He tried to chuckle, but his brows creased tightly as he stared to the spot. Then he looked up to Torrence. Her face aghast.

"I'm so sorry, Tor," he said. "I never should've asked you to do that. I was selfish, and I'm sorry. I am so sorry." His voice trembled, face full of tension as the flesh around his eyes grew red and somewhat blotchy. He looked down, gasping in the outburst of tears. "I'm sorry."

"No, no," Torrence said, brushing his tears from his eyes, falling into the familiarity of their connection as if it'd never been broken, as if she hadn't spent the better half of two decades without him. "I'm the one who should be sorry. Everything that happened…it was my fault. It was only on me. I'm sorry, Alex. God, I am so sorry."

"Torrey, why my parents? Why? We could've been together without them. We could've been free without it. Why?" he cried, experiencing the spiritual weight of it all, of the memories, the images of her arms, protective and comforting, wrapping around him in his pain as he buried his face into her neck. The feelings. The worry. The heartache. It was all so exacerbated here. A clammy hand grabbed at her shoulder as he hunched over. "God, it's horrible here."

"You just need to adjust." She held him up with her impressive, demonic strength, but he used what strength remained in his body to try and stand. "Don't be angry with me," she said. Her efforts to be gentle betrayed by her naturally-commanding tone. "Remember, please, that I was young and impulsive, and didn't perhaps consider all facets of a plan before executing it. I won't lie to you, Alex, I hated them. I hated what they did to you. I hated that they wanted to hurt you, that they did hurt you, and I hated that they wanted to keep you from me, but I…I can't tell you I might have done something different. I don't know that for sure, but I would've figured a way to keep you safe from it. More than anything, Alex, I wanted to keep you safe. I swear it."

He looked up to her now, his eyes red and sorrowful. He ran his hand through his hair, trying to steady himself. "I couldn't sleep at night. I couldn't…I felt so guilty. Why did you even tell me? If you wanted me—you know me. You knew how I'd feel. Why tell me?"

"I didn't want to lie about who I was.

"I want to go back to paradise," he said. "Consciousness is too painful." He looked up to her. "But I don't want to leave you again, either."

"It's always the issue with us, isn't it? Too painful together. Too painful apart."

"It didn't have to be that way."

She lowered her head, her lips pursing. A brow arched over

one of her still-blue eyes. "Yes." She looked up to him now. "It did."

"Tor—."

"This was destiny, Alex. You can't fight what you are, what you're supposed to be. And honestly, I didn't want to. I loved every moment of that gang, every instance of violence. I do now."

His lips tightened, the tension in his muscles tugging at his face in all places. "Tor. I love you. I want to marry you—I wanted to—." His head shook. He was still adjusting to the passage of time. What was the present anyway? Was he seventeen here in this realm or was he thirty-two? Did he love her or had he? "What if that was destiny?"

"We are fate," she said, bringing a hand to his eyes and ridding them of tears. "You wouldn't be here if we weren't. I always knew that, too. Always."

"But it doesn't make sense. The cruelty. How can we be together, meant to be together, when we're so opposite?"

"God and the devil." She shrugged. "Light and darkness. Day and night. I don't think 'opposite' always means 'opponent'."

"What if it does?" Alex asked, a groan overtaking him. He grabbed at his side, his stomach.

"Enemies are as bound together as soulmates. I'd rather be your enemy than be nothing."

"I don't want nothing. I'd rather be anything to you than nothing." He winced, hunching over. "Torrence, I don't…I don't think I'm fully here yet."

She nodded, her hands going to his shoulder and his forearm respectively as she gazed at him in consideration. "You're newly alive. Dirty. Come into my chambers," she said. "I'll clean you. Put you to bed. It's…" she paused, considering the murals on her bedroom walls, the Hell-made-Heaven for her angelic War. The synchronization of all she'd been planning, all she'd planned for her life since meeting Alex and falling in love with him, and how it, as if by miracle, divine or otherwise, seemed to manifest now, all falling into place. "It's actually pretty lovely in there. You can rest. Then we can discuss everything."

"Okay," Alex choked out, his pulse a great thudding in his throat. He tried to swallow it away, but no use. It was very humid here, very dark, very unsettling, and his body was not full his own—not yet. He wondered if it ever would be. "Thank you."

"Of course," Torrence said, aiding him in standing, in straightening his back, in walking.

Alex looked about the room, his eyes fixing on the humanesque creature strapped to an upright slab on concrete, which was next to a metal table littered with weaponry. He recognized the creature's glistening skin, his luminescent hair as almost identical to that of War, of Mecial and Virtutdeus. He swallowed his nerves harshly, as if they were palpable and therefore able to be pushed down and hidden away.

"Is that an angel?" he asked, his words quick and uneasy.

"Yes."

"What are you doing to him?"

"Talking," she said, placing her hands on him and urging him to the door. "Come on. You don't need to be here."

When they exited the doorway, all illumination ceased. Darkness encompassed the entrance and all turmoil within was lost to Alex.

As they walked through the stone and marble hallways, so dimly-lit by hanging candelabra, a drowsiness came over Alex. He stumbled a bit, but Torrence held him up.

"My bed is the most comfortable," she said, her visage blurring. "No one will harm you there. I promise."

He blinked once more, twice, then all was gone.

CHAPTER TWENTY-FOUR

As planned, War snuck back into Hell when Alex had, masking the delicate human from the horrors passing by. After dropping the resurrected man off outside the torture chamber slipping into the angel room to mask his goodness from the demons, from Torrence.

Now he went to check on the young man, feeling guilty for bringing a sensitive human back into the cruel world from which he'd been relieved.

He looked into Torrence's room, observing the long satin of the canopy rippling in response to the heated waves of the stone fireplace. Inside this blackened bed laid a devout spirit, thrust back into rotted flesh to be made whole again.

He hadn't come to the earthly plane on his own accord. He hadn't returned to it by choice. And he'd been instructed to leave paradise behind him to descend into Hell.

War had always considered free will one of humanity's greatest gifts; a present given them by a father who had not realized he was spoiling his children. But now he realized that humanity had as little say in their existence as angels had. They had been created in spirit and in skin and thrown into a realm that required of their souls a receptacle. Forced into that vessel as it grew through blood and tissue around their eternal being, these humans had no choice in how big or how little their bodies would be. They had no choice in where these bodies would be birthed. They had no choice in who would raise them; no say in what type of caretaker they received. If they were loved or if they were resented, if they were fed or not, washed or not, if they were beaten or not.

Oh, this flesh. This prison. Trapped inside bone and easy to break and bleed.

Perhaps their ability to choose to sin—to drink wine, to become drunk on it, to feel the sensations of another's body, and to experience some great, insurmountable pleasure through it—were an apology from God for all this fragility, all this vulnerability, all this forced existence into circumstance and chance.

Angels had orders to obey, yes, but War realized now as he watched Alex, knocked unconscious in a kingdom he hadn't chosen to enter, that he, War, had been far freer as an angel than he'd even be as humanity.

He would not break bones. He would not bleed. He was not born and would not die. There were bindings or bonds to be raised within. There were states from which to rise. He would not need education or athletic ability or manual labor to obtain money, for he would never need money. He would never have to eat or drink or sleep, and he would need a shelter or a home.

So many needs these humans had, and they were birthed into a culture that did not care for their happiness or their emotional well-being. They were given to the dollar, to the pound, to the euro. They were slaves to it, to the forces surrounding it, to other humans who had a lot of it and who sought only to profit still.

No wonder so many of Torrence's followers found appeal in what she offered. With the slaying of virtues came the taking of their jewels and their wallets, the selling of their china or the breaking of it and what it represented—opulence, obnoxious opulence, and how unobtainable it was.

It seemed a rebellion more against the synthetic society than any godly reign. They did not suffer the mental or physical turmoil associated with forced labor, and by forced labor, of course, War meant even most careers the human chose, for they needed money, they required it to live as it was the only means to attain the true necessities of life, which he'd already considered as food and water and shelter.

Torrence's Bad Boy Brethren merely took these things. They took life, yes, but along with each life came the monetary value associated with it.

Torrence may have been providing the sensations of strength and power to those poor souls who had been bullied or beaten or abused into thinking they were not worthy of such mental and emotional securities, but she had also been providing as a great leader provided, as a ruler or a king might have in centuries passed. Her people did not hunger. They did not thirst. They had homes and running water and they did not have to sell their soul to some wealthy corporation to afford any of it.

War realized he had been foolish. He had been the freer of God's creations, and for love of art and expression and of Torrence, he'd lost sight of it.

He looked into the room opposite this bed chamber, watching Torrence as she instructed a demon to guard the soul in her bed, to ensure that no harm came to him, but to allow him exit when he awoke.

So Alex was safe. War inhaled relief, and went to find Wesley's room next.

CHAPTER TWENTY-FIVE

Torrence moved through Hell frantically. All around her were screams and cries, both of praise and of despair. Her brothers came to her. Her demons came. The sensation of War and his angelic presence lingered in the hellish atmosphere. It became overbearing, all of this. Such pressure and such great noise. She wanted only to think, to have silence for a moment of contemplation. Merely to think.

She decided finally to go to Conrad's chambers, to find solace there, to relax into his calm, his easy manner of being, and his softly-handsome features and honey-smooth voice.

"Torrence," he said, rising from his desk as she entered.

She raised a hand to stifle his movement, then brought it to her temple. "I just need to sit," she said.

"Of course." He extended his hand toward the long table on his left.

She sat at the head of it, her elbows resting on either side of the gold-lined, red, velvet runner, which spread across the length of the old, ornately-carved wood. In its center loomed a grand candelabra, which, along with the stony fireplace to Conrad's right, kept the dimly-lit room from encompassing darkness.

"Would you like some wine?"

"Yes."

With his ever-present ease of motion and of demeanor, he went to the back of the study and returned with a glass of white wine. Offering it to Torrence, Conrad held the stem of it between his fingers. All about him was smooth. All was calming. All was beauty.

"May I sit with you?"

"Please."

His eyes were fixated onto her. Silently studying her as she brought the glass to her lips and drank the entirety of the wine, he eased himself into the seat beside her.

"There's an innocent soul here," he said when she sat the empty glass onto the table. He watched her rub at her temple.

"Yes."

"Is there a reason this is so troubling?" He leaned forward, bending his elbows and resting them on the table. His hands folded together before him. "You tend to enjoy them."

"I knew this one," she said, her eyes staring at nothing in particular before her, as if she were gazing into a dream or at a hallucination.

"Before the skies?"

"Before everything." She looked to him now. "I killed him."

Conrad's brows creased. "You killed him?"

"In another life, you could say." Her eyes moved about the room, scanning the silence for a thought that would not form.

"He isn't a spirit," Conrad said. "I can smell his flesh on you. If you killed him—."

"I'll show you," Torrence said quickly, grabbing Conrad's hand and thrusting him into the memories. "We'll walk to him as you learn of us."

Before Conrad came the images of Alex, of his dirty-blond hair, his thin frame, his jean jackets. He saw Torrence leading him into the woods. He watched them climb the moss-covered stairs into her hidden sanctuary where the first of her flock had formed.

He saw Alex deny her. He saw it repeatedly. And he saw the one denial that had sealed his fate.

A switchblade and a stomach. And he was no more.

"Your enemy," Conrad whispered as he sank into the vision, becoming more a voyeur than a visitor within the recollection as the blurred lines of Torrence's body became sharp and more substantial.

She moved to the vanity in her room and sat upon the plush cushion of its chair. Bringing her silver brush to her long, dark hair, Torrence stared at her reflection. She hated what she saw.

Her eyes were dull. Beneath them were the deep, dark crescents of sleepless nights. It was unappealing. Ugly. She couldn't imagine attending the funeral. Not like this, especially. She couldn't.

But who else would be there for Alex? His uncles and his aunts and his cousins, maybe. No one close. There was no one close. Except her.

A debate arose within her. She wanted to distance herself from the body, the suffering of those in mourning, for she did not want to appear as if she were reliving her crime, but logic told her, as Alex's girlfriend, it might appear suspicious if she did not go.

Luckily the sincere turmoil she felt in his loss aided her in any alibi or excuse she might have needed. Nothing seemed odd from her, not when the bruise-like crescents of exhaustion underlined her bloodshot, swollen eyes.

Torrence had never been one to cry. She had never been one to empathize or emote, not when the appearance of these things had not benefited her in some way, but she could not twist or spin or strangle the situation in her mind into something that seemed beneficial.

Alex was beautiful. An angelic countenance that resembled those delicate, strong-jawed figures of renaissance paintings. She'd looked at him myriad occasions and imagined his likeness splayed upon the walls of churches; his creamy skin replicated by cracked paint upon the ceilings of great cathedrals, framed in ornate, studded gold, surrounded by cherubs and protected closely by Saint Michael.

Inside this handsome structure of flesh-and-bone, a spirit unparalleled. His body had not been the house of his soul, but rather his soul seemed to possess the flesh, vibrating within it so that every small motion of his head, every slow blink of his eyelashes, every tiny intake of air through his pink lips appeared fluid; a reflective surface was his flesh, shimmering not in the light of the moon or the sun, but in the effervescence of the being beneath it.

Alex, though soft and hesitant, had been filled with the essence of his spirit. He lived. It was beyond existence. It was not action. It was choice. Decision. The desire to act but the strong will to not. The intelligence by way of books and advanced studies, the memorization of important passages of his Bible, retained by him for the way they struck his spirit, not because he was instructed to or tested on their meaning, and the inability to be convinced or even manipulated away from his convictions.

The only benefit in losing such an asset, such a great extension of herself through their shared affection, was the cause of his demise; without his righteous spirit urging him to confess sins that were not his own, Torrence continued a life of freedom, a life of her own decision and personal choice, a life without facing the consequences of not only her actions but of the actions of others carried out by her word.

There was no greater benefit than that. The ridiculous silencing of someone who knew too much.

She sat in her room, alone and without communication, for the entirety of two days. No food. Little water. Little sleep. Visions came to her. Awful, dreadful things. Pictures of his lovely skin becoming gray, his gleaming eyes dulled and surrounded by decay. She saw worms crawling into his ears, just above the lobes of which she'd so often stolen small tastes.

She winced. Shut her eyes as if that could block out the images in her mind. Nothing took them away. Sometimes she'd flinch as if the images brought with them a great physical hurt.

On the third day after Alex's death, Torrence awoke before noon. She checked her phone but found it held no charge. She stood from her bed, put on a pair of clean jeans, and went into the woods.

Todd had been excited to see her, more so than Aaron had been, and he welcomed her with the open arms of a comforting embrace.

Allowing this, Torrence sank in silence into his warmth. She lifted her hands to his back and gripped the fabric there. Her face, buried into the crook of his neck, angled slightly so that she might kiss his flesh there.

Todd responded accordingly. He let her kiss him and touch him. He remembered the old days in the cemetery when his best friend had died and Torrence came to him in comfort and offered herself to him upon the loosened dirt.

His lips parted in understanding, eyes raking over the small common area of their hideout. When they found the old couch, he nestled his face against hers. "It's okay," he whispered. "It's okay."

He looked to Aaron and signaled for him to leave the room. When he obliged, taking a beer and his book with him, Todd pulled back from Torrence.

He kept his arms around her, leaning down to kiss her lips as he moved them in their embrace toward the couch.

Torrence was quick to deepen their connection, to urge his lips further apart, to rip at his shirt as if she were an animal, enraged now instead of sorrowful, eager to release him of his clothing and wear her emotions out with him.

When they fell onto the old, green velvet, Todd was atop her.

She remedied this quickly, pushing at him as she removed her jeans and straddled him.

She did not wait for his consent before encompassing him, for she only had disregard and disconnection on her mind, but every time Todd's lips touched hers, she imagined them Alex's, and when he grabbed at her hips, she became acutely aware that she'd never again have the opportunity to feel Alex's fingers pressing into her skin.

She pulled away from him, keeping only the attachments of their lust as their sole connection. She could not close her eyes for fear of the images' return, so she tried, instead, to focus on any image in the room that might bring her awareness away from reality, but on the wall were the remaining licenses of her brothers' victims, and they reminded her of Alex's sudden knowledge of her there.

She looked away, but found nothing in the room but reminders of his distaste for her hobbies, for her lifestyle. She moved more quickly now, trying to force her focus onto achieving her release, hoping that release from all things would accompany the pleasurable end of this distracting act. Her movements became sharp and chaotic, and though her eyes ran rampantly throughout the darkened room, she began to feel herself slipping into a rhythm.

Pants came to accompany the motions; senses of sound blending with touch to create that delicious atmosphere of attraction and ardor. She groaned, her eyes finally closing, and after a few disassociating moments, Torrence felt the height of this dance upon her.

Gritting her teeth, she let the rapturous sensation encompass her, her eyes opening in time with in, glancing at the body beneath her, realizing that it was Todd, and quickly looking away, for she did not want to see his face in her moment of climax. Instead, as her head turned away from him, downcast and dissatisfied with the image before her, Torrence found herself, in her orgasm, staring at the disheveled rugs before the door, which had been torn up as Alex fled the hideout, as he fled and died.

"Fuck." She gasped, her body ceasing its motions, her eyes staring at the evidence of Alex's demise as she pulsated in the aftershocks of her achieved pleasure. "Motherfucker."

Guilt was not a common emotion. Torrence often acted as she pleased without second thought. Now everything seemed tarnished. She'd tainted it. She'd taken something holy and pure and destroyed it, and now she'd replaced the lingering of his taste on her lips with that of another. It was wretched. She was wretched. She knew it.

Some days later, she wasn't sure how many, she finally concerned herself enough with her phone to charge it. Torrence instructed Todd to bring the third and fourth licenses to her house tonight. They'd do this thing together.

"What about you not wanting to leave any trace of you at the crime scenes?" Aaron asked when Torrence arrived at the victim's home with Todd.

"Things change," she said, switching open her knife, this thrilling little tool she only acquired because it had been illegal to do so, and treading aggressively toward the house.

The two men followed her. They watched her. When she paused before the door, they each reached for the handle, eager to open it for her.

She stood there at the threshold of this home, staring straight ahead as the door opened before her. Eyes flickering about the room, consuming photos and car keys, socks tossed wantonly on the floor, one near the tennis shoes by the door, the other somewhere in the distance near the couch. Signs of life everywhere.

A brow arched over her left eye. She grinned. "After you," she said, "little brothers."

Todd and Aaron shared only a brief look before heading inside, each quick and careful in their execution of all Torrence commanded.

"Let her know I'm here," Torrence called as she watched her boys run up the staircase.

It was surprising, and perhaps quite frightening, how quickly and witch such ease she fell into the rhythm of her murderous routine, the same routine she'd carry with her into adulthood and into ritual. Go on, little brothers, she thought as she stepped inside the house in a slow, deliberate pace, Wake the almost-dead for me.

Torrence had often felt powerful, but when she heard a shocked and sudden scream muffled by sweaty palms, its owner threatened into silence with the threat of violence, an all-new sensation of strength rushed to her.

She heard Todd's shaking voice instructing Aaron to bind the victim at her ankles. "No," he said, stammering a bit. "Like we did the last guy."

"Don did the last guy," Aaron argued.

"Well, Don's not here, so get it right. She wants them to look identical. Left ankle over right."

Delight entered Torrence, mingling with the pain she felt. She found that when she knocked over something made of glass and watched it shatter in pieces the delight increased, driving away more of the pain, little by very little.

She ascended the staircase now, each step methodical and careful, for she wanted to savor this moment, this moment of great change. She'd climb the stairs a deviant mastermind, but she'd descend them as something new. Something worse. Something to be feared.

"She's coming," Todd said as the floorboards creaked beneath her feet.

"What?" The woman gasped. "Who?"

"Torrence."

She entered the room as if she were an actor and her cue had been called. The woman's eyes darted to Torrence.

Acknowledgement flickered there begins the fear. Oh, Torrence liked that.

To be the leader, yes. To be the ruler, yes. But to be seen, to be known, to be labeled the deliverer, not only the plotter, of one's demise, this evoked something new.

Torrence lifted her hand, the silver of the blade shining in the sliver of moonlight cast through the window behind the woman—her head against the wall beneath the glass, a little brother on each side of her, holding her by the wrists. With her legs crossed and taped together, the woman appeared almost as the Christ, her body becoming the very cross upon which she might die.

"Well," Torrence said, smirking, "blessed be."

The first entry of her blade into the woman felt too familiar. Torrence hadn't aimed for her abdomen, but that's where the knife touched flesh first. Just as it had been with Alex. No, Torrence thought, shaking her head, Not now. Not in a time of such fun. She raised the blade again and aimed this time. It pierced the flesh of the woman's chest, then her neck, then her face.

As the woman gurgled and bled, Todd looked away. He could hear the sound of the blade as it cut through the air and as it cut through the flesh. He heard weeping, wailing. He thought he heard laughing.

Glancing up to Torrence, seeing the sparkle in widened eyes, Todd slipped away from the dying victim. Looking over to Aaron and watching him jerk away from the woman's wrists as Torrence's blade came down upon the victim's palm, Todd gasped.

Torrence shot a glare at him. She moved to the woman's opposite arm now and, as she stared into Todd's eyes, brought the blade of the down into the victim's other palm.

Torrence grinned. "Christ-like, huh?"

Hesitantly and in fear, Todd nodded, agreeing. He tried to

lower his shoulders, tried to move his legs and straighten his knees; he hadn't even realized he'd closed himself up so tightly, but the fervor within Torrence as she committed this great and deadly assault had been terrifying to him.

Torrence stood now. She straddled the woman's body, moving to her bounded ankles and driving the blade now into her feet.

She did not know why the wounds of crucifixion seemed necessary here, but they were. She liked the way they looked, liked the positioning of the body, liked the white robe she'd been dressed in.

Torrence turned now to face her brothers, her eyes consuming the sight of a dying body before her and, on its respective sides, a cowering man.

"Your turn," she said.

"Turn?" Todd asked, his words stammering. "Turn to what?"

"To bleed."

"What?" Aaron asked, but before he could speak another syllable, she'd taken him by the wrist. "Hey, what the fuck?"

"Open your palm," she commanded. "You're my brother, aren't you? Let's make it by blood."

Aaron licked his lips, his nostrils flared. He glanced over to Todd, who only sat in frozen confusion, then he found Torrence's steady gaze again.

"By blood," he said, revealing to her his palm.

When she yanked him closer, he fell forward, catching himself with his free hand. Torrence kept hold of the hand in hers, ignoring the cracking of Aaron's shoulder as he contorted. She dragged the blade across his palm, then released it.

"What about you?" She nodded over to Todd, who merely shook his head in response and, trembling, offered his own palm to her.

She watched him willingly bleed for her, then looked back to her victim. She took the next victim's license from her boot and threw it down into the mess. "In the wallet," she said, then exited.

The sixth day after Alex's death was different from the previous five. Torrence, still consumed by the loss, felt more herself than ever before.

As she had explained to Alex, as she tried to make him understand, this was what she was meant to do. This was her future. This could've been their future together.

She felt sick but considered perhaps it was this new combination of who she'd been and who she was becoming. She'd been the daughter of an award-winning journalist and author. She'd been a high school student too smart for even her teachers. She'd been faking smiles and solicitude and concern. Now she was finding herself inside the insincerity. Every step she took on this path of power and bloodshed felt an inevitable direction for her to travel. She felt freed. She was alive. She did not know why, but reason mattered little.

She couldn't imagine why, with her stars seeming to align so perfectly now, Alex was not a part of this ultimate future. She could not see a wholly-successful or perfectly-achieved life without this cherubic figure acting as her closest consort, even if she were to attain this great leadership of boys then men then mankind then the world. She could not close her eyes and see herself seated at the head of an impressive table without her angelic lover at her side. A hand to hold. The body with which she'd spend not merely nights, but entire lives. A future without Alex and the piety which equally drove her mad and melted her uncaring heart, it was unimaginable. She could not accept it. But recovery or remedy from the reality of it was just as impossible.

She put on a black dress. Wore her mother's pearl necklace. A small heel.

She intended to go into the church, the one in which Alex's father used to preach, but she remained in her car.

She watched Alex's cousins, his uncle, his best friend carrying the wooden box down the stairs of the church. Watched as they placed it into the back of a hearse. Watched the cars follow it. Then she exited her car and went inside the church.

Looking at the Christ in the center of the pulpit, Torrence placed her hand on the wooden pew of the humble church.

"Why did you do this?" she asked the crucified savior. "He loved you. He worshipped you. He would've done anything for you." She exhaled through her solemn lips a small, shaken laugh. Painful to smile, she gritted her teeth. It was better than crying. "I don't get you," she said after a long moment, letting her hand fall away from the wood. Her eyes narrowed as she stared to Christ. "What else did you want from him? What else could've been done?" Her words quickened, accompanied now by the clicking of her heels as she made her way through the aisle of the church. "He was being beaten. He wore bruises. That night wasn't the first time, and you knew it! You knew it."

She grabbed onto the lectern, her weight falling into it, her knees starting to buckle. "Oh, God," she whined, her features twisting in the agony of all she felt. A deep breath in, her lung punctuating the silence of the air as they filled shakily with it. Her eyes darted by to the Savior, and with great effort she rose again, straightening her back to stare in defiance to him. "I protected him. I saved him. Me. Not you."

Adrenaline rushed through her body, and she used it to grab from beside her one of the great altar candelabras. As she rushed toward the crucified Christ, she screamed, hurling the altar candles at his downcast face. "I saved him!" she cried, grabbing at the other candelabra and wielding it like a baseball bat, beating at the crossed legs of the Christ on his crucifix until they broke away from his body. "You took him from me! You did this! He's gone because of you!" She wailed and screamed and cursed at him, inflicting blow after damaging blow upon his body, sending large shards of the wooden statue flying throughout the pulpit.

When the Christ had no longer a body, she hurled the candelabra at his face, busting the wood in two. As a hunk of it fell, Torrence stared at it. Her chest heaved, the air rushing in and out of her lips in great gasps of exhaustion and emotion.

Her hand rushed to her forehead. She rubbed at her eyes and her mouth. When she steadied, she walked around the lectern and made for the aisle again.

Her heels clicked as she moved for the door, the sound pounding into her ears and against her head in tangible pulses. She reached for the door, turning to gaze at the remnants of the Christ. "Remember me," she said. "Know my face. I'll make you suffer as you've made me suffer. You'll sit in the heavens and watch your children fall before me in brotherhood or in blood."

Cautiously, Torrence went to the grave-site, driving her car under the speed limit, careful not to draw attention to her or to the church of her first desecration.

She parked two blocks away from the cemetery, pulling the hood of her maroon sweater over her head and zipping up her biker jacket over it. Her black dress clung to her body beneath her winter layers. Her heels skidded in the slush and snow.

She wanted to go home, but not to hers. She wanted to be anywhere but where she was. How could she have lost Alex? How could she have hurt him? She never meant to hurt Alex. He was destiny. She'd been so sure of it.

She entered the cemetery slowly, realizing now that it hadn't simply been the switching of a blade that killed Alex, but every action Torrence had taken up to that point in the hideout. Every time she opened her blade, it was a despicable action made normal. Every assault, an unfathomable action made common. Violence had become mundane, so much so that Torrence's reaction to losing Alex was to have him lost to the world, too.

It had been impulse, disorganization, desire. A welling up of emotions she'd hadn't ever had to face to that point: denial, rejection, dislike, and by her most beloved.

She wrapped her arms around her body tightly, trying to

protect her core as much as possible from the frigid air. As she walked along the concrete pathway of the cemetery, she looked at the stones, the names upon them, the titles.

How many beloved daughters had been chastised for their choices? How many loving husbands had been unfaithful? What would Alex's stone say about him? That he was a son? He was so much more than that; he was a person.

She could never understand why people only seemed to matter when their relationships to others were brought into perspective. Why did what happened to a person only matter so long as someone else loved them?

These people, buried beneath the earth, didn't matter because they'd been sons or wives. Maybe they didn't matter at all. But if they did, it should've been merely because they'd existed. They'd lived. At one point in time, they had breathed the air the living don't even consider until the threat of its ceasing arises.

Alex wasn't just a sin and nothing else. Alex was a deeply complicated person; a person who bought into everything he'd been force-fed even as he questioned the reality around him.

God's love was true for Alex, no matter how many people died or killed in its name, but Alex had never seen God. But Torrence's love was questionable because people died for her, killed for her, and Torrence had been real. A body housed her spirit, and made it recognizable by the eye and by the mind, the memory, the emotion.

She realized as she walked that Alex hadn't denied her. This hadn't been rejection of her; it had been a break in his faith, in his reality, his sense of the world around him.

Torrence, as the liberator of Alex from his old life, had forgotten the title would be a dual one; she'd also be the bringer of his new life. She knew he needed time to consider it, but she was impulsive in her youth and impatient and fearful; losing Alex was the only worry she'd ever had.

As she collapsed into the dirt, Torrence stared

dumbfoundedly as if in a trace at his headstone. Lifting a hand toward the slab, which marked now the resting place of Alex's body, she pressed her fingers into the indentations, trying to remember what it felt like to feel his flesh, living and soft and warm, beneath her fingertips.

She'd never touch Alex again, she realized, as she stared, slack-jawed at the carving in the headstone, which read simply:

ALEXANDER MILTON
BELOVED SON
1989-2006

Her fingertips slipped away from it, this physical evidence of a unfathomable loss, and fell unceremoniously into the grass-less soil of the newly-covered grave. Hands gripping fistfuls of the fresh dirt, Torrence fell forward, her chest pressing against her knees and wept. Tears streamed from her eyes as she screamed. Her face reddened. Her head throbbed. Wailing as a dying animal, Torrence expounded every bit of energy she had, giving in to this all encompassing sorrow and exhaling it out of her body in scream after painful, bloodcurdling, scream.

She knew that this was not something she could ever experience again, that love and its enjoyments could never seep into her mind again. She'd been corrupted, however briefly, by the considerations that came with any gained and beloved part of life—that one could lose what was obtained—and people were too much their own to ever say with certainty that their presence would never become absence.

She didn't need the worry of it, especially when it took her calculating and controlled demeanor away from her, even if for only a second or two of emotional outburst. It was not worth it. She would never lose sight of her work again.

But Alex, oh, how she wished she could simply go back in time to that day when she'd first seen him, first desired him and decided against knowing him. She wished she would've driven away without ever speaking a word to him. She wished she wouldn't have pursued him in reality so she could've kept him forever as a fantasy within her mind.

She went home. She sat at the breakfast table, her temple pressed against her fist, as she picked at the eggs on her plate.

"You know, honey," her father started.

She didn't look up to him. She didn't move.

A member of their staff came in to refill the cups with coffee and orange juice.

After some time, he tried again. "Honey, I can't imagine what you must be feeling."

"It's for the best," her mother interrupted.

Torrence's body went rigid. In an instant she was glaring up to her mother, rage and confusion painting her features in an uncanny state

"He was from a poor family. An orphan."

"Delia—."

"You could do so much better," she continued, though her husband begged her to stop. "And now you will."

Torrence rose from the table in a sharp, fluid motion. "Go fuck yourself, Mother."

She stormed out. Her father pursued, but she wasn't in the mood for fights or explanations. With tears in her eyes, she turned to him there on the porch. "I just need to go for a drive, okay?"

He nodded, a defeated half-smile of understanding on his lips. "Yeah," he said, his hand falling from her arm. "Yeah, okay. Be safe."

She returned the same insincere smile, turning to the door and exiting.

She got into her car, drove in the direction of the sunset, and never looked back.

Torrence didn't know where her parents were now. Frankly, she didn't care. As they moved down the hallways of Hell now, ready to witness in flesh this resurrected lover, Torrence stared to Conrad, her Awakener, spiritual counterpart, teacher, brother, lover. The connection they shared crafted by fate, by great prophecy, but not defined by it.

"You are my family," she said.

"And you are mine," he replied, placing a hand at the small of her back as they entered the room where Alex laid sleeping.

"See," she said, staring down to him. "He's alive. He's him."

"I see," he said, "but, Torrence, I think you may be too close to see it."

"To see what?"

"A soul born beneath broken skies," he said.

"Yes…"

"He died…But he is risen. He is resurrected. He is reborn."

"Reborn," Torrence said, eyeing Conrad.

"Reborn…"

"No…"

"Beneath the broken sky," Conrad finished.

"No," Torrence whispered, eyes gazing at Alex, returned to her, returned and reborn, as the pressure of her switchblade in her boot seemed suddenly so present against her ankle. "Don't make me."